SHORT STORY MASTERPIECES
by American Women Writers

DOVER THRIFT EDITIONS

Edited by
Clarence C. Strowbridge

DOVER PUBLICATIONS
GARDEN CITY, NEW YORK

DOVER THRIFT EDITIONS

GENERAL EDITOR: MARY CAROLYN WALDREP

Bibliographical Note

Short Story Masterpieces by American Women Writers, first published by Dover Publications in 2013, is a new anthology of short stories reprinted from standard sources with a Note by the editor, Clarence C. Strowbridge.

Library of Congress Cataloging-in-Publication Data

Short story masterpieces by American women writers / edited by Clarence C. Strowbridge.
pages cm. — (Dover Thrift Editions)
ISBN-13: 978-0-486-49994-9
ISBN-10: 0-486-49994-4
1. American fiction—Women authors. 2. Short stories, American. I. Strowbridge, Clarence C., editor of compilation.
PS647.W6S54 2013
813'.01089287—dc23
2013010224

Manufactured in the United States by LSC Communications Book LLC
49994407 2021
www.doverpublications.com

Contents

NOTE

"One reason I like to publish short stories is that nobody pays any attention to them. In ten years or so they begin to be known but the process has not been obnoxious. When you publish a novel, the racket is like a fox in the hen house."

FLANNERY O'CONNOR'S WITTY observation about the small impact short stories generally make upon initial publication holds true for most of the stories in this collection; as noted in the bibliographical notes, the majority were first published in limited-circulation literary magazines and went unnoticed by most readers of fiction. In several instances it took much longer than ten years for them to become the universally acknowledged classics they are today.

But once these stories took hold, they made lasting impressions because of their creative imagination and intensity. I first read many of these stories in college over fifty years ago; they impressed me tremendously back then, but I find my enjoyment and appreciation of them grow with each subsequent reading.

American literature is particularly rich in the genre of the short story, and Dover has published several excellent, inexpensive anthologies that have found large academic and general audiences. Over fifteen years ago Candace Ward spotlighted the outstanding role that American women played in the development of the genre in her Dover Thrift Editions anthology *Great Short Stories by American Women,* comprising thirteen great stories by as many writers. It remains one of the best and most affordable collections available (see the full table of contents at www.doverpublications.com).

I was delighted when the editors at Dover invited me to select the stories for a second volume from the same rich vein. I have been careful to choose different and equally strong stories so that the two anthologies complement one another. Either book will make a fine introduction to the subject, but together they provide a much more comprehensive reading experience with twenty-seven stories (dating from 1861 to 2001) by twenty-three different authors. While I am pleased to have been able to obtain permission to include several relatively recent, copyrighted stories in this collection, I am equally excited to include a few "rediscoveries," such as the extraordinarily fine works by Constance Fenimore Woolson and Margaret Prescott Montague.

ACKNOWLEDGMENTS

Louise Erdrich: "The Shawl," originally published in *The New Yorker* and currently collected in *The Red Convertible,* by Louise Erdrich. Copyright © 1980 by Louise Erdrich, used by permission of The Wylie Agency LLC.

Joyce Carol Oates: "Heat" from *Heat and Other Stories* by Joyce Carol Oates. Copyright © 1992 Ontario Review, Inc. Reprinted by permission of John Hawkins & Associates, Inc.

Flannery O'Connor: "The Life You Save May Be Your Own" from *A Good Man Is Hard to Find and Other Stories* by Flannery O'Connor, © 1955, 1954, 1953, 1948 by Flannery O'Connor. Copyright © renewed 1976 by Mrs. Edward F. O'Connor. Copyright © renewed 1981, 1982, 1983 by Regina O'Connor. Reprinted by permission of Houghton Mifflin Harcourt Publishing Company and the Mary Flannery O'Connor Charitable Trust via Harold Matson Co., Inc. All rights reserved.

Marjorie Kinnan Rawlings: "Gal Young 'Un" by Marjorie Kinnan Rawlings. Used by permission of John Sundeman, Trustee of the Norton S. Baskin Literary Trust, P.O. Box 3443, Saint Augustine, Florida 32085-3443, U.S.A.

Alice Walker: "Everyday Use" from *In Love & Trouble: Stories of Black Women* by Alice Walker. Copyright © 1973, and renewed 2001 by Alice Walker. Reprinted by permission of Houghton Mifflin Harcourt Publishing Company. All rights reserved.

Eudora Welty: "Why I Live at the P.O." from *A Curtain of Green and Other Stories* by Eudora Welty. Copyright © 1941 by Eudora Welty. Copyright © Renewed 1969 by Eudora Welty. Reprinted by permission of Houghton Mifflin Harcourt Publishing Company. All rights reserved. Reprinted by permission of Eudora Welty LLC and Russell & Volkening as agents for the author. Copyright © 1941 Eudora Welty, renewed © 1980.

MISS GRIEF

by Constance Fenimore Woolson

Although but little remembered today, Constance Fenimore Woolson can be considered to be the first female American to achieve a worldwide reputation as a writer of fiction. Her earliest works, dealing with life on the Great Lakes frontier, and her middle-period stories of the Reconstruction South, had been published in *The Atlantic Monthly*, *Harper's*, and *Scribner's* since the early 1900s. Ms. Woolson, who was a grandniece of James Fenimore Cooper, wrote "Miss Grief" soon after her removal to Europe in 1879, following her mother's death. It was first published in *Lippincott's Magazine* in 1880. Her deep friendship with Henry James began that year and continued until she died at the age of 53 after falling or jumping from a window at her home in Venice.

"A CONCEITED FOOL" is a not uncommon expression. Now, I know that I am not a fool, but I also know that I am conceited. But, candidly, can it be helped if one happens to be young, well and strong, passably good-looking, with some money that one has inherited and more that one has earned—in all, enough to make life comfortable—and if upon this foundation rests also the pleasant superstructure of a literary success? The success is deserved, I think: certainly it was not lightly gained. Yet even with this I fully appreciate its rarity. Thus, I find myself very well entertained in life: I have all I wish in the way of society, and a deep, though of course carefully concealed, satisfaction in my own little fame; which fame I foster by a gentle system of non-interference. I know that I am spoken of as "that quiet young fellow who writes those delightful little studies of society, you know"; and I live up to that definition.

A year ago I was in Rome, and enjoying life particularly. I had a large number of my acquaintances there, both American and

English, and no day passed without its invitation. Of course I understood it: it is seldom that you find a literary man who is good-tempered, well-dressed, sufficiently provided with money, and amiably obedient to all the rules and requirements of "society." "When found, make a note of it"; and the note was generally an invitation.

One evening, upon returning to my lodgings, my man Simpson informed me that a person had called in the afternoon, and upon learning that I was absent had left not a card, but her name—"Miss Grief." The title lingered—Miss Grief! "Grief has not so far visited me here," I said to myself, dismissing Simpson and seeking my little balcony for a final smoke, "and she shall not now. I shall take care to be 'not at home' to her if she continues to call." And then I fell to thinking of Isabel Abercrombie, in whose society I had spent that and many evenings: they were golden thoughts.

The next day there was an excursion; it was late when I reached my rooms, and again Simpson informed me that Miss Grief had called.

"Is she coming continuously?" I said, half to myself.

"Yes, sir: she mentioned that she should call again."

"How does she look?"

"Well, sir, a lady, but not so prosperous as she was, I should say," answered Simpson, discreetly.

"Young?"

"No, sir."

"Alone?"

"A maid with her, sir."

But once outside in my little high-up balcony with my cigar, I again forgot Miss Grief and whatever she might represent. Who would not forget in that moonlight, with Isabel Abercrombie's face to remember?

The stranger came a third time, and I was absent; then she let two days pass, and began again. It grew to be a regular dialogue between Simpson and myself when I came in at night: "Grief today?"

"Yes, sir."

"What time?"

"Four, sir."

"Happy the man," I thought, "who can keep her confined to a particular hour!"

But I should not have treated my visitor so cavalierly if I had not felt sure that she was eccentric and unconventional—qualities extremely tiresome in a woman no longer young or attractive. If she were not eccentric, she would not have persisted in coming to my door day after day in this silent way, without stating her errand, leaving a note, or presenting her credentials in any shape. I made up my mind that she had something to sell—a bit of carving or some intaglio supposed to be antique. It was known that I had a fancy for oddities. I said to myself, "She has read or heard of my 'Old Gold' story, or else 'The Buried God,' and she thinks me an idealizing ignoramus upon whom she can impose. Her sepulchral name is at least not Italian; probably she is a sharp countrywoman of mine, turning, by means of the present æsthetic craze, an honest penny when she can."

She had called seven times during a period of two weeks without seeing me, when one day I happened to be at home in the afternoon, owing to a pouring rain and a fit of doubt concerning Miss Abercrombie. For I had constructed a careful theory of that young lady's characteristics in my own mind, and she had lived up to it delightfully until the previous evening, when with one word she had blown it to atoms and taken flight, leaving me standing, as it were, on a desolate shore, with nothing but a handful of mistaken inductions wherewith to console myself. I do not know a more exasperating frame of mind, at least for a constructor of theories. I could not write, and so I took up a French novel (I model myself a little on Balzac). I had been turning over its pages but a few moments when Simpson knocked, and, entering softly, said, with just a shadow of a smile on his well-trained face, "Miss Grief." I briefly consigned Miss Grief to all the Furies, and then, as he still lingered—perhaps not knowing where they resided—I asked where the visitor was.

"Outside, sir—in the hall. I told her I would see if you were at home."

"She must be unpleasantly wet if she had no carriage."

"No carriage, sir: they always come on foot. I think she *is* a little damp, sir."

"Well, let her in; but I don't want the maid. I may as well see her now, I suppose, and end the affair."

"Yes, sir."

I did not put down my book. My visitor should have a hearing, but not much more: she had sacrificed her womanly claims by her persistent attacks upon my door. Presently Simpson ushered her in. "Miss Grief," he said, and then went out, closing the curtain behind him.

A woman—yes, a lady—but shabby, unattractive, and more than middle-aged.

I rose, bowed slightly, and then dropped into my chair again, still keeping the book in my hand. "Miss Grief?" I said interrogatively as I indicated a seat with my eyebrows.

"Not Grief," she answered—"Crief: my name is Crief."

She sat down, and I saw that she held a small flat box.

"Not carving, then," I thought—"probably old lace, something that belonged to Tullia or Lucrezia Borgia." But, as she did not speak, I found myself obliged to begin: "You have been here, I think, once or twice before?"

"Seven times; this is the eighth."

A silence.

"I am often out; indeed, I may say that I am never in," I remarked carelessly.

"Yes; you have many friends."

"—Who will perhaps buy old lace," I mentally added. But this time I too remained silent; why should I trouble myself to draw her out? She had sought me; let her advance her idea, whatever it was, now that entrance was gained.

But Miss Grief (I preferred to call her so) did not look as though she could advance anything; her black gown, damp with rain, seemed to retreat fearfully to her thin self, while her thin self retreated as far as possible from me, from the chair, from everything. Her eyes were cast down; an old-fashioned lace veil with a heavy border shaded her face. She looked at the floor, and I looked at her.

I grew a little impatient, but I made up my mind that I would continue silent and see how long a time she would consider necessary to give due effect to her little pantomime. Comedy? Or was it tragedy? I suppose full five minutes passed thus in our double silence; and that is a long time when two persons are sitting opposite each other alone in a small still room.

At last my visitor, without raising her eyes, said slowly, "You are very happy, are you not, with youth, health, friends, riches, fame?"

It was a singular beginning. Her voice was clear, low, and very sweet as she thus enumerated my advantages one by one in a list.

I was attracted by it, but repelled by her words, which seemed to me flattery both dull and bold.

"Thanks," I said, "for your kindness, but I fear it is undeserved. I seldom discuss myself even when with my friends."

"I am your friend," replied Miss Grief. Then, after a moment, she added slowly, "I have read every word you have written."

I curled the edges of my book indifferently; I am not a fop, I hope, but—others have said the same.

"What is more, I know much of it by heart," continued my visitor. "Wait: I will show you"; and then, without pause, she began to repeat something of mine word for word, just as I had written it. On she went, and I—listened. I intended interrupting her after a moment, but I did not, because she was reciting so well, and also because I felt a desire gaining upon me to see what she would make of a certain conversation which I knew was coming—a conversation between two of my characters which was, to say the least, sphinx-like, and somewhat incandescent as well. What won me a little, too, was the fact that the scene she was reciting (it was hardly more than that, though called a story) was secretly my favorite among all the sketches from my pen which a gracious public has received with favor. I never said so, but it was; and I had always felt a wondering annoyance that the aforesaid public, while kindly praising beyond their worth other attempts of mine, had never noticed the higher purpose of this little shaft, aimed not at the balconies and lighted windows of society, but straight up toward the distant stars. So she went on, and presently reached the conversation: my two people began to talk. She had raised her eyes now, and was looking at me soberly as she gave the words of the woman, quiet, gentle, cold, and the replies of the man, bitter, hot, and scathing. Her very voice changed, and took, though always sweetly, the different tones required, while no point of meaning, however small, no breath of delicate emphasis which I had meant, but which the dull types could not give, escaped an appreciative and full, almost overfull, recognition which startled me. For she had understood me—understood me almost better than I had understood myself. It seemed to me that while I had labored to interpret, partially, a psychological riddle, she, coming after, had comprehended its bearings better than I had, though confining herself strictly to my own words and emphasis. The scene ended (and it ended rather suddenly), she dropped her eyes, and moved her hand nervously to and fro over the box she held; her gloves were old and shabby, her hands small.

I was secretly much surprised by what I had heard, but my ill-humor was deep-seated that day, and I still felt sure, besides, that the box contained something which I was expected to buy.

"You recite remarkably well," I said carelessly, "and I am much flattered also by your appreciation of my attempt. But it is not, I presume, to that alone that I owe the pleasure of this visit?"

"Yes," she answered, still looking down, "it is, for if you had not written that scene I should not have sought you. Your other sketches are interiors—exquisitely painted and delicately finished, but of small scope. *This* is a sketch in a few bold, masterly lines—work of entirely different spirit and purpose."

I was nettled by her insight. "You have bestowed so much of your kind attention upon me that I feel your debtor," I said, conventionally. "It may be that there is something I can do for you—connected, possibly, with that little box?"

It was impertinent, but it was true; for she answered, "Yes."

I smiled, but her eyes were cast down and she did not see the smile.

"What I have to show you is a manuscript," she said after a pause which I did not break; "it is a drama. I thought that perhaps you would read it."

"An authoress! This is worse than old lace," I said to myself in dismay.—Then, aloud, "My opinion would be worth nothing, Miss Crief."

"Not in a business way, I know. But it might be—an assistance personally." Her voice had sunk to a whisper; outside, the rain was pouring steadily down. She was a very depressing object to me as she sat there with her box.

"I hardly think I have the time at present—" I began.

She had raised her eyes and was looking at me; then, when I paused, she rose and came suddenly toward my chair. "Yes, you will read it," she said with her hand on my arm—"you will read it. Look at this room; look at yourself; look at all you have. Then look at me, and have pity."

I had risen, for she held my arm, and her damp skirt was brushing my knees.

Her large dark eyes looked intently into mine as she went on: "I have no shame in asking. Why should I have? It is my last endeavor; but a calm and well-considered one. If you refuse I shall go away, knowing that Fate has willed it so. And I shall be content."

"She is mad," I thought. But she did not look so, and she had spoken quietly, even gently. "Sit down," I said, moving away from her. I felt as if I had been magnetized; but it was only the nearness of her eyes to mine, and their intensity. I drew forward a chair, but she remained standing.

"I cannot," she said in the same sweet, gentle tone, "unless you promise."

"Very well, I promise; only sit down."

As I took her arm to lead her to the chair, I perceived that she was trembling, but her face continued unmoved.

"You do not, of course, wish me to look at your manuscript now?" I said, temporizing; "it would be much better to leave it. Give me your address, and I will return it to you with my written opinion; though, I repeat, the latter will be of no use to you. It is the opinion of an editor or publisher that you want."

"It shall be as you please. And I will go in a moment," said Miss Grief, pressing her palms together, as if trying to control the tremor that had seized her slight frame.

She looked so pallid that I thought of offering her a glass of wine; then I remembered that if I did it might be a bait to bring her here again, and this I was desirous to prevent. She rose while the thought was passing through my mind. Her pasteboard box lay on the chair she had first occupied; she took it, wrote an address on the cover, laid it down, and then, bowing with a little air of formality, drew her black shawl round her shoulders and turned toward the door.

I followed, after touching the bell. "You will hear from me by letter," I said.

Simpson opened the door, and I caught a glimpse of the maid, who was waiting in the anteroom. She was an old woman, shorter than her mistress, equally thin, and dressed like her in rusty black. As the door opened she turned toward it a pair of small, dim blue eyes with a look of furtive suspense. Simpson dropped the curtain, shutting me into the inner room; he had no intention of allowing me to accompany my visitor further. But I had the curiosity to go to a bay window in an angle from whence I could command the street door, and presently I saw them issue forth in the rain and walk away side by side, the mistress, being the taller, holding the umbrella: probably there was not much difference in rank between persons so poor and forlorn as these.

It grew dark. I was invited out for the evening, and I knew that if I should go I should meet Miss Abercrombie. I said to myself that I would not go. I got out my paper for writing, I made my preparations for a quiet evening at home with myself; but it was of no use. It all ended slavishly in my going. At the last allowable moment I presented myself, and—as a punishment for my vacillation, I suppose—I never passed a more disagreeable evening. I drove homeward in a murky temper; it was foggy without, and very foggy within. What Isabel really was, now that she had broken through my elaborately built theories, I was not able to decide. There was, to tell the truth, a certain young Englishman—But that is apart from this story.

I reached home, went up to my rooms, and had a supper. It was to console myself; I am obliged to console myself scientifically once in a while. I was walking up and down afterward, smoking and feeling somewhat better, when my eye fell upon the pasteboard box. I took it up; on the cover was written an address which showed that my visitor must have walked a long distance in order to see me: "A. Crief."—"A Grief," I thought; "and so she is. I positively believe she has brought all this trouble upon me: she has the evil eye." I took out the manuscript and looked at it. It was in the form of a little volume, and clearly written; on the cover was the word "Armor" in German text, and, underneath, a pen-and-ink sketch of a helmet, breastplate, and shield.

"Grief certainly needs armor," I said to myself, sitting down by the table and turning over the pages. "I may as well look over the thing now; I could not be in a worse mood." And then I began to read.

Early the next morning Simpson took a note from me to the given address, returning with the following reply: "No; I prefer to come to you; at four; A. Crief." These words, with their three semicolons, were written in pencil upon a piece of coarse printing paper, but the handwriting was as clear and delicate as that of the manuscript in ink.

"What sort of a place was it, Simpson?"

"Very poor, sir, but I did not go all the way up. The elder person came down, sir, took the note, and requested me to wait where I was."

"You had no chance, then, to make inquiries?" I said, knowing full well that he had emptied the entire neighborhood of any information it might possess concerning these two lodgers.

"Well, sir, you know how these foreigners will talk, whether one wants to hear or not. But it seems that these two persons have been there but a few weeks; they live alone, and are uncommonly silent and reserved. The people round there call them something that signifies 'the Madames American, thin and dumb.'"

At four the "Madames American" arrived; it was raining again, and they came on foot under their old umbrella. The maid waited in the anteroom, and Miss Grief was ushered into my bachelor's parlor. I had thought that I should meet her with great deference; but she looked so forlorn that my deference changed to pity. It was the woman that impressed me then, more than the writer—the fragile, nerveless body more than the inspired mind. For it was inspired: I had sat up half the night over her drama, and had felt thrilled through and through more than once by its earnestness, passion, and power.

No one could have been more surprised than I was to find myself thus enthusiastic. I thought I had outgrown that sort of thing. And one would have supposed, too (I myself should have supposed so the day before), that the faults of the drama, which were many and prominent, would have chilled any liking I might have felt, I being a writer myself, and therefore critical; for writers are as apt to make much of the "how," rather than the "what," as painters, who, it is well known, prefer an exquisitely rendered representation of a commonplace theme to an imperfectly executed picture of even the most striking subject. But in this case, on the contrary, the scattered rays of splendor in Miss Grief's drama had made me forget the dark spots, which were numerous and disfiguring; or, rather, the splendor had made me anxious to have the spots removed. And this also was a philanthropic state very unusual with me. Regarding unsuccessful writers, my motto had been "Væ victis!"

My visitor took a seat and folded her hands; I could see, in spite of her quiet manner, that she was in breathless suspense. It seemed so pitiful that she should be trembling there before me—a woman so much older than I was, a woman who possessed the divine spark of genius, which I was by no means sure (in spite of my success) had been granted to me—that I felt as if I ought to go down on my knees before her, and entreat her to take her proper place of supremacy at once. But there! one does not go down on one's knees, combustively, as it were, before a woman over fifty, plain in feature, thin, dejected, and ill-dressed. I contented myself with taking her hands (in their miserable old gloves) in mine, while I said cordially, "Miss Crief, your drama seems to me full of original power. It has roused my enthusiasm: I sat up half the night reading it."

The hands I held shook, but something (perhaps a shame for having evaded the knees business) made me tighten my hold and bestow upon her also a reassuring smile. She looked at me for a moment, and then, suddenly and noiselessly, tears rose and rolled down her cheeks. I dropped her hands and retreated. I had not thought her tearful: on the contrary, her voice and face had seemed rigidly controlled. But now here she was bending herself over the side of the chair with her head resting on her arms, not sobbing aloud, but her whole frame shaken by the strength of her emotion. I rushed for a glass of wine; I pressed her to take it. I did not quite know what to do, but, putting myself in her place, I decided to praise the drama; and praise it I did. I do not know when I have used so many adjectives. She raised her head and began to wipe her eyes.

"Do take the wine," I said, interrupting myself in my cataract of language.

"I dare not," she answered; then added humbly, "that is, unless you have a biscuit here or a bit of bread."

I found some biscuit; she ate two, and then slowly drank the wine, while I resumed my verbal Niagara. Under its influence—and that of the wine too, perhaps—she began to show new life. It was not that she looked radiant—she could not—but simply that she looked warm. I now perceived what had been the principal discomfort of her appearance heretofore: it was that she had looked all the time as if suffering from cold.

At last I could think of nothing more to say, and stopped. I really admired the drama, but I thought I had exerted myself sufficiently as an anti-hysteric, and that adjectives enough, for the present at least, had been administered. She had put down her empty wineglass, and was resting her hands on the broad cushioned arms of her chair with, for a thin person, a sort of expanded content.

"You must pardon my tears," she said, smiling; "it was the revulsion of feeling. My life was at a low ebb: if your sentence had been against me, it would have been my end."

"Your end?"

"Yes, the end of my life; I should have destroyed myself."

"Then you would have been a weak as well as wicked woman," I said in a tone of disgust. I do hate sensationalism.

"Oh no, you know nothing about it. I should have destroyed only this poor worn tenement of clay. But I can well understand how *you* would look upon it. Regarding the desirableness of life, the prince and the beggar may have different opinions. We will say no more of it, but talk of the drama instead." As she spoke the word "drama" a triumphant brightness came into her eyes.

I took the manuscript from a drawer and sat down beside her. "I suppose you know that there are faults," I said, expecting ready acquiescence.

"I was not aware that there were any," was her gentle reply.

Here was a beginning! After all my interest in her—and, I may say under the circumstances, my kindness—she received me in this way! However, my belief in her genius was too sincere to be altered by her whimsies; so I persevered. "Let us go over it together," I said. "Shall I read it to you, or will you read it to me?"

"I will not read it, but recite it."

"That will never do; you will recite it so well that we shall see only the good points, and what we have to concern ourselves with now is the bad ones."

"I will recite it," she repeated.

"Now, Miss Crief," I said bluntly, "for what purpose did you come to me? Certainly not merely to recite: I am no stage manager. In plain English, was it not your idea that I might help you in obtaining a publisher?"

"Yes, yes," she answered, looking at me apprehensively, all her old manner returning.

I followed up my advantage, opened the little paper volume and began. I first took the drama line by line, and spoke of the faults of expression and structure; then I turned back and touched upon two or three glaring impossibilities in the plot. "Your absorbed interest in the motive of the whole no doubt made you forget these blemishes," I said apologetically.

But, to my surprise, I found that she did not see the blemishes—that she appreciated nothing I had said, comprehended nothing. Such unaccountable obtuseness puzzled me. I began again, going over the whole with even greater minuteness and care. I worked hard: the perspiration stood in beads upon my forehead as I struggled with her—what shall I call it—obstinacy? But it was not exactly obstinacy. She simply could not see the faults of her own work, any more than a blind man can see the smoke that dims a patch of blue sky. When I had finished my task the second time, she still remained as gently impassive as before. I leaned back in my chair exhausted, and looked at her.

Even then she did not seem to comprehend (whether she agreed with it or not) what I must be thinking. "It is such a heaven to me that you like it!" she murmured dreamily, breaking the silence. Then, with more animation, "And *now* you will let me recite it?"

I was too weary to oppose her; she threw aside her shawl and bonnet, and, standing in the centre of the room, began.

And she carried me along with her: all the strong passages were doubly strong when spoken, and the faults, which seemed nothing to her, were made by her earnestness to seem nothing to me, at least for that moment. When it was ended, she stood looking at me with a triumphant smile.

"Yes," I said, "I like it, and you see that I do. But I like it because my taste is peculiar. To me originality and force are everything—perhaps because I have them not to any marked degree myself—but the world at large will not overlook as I do your absolutely barbarous shortcomings on account of them. Will you trust me to go over the drama and correct it at my pleasure?" This was a vast deal for me to offer; I was surprised at myself.

"No," she answered softly, still smiling. "There shall not be so much as a comma altered." Then she sat down and fell into a reverie as though she were alone.

"Have you written anything else?" I said after a while, when I had become tired of the silence.

"Yes."

"Can I see it? Or is it *them*?"

"It is *them*. Yes, you can see all."

"I will call upon you for the purpose."

"No, you must not," she said, coming back to the present nervously. "I prefer to come to you."

At this moment Simpson entered to light the room, and busied himself rather longer than was necessary over the task. When he finally went out I saw that my visitor's manner had sunk into its former depression: the presence of the servant seemed to have chilled her.

"When did you say I might come?" I repeated, ignoring her refusal.

"I did not say it. It would be impossible."

"Well, then, when will you come here?" There was, I fear, a trace of fatigue in my tone.

"At your good pleasure, sir," she answered humbly.

My chivalry was touched by this: after all, she was a woman. "Come tomorrow," I said. "By the way, come and dine with me then; why not?" I was curious to see what she would reply.

"Why not, indeed? Yes, I will come. I am forty-three: I might have been your mother."

This was not quite true, as I am over thirty: but I look young, while she—Well, I had thought her over fifty. "I can hardly call you 'mother,' but we might compromise upon 'aunt,'" I said, laughing. "Aunt what?"

"My name is Aaronna," she gravely answered. "My father was much disappointed that I was not a boy, and gave me as nearly as possible the name he had prepared—Aaron."

"Then come and dine with me tomorrow, and bring with you the other manuscripts, Aaronna," I said, amused at the quaint sound of the name. On the whole, I did not like "aunt."

"I will come," she answered.

It was twilight and still raining, but she refused all offers of escort or carriage, departing with her maid, as she had come, under the brown umbrella. The next day we had the dinner. Simpson was astonished—and more than astonished, grieved—when I told him that he was to dine with the maid; but he could not complain in words, since my own guest, the mistress, was hardly more attractive. When our preparations were complete, I could not help laughing: the two prim little tables, one in the parlor and one in the anteroom, and Simpson disapprovingly going back and forth between them, were irresistible.

I greeted my guest hilariously when she arrived, and, fortunately, her manner was not quite so depressed as usual: I could never have accorded myself with a tearful mood. I had thought that perhaps she would make, for the occasion, some change in her attire; I have never known a woman who had not some scrap of finery, however small, in reserve for that unexpected occasion of which she is ever dreaming. But no: Miss Grief wore the same black gown, unadorned and unaltered. I was glad that there was no rain that day, so that the skirt did not at least look so damp and rheumatic.

She ate quietly, almost furtively, yet with a good appetite, and she did not refuse the wine. Then, when the meal was over and Simpson had removed the dishes, I asked for the new manuscripts. She gave me an old green copybook filled with short poems, and a prose sketch by itself; I lit a cigar and sat down at my desk to look them over.

"Perhaps you will try a cigarette?" I suggested, more for amusement than anything else, for there was not a shade of Bohemianism about her; her whole appearance was puritanical.

"I have not yet succeeded in learning to smoke."

"You have tried?" I said, turning round.

"Yes: Serena and I tried, but we did not succeed."

"Serena is your maid?"

"She lives with me."

I was seized with inward laughter, and began hastily to look over her manuscripts with my back toward her, so that she might not see it. A vision had risen before me of those two forlorn women, alone in their room with locked doors, patiently trying to acquire the smoker's art.

But my attention was soon absorbed by the papers before me. Such a fantastic collection of words, lines, and epithets I had never before seen, or even in dreams imagined. In truth, they were like the work of dreams: they were *Kubla Khan*, only more so. Here and there was radiance like the flash of a diamond, but each poem, almost each verse and line, was marred by some fault or lack which seemed wilful perversity, like the work of an evil sprite. It was like a case of jeweller's wares set before you, with each ring unfinished, each bracelet too large or too small for its purpose, each breastpin without its fastening, each necklace purposely broken. I turned the pages, marvelling. When about half an hour had passed, and I was leaning back for a moment to light another cigar, I glanced toward my visitor. She was behind me, in an easy chair before my small fire, and she was—fast asleep! In the relaxation of her unconsciousness I was struck anew by the poverty her appearance expressed; her feet were visible, and I saw the miserable worn old shoes which hitherto she had kept concealed.

After looking at her for a moment, I returned to my task and took up the prose story; in prose she must be more reasonable. She was less fantastic perhaps, but hardly more reasonable. The story was that of a profligate and commonplace man forced by two of his friends, in order not to break the heart of a dying girl who loves him, to live up to a high imaginary ideal of himself which her pure but mistaken mind has formed. He has a handsome face and sweet voice, and repeats what they tell him. Her long, slow decline and happy death, and his own inward ennui and profound weariness of the rôle he has to play, made the vivid points of the story. So far, well enough, but here was the trouble: through the whole narrative moved another character, a physician of tender heart and exquisite mercy, who practiced murder as a fine art, and was regarded (by the author) as a second Messiah! This was monstrous. I read it through twice, and threw it down; then, fatigued, I turned round and leaned back, waiting for her to wake. I could see her profile against the dark hue of the easy chair.

Presently she seemed to feel my gaze, for she stirred, then opened her eyes. "I have been asleep," she said, rising hurriedly.

"No harm in that, Aaronna."

But she was deeply embarrassed and troubled, much more so than the occasion required; so much so, indeed, that I turned the conversation back upon the manuscripts as a diversion. "I cannot stand that doctor of yours," I said, indicating the prose story; "no one would. You must cut him out."

Her self-possession returned as if by magic. "Certainly not," she answered haughtily.

"Oh, if you do not care—I had labored under the impression that you were anxious these things should find a purchaser."

"I am, I am," she said, her manner changing to deep humility with wonderful rapidity. With such alternations of feeling as this sweeping over her like great waves, no wonder she was old before her time.

"Then you must take out that doctor."

"I am willing, but do not know how," she answered, pressing her hands together helplessly. "In my mind he belongs to the story so closely that he cannot be separated from it."

Here Simpson entered, bringing a note for me: it was a line from Mrs. Abercrombie inviting me for that evening—an unexpected gathering, and therefore likely to be all the more agreeable. My heart bounded in spite of me; I forgot Miss Grief and her manuscripts for the moment as completely as though they had never existed. But, bodily, being still in the same room with her, her speech brought me back to the present.

"You have had good news?" she said.

"Oh no, nothing especial—merely an invitation."

"But good news also," she repeated. "And now, as for me, I must go."

Not supposing that she would stay much later in any case, I had that morning ordered a carriage to come for her at about that hour. I told her this. She made no reply beyond putting on her bonnet and shawl.

"You will hear from me soon," I said; "I shall do all I can for you."

She had reached the door, but before opening it she stopped, turned and extended her hand. "You are good," she said: "I give you thanks. Do not think me ungrateful or envious. It is only that you are young, and I am so—so old." Then she opened the door and passed through the anteroom without pause, her maid accompanying her and Simpson with gladness lighting the way. They were gone. I dressed hastily and went out—to continue my studies in psychology.

Time passed; I was busy, amused and perhaps a little excited (sometimes psychology is exciting). But, though much occupied with my own affairs, I did not altogether neglect my self-imposed task regarding Miss Grief. I began by sending her prose story to a friend, the editor of a monthly magazine, with a letter making a strong plea for its admittance. It should have a chance first on its own merits. Then I forwarded the drama to a publisher, also an acquaintance, a man with a taste for phantasms and a soul above mere common popularity, as his own coffers knew to their cost. This done, I waited with conscience clear.

Four weeks passed. During this waiting period I heard nothing from Miss Grief. At last one morning came a letter from my editor. "The story has force, but I cannot stand that doctor," he wrote. "Let her cut him out, and I might print it." Just what I myself had said. The package lay there on my table, travel worn and grimed; a returned manuscript is, I think, the most melancholy object on earth. I decided to wait, before writing to Aaronna, until the second letter was received. A week later it came. "Armor" was declined. The publisher had been "impressed" by the power displayed in certain passages, but the "impossibilities of the plot" rendered it "unavailable for publication"—in fact, would "bury it in ridicule" if brought before the public, a public "lamentably" fond of amusement, "seeking it, undaunted, even in the cannon's mouth." I doubt if he knew himself what he meant. But one thing, at any rate, was clear: "Armor" was declined.

Now, I am, as I have remarked before, a little obstinate. I was determined that Miss Grief's work should be received. I would alter and improve it myself, without letting her know: the end justified the means. Surely the sieve of my own good taste, whose mesh had been pronounced so fine and delicate, would serve for two. I began; and utterly failed.

I set to work first upon "Armor." I amended, altered, left out, put in, pieced, condensed, lengthened; I did my best, and all to no avail. I could not succeed in completing anything that satisfied me, or that approached, in truth, Miss Grief's own work just as it stood. I suppose I went over that manuscript twenty times: I covered sheets of paper with my copies. But the obstinate drama refused to be corrected; as it was it must stand or fall.

Wearied and annoyed, I threw it aside and took up the prose story: that would be easier. But, to my surprise, I found that that apparently gentle "doctor" would not out: he was so closely interwoven with every part of the tale that to take him out was like taking out one especial figure in a carpet: that is, impossible, unless you unravel the whole. At last I did unravel the whole, and then the story was no longer good, or Aaronna's: it was weak, and mine. All this took time, for of course I had much to do in connection with my own life and tasks. But, though slowly and at my leisure, I really did try my best as regarded Miss Grief, and without success. I was forced at last to make up my mind that either my own powers were not equal to the task, or else that her perversities were as essential a part of her work as her inspirations, and not to be separated from it. Once during this period I showed two of the short poems to Isabel, withholding of course the writer's name. "They were written by a woman," I explained.

"Her mind must have been disordered, poor thing!" Isabel said in her gentle way when she returned them—"at least, judging by these. They are hopelessly mixed and vague."

Now, they were not vague so much as vast. But I knew that I could not make Isabel comprehend it, and (so complex a creature is man) I do not know that I wanted her to comprehend it. These were the only ones in the whole collection that I would have shown her, and I was rather glad that she did not like even these. Not that poor Aaronna's poems were evil: they were simply unrestrained, large, vast, like the skies or the wind. Isabel was bounded on all sides, like a violet in a garden bed. And I liked her so.

One afternoon, about the time when I was beginning to see that I could not "improve" Miss Grief, I came upon the maid. I was driving, and she had stopped on the crossing to let the carriage pass. I recognized her at a glance (by her general forlornness), and called to the driver to stop: "How is Miss Grief?" I said. "I have been intending to write to her for some time."

"And your note, when it comes," answered the old woman on the crosswalk fiercely, "she shall not see."

"What?"

"I say she shall not see it. Your patronizing face shows that you have no good news, and you shall not rack and stab her any more on *this* earth, please God, while I have authority."

"Who has racked or stabbed her, Serena?"

"Serena, indeed! Rubbish! I'm no Serena: I'm her aunt. And as to who has racked and stabbed her, I say you, *you*—YOU literary men!" She had put her old head inside my carriage, and flung out these words at me in a shrill, menacing tone. "But she shall die in peace in spite of you," she continued. "Vampires! you take her ideas and fatten on them, and leave her to starve. You know you do—*you* who have had her poor manuscripts these months and months!"

"Is she ill?" I asked in real concern, gathering that much at least from the incoherent tirade.

"She is dying," answered the desolate old creature, her voice softening and her dim eyes filling with tears.

"Oh, I trust not. Perhaps something can be done. Can I help you in any way?"

"In all ways if you would," she said, breaking down and beginning to sob weakly, with her head resting on the sill of the carriage window. "Oh, what have we not been through together, we two! Piece by piece I have sold all."

I am goodhearted enough, but I do not like to have old women weeping across my carriage door. I suggested, therefore, that she should come inside and let me take her home. Her shabby old skirt was soon beside me, and, following her directions, the driver turned toward one of the most wretched quarters of the city, the abode of poverty, crowded and unclean. Here, in a large bare chamber up many flights of stairs, I found Miss Grief.

As I entered I was startled: I thought she was dead. There seemed no life present until she opened her eyes, and even then they rested upon us vaguely, as though she did not know who we were. But as I approached a light came into them: she recognized me, and this sudden revivification, this return of the soul to the almost deserted body, was the most wonderful thing I ever saw. "You have good news of the drama?" she whispered as I bent over her: "tell me. I *know* you have good news."

What was I to answer? Pray, what would you have answered, puritan?

"Yes, I have good news, Aaronna," I said. "The drama will appear." (And who knows? Perhaps it will in some other world.)

She smiled, and her now brilliant eyes did not leave my face.

"He knows I'm your aunt: I told him," said the old woman, coming to the bedside.

"Did you?" whispered Miss Grief, still gazing at me with a smile. "Then please, dear Aunt Martha, give me something to eat."

Aunt Martha hurried across the room, and I followed her. "It's the first time she's asked for food in weeks," she said in a husky tone.

She opened a cupboard door vaguely, but I could see nothing within. "What have you for her?" I asked with some impatience, though in a low voice.

"Please God, nothing!" answered the poor old woman, hiding her reply and her tears behind the broad cupboard door. "I was going out to get a little something when I met you."

"Good Heavens! is it money you need? Here, take this and send; or go yourself in the carriage waiting below."

She hurried out breathless, and I went back to the bedside, much disturbed by what I had seen and heard. But Miss Grief's eyes were full of life, and as I sat down beside her she whispered earnestly, "Tell me."

And I did tell her—a romance invented for the occasion. I venture to say that none of my published sketches could compare with it. As for the lie involved, it will stand among my few good deeds, I know, at the judgment bar.

And she was satisfied. "I have never known what it was," she whispered, "to be fully happy until now." She closed her eyes, and when the lids fell I again thought that she had passed away. But no, there was still pulsation in her small, thin wrist. As she perceived my touch she smiled. "Yes, I am happy," she said again, though without audible sound.

The old aunt returned; food was prepared, and she took some. I myself went out after wine that should be rich and pure. She rallied a little, but I did not leave her: her eyes dwelt upon me and compelled me to stay, or rather my conscience compelled me. It was a damp night, and I had a little fire made. The wine, fruit, flowers, and candles I had ordered made the bare place for the time being bright and fragrant. Aunt Martha dozed in her chair from sheer fatigue—she had watched many nights—but Miss Grief was awake, and I sat beside her.

"I make you my executor," she murmured, "as to the drama. But my other manuscripts place, when I am gone, under my head, and let them be buried with me. They are not many—those you have and these. See!"

I followed her gesture, and saw under her pillows the edges of two more copybooks like the one I had. "Do not look at them—my poor dead children!" she said tenderly. "Let them depart with me—unread, as I have been."

Later she whispered, "Did you wonder why I came to you? It was the contrast. You were young—strong—rich—praised—loved—successful: all that I was not. I wanted to look at you—and imagine how it would feel. You had success—but I had the greater power. Tell me, did I not have it?"

"Yes, Aaronna."

"It is all in the past now. But I am satisfied."

After another pause she said with a faint smile, "Do you remember when I fell asleep in your parlor? It was the good and rich food. It was so long since I had had food like that!"

I took her hand and held it, conscience stricken, but now she hardly seemed to perceive my touch. "And the smoking?" she whispered. "Do you remember how you laughed? I saw it. But I had heard that smoking soothed—that one was no longer tired and hungry—with a cigar."

In little whispers of this sort, separated by long rests and pauses, the night passed. Once she asked if her aunt was asleep, and when I answered in the affirmative she said, "Help her to return home—to America: the drama will pay for it. I ought never to have brought her away."

I promised, and she resumed her bright-eyed silence.

I think she did not speak again. Toward morning the change came, and soon after sunrise, with her old aunt kneeling by her side, she passed away.

All was arranged as she had wished. Her manuscripts, covered with violets, formed her pillow. No one followed her to the grave save her aunt and myself; I thought she would prefer it so. Her name was not "Crief," after all, but "Moncrief"; I saw it written out by Aunt Martha for the coffin plate, as follows: "Aaronna Moncrief, aged forty-three years, two months, and eight days."

I never knew more of her history than is written here. If there was more that I might have learned, it remained unlearned, for I did not ask.

And the drama? I keep it here in this locked case. I could have had it published at my own expense; but I think that now she knows its faults herself, perhaps, and would not like it.

I keep it; and, once in a while, I read it over—not as a *memento mori* exactly, but rather as a memento of my own good fortune, for which I should continually give thanks. The want of one grain made all her work void, and that one grain was given to me. She, with the greater power, failed—I, with the less, succeeded. But no praise is due to me for that. When I die "Armor" is to be destroyed unread: not even Isabel is to see it. For women will misunderstand each other; and, dear and precious to me as my sweet wife is, I could not bear that she or any one should cast so much as a thought of scorn upon the memory of the writer, upon my poor dead, "unavailable," unaccepted "Miss Grief."

THE REVOLT OF "MOTHER"

by Mary E. Wilkins Freeman

Mary Eleanor Wilkins Freeman lived most of her life in rural Massachusetts and Vermont. She started writing stories as a teenager, and was quite successful. By 1890, when "The Revolt of 'Mother'" was published in *Harper's Bazaar*, she was one of the most widely read writers in the English language. This story was included in *A New England Nun and Other Stories* (1891).

"FATHER!"

"What is it?"

"What are them men diggin' over there in the field for?"

There was a sudden dropping and enlarging of the lower part of the old man's face, as if some heavy weight had settled therein; he shut his mouth tight, and went on harnessing the great bay mare. He hustled the collar on to her neck with a jerk.

"Father!"

The old man slapped the saddle upon the mare's back.

"Look here, father, I want to know what them men are diggin' over in the field for, an' I'm goin' to know."

"I wish you'd go into the house, mother, an' 'tend to your own affairs," the old man said then. He ran his words together, and his speech was almost as inarticulate as a growl.

But the woman understood; it was her most native tongue. "I ain't goin' into the house till you tell me what them men are doin' over there in the field," said she.

Then she stood waiting. She was a small woman, short and straight-waisted like a child in her brown cotton gown. Her forehead was mild and benevolent between the smooth curves of gray hair; there were meek downward lines about her nose and mouth; but her eyes, fixed upon the old man, looked as if the meekness had been the result of her own will, never of the will of another.

They were in the barn, standing before the wide open doors. The spring air, full of the smell of growing grass and unseen blossoms, came in their faces. The deep yard in front was littered with farm wagons and piles of wood; on the edges, close to the fence and the house, the grass was a vivid green, and there were some dandelions.

The old man glanced doggedly at his wife as he tightened the last buckles on the harness. She looked as immovable to him as one of the rocks in his pasture-land, bound to the earth with generations of blackberry vines. He slapped the reins over the horse, and started forth from the barn.

"*Father!*" said she.

The old man pulled up. "What is it?"

"I want to know what them men are diggin' over there in that field for."

"They're diggin' a cellar, I s'pose, if you've got to know."

"A cellar for what?"

"A barn."

"A barn? You ain't goin' to build a barn over there where we was goin' to have a house, father?"

The old man said not another word. He hurried the horse into the farm wagon, and clattered out of the yard, jouncing as sturdily on his seat as a boy.

The woman stood a moment looking after him, then she went out of the barn across a corner of the yard to the house. The house, standing at right angles with the great barn and a long reach of sheds and out-buildings, was infinitesimal compared with them. It was scarcely as commodious for people as the little boxes under the barn eaves were for doves.

A pretty girl's face, pink and delicate as a flower, was looking out of one of the house windows. She was watching three men who were digging over in the field which bounded the yard near the road line. She turned quietly when the woman entered.

"What are they diggin' for, mother?" said she. "Did he tell you?"

"They're diggin' for—a cellar for a new barn."

"Oh, mother, he ain't goin' to build another barn?"

"That's what he says."

A boy stood before the kitchen glass combing his hair. He combed slowly and painstakingly, arranging his brown hair in a smooth hillock over his forehead. He did not seem to pay any attention to the conversation.

"Sammy, did you know father was goin' to build a new barn?" asked the girl.

The boy combed assiduously.

"Sammy!"

He turned, and showed a face like his father's under his smooth crest of hair. "Yes, I s'pose I did," he said, reluctantly.

"How long have you known it?" asked his mother.

" 'Bout three months, I guess."

"Why didn't you tell of it?"

"Didn't think 'twould do no good."

"I don't see what father wants another barn for," said the girl, in her sweet, slow voice. She turned again to the window, and stared out at the digging men in the field. Her tender, sweet face was full of a gentle distress. Her forehead was as bald and innocent as a baby's, with the light hair strained back from it in a row of curl-papers. She was quite large, but her soft curves did not look as if they covered muscles.

Her mother looked sternly at the boy. "Is he goin' to buy more cows?" said she.

The boy did not reply; he was tying his shoes.

"Sammy, I want you to tell me if he's goin' to buy more cows."

"I s'pose he is."

"How many?"

"Four, I guess."

His mother said nothing more. She went into the pantry, and there was a clatter of dishes. The boy got his cap from a nail behind the door, took an old arithmetic from the shelf, and started for school. He was lightly built, but clumsy. He went out of the yard with a curious spring in the hips, that made his loose home-made jacket tilt up in the rear.

The girl went to the sink, and began to wash the dishes that were piled up there. Her mother came promptly out of the pantry, and shoved her aside. "You wipe 'em," said she; "I'll wash. There's a good many this mornin'."

The mother plunged her hands vigorously into the water, the girl wiped the plates slowly and dreamily. "Mother," said she, "don't you think it's too bad father's goin' to build that new barn, much as we need a decent house to live in?"

Her mother scrubbed a dish fiercely. "You ain't found out yet we're women-folks, Nanny Penn," said she. "You ain't seen enough of men-folks yet to. One of these days you'll find it out, an' then you'll know that we know only what men-folks think we do, so far as any use of it goes, an' how we'd ought to reckon men-folks in with Providence, an' not complain of what they do any more than we do of the weather."

"I don't care; I don't believe George is anything like that, anyhow," said Nanny. Her delicate face flushed pink, her lips pouted softly, as if she were going to cry.

"You wait an' see. I guess George Eastman ain't no better than other men. You hadn't ought to judge father, though. He can't help it, 'cause he don't look at things jest the way we do. An' we've been pretty comfortable here, after all. The roof don't leak—ain't never but once—that's one thing. Father's kept it shingled right up."

"I do wish we had a parlor."

"I guess it won't hurt George Eastman any to come to see you in a nice clean kitchen. I guess a good many girls don't have as good a place as this. Nobody's ever heard me complain."

"I ain't complained either, mother."

"Well, I don't think you'd better, a good father an' a good home as you've got. S'pose your father made you go out an' work for your livin'? Lots of girls have to that ain't no stronger an' better able to than you be."

Sarah Penn washed the frying-pan with a conclusive air. She scrubbed the outside of it as faithfully as the inside. She was a masterly keeper of her box of a house. Her one living-room never seemed to have in it any of the dust which the friction of life with inanimate matter produces. She swept, and there seemed to be no dirt to go before the broom; she cleaned, and one could see no difference. She was like an artist so perfect that he has apparently no art. To-day she got out a mixing bowl and a board, and rolled some pies, and there was no more flour upon her than upon her daughter who was doing finer work. Nanny was to be married in the fall, and she was sewing on some white cambric and embroidery. She sewed industriously while her mother cooked, her soft milk-white hands and wrists showed whiter than her delicate work.

"We must have the stove moved out in the shed before long," said Mrs. Penn. "Talk about not havin' things, it's been a real blessin' to be able to put a stove up in that shed in hot weather. Father did one good thing when he fixed that stove-pipe out there."

Sarah Penn's face as she rolled her pies had that expression of meek vigor which might have characterized one of the New Testament saints. She was making mince-pies. Her husband, Adoniram Penn, liked them better than any other kind. She baked twice a week. Adoniram often liked a piece of pie between meals. She hurried this morning. It had been later than usual when she began, and she wanted to have a pie baked for dinner. However deep a resentment she might be forced to hold against her husband, she would never fail in sedulous attention to his wants.

Nobility of character manifests itself at loop-holes when it is not provided with large doors. Sarah Penn's showed itself to-day in flaky dishes of pastry. So she made the pies faithfully, while across the table she could see, when she glanced up from her work, the sight that rankled in her patient and steadfast soul—the digging of the cellar of the new barn in the place where Adoniram forty years ago had promised her their new house should stand.

The pies were done for dinner. Adoniram and Sammy were home a few minutes after twelve o'clock. The dinner was eaten with serious haste. There was never much conversation at the table in the Penn family. Adoniram asked a blessing, and they ate promptly, then rose up and went about their work.

Sammy went back to school, taking soft sly lopes out of the yard like a rabbit. He wanted a game of marbles before school, and feared his father would give him some chores to do. Adoniram hastened to the door and called after him, but he was out of sight.

"I don't see what you let him go for, mother," said he. "I wanted him to help me unload that wood."

Adoniram went to work out in the yard unloading wood from the wagon. Sarah put away the dinner dishes, while Nanny took down her curl-papers and changed her dress. She was going down to the store to buy some more embroidery and thread.

When Nanny was gone, Mrs. Penn went to the door. "Father!" she called.

"Well, what is it!"

"I want to see you jest a minute, father."

"I can't leave this wood nohow. I've got to git it unloaded an' go for a load of gravel afore two o'clock. Sammy had ought to helped me. You hadn't ought to let him go to school so early."

"I want to see you jest a minute."

"I tell ye I can't, nohow, mother."

"Father, you come here." Sarah Penn stood in the door like a queen; she held her head as if it bore a crown; there was that patience which makes authority royal in her voice. Adoniram went.

Mrs. Penn led the way into the kitchen, and pointed to a chair. "Sit down, father," said she; "I've got somethin' I want to say to you."

He sat down heavily; his face was quite stolid, but he looked at her with restive eyes. "Well, what is it, mother?"

"I want to know what you're buildin' that new barn for, father?"

"I ain't got nothin' to say about it."

"It can't be you think you need another barn?"

"I tell ye I ain't got nothin' to say about it, mother; an' I ain't goin' to say nothin'."

"Be you goin' to buy more cows?"

Adoniram did not reply; he shut his mouth tight.

"I know you be, as well as I want to. Now, father, look here"—Sarah Penn had not sat down; she stood before her husband in the humble fashion of a Scripture woman—"I'm goin' to talk real plain to you; I never have sence I married you, but I'm goin' to now. I ain't never complained, an' I ain't goin' to complain now, but I'm goin' to talk plain. You see this room here, father; you look at it well. You see there ain't no carpet on the floor, an' you see the paper is all dirty, an' droppin' off the walls. We ain't had no new paper on it for ten year, an' then I put it on myself, an' it didn't cost but ninepence a roll. You see this room, father; it's all the one I've had to work in an' eat in an' sit in sence we was married. There ain't another woman in the whole town whose husband ain't got half the means you have but what's got better. It's all the room Nanny's got to have her company in; an' there ain't one of her mates but what's got better, an' their fathers not so able as hers is. It's all the room she'll have to be married in. What would you have thought, father, if we had had our weddin' in a room no better than this? I was married in my mother's parlor, with a carpet on the floor, an' stuffed furniture, an' a mahogany card-table. An' this is all the room my daughter will have to be married in. Look here, father!"

Sarah Penn went across the room as though it were a tragic stage. She flung open a door and disclosed a tiny bedroom, only large enough for a bed and bureau, with a path between. "There, father," said she—"there's all the room I've had to sleep in forty year. All my children were born there—the two that died, an' the two that's livin'. I was sick with a fever there."

She stepped to another door and opened it. It led into the small, ill-lighted pantry. "Here," said she, "is all the buttery I've got—every place I've got for my dishes, to set away my victuals in, an' to keep my milk-pans in. Father, I've been takin' care of the milk of six cows in this place, an' now you're goin' to build a new barn, an' keep more cows, an' give me more to do in it."

She threw open another door. A narrow crooked flight of stairs wound upward from it. "There, father," said she, "I want you to look at the stairs that go up to them two unfinished chambers that are all the places our son an' daughter have had to sleep in all their lives. There ain't a prettier girl in town nor a more ladylike one than Nanny, an' that's the place she has to sleep in. It ain't so good as your horse's stall; it ain't so warm an' tight."

Sarah Penn went back and stood before her husband. "Now, father," said she, "I want to know if you think you're doin' right an' accordin' to what you profess. Here, when we was married, forty year ago, you promised me faithful that we should have a new house built in that lot over in the field before the year was out. You said you had money enough, an' you wouldn't ask me to live in no such place as this. It is forty year now, an' you've been makin' more money, an' I've been savin' of it for you ever since, an' you ain't built no house yet. You've built sheds an' cow-houses an' one new barn, an' now you're goin' to build another. Father, I want to know if you think it's right. You're lodgin' your dumb beasts better than you are your own flesh an' blood. I want to know if you think it's right."

"I ain't got nothin' to say."

"You can't say nothin' without ownin' it ain't right, father. An' there's another thing—I ain't complained; I've got along forty year, an' I s'pose I should forty more, if it wa'n't for that—if we don't have another house. Nanny she can't live with us after she's married. She'll have to go somewheres else to live away from us, an' it don't seem as if I could have it so, noways, father. She wa'n't ever strong. She's got considerable color, but there wa'n't never any backbone to her. I've always took the heft of everything off her, an' she ain't fit to keep house an' do everything herself. She'll be all worn out inside of a year. Think of her doin' all the washin' an' ironin' an' bakin' with them soft white hands an' arms, an' sweepin'! I can't have it so, noways, father."

Mrs. Penn's face was burning; her mild eyes gleamed. She had pleaded her little cause like a Webster; she had ranged from severity to pathos; but her opponent employed that obstinate silence which makes eloquence futile with mocking echoes. Adoniram arose clumsily.

"Father, ain't you got nothin' to say?" said Mrs. Penn.

"I've got to go off after that load of gravel. I can't stan' here talkin' all day."

"Father, won't you think it over, an' have a house built there instead of a barn?"

"I ain't got nothin' to say."

Adoniram shuffled out. Mrs. Penn went into her bedroom. When she came out, her eyes were red. She had a roll of unbleached cotton cloth. She spread it out on the kitchen table, and began cutting out some shirts for her husband. The men over in the field had a team to help them this afternoon; she could hear their halloos. She had a scanty pattern for the shirts; she had to plan and piece the sleeves.

Nanny came home with her embroidery, and sat down with her needlework. She had taken down her curl-papers, and there was a soft roll of fair hair like an aureole over her forehead; her face was as delicately fine and clear as porcelain. Suddenly she looked up, and the tender red flamed all over her face and neck. "Mother," said she.

"What say?"

"I've been thinking—I don't see how we're goin' to have any—wedding in this room. I'd be ashamed to have his folks come if we didn't have anybody else."

"Mebbe we can have some new paper before then; I can put it on. I guess you won't have no call to be ashamed of your belongin's."

"We might have the wedding in the new barn," said Nanny, with gentle pettishness. "Why, mother, what makes you look so?"

Mrs. Penn had started, and was staring at her with a curious expression. She turned again to her work, and spread out a pattern carefully on the cloth. "Nothin'," said she.

Presently Adoniram clattered out of the yard in his two-wheeled dump cart, standing as proudly upright as a Roman charioteer. Mrs. Penn opened the door and stood there a minute looking out; the halloos of the men sounded louder.

It seemed to her all through the spring months that she heard nothing but the halloos and the noises of saws and hammers. The new barn grew fast. It was a fine edifice for this little village. Men came on pleasant Sundays, in their meeting suits and clean shirt bosoms, and stood around it admiringly. Mrs. Penn did not speak of it, and Adoniram did not mention it to her, although sometimes, upon a return from inspecting it, he bore himself with injured dignity.

"It's a strange thing how your mother feels about the new barn," he said, confidentially, to Sammy one day.

Sammy only grunted after an odd fashion for a boy; he had learned it from his father.

The barn was all completed ready for use by the third week in July. Adoniram had planned to move his stock in on Wednesday; on Tuesday he received a letter which changed his plans. He came in with it early in the morning. "Sammy's been to the post-office," said he, "an' I've got a letter from Hiram." Hiram was Mrs. Penn's brother, who lived in Vermont.

"Well," said Mrs. Penn, "what does he say about the folks?"

"I guess they're all right. He says he thinks if I come up country right off there's a chance to buy jest the kind of a horse I want." He stared reflectively out of the window at the new barn.

Mrs. Penn was making pies. She went on clapping the rolling-pin into the crust, although she was very pale, and her heart beat loudly.

"I dun' know but what I'd better go," said Adoniram. "I hate to go off jest now, right in the midst of hayin', but the ten-acre lot's cut, an' I guess Rufus an' the others can git along without me three or four days. I can't get a horse round here to suit me, nohow, an' I've got to have another for all that wood-haulin' in the fall. I told Hiram to watch out, an' if he got wind of a good horse to let me know. I guess I'd better go."

"I'll get out your clean shirt an' collar," said Mrs. Penn calmly.

She laid out Adoniram's Sunday suit and his clean clothes on the bed in the little bedroom. She got his shaving-water and razor ready. At last she buttoned on his collar and fastened his black cravat.

Adoniram never wore his collar and cravat except on extra occasions. He held his head high, with a rasped dignity. When he was all ready, with his coat and hat brushed, and a lunch of pie and cheese in a paper bag, he hesitated on the threshold of the door. He looked at his wife, and his manner was defiantly apologetic. "*If* them cows come to-day, Sammy can drive 'em into the new barn," said he; "an' when they bring the hay up, they can pitch it in there."

"Well," replied Mrs. Penn.

Adoniram set his shaven face ahead and started. When he had cleared the door-step, he turned and looked back with a kind of nervous solemnity. "I shall be back by Saturday if nothin' happens," said he.

"Do be careful, father," returned his wife.

She stood in the door with Nanny at her elbow and watched him out of sight. Her eyes had a strange, doubtful expression in them; her peaceful forehead was contracted. She went in, and about her baking again. Nanny sat sewing. Her wedding-day was drawing nearer, and she was getting pale and thin with her steady sewing. Her mother kept glancing at her.

"Have you got that pain in your side this mornin'?" she asked.

"A little."

Mrs. Penn's face, as she worked, changed, her perplexed forehead smoothed, her eyes were steady, her lips firmly set. She formed a maxim for herself, although incoherently with her unlettered thoughts. "Unsolicited opportunities are the guide-posts of the Lord to the new roads of life," she repeated in effect, and she made up her mind to her course of action.

"S'posin' I *had* wrote to Hiram," she muttered once, when she was in the pantry—"s'posin' I had wrote, an' asked him if he knew of any horse? But I didn't, an' father's goin' wa'n't none of my doin'. It looks like a providence." Her voice rang out quite loud at the last.

"What you talkin' about, mother?" called Nanny.

"Nothin'."

Mrs. Penn hurried her baking; at eleven o'clock it was all done. The load of hay from the west field came slowly down the cart track, and drew up at the new barn. Mrs. Penn ran out. "Stop!" she screamed—"stop!"

The men stopped and looked; Sammy upreared from the top of the load, and stared at his mother.

"Stop!" she cried out again. "Don't you put the hay in that barn; put it in the old one."

"Why, he said to put it in here," returned one of the haymakers, wonderingly. He was a young man, a neighbor's son, whom Adoniram hired by the year to help on the farm.

"Don't you put the hay in the new barn; there's room enough in the old one, ain't there?" said Mrs. Penn.

"Room enough," returned the hired man, in his thick, rustic tones. "Didn't need the new barn, nohow, far as room's concerned. Well, I s'pose he changed his mind." He took hold of the horses' bridles.

Mrs. Penn went back to the house. Soon the kitchen windows were darkened, and a fragrance like warm honey came into the room.

Nanny laid down her work. "I thought father wanted them to put the hay into the new barn?" she said, wonderingly.

"It's all right," replied her mother.

Sammy slid down from the load of hay, and came in to see if dinner was ready.

"I ain't goin' to get a regular dinner to-day, as long as father's gone," said his mother. "I've let the fire go out. You can have some bread an' milk an' pie. I thought we could get along." She set out some bowls of milk, some bread, and a pie on the kitchen table. "You'd better eat your dinner now," said she. "You might jest as well get through with it. I want you to help me afterward."

Nanny and Sammy stared at each other. There was something strange in their mother's manner. Mrs. Penn did not eat anything herself. She went into the pantry, and they heard her moving dishes while they ate. Presently she came out with a pile of plates. She got the clothes-basket out of the shed, and packed them in it. Nanny and Sammy watched. She brought out cups and saucers, and put them in with the plates.

"What you goin' to do, mother?" inquired Nanny, in a timid voice. A sense of something unusual made her tremble, as if it were a ghost. Sammy rolled his eyes over his pie.

"You'll see what I'm goin' to do," replied Mrs. Penn. "If you're through, Nanny, I want you to go up-stairs an' pack up your things; an' I want you, Sammy, to help me take down the bed in the bedroom."

"Oh, mother, what for?" gasped Nanny.

"You'll see."

During the next few hours a feat was performed by this simple, pious New England mother which was equal in its way to Wolfe's storming of the Heights of Abraham. It took no more genius and audacity of bravery for Wolfe to cheer his wondering soldiers up those steep precipices, under the sleeping eyes of the enemy, than for Sarah Penn, at the head of her children, to move all their little household goods into the new barn while her husband was away.

Nanny and Sammy followed their mother's instructions without a murmur; indeed, they were overawed. There is a certain uncanny and superhuman quality about all such purely original undertakings as their mother's was to them. Nanny went back and forth with her light loads, and Sammy tugged with sober energy.

At five o'clock in the afternoon the little house in which the Penns had lived for forty years had emptied itself into the new barn.

Every builder builds somewhat for unknown purposes, and is in a measure a prophet. The architect of Adoniram Penn's barn, while he designed it for the comfort of four-footed animals, had planned better than he knew for the comfort of humans. Sarah Penn saw at a glance its possibilities. Those great box-stalls, with quilts hung before them, would make better bedrooms than the one she had occupied for forty years, and there was a tight carriage-room. The harness-room, with its chimney and shelves, would make a kitchen of her dreams. The great middle space would make a parlor, by-and-by, fit for a palace. Up-stairs there was as much room as down. With partitions and windows, what a house would there be! Sarah looked at the row of stanchions before the allotted space for cows, and reflected that she would have her front entry there.

At six o'clock the stove was up in the harness-room, the kettle was boiling, and the table set for tea. It looked almost as home-like as the abandoned house across the yard had ever done. The young hired man milked, and Sarah directed him calmly to bring the milk to the new barn. He came gaping, dropping little blots of foam from the brimming pails on the grass. Before the next morning he had spread the story of Adoniram Penn's wife moving into the new barn all over the little village. Men assembled in the store and talked it over, women with shawls over their heads scuttled into each other's houses before their work was done. Any deviation from the ordinary course of life in this quiet town was enough to stop all progress in it. Everybody paused to look at the staid, independent figure on the side track. There was a difference of opinion with regard to her. Some held her to be insane; some, of a lawless and rebellious spirit.

Friday the minister went to see her. It was in the forenoon, and she was at the barn door shelling pease for dinner. She looked up and returned his salutation with dignity, then she went on with her work. She did not invite him in. The saintly expression of her face remained fixed, but there was an angry flush over it.

The minister stood awkwardly before her, and talked. She handled the pease as if they were bullets. At last she looked up, and her eyes showed the spirit that her meek front had covered for a lifetime.

"There ain't no use talkin', Mr. Hersey," said she. "I've thought it all over an' over, an' I believe I'm doin' what's right. I've made it the subject of prayer, an' it's betwixt me an' the Lord an' Adoniram. There ain't no call for nobody else to worry about it."

"Well, of course, if you have brought it to the Lord in prayer, and feel satisfied that you are doing right, Mrs. Penn," said the minister, helplessly. His thin gray-bearded face was pathetic. He was a sickly man; his youthful confidence had cooled; he had to scourge himself up to some of his pastoral duties as relentlessly as a Catholic ascetic, and then he was prostrated by the smart.

"I think it's right jest as much as I think it was right for our forefathers to come over from the old country 'cause they didn't have what belonged to 'em," said Mrs. Penn. She arose. The barn threshold might have been Plymouth Rock from her bearing. "I don't doubt you mean well, Mr. Hersey," said she, "but there are things people hadn't ought to interfere with. I've been a member of the church for over forty year. I've got my own mind an' my own feet, an' I'm goin' to think my own thoughts an' go my own ways, an' nobody but the Lord is goin' to dictate to me unless I've a mind to have him. Won't you come in an' set down? How is Mis' Hersey?"

"She is well, I thank you," replied the minister. He added some more perplexed apologetic remarks; then he retreated.

He could expound the intricacies of every character study in the Scriptures, he was competent to grasp the Pilgrim Fathers and all historical innovators, but Sarah Penn was beyond him. He could deal with primal cases, but parallel ones worsted him. But, after all, although it was aside from his province, he wondered more how Adoniram Penn would deal with his wife than how the Lord would. Everybody shared the wonder. When Adoniram's four new cows arrived, Sarah ordered three to be put in the old barn, the other in the house shed where the cooking-stove had stood. That added to the excitement. It was whispered that all four cows were domiciled in the house.

Toward sunset on Saturday, when Adoniram was expected home, there was a knot of men in the road near the new barn. The hired man had milked, but he still hung around the premises. Sarah Penn had supper all ready. There were brown-bread and baked beans and a custard pie; it was the supper that Adoniram loved on a Saturday night. She had on a clean calico, and she bore herself imperturbably. Nanny and Sammy kept close at her heels. Their eyes were large, and Nanny was full of nervous tremors. Still there was to them more pleasant excitement than anything else. An inborn confidence in their mother over their father asserted itself.

Sammy looked out of the harness-room window. "There he is," he announced, in an awed whisper. He and Nanny peeped around the casing. Mrs. Penn kept on about her work. The children watched Adoniram leave the new horse standing in the drive while he went to the house door. It was fastened. Then he went around to the shed. That door was seldom locked, even when the family was away. The thought how her father would be confronted by the cow flashed upon Nanny. There was a hysterical sob in her throat. Adoniram emerged from the shed and stood looking about in a dazed fashion. His lips moved; he was saying something, but they could not hear what it was. The hired man was peeping around a corner of the old barn, but nobody saw him.

Adoniram took the new horse by the bridle and led him across the yard to the new barn. Nanny and Sammy slunk close to their mother. The barn doors rolled back, and there stood Adoniram, with the long mild face of the great Canadian farm horse looking over his shoulder.

Nanny kept behind her mother, but Sammy stepped suddenly forward, and stood in front of her.

Adoniram stared at the group. "What on airth you all down here for?" said he. "What's the matter over to the house?"

"We've come here to live, father," said Sammy. His shrill voice quavered out bravely.

"What"—Adoniram sniffed—"what is it smells like cookin'?" said he. He stepped forward and looked in the open door of the harness-room. Then he turned to his wife. His old bristling face was pale and frightened. "What on airth does this mean, mother?" he gasped.

"You come in here, father," said Sarah. She led the way into the harness-room and shut the door. "Now, father," said she, "you needn't be scared. I ain't crazy. There ain't nothin' to be upset over. But we've come here to live, an' we're goin' to live here. We've got jest as good a right here as new horses an' cows. The house wa'n't fit for us to live in any longer, an' I made up my mind I wa'n't goin' to stay there. I've done my duty by you forty year, an' I'm goin' to do it now; but I'm goin' to live here. You've got to put in some windows and partitions; an' you'll have to buy some furniture."

"Why, mother!" the old man gasped.

"You'd better take your coat off an' get washed—there's the wash-basin—an' then we'll have supper."

* * *

"Why, mother!"

Sammy went past the window, leading the new horse to the old barn. The old man saw him, and shook his head speechlessly. He tried to take off his coat, but his arms seemed to lack the power. His wife helped him. She poured some water into the tin basin, and put in a piece of soap. She got the comb and brush, and smoothed his thin gray hair after he had washed. Then she put the beans, hot bread, and tea on the table. Sammy came in, and the family drew up. Adoniram sat looking dazedly at his plate, and they waited.

"Ain't you goin' to ask a blessin', father?" said Sarah.

And the old man bent his head and mumbled.

All through the meal he stopped eating at intervals, and stared furtively at his wife; but he ate well. The home food tasted good to him, and his old frame was too sturdily healthy to be affected by his mind. But after supper he went out, and sat down on the step of the smaller door at the right of the barn, through which he had meant his Jerseys to pass in stately file, but which Sarah designed for her front house door, and he leaned his head on his hands.

After the supper dishes were cleared away and the milk-pans washed, Sarah went out to him. The twilight was deepening. There was a clear green glow in the sky. Before them stretched the smooth level of field; in the distance was a cluster of hay-stacks like the huts of a village; the air was very cool and calm and sweet. The landscape might have been an ideal one of peace.

Sarah bent over and touched her husband on one of his thin, sinewy shoulders. "Father!"

The old man's shoulders heaved: he was weeping.

"Why, don't do so, father," said Sarah.

"I'll—put up the—partitions, an'—everything you—want, mother."

Sarah put her apron up to her face; she was overcome by her own triumph.

Adoniram was like a fortress whose walls had no active resistance, and went down the instant the right besieging tools were used. "Why, mother," he said, hoarsely, "I hadn't no idee you was so set on't as all this comes to."

DÉSIRÉE'S BABY

by Kate Chopin

Virtually all of Kate O'Flaherty Chopin's creative work was done in the last decade of the nineteenth century, when she was in her forties and a widow with six children. "Desirée's Baby" was first published in *Vogue* in 1893, six years before her masterpiece *The Awakening.*

As THE DAY was pleasant, Madame Valmondé drove over to L'Abri to see Désirée and the baby.

It made her laugh to think of Désirée with a baby. Why, it seemed but yesterday that Désirée was little more than a baby herself; when Monsieur in riding through the gateway of Valmondé had found her lying asleep in the shadow of the big stone pillar.

The little one awoke in his arms and began to cry for "Dada." That was as much as she could do or say. Some people thought she might have strayed there of her own accord, for she was of the toddling age. The prevailing belief was that she had been purposely left by a party of Texans, whose canvas-covered wagon, late in the day, had crossed the ferry that Coton Maïs kept, just below the plantation. In time Madame Valmondé abandoned every speculation but the one that Désirée had been sent to her by a beneficent Providence to be the child of her affection, seeing that she was without child of the flesh. For the girl grew to be beautiful and gentle, affectionate and sincere,—the idol of Valmondé.

It was no wonder, when she stood one day against the stone pillar in whose shadow she had lain asleep, eighteen years before, that Armand Aubigny riding by and seeing her there, had fallen in love with her. That was the way all the Aubignys fell in love, as if struck by a pistol shot. The wonder was that he had not loved her before; for he had known her since his father brought him home from Paris, a boy of eight, after his mother died there. The passion that awoke in him that day, when he saw her at the gate, swept along like an avalanche, or like a prairie fire, or like anything that drives headlong over all obstacles.

Monsieur Valmondé grew practical and wanted things well considered: that is, the girl's obscure origin. Armand looked into her eyes and did not care. He was reminded that she was nameless. What did it matter about a name when he could give her one of the oldest and proudest in Louisiana? He ordered the *corbeille* from Paris, and contained himself with what patience he could until it arrived; then they were married.

Madame Valmondé had not seen Désirée and the baby for four weeks. When she reached L'Abri she shuddered at the first sight of it, as she always did. It was a sad looking place, which for many years had not known the gentle presence of a mistress, old Monsieur Aubigny having married and buried his wife in France, and she having loved her own land too well ever to leave it. The roof came down steep and black like a cowl, reaching out beyond the wide galleries that encircled the yellow stuccoed house. Big, solemn oaks grew close to it, and their thick-leaved, far-reaching branches shadowed it like a pall. Young Aubigny's rule was a strict one, too, and under it his negroes had forgotten how to be gay, as they had been during the old master's easy-going and indulgent lifetime.

The young mother was recovering slowly, and lay full length, in her soft white muslins and laces, upon a couch. The baby was beside her, upon her arm, where he had fallen asleep, at her breast. The yellow nurse woman sat beside a window fanning herself.

Madame Valmondé bent her portly figure over Désirée and kissed her, holding her an instant tenderly in her arms. Then she turned to the child.

"This is not the baby!" she exclaimed, in startled tones. French was the language spoken at Valmondé in those days.

"I knew you would be astonished," laughed Désirée, "at the way he has grown. The little *cochon de lait!* Look at his legs, mamma, and his hands and finger-nails—real finger-nails. Zandrine had to cut them this morning. Isn't it true, Zandrine?"

The woman bowed her turbaned head majestically, "Mais si, Madame."

"And the way he cries," went on Désirée, "is deafening. Armand heard him the other day as far away as La Blanche's cabin."

Madame Valmondé had never removed her eyes from the child. She lifted it and walked with it over to the window that was lightest. She scanned the baby narrowly, then looked as searchingly at Zandrine, whose face was turned to gaze across the fields.

"Yes, the child has grown, has changed," said Madame Valmondé, slowly, as she replaced it beside its mother. "What does Armand say?"

Désirée's face became suffused with a glow that was happiness itself.

"Oh, Armand is the proudest father in the parish, I believe, chiefly because it is a boy, to bear his name; though he says not,—that he would have loved a girl as well. But I know it isn't true. I know he says that to please me. And mamma," she added, drawing Madame Valmondé's head down to her, and speaking in a whisper, "he hasn't punished one of them—not one of them—since baby is born. Even Négrillon, who pretended to have burnt his leg that he might rest from work—he only laughed, and said Négrillon was a great scamp. Oh, mamma, I'm so happy; it frightens me."

What Désirée said was true. Marriage, and later the birth of his son had softened Armand Aubigny's imperious and exacting nature greatly. This was what made the gentle Désirée so happy, for she loved him desperately. When he frowned she trembled, but loved him. When he smiled, she asked no greater blessing of God. But Armand's dark, handsome face had not often been disfigured by frowns since the day he fell in love with her.

When the baby was about three months old, Désirée awoke one day to the conviction that there was something in the air menacing her peace. It was at first too subtle to grasp. It had only been a disquieting suggestion; an air of mystery among the blacks; unexpected visits from far-off neighbors who could hardly account for their coming. Then a strange, an awful change in her husband's manner, which she dared not ask him to explain. When he spoke to her, it was with averted eyes, from which the old love-light seemed to have gone out. He absented himself from home; and when there, avoided her presence and that of her child, without excuse. And the very spirit of Satan seemed suddenly to take hold of him in his dealings with the slaves. Désirée was miserable enough to die.

She sat in her room, one hot afternoon, in her *peignoir,* listlessly drawing through her fingers the strands of her long, silky brown hair that hung about her shoulders. The baby, half naked, lay asleep upon her own great mahogany bed, that was like a sumptuous throne, with its satin-lined half-canopy. One of La Blanche's little quadroon boys—half naked too—stood fanning the child slowly with a fan of peacock feathers. Désirée's eyes had been fixed absently and sadly upon the baby, while she was striving to penetrate the threatening mist that she felt closing about her. She looked from her child to the boy who stood beside him, and back again; over and over. "Ah!" It was a cry that she could not help; which she was not conscious of having uttered. The blood turned like ice in her veins, and a clammy moisture gathered upon her face.

She tried to speak to the little quadroon boy; but no sound would come, at first. When he heard his name uttered, he looked up, and his mistress was pointing to the door. He laid aside the great, soft fan, and obediently stole away, over the polished floor, on his bare tiptoes.

She stayed motionless, with gaze riveted upon her child, and her face the picture of fright.

Presently her husband entered the room, and without noticing her, went to a table and began to search among some papers which covered it.

"Armand," she called to him, in a voice which must have stabbed him, if he was human. But he did not notice. "Armand," she said again. Then she rose and tottered towards him. "Armand," she panted once more, clutching his arm, "look at our child. What does it mean? Tell me."

He coldly but gently loosened her fingers from about his arm and thrust the hand away from him. "Tell me what it means!" she cried despairingly.

"It means," he answered lightly, "that the child is not white; it means that you are not white."

A quick conception of all that this accusation meant for her nerved her with unwonted courage to deny it. "It is a lie; it is not true, I am white! Look at my hair, it is brown; and my eyes are gray, Armand, you know they are gray. And my skin is fair," seizing his wrist. "Look at my hand; whiter than yours, Armand," she laughed hysterically.

"As white as La Blanche's," he returned cruelly; and went away leaving her alone with their child.

When she could hold a pen in her hand, she sent a despairing letter to Madame Valmondé.

"My mother, they tell me I am not white. Armand has told me I am not white. For God's sake tell them it is not true. You must know it is not true. I shall die. I must die. I cannot be so unhappy, and live."

The answer that came was as brief:

"My own Désirée: Come home to Valmondé; back to your mother who loves you. Come with your child."

When the letter reached Désirée she went with it to her husband's study, and laid it open upon the desk before which he sat. She was like a stone image: silent, white, motionless after she placed it there.

In silence he ran his cold eyes over the written words.

He said nothing. "Shall I go, Armand?" she asked in tones sharp with agonized suspense.

"Yes, go."

"Do you want me to go?"

"Yes, I want you to go."

He thought Almighty God had dealt cruelly and unjustly with him; and felt, somehow, that he was paying Him back in kind when he stabbed thus into his wife's soul. Moreover he no longer loved her, because of the unconscious injury she had brought upon his home and his name.

She turned away like one stunned by a blow, and walked slowly towards the door, hoping he would call her back.

"Good-by, Armand," she moaned.

He did not answer her. That was his last blow at fate.

Désirée went in search of her child. Zandrine was pacing the sombre gallery with it. She took the little one from the nurse's arms with no word of explanation, and descending the steps, walked away, under the live-oak branches.

It was an October afternoon; the sun was just sinking. Out in the still fields the negroes were picking cotton.

Désirée had not changed the thin white garment nor the slippers which she wore. Her hair was uncovered and the sun's rays brought a golden gleam from its brown meshes. She did not take the broad, beaten road which led to the far-off plantation of Valmondé. She walked across a deserted field, where the stubble bruised her tender feet, so delicately shod, and tore her thin gown to shreds.

She disappeared among the reeds and willows that grew thick along the banks of the deep, sluggish bayou; and she did not come back again.

★ ★ ★

Some weeks later there was a curious scene enacted at L'Abri. In the centre of the smoothly swept back yard was a great bonfire. Armand Aubigny sat in the wide hallway that commanded a view of the spectacle; and it was he who dealt out to a half dozen negroes the material which kept this fire ablaze.

A graceful cradle of willow, with all its dainty furbishings, was laid upon the pyre, which had already been fed with the richness of a priceless *layette.* Then there were silk gowns, and velvet and satin ones added to these; laces, too, and embroideries; bonnets and gloves; for the *corbeille* had been of rare quality.

The last thing to go was a tiny bundle of letters; innocent little scribblings that Désirée had sent to him during the days of their espousal. There was the remnant of one back in the drawer from which he took them. But it was not Désirée's; it was part of an old letter from his mother to his father. He read it. She was thanking God for the blessing of her husband's love:—

"But, above all," she wrote, "night and day, I thank the good God for having so arranged our lives that our dear Armand will never know that his mother, who adores him, belongs to the race that is cursed with the brand of slavery."

THE OTHER TWO

by Edith Wharton

"The Other Two" was first published by Edith Wharton in *The Descent of Man, and Other Stories* in 1904, the year before her reputation as a major American writer was firmly established by *The House of Mirth*. During a writing career that lasted almost forty years she published over twenty novels, eighty-five short stories and several works of nonfiction. In 1921 her novel *The Age of Innocence* won the Pulitzer Prize for Fiction.

I

WAYTHORN, ON THE drawing-room hearth, waited for his wife to come down to dinner.

It was their first night under his own roof, and he was surprised at his thrill of boyish agitation. He was not so old, to be sure—his glass gave him little more than the five-and-thirty years to which his wife confessed—but he had fancied himself already in the temperate zone; yet here he was listening for her step with a tender sense of all it symbolized, with some old trail of verse about the garlanded nuptial door-posts floating through his enjoyment of the pleasant room and the good dinner just beyond it.

They had been hastily recalled from their honeymoon by the illness of Lily Haskett, the child of Mrs. Waythorn's first marriage. The little girl, at Waythorn's desire, had been transferred to his house on the day of her mother's wedding, and the doctor, on their arrival, broke the news that she was ill with typhoid, but declared that all the symptoms were favorable. Lily could show twelve years of unblemished health, and the case promised to be a light one. The nurse spoke as reassuringly, and after a moment of alarm Mrs. Waythorn had adjusted herself to the situation. She was very fond of Lily—her affection for the child had perhaps been her decisive charm in Waythorn's eyes—but she had the perfectly balanced nerves which her little girl had inherited, and no woman ever wasted less tissue in unproductive worry. Waythorn was therefore quite prepared to see her come in presently, a little late because of a last look at Lily, but as serene and well-appointed as if her good-night kiss had been laid on the brow of health. Her composure was restful to him; it acted as ballast to his somewhat unstable sensibilities. As he pictured her bending over the child's bed he thought how soothing her presence must be in illness: her very step would prognosticate recovery.

His own life had been a gray one, from temperament rather than circumstance, and he had been drawn to her by the unperturbed gayety which kept her fresh and elastic at an age when most women's activities are growing either slack or febrile. He knew what was said about her; for, popular as she was, there had always been a faint undercurrent of detraction. When she had appeared in New York, nine or ten years earlier, as the pretty Mrs. Haskett whom Gus Varick had unearthed somewhere—was it in Pittsburg or Utica?—society, while promptly accepting her, had reserved the right to cast a doubt on its own discrimination. Enquiry, however, established her undoubted connection with a socially reigning family, and explained her recent divorce as the natural result of a runaway match at seventeen; and as nothing was known of Mr. Haskett it was easy to believe the worst of him.

Alice Haskett's remarriage with Gus Varick was a passport to the set whose recognition she coveted, and for a few years the Varicks were the most popular couple in town. Unfortunately the alliance was brief and stormy, and this time the husband had his champions. Still, even Varick's staunchest supporters admitted that he was not meant for matrimony, and Mrs. Varick's grievances were of a nature to bear the inspection of the New York courts. A New York divorce is in itself a diploma of virtue, and in the semi-widowhood of this second separation Mrs. Varick took on an air of sanctity, and was allowed to confide her wrongs to some of the most scrupulous ears in town. But when it was known that she was to marry Waythorn there was a momentary reaction. Her best friends would have preferred to see her remain in the role of the injured wife, which was as becoming to her as crape to a rosy complexion. True, a decent time had elapsed, and it was not even suggested that Waythorn had supplanted his predecessor. People shook their heads over him, however, and one grudging friend, to whom he affirmed that he took the step with his eyes open, replied oracularly: "Yes—and with your ears shut."

Waythorn could afford to smile at these innuendoes. In the Wall Street phrase, he had "discounted" them. He knew that society has not yet adapted itself to the consequences of divorce, and that till the adaptation takes place every woman who uses the freedom the law accords her must be her own social justification. Waythorn had an amused confidence in his wife's ability to justify herself. His expectations were fulfilled, and before the wedding took place Alice Varick's group had rallied openly to her support. She took it all imperturbably: she had a way of surmounting obstacles without seeming to be aware of them, and Waythorn looked back with wonder at the trivialities over which he had worn his nerves thin. He had the sense of having found refuge in a richer, warmer nature than his own, and his satisfaction, at the moment, was humorously summed up in the thought that his wife, when she had done all she could for Lily, would not be ashamed to come down and enjoy a good dinner.

The anticipation of such enjoyment was not, however, the sentiment expressed by Mrs. Waythorn's charming face when she presently joined him. Though she had put on her most engaging tea-gown she had neglected to assume the smile that went with it, and Waythorn thought he had never seen her look so nearly worried.

"What is it?" he asked. "Is anything wrong with Lily?"

"No; I've just been in and she's still sleeping." Mrs. Waythorn hesitated. "But something tiresome has happened."

He had taken her two hands, and now perceived that he was crushing a paper between them.

"This letter?"

"Yes—Mr. Haskett has written—I mean his lawyer has written."

Waythorn felt himself flush uncomfortably. He dropped his wife's hands.

"What about?"

"About seeing Lily. You know the courts——"

"Yes, yes," he interrupted nervously.

Nothing was known about Haskett in New York. He was vaguely supposed to have remained in the outer darkness from which his wife had been rescued, and Waythorn was one of the few who were aware that he had given up his business in Utica and followed her to New York in order to be near his little girl. In the days of his wooing, Waythorn had often met Lily on the doorstep, rosy and smiling, on her way "to see papa."

"I am so sorry," Mrs. Waythorn murmured.

He roused himself. "What does he want?"

"He wants to see her. You know she goes to him once a week."

"Well—he doesn't expect her to go to him now, does he?"

"No—he has heard of her illness; but he expects to come here."

"*Here?*"

Mrs. Waythorn reddened under his gaze. They looked away from each other.

"I'm afraid he has the right. . . . You'll see. . . ." She made a proffer of the letter.

Waythorn moved away with a gesture of refusal. He stood staring about the softly lighted room, which a moment before had seemed so full of bridal intimacy.

"I'm so sorry," she repeated. "If Lily could have been moved——"

"That's out of the question," he returned impatiently.

"I suppose so."

Her lip was beginning to tremble, and he felt himself a brute.

"He must come, of course," he said. "When is—his day?"

"I'm afraid—to-morrow."

"Very well. Send a note in the morning."

The butler entered to announce dinner.

Waythorn turned to his wife. "Come—you must be tired. It's beastly, but try to forget about it," he said, drawing her hand through his arm.

"You're so good, dear. I'll try," she whispered back.

Her face cleared at once, and as she looked at him across the flowers, between the rosy candle-shades, he saw her lips waver back into a smile.

"How pretty everything is!" she sighed luxuriously.

He turned to the butler. "The champagne at once, please. Mrs. Waythorn is tired."

In a moment or two their eyes met above the sparkling glasses. Her own were quite clear and untroubled: he saw that she had obeyed his injunction and forgotten.

II

Waythorn, the next morning, went down town earlier than usual. Haskett was not likely to come till the afternoon, but the instinct of flight drove him forth. He meant to stay away all day—he had thoughts of dining at his club. As his door closed behind him he reflected that before he opened it again it would have admitted another man who had as much right to enter it as himself, and the thought filled him with a physical repugnance.

He caught the "elevated" at the employees' hour, and found himself crushed between two layers of pendulous humanity. At Eighth Street the man facing him wriggled out and another took his place. Waythorn glanced up and saw that it was Gus Varick. The men were so close together that it was impossible to ignore the smile of recognition on Varick's handsome overblown face. And after all—why not? They had always been on good terms, and Varick had been divorced before Waythorn's attentions to his wife began. The two exchanged a word on the perennial grievance of the congested trains, and when a seat at their side was miraculously left empty the instinct of self-preservation made Waythorn slip into it after Varick.

The latter drew the stout man's breath of relief. "Lord—I was beginning to feel like a pressed flower." He leaned back, looking unconcernedly at Waythorn. "Sorry to hear that Sellers is knocked out again."

"Sellers?" echoed Waythorn, starting at his partner's name.

Varick looked surprised. "You didn't know he was laid up with the gout?"

"No. I've been away—I only got back last night." Waythorn felt himself reddening in anticipation of the other's smile.

"Ah—yes; to be sure. And Sellers's attack came on two days ago. I'm afraid he's pretty bad. Very awkward for me, as it happens, because he was just putting through a rather important thing for me."

"Ah?" Waythorn wondered vaguely since when Varick had been dealing in "important things." Hitherto he had dabbled only in the shallow pools of speculation, with which Waythorn's office did not usually concern itself.

It occurred to him that Varick might be talking at random, to relieve the strain of their propinquity. That strain was becoming momentarily more apparent to Waythorn, and when, at Cortlandt Street, he caught sight of an acquaintance, and had a sudden vision of the picture he and Varick must present to an initiated eye, he jumped up with a muttered excuse.

"I hope you'll find Sellers better," said Varick civilly, and he stammered back: "If I can be of any use to you——" and let the departing crowd sweep him to the platform.

At his office he heard that Sellers was in fact ill with the gout, and would probably not be able to leave the house for some weeks.

"I'm sorry it should have happened so, Mr. Waythorn," the senior clerk said with affable significance. "Mr. Sellers was very much upset at the idea of giving you such a lot of extra work just now."

"Oh, that's no matter," said Waythorn hastily. He secretly welcomed the pressure of additional business, and was glad to think that, when the day's work was over, he would have to call at his partner's on the way home.

He was late for luncheon, and turned in at the nearest restaurant instead of going to his club. The place was full, and the waiter hurried him to the back of the room to capture the only vacant table. In the cloud of cigar-smoke Waythorn did not at once distinguish his neighbors; but presently, looking about him, he saw Varick seated a few feet off. This time, luckily, they were too far apart for conversation, and Varick, who faced another way, had probably not even seen him; but there was an irony in their renewed nearness.

Varick was said to be fond of good living, and as Waythorn sat despatching his hurried luncheon he looked across half enviously at the other's leisurely degustation of his meal. When Waythorn first saw him he had been helping himself with critical deliberation to a bit of Camembert at the ideal point of liquefaction, and now, the cheese removed, he was just pouring his *café double* from its little two-storied earthen pot. He poured slowly, his ruddy profile bent above the task, and one be-ringed white hand steadying the lid of the coffee-pot; then he stretched his other hand to the decanter of cognac at his elbow, filled a liqueur-glass, took a tentative sip, and poured the brandy into his coffee-cup.

Waythorn watched him in a kind of fascination. What was he thinking of—only of the flavour of the coffee and the liqueur? Had the morning's meeting left no more trace in his thoughts than on his face? Had his wife so completely passed out of his life that even this odd encounter with her present husband, within a week after her remarriage, was no more than an incident in his day? And as Waythorn mused, another idea struck him: had Haskett ever met Varick as Varick and he had just met? The recollection of Haskett perturbed him, and he rose and left the restaurant, taking a circuitous way out to escape the placid irony of Varick's nod.

It was after seven when Waythorn reached home. He thought the footman who opened the door looked at him oddly.

"How is Miss Lily?" he asked in haste.

"Doing very well, sir. A gentleman——"

"Tell Barlow to put off dinner for half an hour," Waythorn cut him off, hurrying upstairs.

He went straight to his room and dressed without seeing his wife. When he reached the drawing-room she was there, fresh and radiant. Lily's day had been good; the doctor was not coming back that evening.

At dinner Waythorn told her of Sellers's illness and of the resulting complications. She listened sympathetically, adjuring him not to let himself be overworked, and asking vague feminine questions about the routine of the office. Then she gave him the chronicle of Lily's day; quoted the nurse and doctor, and told him who had called to enquire. He had never seen her more serene and unruffled. It struck him, with a curious pang, that she was very happy in being with him, so happy that she found a childish pleasure in rehearsing the trivial incidents of her day.

After dinner they went to the library, and the servant put the coffee and liqueurs on a low table before her and left the room. She looked singularly soft and girlish in her rosy pale dress, against the dark leather of one of his bachelor armchairs. A day earlier the contrast would have charmed him.

He turned away now, choosing a cigar with affected deliberation.

"Did Haskett come?" he asked, with his back to her.

"Oh, yes—he came."

"You didn't see him, of course?"

She hesitated a moment. "I let the nurse see him."

That was all. There was nothing more to ask. He swung round toward her, applying a match to his cigar. Well, the thing was over for a week, at any rate. He would try not to think of it. She looked up at him, a trifle rosier than usual, with a smile in her eyes.

"Ready for your coffee, dear?"

He leaned against the mantelpiece, watching her as she lifted the coffee-pot. The lamplight struck a gleam from her bracelets and tipped her soft hair with brightness. How light and slender she was, and how each gesture flowed into the next! She seemed a creature all compact of harmonies. As the thought of Haskett receded, Waythorn felt himself yielding again to the joy of possessorship. They were his, those white hands with their flitting motions, his the light haze of hair, the lips and eyes. . . .

She set down the coffee-pot, and reaching for the decanter of cognac, measured off a liqueur-glass and poured it into his cup.

Waythorn uttered a sudden exclamation.

"What is the matter?" she said, startled.

"Nothing; only—I don't take cognac in my coffee."

"Oh, how stupid of me," she cried.

Their eyes met, and she blushed a sudden agonized red.

III

Ten days later, Mr. Sellers, still house-bound, asked Waythorn to call on his way down town.

The senior partner, with his swaddled foot propped up by the fire, greeted his associate with an air of embarrassment.

"I'm sorry, my dear fellow; I've got to ask you to do an awkward thing for me."

Waythorn waited, and the other went on, after a pause apparently given to the arrangement of his phrases: "The fact is, when I was knocked out I had just gone into a rather complicated piece of business for—Gus Varick."

"Well?" said Waythorn, with an attempt to put him at his ease.

"Well—it's this way: Varick came to me the day before my attack. He had evidently had an inside tip from somebody, and had made about a hundred thousand. He came to me for advice, and I suggested his going in with Vanderlyn."

"Oh, the deuce!" Waythorn exclaimed. He saw in a flash what had happened. The investment was an alluring one, but required negotiation. He listened quietly while Sellers put the case before him, and, the statement ended, he said: "You think I ought to see Varick?"

"I'm afraid I can't as yet. The doctor is obdurate. And this thing can't wait. I hate to ask you, but no one else in the office knows the ins and outs of it."

Waythorn stood silent. He did not care a farthing for the success of Varick's venture, but the honor of the office was to be considered, and he could hardly refuse to oblige his partner.

"Very well," he said, "I'll do it."

That afternoon, apprised by telephone, Varick called at the office. Waythorn, waiting in his private room, wondered what the others thought of it. The newspapers, at the time of Mrs. Waythorn's marriage, had acquainted their readers with every detail of her previous matrimonial ventures, and Waythorn could fancy the clerks smiling behind Varick's back as he was ushered in.

Varick bore himself admirably. He was easy without being undignified, and Waythorn was conscious of cutting a much less impressive figure. Varick had no head for business, and the talk prolonged itself for nearly an hour while Waythorn set forth with scrupulous precision the details of the proposed transaction.

"I'm awfully obliged to you," Varick said as he rose. "The fact is I'm not used to having much money to look after, and I don't want to make an ass of myself——" He smiled, and Waythorn could not help noticing that there was something pleasant about his smile. "It feels uncommonly queer to have enough cash to pay one's bills. I'd have sold my soul for it a few years ago!"

Waythorn winced at the allusion. He had heard it rumoured that a lack of funds had been one of the determining causes of the Varick separation, but it did not occur to him that Varick's words were intentional. It seemed more likely that the desire to keep clear of embarrassing topics had fatally drawn him into one. Waythorn did not wish to be outdone in civility.

"We'll do the best we can for you," he said. "I think this is a good thing you're in."

"Oh, I'm sure it's immense. It's awfully good of you——" Varick broke off, embarrassed. "I suppose the thing's settled now—but if——"

"If anything happens before Sellers is about, I'll see you again," said Waythorn quietly. He was glad, in the end, to appear the more self-possessed of the two.

* * *

The course of Lily's illness ran smooth, and as the days passed Waythorn grew used to the idea of Haskett's weekly visit. The first time the day came round, he stayed out late, and questioned his wife as to the visit on his return. She replied at once that Haskett had merely seen the nurse downstairs, as the doctor did not wish any one in the child's sick-room till after the crisis.

The following week Waythorn was again conscious of the recurrence of the day, but had forgotten it by the time he came home to dinner. The crisis of the disease came a few days later, with a rapid decline of fever, and the little girl was pronounced out of danger. In the rejoicing which ensued, the thought of Haskett passed out of Waythorn's mind, and one afternoon, letting himself into the house with a latch-key, he went straight to his library without noticing a shabby hat and umbrella in the hall.

In the library he found a small effaced-looking man with a thinnish gray beard sitting on the edge of a chair. The stranger might have been a piano-tuner, or one of those mysteriously efficient persons who are summoned in emergencies to adjust some detail of the domestic machinery. He blinked at Waythorn through a pair of gold-rimmed spectacles and said mildly: "Mr. Waythorn, I presume? I am Lily's father."

Waythorn flushed. "Oh——" he stammered uncomfortably. He broke off, disliking to appear rude. Inwardly he was trying to adjust the actual Haskett to the image of him projected by his wife's reminiscences. Waythorn had been allowed to infer that Alice's first husband was a brute.

"I am sorry to intrude," said Haskett, with his over-the-counter politeness.

"Don't mention it," returned Waythorn, collecting himself. "I suppose the nurse has been told?"

"I presume so. I can wait," said Haskett. He had a resigned way of speaking, as though life had worn down his natural powers of resistance.

Waythorn stood on the threshold, nervously pulling off his gloves.

"I'm sorry you've been detained. I will send for the nurse," he said; and as he opened the door he added with an effort: "I'm glad we can give you a good report of Lily." He winced as the *we* slipped out, but Haskett seemed not to notice it.

"Thank you, Mr. Waythorn. It's been an anxious time for me."

"Ah, well, that's past. Soon she'll be able to go to you." Waythorn nodded and passed out.

In his own room, he flung himself down with a groan. He hated the womanish sensibility which made him suffer so acutely from the grotesque chances of life. He had known when he married that his wife's former husbands were both living, and that amid the multiplied contacts of modern existence there were a thousand chances to one that he would run against one or the other, yet he found himself as much disturbed by his brief encounter with Haskett as though the law had not obligingly removed all difficulties in the way of their meeting.

Waythorn sprang up and began to pace the room nervously. He had not suffered half so much from his two meetings with Varick. It was Haskett's presence in his own house that made the situation so intolerable. He stood still, hearing steps in the passage.

"This way, please," he heard the nurse say. Haskett was being taken upstairs, then: not a corner of the house but was open to him. Waythorn dropped into another chair, staring vaguely ahead of him. On his dressing-table stood a photograph of Alice, taken when he had first known her. She was Alice Varick then—how fine and exquisite he had thought her! Those were Varick's pearls about her neck. At Waythorn's instance they had been returned before her marriage. Had Haskett ever given her any trinkets—and what had become of them, Waythorn wondered? He realized suddenly that he knew very little of Haskett's past or present situation; but from the man's appearance and manner of speech he could reconstruct with curious precision the surroundings of Alice's first marriage. And it startled him to think that she had, in the background of her life, a phase of existence so different from anything with which he had connected her. Varick, whatever his faults, was a gentleman, in the conventional, traditional sense of the term: the sense which at that moment seemed, oddly enough, to have most meaning to Waythorn. He and Varick had the same social habits, spoke the same language, understood the same allusions. But this other man . . . it was grotesquely uppermost in Waythorn's mind that Haskett had worn a made-up tie attached with an elastic. Why should that ridiculous detail symbolize the whole man? Waythorn was exasperated by his own paltriness, but the fact of the tie expanded, forced itself on him, became as it were the key to Alice's past. He could see her, as Mrs. Haskett, sitting in a "front parlor" furnished in plush, with a pianola, and a copy of "Ben Hur" on the centre-table. He could see her going to the theatre with Haskett—or perhaps even to a "Church Sociable"—she in a "picture hat" and Haskett in a black frock-coat, a little creased, with the made-up tie on an elastic. On the way home they would stop and look at the illuminated shop-windows, lingering over the photographs of New York actresses. On Sunday afternoons Haskett would take her for a walk, pushing Lily ahead of them in a white enamelled perambulator, and Waythorn had a vision of the people they would stop and talk to. He could fancy how pretty Alice must have looked, in a dress adroitly constructed from the hints of a New York fashion-paper, and how she must have looked down on the other women, chafing at her life, and secretly feeling that she belonged in a bigger place.

For the moment his foremost thought was one of wonder at the way in which she had shed the phase of existence which her marriage with Haskett implied. It was as if her whole aspect, every gesture, every inflection, every allusion, were a studied negation of that period of her life. If she had denied being married to Haskett she could hardly have stood more convicted of duplicity than in this obliteration of the self which had been his wife.

Waythorn started up, checking himself in the analysis of her motives. What right had he to create a fantastic effigy of her and then pass judgment on it? She had spoken vaguely of her first marriage as unhappy, had hinted, with becoming reticence, that Haskett had wrought havoc among her young illusions. . . . It was a pity for Waythorn's peace of mind that Haskett's very inoffensiveness shed a new light on the nature of those illusions. A man would rather think that his wife has been brutalized by her first husband than that the process has been reversed.

IV

"Mr. Waythorn, I don't like that French governess of Lily's."

Haskett, subdued and apologetic, stood before Waythorn in the library, revolving his shabby hat in his hand.

Waythorn, surprised in his armchair over the evening paper, stared back perplexedly at his visitor.

"You'll excuse my asking to see you," Haskett continued. "But this is my last visit, and I thought if I could have a word with you it would be a better way than writing to Mrs. Waythorn's lawyer."

Waythorn rose uneasily. He did not like the French governess either; but that was irrelevant.

"I am not so sure of that," he returned stiffly; "but since you wish it I will give your message to—my wife." He always hesitated over the possessive pronoun in addressing Haskett.

The latter sighed. "I don't know as that will help much. She didn't like it when I spoke to her."

Waythorn turned red. "When did you see her?" he asked.

"Not since the first day I came to see Lily—right after she was taken sick. I remarked to her then that I didn't like the governess."

Waythorn made no answer. He remembered distinctly that, after that first visit, he had asked his wife if she had seen Haskett. She had lied to him then, but she had respected his wishes since; and the incident cast a curious light on her character. He was sure she would not have seen Haskett that first day if she had divined that Waythorn would object, and the fact that she did not divine it was almost as disagreeable to the latter as the discovery that she had lied to him.

"I don't like the woman," Haskett was repeating with mild persistency. "She ain't straight, Mr. Waythorn—she'll teach the child to be underhand. I've noticed a change in Lily—she's too anxious to please—and she don't always tell the truth. She used to be the straightest child, Mr. Waythorn——" He broke off, his voice a little thick. "Not but what I want her to have a stylish education," he ended.

Waythorn was touched. "I'm sorry, Mr. Haskett; but frankly, I don't quite see what I can do."

Haskett hesitated. Then he laid his hat on the table, and advanced to the hearth-rug, on which Waythorn was standing. There was nothing aggressive in his manner, but he had the solemnity of a timid man resolved on a decisive measure.

"There's just one thing you can do, Mr. Waythorn," he said. "You can remind Mrs. Waythorn that, by the decree of the courts, I am entitled to have a voice in Lily's bringing up." He paused, and went on more deprecatingly: "I'm not the kind to talk about enforcing my rights, Mr. Waythorn. I don't know as I think a man is entitled to rights he hasn't known how to hold on to; but this business of the child is different. I've never let go there—and I never mean to."

* * *

The scene left Waythorn deeply shaken. Shamefacedly, in indirect ways, he had been finding out about Haskett; and all that he had learned was favourable. The little man, in order to be near his daughter, had sold out his share in a profitable business in Utica, and accepted a modest clerkship in a New York manufacturing house. He boarded in a shabby street and had few acquaintances. His passion for Lily filled his life. Waythorn felt that this exploration of Haskett was like groping about with a dark-lantern in his wife's past; but he saw now that there were recesses his lantern had not explored. He had never enquired into the exact circumstances of his wife's first matrimonial rupture. On the surface all had been fair. It was she who had obtained the divorce, and the court had given her the child. But Waythorn knew how many ambiguities such a verdict might cover. The mere fact that Haskett retained a right over his daughter implied an unsuspected compromise. Waythorn was an idealist. He always refused to recognize unpleasant contingencies till he found himself confronted with them, and then he saw them followed by a special train of consequences. His next days were thus haunted, and he determined to try to lay the ghosts by conjuring them up in his wife's presence.

When he repeated Haskett's request a flame of anger passed over her face; but she subdued it instantly and spoke with a slight quiver of outraged motherhood.

"It is very ungentlemanly of him," she said.

The word grated on Waythorn. "That is neither here nor there. It's a bare question of rights."

She murmured: "It's not as if he could ever be a help to Lily——"

Waythorn flushed. This was even less to his taste. "The question is," he repeated, "what authority has he over her?"

She looked downward, twisting herself a little in her seat. "I am willing to see him—I thought you objected," she faltered.

In a flash he understood that she knew the extent of Haskett's claims. Perhaps it was not the first time she had resisted them.

"My objecting has nothing to do with it," he said coldly; "if Haskett has a right to be consulted you must consult him."

She burst into tears, and he saw that she expected him to regard her as a victim.

Haskett did not abuse his rights. Waythorn had felt miserably sure that he would not. But the governess was dismissed, and from time to time the little man demanded an interview with Alice. After the first outburst she accepted the situation with her usual adaptability. Haskett had once reminded Waythorn of the piano-tuner, and Mrs. Waythorn, after a month or two, appeared to class him with that domestic familiar. Waythorn could not but respect the father's tenacity. At first he had tried to cultivate the suspicion that Haskett might be "up to" something, that he had an object in securing a foothold in the house. But in his heart Waythorn was sure of Haskett's single-mindedness; he even guessed in the latter a mild contempt for such advantages as his relation with the Waythorns might offer. Haskett's sincerity of purpose made him invulnerable, and his successor had to accept him as a lien on the property.

⋆ ⋆ ⋆

Mr. Sellers was sent to Europe to recover from his gout, and Varick's affairs hung on Waythorn's hands. The negotiations were prolonged and complicated; they necessitated frequent conferences between the two men, and the interests of the firm forbade Waythorn's suggesting that his client should transfer his business to another office.

Varick appeared well in the transaction. In moments of relaxation his coarse streak appeared, and Waythorn dreaded his geniality; but in the office he was concise and clear-headed, with a flattering deference to Waythorn's judgment. Their business relations being so affably established, it would have been absurd for the two men to ignore each other in society. The first time they met in a drawing-room, Varick took up their intercourse in the same easy key, and his hostess's grateful glance obliged Waythorn to respond to it. After that they ran across each other frequently, and one evening at a ball Waythorn, wandering through the remoter rooms, came upon Varick seated beside his wife. She coloured a little, and faltered in what she was saying; but Varick nodded to Waythorn without rising, and the latter strolled on.

In the carriage, on the way home, he broke out nervously: "I didn't know you spoke to Varick."

Her voice trembled a little. "It's the first time—he happened to be standing near me; I didn't know what to do. It's so awkward, meeting everywhere—and he said you had been very kind about some business."

"That's different," said Waythorn.

She paused a moment. "I'll do just as you wish," she returned pliantly. "I thought it would be less awkward to speak to him when we meet."

Her pliancy was beginning to sicken him. Had she really no will of her own—no theory about her relation to these men? She had accepted Haskett—did she mean to accept Varick? It was "less awkward," as she had said, and her instinct was to evade difficulties or to circumvent them. With sudden vividness Waythorn saw how the instinct had developed. She was "as easy as an old shoe"—a shoe that too many feet had worn. Her elasticity was the result of tension in too many different directions. Alice Haskett—Alice Varick—Alice Waythorn—she had been each in turn, and had left hanging to each name a little of her privacy, a little of her personality, a little of the inmost self where the unknown god abides.

"Yes—it's better to speak to Varick," said Waythorn wearily.

V

The winter wore on, and society took advantage of the Waythorns' acceptance of Varick. Harassed hostesses were grateful to them for bridging over a social difficulty, and Mrs. Waythorn was held up as a miracle of good taste. Some experimental spirits could not resist the diversion of throwing Varick and his former wife together, and there were those who thought he found a zest in the propinquity. But Mrs. Waythorn's conduct remained irreproachable. She neither avoided Varick nor sought him out. Even Waythorn could not but admit that she had discovered the solution of the newest social problem.

He had married her without giving much thought to that problem. He had fancied that a woman can shed her past like a man. But now he saw that Alice was bound to hers both by the circumstances which forced her into continued relation with it, and by the traces it had left on her nature. With grim irony Waythorn compared himself to a member of a syndicate. He held so many shares in his wife's personality and his predecessors were his partners in the business. If there had been any element of passion in the transaction he would have felt less deteriorated by it. The fact that Alice took her change of husbands like a change of weather reduced the situation to mediocrity. He could have forgiven her for blunders, for excesses; for resisting Hackett, for yielding to

Varick; for anything but her acquiescence and her tact. She reminded him of a juggler tossing knives; but the knives were blunt and she knew they would never cut her.

And then, gradually, habit formed a protecting surface for his sensibilities. If he paid for each day's comfort with the small change of his illusions, he grew daily to value the comfort more and set less store upon the coin. He had drifted into a dulling propinquity with Haskett and Varick and he took refuge in the cheap revenge of satirizing the situation. He even began to reckon up the advantages which accrued from it, to ask himself if it were not better to own a third of a wife who knew how to make a man happy than a whole one who had lacked opportunity to acquire the art. For it *was* an art, and made up, like all others, of concessions, eliminations and embellishments; of lights judiciously thrown and shadows skillfully softened. His wife knew exactly how to manage the lights, and he knew exactly to what training she owed her skill. He even tried to trace the source of his obligations, to discriminate between the influences which had combined to produce his domestic happiness: he perceived that Haskett's commonness had made Alice worship good breeding, while Varick's liberal construction of the marriage bond had taught her to value the conjugal virtues; so that he was directly indebted to his predecessors for the devotion which made his life easy if not inspiring.

From this phase he passed into that of complete acceptance. He ceased to satirize himself because time dulled the irony of the situation and the joke lost its humor with its sting. Even the sight of Haskett's hat on the hall table had ceased to touch the springs of epigram. The hat was often seen there now, for it had been decided that it was better for Lily's father to visit her than for the little girl to go to his boarding-house. Waythorn, having acquiesced in this arrangement, had been surprised to find how little difference it made. Haskett was never obtrusive, and the few visitors who met him on the stairs were unaware of his identity. Waythorn did not know how often he saw Alice, but with himself Haskett was seldom in contact.

One afternoon, however, he learned on entering that Lily's father was waiting to see him. In the library he found Haskett occupying a chair in his usual provisional way. Waythorn always felt grateful to him for not leaning back.

"I hope you'll excuse me, Mr. Waythorn," he said rising. "I wanted to see Mrs. Waythorn about Lily, and your man asked me to wait here till she came in."

"Of course," said Waythorn, remembering that a sudden leak had that morning given over the drawing-room to the plumbers.

He opened his cigar-case and held it out to his visitor, and Haskett's acceptance seemed to mark a fresh stage in their intercourse. The spring evening was chilly, and Waythorn invited his guest to draw up his chair to the fire. He meant to find an excuse to leave Haskett in a moment; but he was tired and cold, and after all the little man no longer jarred on him.

The two were enclosed in the intimacy of their blended cigar-smoke when the door opened and Varick walked into the room. Waythorn rose abruptly. It was the first time that Varick had come to the house, and the surprise of seeing him, combined with the singular inopportuneness of his arrival, gave a new edge to Waythorn's blunted sensibilities. He stared at his visitor without speaking.

Varick seemed too preoccupied to notice his host's embar -rassment.

"My dear fellow," he exclaimed in his most expansive tone, "I must apologize for tumbling in on you in this way, but I was too late to catch you down town, and so I thought——"

He stopped short, catching sight of Haskett, and his sanguine colour deepened to a flush which spread vividly under his scant blond hair. But in a moment he recovered himself and nodded slightly. Haskett returned the bow in silence, and Waythorn was still groping for speech when the footman came in carrying a tea-table.

The intrusion offered a welcome vent to Waythorn's nerves. "What the deuce are you bringing this here for?" he said sharply.

"I beg your pardon, sir, but the plumbers are still in the drawing-room, and Mrs. Waythorn said she would have tea in the library." The footman's perfectly respectful tone implied a reflection on Waythorn's reasonableness.

"Oh, very well," said the latter resignedly, and the footman proceeded to open the folding tea-table and set out its complicated appointments. While this interminable process continued the three men stood motionless, watching it with a fascinated stare, till Waythorn, to break the silence, said to Varick: "Won't you have a cigar?"

He held out the case he had just tendered to Haskett, and Varick helped himself with a smile. Waythorn looked about for a match, and finding none, proffered a light from his own cigar. Haskett, in the background, held his ground mildly, examining his cigar-tip now and then, and stepping forward at the right moment to knock its ashes into the fire.

The footman at last withdrew, and Varick immediately began: "If I could just say half a word to you about this business——"

"Certainly," stammered Waythorn; "in the dining-room——"

But as he placed his hand on the door it opened from without, and his wife appeared on the threshold.

She came in fresh and smiling, in her street dress and hat, shedding a fragrance from the boa which she loosened in advancing.

"Shall we have tea in here, dear?" she began; and then she caught sight of Varick. Her smile deepened, veiling a slight tremor of surprise.

"Why, how do you do?" she said with a distinct note of pleasure.

As she shook hands with Varick she saw Haskett standing behind him. Her smile faded for a moment, but she recalled it quickly, with a scarcely perceptible side-glance at Waythorn.

"How do you do, Mr. Haskett?" she said, and shook hands with him a shade less cordially.

The three men stood awkwardly before her, till Varick, always the most self-possessed, dashed into an explanatory phrase.

"We—I had to see Waythorn a moment on business," he stammered, brick-red from chin to nape.

Haskett stepped forward with his air of mild obstinacy. "I am sorry to intrude; but you appointed five o'clock——" he directed his resigned glance to the timepiece on the mantel.

She swept aside their embarrassment with a charming gesture of hospitality.

"I'm so sorry—I'm always late; but the afternoon was so lovely." She stood drawing her gloves off, propitiatory and graceful, diffusing about her a sense of ease and familiarity in which the situation lost its grotesqueness. "But before talking business," she added brightly, "I'm sure every one wants a cup of tea."

She dropped into her low chair by the tea-table, and the two visitors, as if drawn by her smile, advanced to receive the cups she held out.

She glanced about for Waythorn, and he took the third cup with a laugh.

ROAST BEEF, MEDIUM

by Edna Ferber

Edna Ferber first won acclaim as a writer of fiction with "Roast Beef, Medium" (1913) and other stories about Emma McChesney, a refreshingly with-it traveling petticoat saleswoman. Ferber is now best remembered as a novelist: *So Big* (1925 Pulitzer Prize for Fiction), *Show Boat*, *Saratoga Trunk*, *Giant*, and several other bestsellers. She was also successful as a dramatist (*Stage Door*, *The Royal Family*, *Dinner at Eight*, etc., written in collaboration with George S. Kaufman).

THERE IS A journey compared to which the travels of Bunyan's hero were a summer-evening's stroll. The Pilgrims by whom this forced march is taken belong to a maligned fraternity, and are known as traveling men. Sample-case in hand, trunk key in pocket, cigar in mouth, brown derby atilt at an angle of ninety, each young and untried traveler starts on his journey down that road which leads through morasses of chicken *à la* Creole, over greasy mountains of queen fritters made doubly perilous by slippery glaciers of rum sauce, into formidable jungles of breaded veal chops threaded by sanguine and deadly streams of tomato gravy, past sluggish mires of dreadful things *en casserole*, over hills of corned-beef hash, across shaking quagmires of veal glacé, plunging into sloughs of slaw, until, haggard, weary, digestion shattered, complexion gone, he reaches the safe haven of roast beef, medium. Once there, he never again strays, although the pompadoured, white-aproned siren sing-songs in his ear the praises of Irish stew, and pork with apple sauce.

Emma McChesney was eating her solitary supper at the Berger house at Three Rivers, Michigan. She had arrived at the Roast Beef haven many years before. She knew the digestive perils of a small town hotel dining-room as a guide on the snow-covered mountain knows each treacherous pitfall and chasm. Ten years on the road had taught her to recognize the deadly snare that lurks in the seemingly calm bosom of minced chicken with cream sauce. Not for her the impenetrable mysteries of a hamburger and onions. It had been a struggle, brief but terrible, from which Emma McChesney had emerged triumphant, her complexion and figure saved.

No more metaphor. On with the story, which left Emma at her safe and solitary supper.

She had the last number of the *Dry Goods Review* propped up against the vinegar cruet, and the Worcestershire, and the salt shaker. Between conscientious, but disinterested mouthfuls of medium roast beef, she was reading the snappy ad set forth by her firm's bitterest competitors, the Strauss Sans-silk Skirt Company. It was a good reading ad. Emma McChesney, who had forgotten more about petticoats than the average skirt salesman ever knew, presently allowed her luke-warm beef to grow cold and flabby as she read. Somewhere in her subconscious mind she realized that the lanky head waitress had placed some one opposite her at the table. Also, subconsciously, she heard him order liver and bacon, with onions. She told herself that as soon as she reached the bottom of the column she'd look up to see who the fool was. She never arrived at the column's end.

"I just hate to tear you away from that love lyric; but if I might trouble you for the vinegar—"

Emma groped for it back of her paper and shoved it across the table without looking up.

"—and the Worcester—"

One eye on the absorbing column, she passed the tall bottle. But at its removal her prop was gone. The *Dry Goods Review* was too weighty for the salt shaker alone.

"—and the salt. Thanks. Warm, isn't it?"

There was a double vertical frown between Emma McChesney's eyes as she glanced up over the top of her *Dry Goods Review*. The frown gave way to a half smile. The glance settled into a stare.

"But then, anybody would have stared. He expected it," she said, afterwards, in telling about it. "I've seen matinée idols, and tailors' supplies salesmen, and Julian Eltinge, but this boy had any male professional beauty I ever saw, looking as handsome and dashing as a bowl of cold oatmeal. And he knew it."

Now, in the ten years that she had been out representing T. A. Buck's Featherloom Petticoats, Emma McChesney had found it necessary to make a rule or two for herself. In the strict observance of one of these she had become past mistress in the fine art of congealing the warm advances of fresh and friendly salesmen of the opposite sex. But this case was different, she told herself. The man across the table was little more than a boy—an amazingly handsome, astonishingly impudent, cockily confident boy, who was staring with insolent approval at Emma McChesney's trim, shirt-waisted figure, and her fresh, attractive coloring, and her well-cared-for hair beneath the smart summer hat.

"It isn't in human nature to be as good-looking as you are," spake Emma McChesney, suddenly, being a person who never trifled with half-way measures. "I'll bet you have bad teeth, or an impediment in your speech."

The gorgeous young man smiled. His teeth were perfect. "Peter Piper picked a peck of pickled peppers," he announced, glibly. "Nothing missing there, is there?"

"Must be your morals then," retorted Emma McChesney. "My! My! And on the road! Why, the trail of bleeding hearts that you must leave all the way from Maine to California would probably make the Red Sea turn white with envy."

The Fresh Young Kid speared a piece of liver and looked soulfully up into the adoring eyes of the waitress who was hovering over him.

"Got any nice hot biscuits to-night, girlie?" he inquired.

"I'll get you some; sure," wildly promised his handmaiden, and disappeared kitchenward.

"Brand new to the road, aren't you?" observed Emma McChesney, cruelly.

"What makes you think—"

"Liver and bacon, hot biscuits, Worcestershire," elucidated she. "No old-timer would commit suicide that way. After you've been out for two or three years you'll stick to the Rock of Gibraltar—roast beef, medium. Oh, I get wild now and then, and order eggs if the girl says she knows the hen that layed 'em, but plain roast beef, unchloroformed, is the one best bet. You can't go wrong if you stick to it."

The god-like young man leaned forward, forgetting to eat.

"You don't mean to tell me you're on the road!"

"Why not?" demanded Emma McChesney, briskly.

"Oh, fie, fie!" said the handsome youth, throwing her a languishing look. "Any woman as pretty as you are, and with those eyes, and that hair, and figure—Say, Little One, what are you going to do to-night?"

Emma McChesney sugared her tea, and stirred it, slowly. Then she looked up. "To-night, you fresh young kid, you!" she said calmly, "I'm going to dictate two letters, explaining why business was rotten last week, and why it's going to pick up next week, and then I'm going to keep an engagement with a nine-hour beauty sleep."

"Don't get sore at a fellow. You'd take pity on me if you knew how I have to work to kill an evening in one of these little town-pump burgs. Kill 'em! It can't be done. They die harder than the heroine in a ten, twenty, thirty. From supper to bedtime is twice as long as from breakfast to supper. Honest!"

But Emma McChesney looked inexorable, as women do just before they relent. Said she: "Oh, I don't know. By the time I get through trying to convince a bunch of customers that T. A. Buck's Featherloom Petticoat has every other skirt in the market looking like a piece of Fourth of July bunting that's been left out in the rain, I'm about ready to turn down the spread and leave a call for six-thirty."

"Be a good fellow," pleaded the unquenchable one. "Let's take in all the nickel shows, and then see if we can't drown our sorrows in—er—"

Emma McChesney slipped a coin under her plate, crumpled her napkin, folded her arms on the table, and regarded the boy across the way with what our best talent calls a long, level look. It was so long and so level that even the airiness of the buoyant youngster at whom it was directed began to lessen perceptibly, long before Emma began to talk.

"Tell me, young 'un, did any one ever refuse you anything? I thought not. I should think that when you realize what you've got to learn it would scare you to look ahead. I don't expect you to believe me when I tell you I never talk to fresh guys like you, but it's true. I don't know why I'm breaking my rule for you, unless it's because you're so unbelievably good-looking that I'm anxious to know where the blemish is. The Lord don't make 'em perfect, you know. I'm going to get out those letters, and then, if it's just the same to you, we'll take a walk. These nickel shows are getting on my nerves. It seems to me that if I have to look at one more

Western picture about a fool girl with her hair in a braid riding a show horse in the wilds of Clapham Junction and being rescued from a band of almost-Indians by the handsome, but despised Eastern tenderfoot, or if I see one more of those historical pictures, with the women wearing costumes that are a pass between early Egyptian and late State Street, I know I'll get hysterics and have to be carried shrieking, up the aisle. Let's walk down Main Street and look in the store windows, and up as far as the park and back."

"Great!" assented he. "Is there a park?"

"I don't know," replied Emma McChesney, "but there is. And for your own good I'm going to tell you a few things. There's more to this traveling game than just knocking down on expenses, talking to every pretty woman you meet, and learning to ask for fresh white-bread heels at the Palmer House in Chicago. I'll meet you in the lobby at eight."

Emma McChesney talked steadily, and evenly, and generously, from eight until eight-thirty. She talked from the great storehouse of practical knowledge which she had accumulated in her ten years on the road. She told the handsome young cub many things for which he should have been undyingly thankful. But when they reached the park—the cool, dim, moon-silvered park, its benches dotted with glimpses of white showing close beside a blur of black, Emma McChesney stopped talking. Not only did she stop talking, but she ceased to think of the boy seated beside her on the bench.

In the band-stand, under the arc-light, in the center of the pretty little square, some neighborhood children were playing a noisy game, with many shrill cries, and much shouting and laughter. Suddenly, from one of the houses across the way, a woman's voice was heard, even above the clamor of the children.

"Fred-dee!" called the voice. "Maybelle! Come, now."

And a boy's voice answered, as boys' voices have since Cain was a child playing in the Garden of Eden, and as boys' voices will as long as boys are:

"Aw, ma, I ain't a bit sleepy. We just begun a new game, an' I'm leader. Can't we just stay out a couple of minutes more?"

"Well, five minutes," agreed the voice. "But don't let me call you again."

Emma McChesney leaned back on the rustic bench and clasped her strong, white hands behind her head, and stared straight ahead into the soft darkness. And if it had been light you could have seen that the bitter lines showing faintly about her mouth were outweighed by the sweet and gracious light which was glowing in her eyes.

"Fred-dee!" came the voice of command again. "May-belle! This minute, now!"

One by one the flying little figures under the arc-light melted away in the direction of the commanding voice and home and bed. And Emma McChesney forgot all about fresh young kids and featherloom petticoats and discounts and bills of lading and sample-cases and grouchy buyers. After all, it had been her protecting maternal instinct which had been aroused by the boy at supper, although she had not known it then. She did not know it now, for that matter. She was busy remembering just such evenings in her own life—summer evenings, filled with the high, shrill laughter of children at play. She too, had stood in the doorway, making a funnel of her hands, so that her clear call through the twilight might be heard above the cries of the boys and girls. She had known how loath the little feet had been to leave their play, and how they had lagged up the porch stairs, and into the house. Years, whose memory she had tried to keep behind her, now suddenly loomed before her in the dim quiet of the little flower-scented park.

A voice broke the silence, and sent her dream-thoughts scattering to the winds.

"Honestly, kid," said the voice, "I could be crazy about you, if you'd let me."

The forgotten figure beside her woke into sudden life. A strong arm encircled her shoulders. A strong hand seized her own, which were clasped behind her head. Two warm, eager lips were pressed upon her lips, checking the little cry of surprise and wrath that rose in her throat.

Emma McChesney wrenched herself free with a violent jerk, and pushed him from her. She did not storm. She did not even rise. She sat very quietly, breathing fast. When she turned at last to look at the boy beside her it seemed that her white profile cut the darkness. The man shrank a little, and would have stammered something, but Emma McChesney checked him.

"You nasty, good-for-nothing, handsome young devil, you!" she said. "So you're married."

He sat up with a jerk. "How did you—what makes you think so?"

"That was a married kiss—a two-year-old married kiss, at least. No boy would get as excited as that about kissing an old stager like me. The chances are you're out of practise. I knew that if it wasn't teeth or impediment it must be morals. And it is."

She moved over on the bench until she was close beside him. "Now, listen to me, boy." She leaned forward, impressively. "Are you listening?"

"Yes," answered the handsome young devil, sullenly.

"What I've got to say to you isn't so much for your sake, as for your wife's. I was married when I was eighteen, and stayed married eight years. I've had my divorce ten years, and my boy is seventeen years old. Figure it out. How old is Ann?"

"I don't believe it," he flashed back. "You're not a day over twenty-six—anyway, you don't look it. I—"

"Thanks," drawled Emma. "That's because you've never seen me in negligée. A woman's as old as she looks with her hair on the dresser and bed only a few minutes away. Do you know why I was decent to you in the first place? Because I was foolish enough to think that you reminded me of my own kid. Every fond mama is gump enough to think that every Greek god she sees looks like her own boy, even if her own happens to squint and have two teeth missing—which mine hasn't, thank the Lord! He's the greatest young— Well, now, look here, young 'un. I'm going to return good for evil. Traveling men and geniuses should never marry. But as long as you've done it, you might as well start right. If you move from this spot till I get through with you, I'll yell police and murder. Are you ready?"

"I'm dead sorry, on the square, I am—"

"Ten minutes late," interrupted Emma McChesney. "I'm dishing up a sermon, hot, for one, and you've got to choke it down. Whenever I hear a traveling man howling about his lonesome evenings, and what a dog's life it is, and no way for a man to live, I always wonder what kind of a summer picnic he thinks it is for his wife. She's really a widow seven months in the year, without any of a widow's privileges. Did you ever stop to think what she's doing evenings? No, you didn't. Well, I'll tell you. She's sitting home, night after night, probably embroidering monograms on your shirt sleeves by way of diversion. And on Saturday night, which is the night when every married woman has the inalienable right to be taken out by her husband, she can listen to the woman in the flat upstairs getting ready to go to the theater. The fact that there's a ceiling between 'em doesn't prevent her from knowing just where they're going, and why he has worked himself into a rage over his white lawn tie, and whether they're taking a taxi or the car and who they're going to meet afterward at supper. Just by listening to them coming downstairs she can tell how much Mrs. Third Flat's silk stockings cost, and if she's wearing her new La Valliere or not. Women have that instinct, you know. Or maybe you don't. There's so much you've missed."

"Say, look here—" broke from the man beside her. But Emma McChesney laid her cool fingers on his lips.

"Nothing from the side-lines, please," she said. "After they've gone she can go to bed, or she can sit up, pretending to read, but really wondering if that squeaky sound coming from the direction of the kitchen is a loose screw in the storm door, or if it's some one trying to break into the flat. And she'd rather sit there, scared green, than go back through that long hall to find out. And when Tillie comes home with her young man at eleven o'clock, though she promised not to stay out later than ten, she rushes back to the kitchen and falls on her neck, she's so happy to see her. Oh, it's a gay life. You talk about the heroism of the early Pilgrim mothers! I'd like to know what they had on the average traveling man's wife."

"Bess goes to the matinée every Saturday," he began, in feeble defense.

"Matinée!" scoffed Emma McChesney. "Do you think any woman goes to matinée by preference? Nobody goes but girls of sixteen, and confirmed old maids without brothers, and traveling men's wives. Matinée! Say, would you ever hesitate to choose between an all-day train and a sleeper? It's the same idea. What a woman calls going to the theater is something very different. It means taking a nap in the afternoon, so her eyes will be bright at night, and then starting at about five o'clock to dress, and lay her husband's clean things out on the bed. She loves it. She even enjoys getting his bath towels ready, and putting his shaving things where he can lay his hands on 'em, and telling the girl to have dinner ready promptly at six-thirty. It means getting out her good dress that hangs in the closet with a cretonne bag covering it, and her black satin coat, and her hat with the paradise aigrettes that she bought with what she saved out of the housekeeping money. It means her best silk stockings, and her diamond sunburst that he's going to have made over into a La Valliere just as soon as business is better. She loves it all, and her cheeks get pinker and pinker, so that she really doesn't need the little dash of rouge that she puts on 'because everybody does it, don't you know?' She gets ready, all but her dress, and then she puts on a kimono and slips out to the kitchen to make the gravy for the chicken because the girl never can get it as smooth as he likes it. That's part of what she calls going to the theater, and having a husband. And if there are children—"

There came a little, inarticulate sound from the boy. But Emma's quick ear caught it.

"No? Well, then, we'll call that one black mark less for you. But if there are children—and for her sake I hope there will be—she's father and mother to them. She brings them up, single-handed, while he's on the road. And the worst she can do is to say to them, 'Just wait until your father gets home. He'll hear of this.' But shucks! When he comes home he can't whip the kids for what they did seven weeks before, and that they've forgotten all about, and for what he never saw, and can't imagine. Besides, he wants his comfort when he gets home. He says he wants a little rest and peace, and he's darned if he's going to run around evenings. Not much, he isn't! But he doesn't object to her making a special effort to cook all those little things that he's been longing for on the road. Oh, there'll be a seat in Heaven for every traveling man's wife—though at that, I'll bet most of 'em will find themselves stuck behind a post."

"You're all right!" exclaimed Emma McChesney's listener, suddenly. "How a woman like you can waste her time on the road is more than I can see. And—I want to thank you. I'm not such a fool—"

"I haven't let you finish a sentence so far, and I'm not going to yet. Wait a minute. There's one more paragraph to this sermon. You remember what I told you about old stagers, and the roast beef diet? Well, that applies right through life. It's all very well to trifle with the little side-dishes at first, but there comes a time when you've got to quit fooling with the minced chicken, and the imitation lamb chops of this world, and settle down to plain, everyday, roast beef, medium. That other stuff may tickle your palate for a while, but sooner or later it will turn on you, and ruin your moral digestion. You stick to roast beef, medium. It may sound prosaic, and unimaginative and dry, but you'll find that it wears in the long run. You can take me over to the hotel now. I've lost an hour's sleep, but I don't consider it wasted. And you'll oblige me by putting the stopper on any conversation that may occur to you between here and the hotel. I've talked until I'm so low on words that I'll probably have to sell featherlooms in sign language to-morrow."

They walked to the very doors of the Berger House in silence. But at the foot of the stairs that led to the parlor floor he stopped, and looked into Emma McChesney's face. His own was rather white and tense.

"Look here," he said. "I've got to thank you. That sounds idiotic, but I guess you know what I mean. And I won't ask you to forgive a hound like me. I haven't been so ashamed of myself since I was a kid. Why, if you knew Bess—if you knew—"

"I guess I know Bess, all right. I used to be a Bess, myself. Just because I'm a traveling man it doesn't follow that I've forgotten the Bess feeling. As far as that goes, I don't mind telling you that I've got neuralgia from sitting in that park with my feet in the damp grass. I can feel it in my back teeth, and by eleven o'clock it will be camping over my left eye, with its little brothers doing a war dance up the side of my face. And, boy, I'd give last week's commissions if there was some one to whom I had the right to say: 'Henry, will you get up and get me a hot-water bag for my neuralgia? It's something awful. And just open the left-hand lower drawer of the chiffonier and get out one of those gauze vests and then get me a safety pin from the tray on my dresser. I'm going to pin it around my head.'"

ENGLAND TO AMERICA

by Margaret Prescott Montague

Although relatively unknown today, Margaret Prescott Montague's fiction had been both critically acclaimed and popular for over a decade when "England to America" garnered the very first O. Henry Memorial Prize in 1919, soon after publication in *The Atlantic Monthly*. The story's sophisticated First-World-War England setting was dramatically different from that of her earlier work, which had dealt with the lives of mountain people in her native Appalachia.

1

"LORD, BUT ENGLISH people are funny!"

This was the perplexed mental ejaculation that young Lieutenant Skipworth Cary, of Virginia, found his thoughts constantly reiterating during his stay in Devonshire. Had he been, he wondered, a confiding fool to accept so trustingly Chev Sherwood's suggestion that he spend a part of his leave, at least, at Bishopsthorpe, where Chev's people lived? But why should he have anticipated any difficulty here, in this very corner of England which had bred his own ancestors, when he had always hit it off so splendidly with his English comrades at the Front? Here, however, though they were all awfully kind,—at least, he was sure they meant to be kind,—something was always bringing him up short: something that he could not lay hold of but which made him feel like a blind man groping in a strange place, or worse, like a bull in a china-shop. He was prepared enough to find differences in the American and English points of view. But this thing that baffled him did not seem to have to do with that; it was something deeper, something very definite, he was sure—and yet, what was it? The worst of it was that he had a curious feeling as if they were all—that is, Lady Sherwood and Gerald; not Sir Charles so much—protecting him from himself—keeping him from making breaks, as he phrased it. That hurt and annoyed him, and piqued his vanity. Was he a social blunderer, and weren't a Virginia gentleman's manners to be trusted in England without leading-strings?

He had been at the Front for several months with the Royal Flying Corps, and when his leave came, his Flight Commander, Captain Cheviot Sherwood, discovering that he meant to spend it in England, where he hardly knew a soul, had said that his people down in Devonshire would be jolly glad to have him stop with them; and Skipworth Cary, knowing that if the circumstances had been reversed, his people down in Virginia would indeed have been jolly glad to entertain Captain Sherwood, had accepted unhesitatingly. The invitation had been seconded by a letter from Lady Sherwood,—Chev's mother,—and after a few days' sight-seeing in London he had come down to Bishopsthorpe, very eager to know his friend's family, feeling as he did about Chev himself. "He's the finest man that ever went up in the air," he had written home; and to his own family's disgust, his letters had been far more full of Chev Sherwood than they had been of Skipworth Cary.

And now here he was, and he almost wished himself away—wished almost that he was back again at the Front, carrying on under Chev. There, at least, you knew what you were up against. The job might be hard enough, but it wasn't baffling and queer, with hidden undercurrents that you couldn't chart. It seemed to him that this baffling feeling of constraint had rushed to meet him on the very threshold of the drawing-room, when he had made his first appearance.

As he entered, he had a sudden sensation that they had been awaiting him in a strained expectancy, and that, as he appeared, they adjusted unseen masks and began to play-act at something. "But English people don't play-act very well," he commented to himself, reviewing the scene afterward.

Lady Sherwood had come forward and greeted him in a manner which would have been pleasant enough if he had not, with quick sensitiveness, felt it to be forced. But perhaps that was English stiffness.

Then she had turned to her husband, who was standing staring into the fireplace, although, as it was June, there was no fire there to stare at.

"Charles," she said, "here is Lieutenant Cary"; and her voice had a certain note in it which at home Cary and his sister Nancy were in the habit of designating "mother-making-dad-mind-his-manners."

At her words the old man—and Cary was startled to see how old and broken he was—turned round and held out his hand. "How d'you do?" he said, jerkily, "how d'you do?" and then turned abruptly back again to the fireplace.

"Hello! What's up! The old boy doesn't like me!" was Cary's quick, startled comment to himself.

He was so surprised by the look the other bent upon him that he involuntarily glanced across to a long mirror to see if there was anything wrong with his uniform. But no, that appeared to be all right. It was himself, then—or his country; perhaps the old sport didn't fall for Americans.

"And here is Gerald," Lady Sherwood went on in her low remote voice, which somehow made the Virginian feel very far away.

It was with genuine pleasure, though with some surprise, that he turned to greet Gerald Sherwood, Chev's younger brother, who had been, tradition in the corps said, as gallant and daring a flyer as Chev himself, until he got his in the face five months ago.

"I'm mighty glad to meet you," he said, eagerly, in his pleasant, muffled Southern voice, grasping the hand the other stretched out, and looking with deep respect at the scarred face and sightless eyes.

Gerald laughed a little, but it was a pleasant laugh, and his hand-clasp was friendly.

"That's real American, isn't it?" he said. "I ought to have remembered and said it first. Sorry."

Skipworth laughed, too. "Well," he conceded, "we generally are glad to meet people in my country, and we don't care who says it first. But," he added, "I didn't think I'd have the luck to find you here."

He remembered that Chev had regretted that he probably wouldn't see Gerald, as the latter was at St. Dunstan's, where they were re-educating the blinded soldiers.

The other hesitated a moment, and then said, rather awkwardly, "Oh, I'm just home for a little while; I only got here this morning, in fact."

Skipworth noted the hesitation. Did the old people get panicky at the thought of entertaining a wild man from Virginia, and send an SOS for Gerald, he wondered.

"We are so glad you could come to us," Lady Sherwood said, rather hastily, just then. And again he could not fail to note that she was prompting her husband.

The latter reluctantly turned round, and said, "Yes, yes, quite so. Welcome to Bishopsthorpe, my boy," as if his wife had pulled a string, and he responded mechanically, without quite knowing what he said. Then, as his eyes rested a moment on his guest, he looked as if he would like to bolt out of the room. He controlled himself, however, and, jerking round again to the fireplace, went on murmuring, "Yes, yes, yes," vaguely—just like the dormouse at the Mad Tea-Party, who went to sleep, saying "Twinkle, twinkle, twinkle," Cary could not help thinking to himself.

But, after all, it wasn't really funny, it was pathetic. Gosh, how doddering the poor old boy was! Skipworth wondered, with a sudden twist at his heart, if the war was playing the deuce with his home people, too. Was his own father going to pieces like this, and had his mother's gay vivacity fallen into that still remoteness of Lady Sherwood's? But of course not! The Carys hadn't suffered as the poor Sherwoods had, with their youngest son, Curtin, killed early in the war, and now Gerald knocked out so tragically. Lord, he thought, how they must all bank on Chev! And of course they would want to hear at once about him. "I left Chev as fit as anything, and he sent all sorts of messages," he reported, thinking it more discreet to deliver Chev's messages thus vaguely than to repeat his actual carefree remark, which had been, "Oh, tell 'em I'm jolly as a tick."

But evidently there was something wrong with the words as they were, for instantly he was aware of that curious sense of withdrawal on their part. Hastily reviewing them, he decided that they had sounded too familiar from a stranger and a younger man like himself. He supposed he ought not to have spoken of Chev by his first name. Gee, what sticklers they were! Wouldn't his family—dad and mother and Nancy—have fairly lapped up any messages from him, even if they had been delivered a bit awkwardly? However, he added, as a concession to their point of view, "But of course, you'll have had later news of Captain Sherwood."

To which, after a pause, Lady Sherwood responded, "Oh, yes," in that remote and colourless voice which might have meant anything or nothing.

At this point dinner was announced.

Lady Sherwood drew her husband away from the empty fireplace, and Gerald slipped his arm through the Virginian's, saying pleasantly, "I'm learning to carry on fairly well at St. Dunstan's, but I confess I still like to have a pilot."

To look at the tall young fellow beside him, whose scarred face was so reminiscent of Chev's untouched good looks, who had known all the immense freedom of the air, but who was now learning to carry on in the dark, moved Skipworth Cary to generous homage.

"You know my saying I'm glad to meet you isn't just American," he said half shyly, but warmly. "It's plain English, and the straight truth. I've wanted to meet you awfully. The oldsters are always holding up your glorious exploits to us newcomers. Withers never gets tired telling about that fight of yours with the four enemy planes. And besides," he rushed on, eagerly, "I'm glad to have a chance to tell Chev's brother—Captain Sherwood's brother, I mean—what l think of him. Only, as a matter of fact, I can't," he broke off with a laugh. "I can't put it exactly into words, but I tell you I'd follow that man straight into hell and out the other side—or go there alone if he told me to. He is the finest chap that ever flew."

And then he felt as if a cold douche had been flung in his face, for after a moment's pause the other returned, "That's awfully good of you," in a voice so distant and formal that the Virginian could have kicked himself. What an ass he was to be so darned enthusiastic with an Englishman! He supposed it was bad form to show any pleasure over praise of a member of your family. Lord, if Chev got the V.C., he reckoned it would be awful to speak of it. Still, you would have thought Gerald might have stood for a little praise of him. But then, glancing sideways at his companion, he surprised on his face a look so strange and suffering that it came to him almost violently what it must be never to fly again; to be on the threshold of life, with endless days of blackness ahead. Good God! How cruel he had been to flaunt Chev in his face! In remorseful and hasty reparation he stumbled on, "But the old fellows are always having great discussions as to which was the best—you or your brother. Withers always maintains you were."

"Withers lies, then!" the other retorted. "I never touched Chev—never came within a mile of him, and never could have."

They reached the dinner-table with that, and young Cary found himself bewildered and uncomfortable. If Gerald hadn't liked praise of Chev, he had liked praise of himself even less, it seemed.

Dinner was not a success. The Virginian found that, if there was to be conversation, the burden of carrying it on was upon him, and gosh! they don't mind silences in this man's island, do they? he commented desperately to himself, thinking how different it was from America. Why, there they acted as if silence was an egg that had just been laid, and everyone had to cackle at once to cover it up. But here the talk constantly fell to the ground, and nobody but himself seemed concerned to pick it up. His attempt to praise Chev had not been successful, and he could understand their not wanting to hear about flying and the war before Gerald.

So at last, in desperation, he wandered off into descriptions of America, finding to his relief, that he had struck the right note at last. They were glad to hear about the States, and Lady Sherwood inquired politely if the Indians still gave them much trouble; and when he assured her that in Virginia, except for the Pocahontas tribe, they were all pretty well subdued, she accepted his statement with complete innocency. And he was so delighted to find at last a subject to which they were evidently cordial, that he was quite carried away, and wound up by inviting them all to visit his family in Richmond, as soon as the war was over.

Gerald accepted at once, with enthusiasm; Lady Sherwood made polite murmurs, smiling at him in quite a warm and almost, indeed, maternal manner. Even Sir Charles, who had been staring at the food on his plate as if he did not quite know what to make of it, came to the surface long enough to mumble, "Yes, yes, very good idea. Countries must carry on together—— What?"

But that was the only hit of the whole evening, and when the Virginian retired to his room, as he made an excuse to do early, he was so confused and depressed that he fell into an acute attack of homesickness.

Heavens, he thought, as he tumbled into bed, just suppose, now, this was little old Richmond, Virginia, U.S.A., instead of being Bishopsthorpe, Avery Cross near Wick, and all the rest of it! And at that, he grinned to himself. England wasn't such an all-fired big country that you'd think they'd have to ticket themselves with addresses a yard long, for fear they'd get lost—now, would you? Well, anyway, suppose it was Richmond, and his train just pulling into the Byrd Street Station. He stretched out luxuriously, and let his mind picture the whole familiar scene. The wind was blowing right, so there was the mellow, homely smell of tobacco in the streets, and plenty of people all along the way to hail him with outstretched hands and shouts of "Hey, Skip Cary, when did you get back?" "Welcome home, my boy!" "Well, with will you *look* what the cat dragged in!" And so he came to his own front door-step, and, walking straight in, surprised the whole family at break-fast; and yes—doggone it! if it wasn't Sunday, and they having waffles! And after that his obliging fancy bore him up Franklin Street, through Monroe Park, and so to Miss Sally Berkeley's door. He was sound asleep before he reached it, but in his dreams, light as a little bird, she came flying down the broad stairway to meet him, and—

But when he waked next morning, he did not find himself in Virginia, but in Devonshire, where, to his unbounded embarrass-ment, a white housemaid was putting up his curtains and whisper-ing something about his bath. And though he pretended profound slumber, he was well aware that people do not turn brick-red in their sleep. And the problem of what was the matter with the Sherwood family was still before him.

2

"They're playing a game," he told himself after a few days. "That is, Lady Sherwood and Gerald are—poor old Sir Charles can't make much of a stab at it. The game is to make me think they are awfully glad to have me, when in reality there's something about me, or something I do, that gets them on the raw."

He almost decided to make some excuse and get away; but after all, that was not easy. In English novels, he remembered, they always had a wire calling them to London; but, darn it all! the Sherwoods knew mighty well there wasn't any one in London who cared a hoot about him.

The thing that got his goat most, he told himself, was that they apparently didn't like his friendship with Chev. Anyway, they didn't seem to want him to talk about him; and whenever he tried to express his warm appreciation for all that the older man had done for him, he was instantly aware of a wall of reserve on their part, a holding of themselves aloof from him. That puzzled and hurt him, and put him on his dignity. He concluded that they thought it was cheeky of a youngster like him to think that a man like Chev could be his friend; and if that was the way they felt, he reckoned he'd jolly well better shut up about it.

But whatever it was that they didn't like about him, they most certainly did want him to have a good time. He and his pleasure appeared to be for the time being their chief consideration. And after the first day or so he began indeed to enjoy himself extremely. For one thing, he came to love the atmosphere of the old place and of the surrounding country, which he and Gerald explored together. He liked to think that ancestors of his own had been inheritors of these green lanes, and pleasant mellow stretches. Then, too, after the first few days, he could not help seeing that they really began to like him, which of course was reassuring, and tapped his own warm friendliness, which was always ready enough to be released. And besides, he got by accident what he took to be a hint as to the trouble. He was passing the half-open door of Lady Sherwood's morning-room when he heard Sir Charles's voice break out, "Good God, Elizabeth, I don't see how you stand it! When I see him so straight and fine-looking, and so untouched, beside our poor lad, and think—and think——"

Skipworth hurried out of earshot, but now he understood that look of aversion in the old man's eyes which had so startled him at first. Of course, the poor old boy might easily hate the sight of him beside Gerald. With Gerald himself he really got along famously. He was a most delightful companion, full of anecdotes and history of the countryside, every foot of which he had apparently explored in the old days with Chev and the younger brother, Curtin. Yet even with Gerald, Cary sometimes felt that aloofness and reserve, and that older protective air that they all showed him. Take, for instance, that afternoon when they were lolling together on the grass in the park. The Virginian, running on in his usual eager manner, had plunged without thinking into an account of a particularly daring bit of flying on Chev's part, when suddenly he realized that Gerald had rolled over on the grass and buried his face in his arms, and interrupted himself awkwardly. "But, of course," he said, "he must have written home about it himself."

"No, or if he did, I didn't hear of it. Go on," Gerald said in a muffled voice.

A great rush of compassion and remorse overwhelmed the Virginian, and he burst out penitently, "What a brute I am! I'm always forgetting and running on about flying, when I know it must hurt like the very devil!"

The other drew a difficult breath. "Yes," he admitted, "what you say does hurt in a way—in a way you can't understand. But all the same I like to hear you. Go on about Chev."

So Skipworth went on and finished his account, winding up, "I don't believe there's another man in the service who could have pulled it off—but I tell you your brother's one in a million."

"Good God, don't I know it!" the other burst out. "We were all three the jolliest pals together," he got out presently in a choked voice, "Chev and the young un and I; and now——"

He did not finish, but Cary guessed his meaning. Now the young un, Curtin, was dead, and Gerald himself knocked out. But, heavens! the Virginian thought, did Gerald think Chev would go back on him now on account of his blindness? Well, you could everlastingly bet he wouldn't!

"Chev thinks the world and all of you!" he cried in eager defense of his friend's loyalty. "Lots of times when we're all awfully jolly together, he makes some excuse and goes off by himself; and Withers told me it was because he was so frightfully cut up about you. Withers said he told him once that he'd a lot rather have got it himself—so you can everlastingly bank on him!"

Gerald gave a terrible little gasp. "I—I knew he'd feel like that," he got out. "We've always cared such a lot for each other." And then he pressed his face harder than ever into the grass, and his long body quivered all over. But not for long. In a moment he took fierce hold on himself, muttering, "Well, one must carry on, whatever happens," and apologized disjointedly. "What a fearful fool you must think me! And—and this isn't very pippy for you, old chap." Presently, after that, he sat up, and said, brushing it all aside, "We're facing the old moat, aren't we? There's an interesting bit of tradition about it that I must tell you."

And there you were, Cary thought: no matter how much Gerald might be suffering from his misfortune, he must carry on just the same, and see that his visitor had a pleasant time. It made the Virginian feel like an outsider and very young, as if he were not old enough for them to show him their real feelings.

Another thing that he noticed was that they did not seem to want him to meet people. They never took him anywhere to call, and if visitors came to the house, they showed an almost panicky desire to get him out of the way. That again hurt his pride. What in heaven's name was the matter with him, anyway!

3

However, on the last afternoon of his stay at Bishopsthorpe, he told himself with a rather rueful grin that his manners must have improved a little, for they took him to tea at the rectory.

He was particularly glad to go there because, from certain jokes of Withers's, who had known the Sherwoods since boyhood, he gathered that Chev and the rector's daughter were engaged. And just as he would have liked Chev to meet Sally Berkeley, so he wanted to meet Miss Sybil Gaylord.

He had little hope of having a tête-à-tête with her, but as it fell out he did. They were all in the rectory garden together, Gerald and the rector a little behind Miss Gaylord and himself, as they strolled down a long walk with high hedges bordering it. On the other side of the hedge Lady Sherwood and her hostess still sat at the tea-table, and then it was that Cary heard Mrs. Gaylord say distinctly: "I'm afraid the strain has been too much for you—you should have let us have him."

To which Lady Sherwood returned quickly, "Oh, no, that would have been impossible with——"

"Come—come this way—I must show you the view from the arbour," Miss Gaylord broke in breathlessly; and laying a hand on his arm, she turned him abruptly into a side path.

Glancing down at her, the Southerner could not but note the panic and distress in her fair face. It was so obvious that the overheard words referred to him, and he was so bewildered by the whole situation, that he burst out impulsively, "I say, what *is* the matter with me? Why do they find me so hard to put up with? Is it something I do—or don't they like Americans? Honestly, I wish you'd tell me."

She stood still at that, looking at him, her blue eyes full of distress and concern.

"Oh, I am so sorry!" she cried. "They would be so sorry to have you think anything like that."

"But what is it?" he persisted. "Don't they like Americans?"

"Oh, no, it isn't that—Oh, quite the contrary!" she returned, eagerly.

"Then it's something about me they don't like?"

"Oh, no, no! Least of all, that—*don't* think that!" she begged.

"But what am I to think then?"

"Don't think anything just yet," she pleaded. "Wait a little, and you will understand."

She was so evidently distressed that he could not press her further; and fearing she might think him unappreciative, he said, "Well, whatever it is, it hasn't prevented me from having a ripping good time. They've seen to that, and just done everything for my pleasure."

She looked up quickly, and to his relief he saw that for once he had said the right thing.

"You have enjoyed it, then?" she questioned, eagerly.

"Most awfully," he assured her, warmly. "I shall always remember what a happy leave they gave me."

She gave a little sigh of satisfaction. "I am so glad," she said. "They wanted you to have a good time—that was what we all wanted."

He looked at her gratefully, thinking how sweet she was in her fair English beauty, and how good to care that he should have enjoyed his leave. How different she was too from Sally Berkeley—why, she would have made two of his little girl! And how quiet! Sally Berkeley, with her quick glancing vivacity, would have been all around her and off again like a humming-bird before she could have uttered two words. And yet he was sure that they would have been friends, just as he and Chev were. Perhaps they all would be, after the war. And then he began to talk about Chev, being sure that, had the circumstances been reversed, Sally Berkeley would have wanted news of him. Instantly he was aware of a tense listening stillness on her part. That pleased him. Well, she did care for the old fellow all right, he thought; and though she made no response, averting her face, and plucking nervously at the leaves of the hedge as they passed slowly along, he went on pouring out his eager admiration for his friend.

At last they came to a seat in an arbour, from which one looked out upon a green, beneficent landscape. It was an intimate, secluded little spot—and oh, if Sally Berkeley were only there to sit beside him! And as he thought of this, it came to him whimsically that in all probability Miss Gaylord must be longing for Chev, just as he was for Sally.

Dropping down on the bench beside her, he leaned over, and said with a friendly, almost brotherly, grin of understanding, "I reckon you're wishing Captain Sherwood was sitting here instead of Lieutenant Cary."

The minute the impulsive words were out of his mouth, he knew he had blundered, been awkward, and inexcusably intimate. She gave a little choked gasp, and her blue eyes stared up at him, wide and startled. Good heavens, what a break he had made! No wonder the Sherwoods couldn't trust him in company! There seemed no apology that he could offer in words, but at least, he thought, he would show her that he would not have intruded on her secret without being willing to share his with her. With awkward haste he put his hand into his breast-pocket, and dragged forth the picture of Sally Berkeley that he always carried there.

"This is the little girl I'm thinking about," he said, turning very red, yet boyishly determined to make amends, and also proudly confident of Sally Berkeley's charms. "I'd like mighty well for you two to know one another."

She took the picture in silence, and for a long moment stared down at the soft little face, so fearless, so confident and gay, that smiled appealingly back at her. Then she did something astonishing,—something which seemed to him wholly un-English,—and yet he thought it the sweetest thing he had ever seen. Cupping her strong hands about the picture with a quick protectiveness, she suddenly raised it to her lips, and kissed it lightly. "O little girl!" she cried, "I hope you will be very happy!"

The little involuntary act, so tender, so sisterly and spontaneous, touched the Virginian extremely.

"Thanks awfully," he said, unsteadily. "She'll think a lot of that, just as I do—and I know she'd wish you the same."

She made no reply to that, and as she handed the picture back to him he saw that her hands were trembling, and he had a sudden conviction that, if she had been Sally Berkeley, her eyes would have been full of tears. As she was Sybil Gaylord, however, there were no tears there, only a look that he never forgot. The look of one much older, protective, maternal almost, and as if she were gazing back at Sally Berkeley and himself from a long way ahead on the road of life. He supposed it was the way most English people felt nowadays. He had surprised it so often on all their faces that he could not help speaking of it.

"You all think we Americans are awfully young and raw, don't you?" he questioned.

"Oh, no, not that," she deprecated. "Young perhaps for these days, yes—but it is more that you—that your country is so—so unsuffered. And we don't want you to suffer!" she added quickly.

Yes, that was it! He understood now, and, heavens, how fine it was! Old England was wounded deep—deep. What she suffered herself she was too proud to show; but out of it she wrought a great maternal care for the newcomer. Yes, it *was* fine—he hoped his country would understand.

Miss Gaylord rose. "There are Gerald and father looking for you," she said, "and I must go now." She held out her hand. "Thank you for letting me see her picture, and for everything you said about Captain Sherwood—for *everything*, remember—I want you to remember."

With a light pressure of her fingers she was gone, slipping away through the shrubbery, and he did not see her again.

4

So he came to his last morning at Bishopsthorpe; and as he dressed, he wished it could have been different; that he were not still conscious of that baffling wall of reserve between himself and Chev's people, for whom, despite all, he had come to have a real affection.

In the breakfast-room he found them all assembled, and his last meal there seemed to him as constrained and difficult as any that had preceded it. It was over finally, however, and in a few minutes he would be leaving.

"I can never thank you enough for the splendid time I've had here," he said as he rose. "I'll be seeing Chev to-morrow, and I'll tell him all about everything."

Then he stopped dead. With a smothered exclamation, old Sir Charles had stumbled to his feet, knocking over his chair, and hurried blindly out of the room; and Gerald said, *"Mother!"* in a choked appeal.

As if it were a signal between them. Lady Sherwood pushed her chair back a little from the table, her long delicate fingers dropped together loosely in her lap; she gave a faint sigh as if a restraining mantle slipped from her shoulders, and, looking up at the youth before her, her fine pale face lighted with a kind of glory, she said, "No, dear lad, no. You can never tell Chev, for he is gone."

"*Gone!*" he cried.

"Yes," she nodded back at him, just above a whisper; and now her face quivered, and the tears began to rush down her cheeks.

"Not *dead!*" he cried. "Not Chev—not that! O my God, Gerald, not *that!*"

"Yes," Gerald said. "They got him two days after you left."

It was so overwhelming, so unexpected and shocking, above all so terrible, that the friend he had so greatly loved and admired was gone out of his life forever, that young Cary stumbled back into his seat, and crumpling over, buried his face in his hands, making great uncouth gasps as he strove to choke back his grief.

Gerald groped hastily around the table and flung an arm about his shoulders.

"Steady on, dear fellow, steady," he said, though his own voice broke.

"When did you hear?" Cary got out at last.

"We got the official notice just the day before you came—and Withers has written us particulars since."

"And you *let* me come in spite of it! And stay on, when every word I said about him must have—have fairly *crucified* each one of you! Oh, forgive me! Forgive me!" he cried distractedly. He saw it all now; he understood at last. It was not on Gerald's account that they could not talk of flying and of Chev, it was because—because their hearts were broken over Chev himself. "Oh, forgive me!" he gasped again.

"Dear lad, there is nothing to forgive," Lady Sherwood returned. "How could we help loving your generous praise of our poor darling? We loved it, and you for it; we wanted to hear it, but we were afraid. We were afraid we might break down, and that you would find out."

The tears were still running down her cheeks. She did not brush them away now; she seemed glad to have them there at last.

Sinking down on his knees, he caught her hands. "Why did you *let* me do such a horrible thing?" he cried. "Couldn't you have trusted me to understand? Couldn't you *see* I loved him just as you did——No, no!" he broke down, humbly. "Of course I couldn't love him as his own people did. But you must have seen how I felt about him—how I admired him, and would have followed him anywhere—and *of course* if I had known, I should have gone away at once."

"Ah, but that was just what we were afraid of," she said, quickly. "We were afraid you would go away and have a lonely leave somewhere. And in these days a boy's leave is so precious a thing that nothing must spoil it—*nothing*," she reiterated; and her tears fell upon his hands like a benediction. "But we didn't do it very well, I'm afraid," she went on, presently, with gentle contrition. "You were too quick and understanding; you guessed there was something wrong. We were sorry not to manage better," she apologized.

"Oh, you wonderful, wonderful people!" he gasped. "Doing everything for my happiness, when all the time—all the time——"

His voice went out sharply, as his mind flashed back to scene after scene: to Gerald's long body lying quivering on the grass; to Sybil Gaylord wishing Sally Berkeley happiness out of her own tragedy; and to the high look on Lady Sherwood's face. They seemed to him themselves, and yet more than themselves—shining bits in the mosaic of a great nation. Disjointedly there passed through his mind familiar words—"these are they who have washed their garments—having come out of great tribulation." No wonder they seemed older.

"We—we couldn't have done it in America," he said, humbly.

He had a desperate desire to get away to himself; to hide his face in his arms, and give vent to the tears that were stifling him; to weep for his lost friend, and for this great, heartbreaking heroism of theirs.

"But why did you do it?" he persisted. "Was it because I was his friend?"

"Oh, it was much more than that," Gerald said quickly. "It was a matter of the two countries. Of course, we jolly well knew you didn't belong to us, and didn't want to, but for the life of us we couldn't help a sort of feeling that you did. And when America was in at last, and you fellows began to come, you seemed like our very own come back after many years, and," he added, a throb in his voice, "we were most awfully glad to see you—we wanted a chance to show you how England felt."

Skipworth Cary rose to his feet. The tears for his friend were still wet upon his lashes. Stooping, he took Lady Sherwood's hands in his and raised them to his lips. "As long as I live, I shall never forget," he said. "And others of us have seen it too in other ways—be sure America will never forget, either."

She looked up at his untouched youth out of her beautiful sad eyes, the exalted light still shining through her tears. "Yes," she said, "you see it was—I don't know exactly how to put it—but it was England to America."

COMING, APHRODITE!

by Willa Cather

Some of Willa Cather's short stories about artists rank with *My Ántonia* and *Death Comes for the Archbishop* as her best work. This story was first published in *Smart Set* in 1920 under the title "Coming, Eden Bower!"; later that same year it was included, with minor changes and the present title, in her collection entitled *Youth and the Bright Medusa.*

I

DON HEDGER HAD lived for four years on the top floor of an old house on the south side of Washington Square, and nobody had ever disturbed him. He occupied one big room with no outside exposure except on the north, where he had built in a many-paned studio window that looked upon a court and upon the roofs and walls of other buildings. His room was very cheerless, since he never got a ray of direct sunlight; the south corners were always in shadow. In one of the corners was a clothes closet, built against the partition, in another a wide divan, serving as a seat by day and a bed by night. In the front corner, the one farther from the window, was a sink, and a table with two gas burners where he sometimes cooked his food. There, too, in the perpetual dusk, was the dog's bed, and often a bone or two for his comfort.

The dog was a Boston bull terrier, and Hedger explained his surly disposition by the fact that he had been bred to the point where it told on his nerves. His name was Caesar III, and he had taken prizes at very exclusive dog shows. When he and his master went out to prowl about University Place or to promenade along West Street, Caesar III was invariably fresh and shining. His pink skin showed through his mottled coat, which glistened as if it had just been rubbed with olive oil, and he wore a brass-studded collar, bought at the smartest saddler's. Hedger, as often as not, was hunched up in an old striped blanket coat, with a shapeless felt hat pulled over his bushy hair, wearing black shoes that had become grey, or brown ones that had become black, and he never put on gloves unless the day was biting cold.

Early in May, Hedger learned that he was to have a new neighbour in the rear apartment—two rooms, one large and one small, that faced the west. His studio was shut off from the larger of these rooms by double doors, which, though they were fairly tight, left him a good deal at the mercy of the occupant. The rooms had been leased, long before he came there, by a trained nurse who considered herself knowing in old furniture. She went to auction sales and bought up mahogany and dirty brass and stored it away here, where she meant to live when she retired from nursing. Meanwhile, she sub-let her rooms, with their precious furniture, to young people who came to New York to "write" or to "paint"—who proposed to live by the sweat of the brow rather than of the hand, and who desired artistic surroundings. When Hedger first moved in, these rooms were occupied by a young man who tried to write plays,—and who kept on trying until a week ago, when the nurse had put him out for unpaid rent.

A few days after the playwright left, Hedger heard an ominous murmur of voices through the bolted double doors: the lady-like intonation of the nurse—doubtless exhibiting her treasures—and another voice, also a woman's, but very different; young, fresh, unguarded, confident. All the same, it would be very annoying to have a woman in there. The only bath-room on the floor was at the top of the stairs in the front hall, and he would always be running into her as he came or went from his bath. He would have to be more careful to see that Caesar didn't leave bones about the hall, too; and she might object when he cooked steak and onions on his gas burner.

As soon as the talking ceased and the women left, he forgot them. He was absorbed in a study of paradise fish at the Aquarium, staring out at people through the glass and green water of their tank. It was a highly gratifying idea; the incommunicability of one stratum of animal life with another,—though Hedger pretended it was only an experiment in unusual lighting. When he heard trunks knocking against the sides of the narrow hall, then he realized that she was moving in at once. Toward noon, groans and deep gasps and the creaking of ropes, made him aware that a piano was arriving. After the tramp of the movers died away down the stairs, somebody touched off a few scales and chords on the instrument, and then there was peace. Presently he heard her lock her door and go down the hall humming something; going out to lunch, probably. He stuck his brushes in a can of turpentine and put on his hat, not stopping to wash his hands. Caesar was smelling along the crack under the bolted doors; his bony tail stuck out hard as a hickory withe, and the hair was standing up about his elegant collar.

Hedger encouraged him. "Come along, Caesar. You'll soon get used to a new smell."

In the hall stood an enormous trunk, behind the ladder that led to the roof, just opposite Hedger's door. The dog flew at it with a growl of hurt amazement. They went down three flights of stairs and out into the brilliant May afternoon.

Behind the Square, Hedger and his dog descended into a basement oyster house where there were no tablecloths on the tables and no handles on the coffee cups, and the floor was covered with sawdust, and Caesar was always welcome,—not that he needed any such precautionary flooring. All the carpets of Persia would have been safe for him. Hedger ordered steak and onions absentmindedly, not realizing why he had an apprehension that this dish might be less readily at hand hereafter. While he ate, Caesar sat beside his chair, gravely disturbing the sawdust with his tail.

After lunch Hedger strolled about the Square for the dog's health and watched the stages pull out;—that was almost the very last summer of the old horse stages on Fifth Avenue. The fountain had but lately begun operations for the season and was throwing up a mist of rainbow water which now and then blew south and sprayed a bunch of Italian babies that were being supported on the outer rim by older, very little older, brothers and sisters. Plump robins were hopping about on the soil; the grass was newly cut and blindingly green. Looking up the Avenue through the Arch, one could see the young poplars with their bright, sticky leaves, and the Brevoort glistening in its spring coat of paint, and shining horses and carriages,—occasionally an automobile, misshapen and sullen, like an ugly threat in a stream of things that were bright and beautiful and alive.

While Caesar and his master were standing by the fountain, a girl approached them, crossing the Square. Hedger noticed her because she wore a lavender cloth suit and carried in her arms a big bunch of fresh lilacs. He saw that she was young and handsome,—beautiful, in fact, with a splendid figure and good action. She, too, paused by the fountain and looked back through the Arch up the Avenue. She smiled rather patronizingly as she looked, and at the same time seemed delighted. Her slowly curving upper lip and half-closed eyes seemed to say: "You're gay, you're exciting, you are quite the right sort of thing; but you're none too fine for me!"

In the moment she tarried, Caesar stealthily approached her and sniffed at the hem of her lavender skirt, then, when she went south like an arrow, he ran back to his master and lifted a face full of emotion and alarm, his lower lip twitching under his sharp white teeth and his hazel eyes pointed with a very definite discovery. He stood thus, motionless, while Hedger watched the lavender girl go up the steps and through the door of the house in which he lived.

"You're right, my boy, it's she! She might be worse looking, you know."

When they mounted to the studio, the new lodger's door, at the back of the hall, was a little ajar, and Hedger caught the warm perfume of lilacs just brought in out of the sun. He was used to the musty smell of the old hall carpet. (The nurse-lessee had once knocked at his studio door and complained that Caesar must be somewhat responsible for the particular flavour of that mustiness, and Hedger had never spoken to her since.) He was used to the old smell, and he preferred it to that of the lilacs, and so did his companion, whose nose was so much more discriminating. Hedger shut his door vehemently, and fell to work.

Most young men who dwell in obscure studios in New York have had a beginning, come out of something, have somewhere a home town, a family, a paternal roof. But Don Hedger had no such background. He was a foundling, and had grown up in a school for homeless boys, where book-learning was a negligible part of the curriculum. When he was sixteen, a Catholic priest took him to Greensburg, Pennsylvania, to keep house for him. The priest did something to fill in the large gaps in the boy's education,—taught him to like "Don Quixote" and "The Golden Legend," and encouraged him to mess with paints and crayons in his room up under the slope of the mansard. When Don wanted to go to New York to study at the Art League, the priest got him a night job as packer in one of the big department stores. Since then, Hedger had taken care of himself; that was his only responsibility. He was singularly unencumbered; had no family duties, no social ties, no obligations toward any one but his landlord. Since he travelled light, he had travelled rather far. He had got over a good deal of the earth's surface, in spite of the fact that he never in his life had more than three hundred dollars ahead at any one time, and he had already outlived a succession of convictions and revelations about his art.

Though he was now but twenty-six years old, he had twice been on the verge of becoming a marketable product; once through some studies of New York streets he did for a magazine, and once through a collection of pastels he brought home from New Mexico, which Remington, then at the height of his popularity, happened to see, and generously tried to push. But on both occasions Hedger decided that this was something he didn't wish to carry further,—simply the old thing over again and got nowhere,—so he took enquiring dealers experiments in a "later manner," that made them put him out of the shop. When he ran short of money, he could always get any amount of commercial work; he was an expert draughtsman and worked with lightning speed. The rest of his time he spent in groping his way from one kind of painting into another, or travelling about without luggage, like a tramp, and he was chiefly occupied with getting rid of ideas he had once thought very fine.

Hedger's circumstances, since he had moved to Washington Square, were affluent compared to anything he had ever known before. He was now able to pay advance rent and turn the key on his studio when he went away for four months at a stretch. It didn't occur to him to wish to be richer than this. To be sure, he did without a great many things other people think necessary, but he didn't miss them, because he had never had them. He belonged to no clubs, visited no houses, had no studio friends, and he ate his dinner alone in some decent little restaurant, even on Christmas and New Year's. For days together he talked to nobody but his dog and the janitress and the lame oysterman.

After he shut the door and settled down to his paradise fish on that first Tuesday in May, Hedger forgot all about his new neighbour. When the light failed, he took Caesar out for a walk. On the way home he did his marketing on West Houston Street, with a one-eyed Italian woman who always cheated him. After he had cooked his beans and scallopini, and drunk half a bottle of Chianti, he put his dishes in the sink and went up on the roof to smoke. He was the only person in the house who ever went to the roof, and he had a secret understanding with the janitress about it. He was to have "the privilege of the roof," as she said, if he opened the heavy trapdoor on sunny days to air out the upper hall, and was watchful to close it when rain threatened. Mrs. Foley was fat and dirty and hated to climb stairs,—besides, the roof was reached by a perpendicular iron ladder, definitely inaccessible to a woman of her bulk, and the iron door at the top of it was too heavy for any but Hedger's strong arm to lift. Hedger was not above medium height, but he practised with weights and dumb-bells, and in the shoulders he was as strong as a gorilla.

So Hedger had the roof to himself. He and Caesar often slept up there on hot nights, rolled in blankets he had brought home from Arizona. He mounted with Caesar under his left arm. The dog had never learned to climb a perpendicular ladder, and never did he feel so much his master's greatness and his own dependence upon him, as when he crept under his arm for this perilous ascent. Up there was even gravel to scratch in, and a dog could do whatever he liked, so long as he did not bark. It was a kind of Heaven, which no one was strong enough to reach but his great, paint-smelling master.

On this blue May night there was a slender, girlish looking young moon in the west, playing with a whole company of silver stars. Now and then one of them darted away from the group and shot off into the gauzy blue with a soft little trail of light, like laughter. Hedger and his dog were delighted when a star did this. They were quite lost in watching the glittering game, when they were suddenly diverted by a sound,—not from the stars, though it was music. It was not the Prologue to Pagliacci, which rose ever and anon on hot evenings from an Italian tenement on Thompson Street, with the gasps of the corpulent baritone who got behind it; nor was it the hurdy-gurdy man, who often played at the corner in the balmy twilight. No, this was a woman's voice, singing the tempestuous, over-lapping phrases of Signor Puccini, then comparatively new in the world, but already so popular that even Hedger recognized his unmistakable gusts of breath. He looked about over the roofs; all was blue and still, with the well-built chimneys that were never used now standing up dark and mournful. He moved softly toward the yellow quadrangle where the gas from the hall shone up through the half-lifted trapdoor. Oh yes! It came up through the hole like a strong draught, a big, beautiful voice, and it sounded rather like a professional's. A piano had arrived in the morning, Hedger remembered. This might be a very great nuisance. It would be pleasant enough to listen to, if you could turn it on and off as you wished; but you couldn't. Caesar, with the gas light shining on his collar and his ugly but sensitive face, panted and looked up for information. Hedger put down a reassuring hand.

"I don't know. We can't tell yet. It may not be so bad."

He stayed on the roof until all was still below, and finally descended, with quite a new feeling about his neighbour. Her voice, like her figure, inspired respect,—if one did not choose to call it admiration. Her door was shut, the transom was dark; nothing remained of her but the obtrusive trunk, unrightfully taking up room in the narrow hall.

II

For two days Hedger didn't see her. He was painting eight hours a day just then, and only went out to hunt for food. He noticed that she practised scales and exercises for about an hour in the morning; then she locked her door, went humming down the hall, and left him in peace. He heard her getting her coffee ready at about the same time he got his. Earlier still, she passed his room on her way to her bath. In the evening she sometimes sang, but on the whole she didn't bother him. When he was working well he did not notice anything much. The morning paper lay before his door until he reached out for his milk bottle, then he kicked the sheet inside and it lay on the floor until evening. Sometimes he read it and sometimes he did not. He forgot there was anything of importance going on in the world outside of his third floor studio. Nobody had ever taught him that he ought to be interested in other people; in the Pittsburgh steel strike, in the Fresh Air Fund, in the scandal about the Babies' Hospital. A grey wolf, living in a Wyoming canyon, would hardly have been less concerned about these things than was Don Hedger.

One morning he was coming out of the bathroom at the front end of the hall, having just given Caesar his bath and rubbed him into a glow with a heavy towel. Before the door, lying in wait for him, as it were, stood a tall figure in a flowing blue silk dressing gown that fell away from her marble arms. In her hands she carried various accessories of the bath.

"I wish," she said distinctly, standing in his way, "I wish you wouldn't wash your dog in the tub. I never heard of such a thing! I've found his hair in the tub, and I've smelled a doggy smell, and now I've caught you at it. It's an outrage!".

Hedger was badly frightened. She was so tall and positive, and was fairly blazing with beauty and anger. He stood blinking, holding on to his sponge and dog-soap, feeling that he ought to bow very low to her. But what he actually said was:

"Nobody has ever objected before. I always wash the tub,—and, anyhow, he's cleaner than most people."

"Cleaner than me?" her eyebrows went up, her white arms and neck and her fragrant person seemed to scream at him like a band of outraged nymphs. Something flashed through his mind about a man who was turned into a dog, or was pursued by dogs, because he unwittingly intruded upon the bath of beauty.

"No, I didn't mean that," he muttered, turning scarlet under the bluish stubble of his muscular jaws. "But I know he's cleaner than I am."

"That I don't doubt!" Her voice sounded like a soft shivering of crystal, and with a smile of pity she drew the folds of her voluminous blue robe close about her and allowed the wretched man to pass. Even Caesar was frightened; he darted like a streak down the hall, through the door and to his own bed in the corner among the bones.

Hedger stood still in the doorway, listening to indignant sniffs and coughs and a great swishing of water about the sides of the tub. He had washed it; but as he had washed it with Caesar's sponge, it was quite possible that a few bristles remained; the dog was shedding now. The playwright had never objected, nor had the jovial illustrator who occupied the front apartment,—but he, as he admitted, "was usually pye-eyed, when he wasn't in Buffalo." He went home to Buffalo sometimes to rest his nerves.

It had never occurred to Hedger that any one would mind using the tub after Caesar;—but then, he had never seen a beautiful girl caparisoned for the bath before. As soon as he beheld her standing there, he realized the unfitness of it. For that matter, she ought not to step into a tub that any other mortal had bathed in; the illustrator was sloppy and left cigarette ends on the moulding.

All morning as he worked he was gnawed by a spiteful desire to get back at her. It rankled that he had been so vanquished by her disdain. When he heard her locking her door to go out for lunch, he stepped quickly into the hall in his messy painting coat, and addressed her.

"I don't wish to be exigent, Miss,"—he had certain grand words that he used upon occasion—"but if this is your trunk, it's rather in the way here."

"Oh, very well!" she exclaimed carelessly, dropping her keys into her handbag. "I'll have it moved when I can get a man to do it," and she went down the hall with her free, roving stride.

Her name, Hedger discovered from her letters, which the postman left on the table in the lower hall, was Eden Bower.

III

In the closet that was built against the partition separating his room from Miss Bower's, Hedger kept all his wearing apparel, some of it on hooks and hangers, some of it on the floor. When he opened his closet door now-a-days, little dust-coloured insects flew out on downy wing, and he suspected that a brood of moths were hatching in his winter overcoat. Mrs. Foley, the janitress, told him to bring down all his heavy clothes and she would give them a beating and hang them in the court. The closet was in such disorder that he shunned the encounter, but one hot afternoon he set himself to the task. First he threw out a pile of forgotten laundry and tied it up in a sheet. The bundle stood as high as his middle when he had knotted the corners. Then he got his shoes and overshoes together. When he took his overcoat from its place against the partition, a long ray of yellow light shot across the dark enclosure,—a knot hole, evidently, in the high wainscoating of the west room. He had never noticed it before, and without realizing what he was doing, he stooped and squinted through it.

Yonder, in a pool of sunlight, stood his new neighbour, wholly unclad, doing exercises of some sort before a long gilt mirror. Hedger did not happen to think how unpardonable it was of him to watch her. Nudity was not improper to any one who had worked so much from the figure, and he continued to look, simply because he had never seen a woman's body so beautiful as this one,—positively glorious in action. As she swung her arms and changed from one pivot of motion to another, muscular energy seemed to flow through her from her toes to her finger-tips. The soft flush of exercise and the gold of afternoon sun played over her flesh together, enveloped her in a luminous mist which, as she turned and twisted, made now an arm, now a shoulder, now a thigh, dissolve in pure light and instantly recover its outline with the next gesture. Hedger's fingers curved as if he were holding a crayon; mentally he was doing the whole figure in a single running line, and the charcoal seemed to explode in his hand at the point where the energy of each gesture was discharged into the whirling disc of light, from a foot or shoulder, from the up-thrust chin or the lifted breasts.

He could not have told whether he watched her for six minutes or sixteen. When her gymnastics were over, she paused to catch up a lock of hair that had come down, and examined with solicitude a little reddish mole that grew under her left arm-pit. Then, with her hand on her hip, she walked unconcernedly across the room and disappeared through the door into her bedchamber.

Disappeared—Don Hedger was crouching on his knees, staring at the golden shower which poured in through the west windows, at the lake of gold sleeping on the faded Turkish carpet. The spot was enchanted; a vision out of Alexandria, out of the remote pagan past, had bathed itself there in Helianthine fire.

When he crawled out of his closet, he stood blinking at the grey sheet stuffed with laundry, not knowing what had happened to him. He felt a little sick as he contemplated the bundle. Everything here was different; he hated the disorder of the place, the grey prison light, his old shoes and himself and all his slovenly habits. The black calico curtains that ran on wires over his big window were white with dust. There were three greasy frying pans in the sink, and the sink itself—He felt desperate. He couldn't stand this another minute. He took up an armful of winter clothes and ran down four flights into the basement.

"Mrs. Foley," he began, "I want my room cleaned this afternoon, thoroughly cleaned. Can you get a woman for me right away?"

"Is it company you're having?" the fat, dirty janitress enquired. Mrs. Foley was the widow of a useful Tammany man, and she owned real estate in Flatbush. She was huge and soft as a feather bed. Her face and arms were permanently coated with dust, grained like wood where the sweat had trickled.

"Yes, company. That's it."

"Well, this is a queer time of the day to be asking for a cleaning woman. It's likely I can get you old Lizzie, if she's not drunk. I'll send Willy round to see."

Willy, the son of fourteen, roused from the stupor and stain of his fifth box of cigarettes by the gleam of a quarter, went out. In five minutes he returned with old Lizzie,—she smelling strong of spirits and wearing several jackets which she had put on one over the other, and a number of skirts, long and short, which made her resemble an animated dish-clout. She had, of course, to borrow her equipment from Mrs. Foley, and toiled up the long flights, dragging mop and pail and broom. She told Hedger to be of good cheer, for he had got the right woman for the job, and showed him a great leather strap she wore about her wrist to prevent dislocation of tendons. She swished about the place, scattering dust and splashing soapsuds, while he watched her in nervous despair. He stood over Lizzie and made her scour the sink, directing her roughly, then paid her and got rid of her. Shutting the door on his failure, he hurried off with his dog to lose himself among the stevedores and dock labourers on West Street.

A strange chapter began for Don Hedger. Day after day, at that hour in the afternoon, the hour before his neighbour dressed for dinner, he crouched down in his closet to watch her go through her mysterious exercises. It did not occur to him that his conduct was detestable; there was nothing shy or retreating about this unclad girl,—a bold body, studying itself quite coolly and evidently well pleased with itself, doing all this for a purpose. Hedger scarcely regarded his action as conduct at all; it was something that had happened to him. More than once he went out and tried to stay away for the whole afternoon, but at about five o'clock he was sure to find himself among his old shoes in the dark. The pull of that aperture was stronger than his will,—and he had always considered his will the strongest thing about him. When she threw herself upon the divan and lay resting, he still stared, holding his breath. His nerves were so on edge that a sudden noise made him start and brought out the sweat on his forehead. The dog would come and tug at his sleeve, knowing that something was wrong with his master. If he attempted a mournful whine, those strong hands closed about his throat.

When Hedger came slinking out of his closet, he sat down on the edge of the couch, sat for hours without moving. He was not painting at all now. This thing, whatever it was, drank him up as ideas had sometimes done, and he sank into a stupor of idleness as deep and dark as the stupor of work. He could not understand it; he was no boy, he had worked from models for years, and a woman's body was no mystery to him. Yet now he did nothing but sit and think about one. He slept very little, and with the first light of morning he awoke as completely possessed by this woman as if he had been with her all the night before. The unconscious operations of life went on in him only to perpetuate this excitement. His brain held but one image now—vibrated, burned with it. It was a heathenish feeling; without friendliness, almost without tenderness.

Women had come and gone in Hedger's life. Not having had a mother to begin with, his relations with them, whether amorous or friendly, had been casual. He got on well with janitresses and wash-women, with Indians and with the peasant women of foreign countries. He had friends among the silk-skirt factory girls who came to eat their lunch in Washington Square, and he sometimes took a model for a day in the country. He felt an unreasoning antipathy toward the well-dressed women he saw coming out of big shops, or driving in the Park. If, on his way to the Art Museum, he noticed a pretty girl standing on the steps of one of the houses on upper Fifth Avenue, he frowned at her and went by with his shoulders hunched up as if he were cold. He had never known such girls, or heard them talk, or seen the inside of the houses in which they lived; but he believed them all to be artificial and, in an aesthetic sense, perverted. He saw them enslaved by desire of merchandise and manufactured articles, effective only in making life complicated and insincere and in embroidering it with ugly and meaningless trivialities. They were enough, he thought, to make one almost forget woman as she existed in art, in thought, and in the universe.

He had no desire to know the woman who had, for the time at least, so broken up his life,—no curiosity about her every-day personality. He shunned any revelation of it, and he listened for Miss Bower's coming and going, not to encounter, but to avoid her. He wished that the girl who wore shirt-waists and got letters from Chicago would keep out of his way, that she did not exist. With her he had naught to make. But in a room full of sun, before an old mirror, on a little enchanted rug of sleeping colours, he had seen a woman who emerged naked through a door, and disappeared naked. He thought of that body as never having been clad, or as having worn the stuffs and dyes of all the centuries but his own. And for him she had no geographical associations; unless with Crete, or Alexandria, or Veronese's Venice. She was the immortal conception, the perennial theme.

The first break in Hedger's lethargy occurred one afternoon when two young men came to take Eden Bower out to dine. They went into her music room, laughed and talked for a few minutes, and then took her away with them. They were gone a long while, but he did not go out for food himself; he waited for them to come back. At last he heard them coming down the hall, gayer and more talkative than when they left. One of them sat down at the piano, and they all began to sing. This Hedger found absolutely unendurable. He snatched up his hat and went running down the stairs. Caesar leaped beside him, hoping that old times were coming back. They had supper in the oysterman's basement and then sat down in front of their own doorway. The moon stood full over the Square, a thing of regal glory; but Hedger did not see the moon; he was looking, murderously, for men. Presently two, wearing straw hats and white trousers and carrying canes, came down the steps from his house. He rose and dogged them across the Square. They were laughing and seemed very much elated about something. As one stopped to light a cigarette, Hedger caught from the other:

"Don't you think she has a beautiful talent?"

His companion threw away his match. "She has a beautiful figure." They both ran to catch the stage.

Hedger went back to his studio. The light was shining from her transom. For the first time he violated her privacy at night, and peered through that fatal aperture. She was sitting, fully dressed, in the window, smoking a cigarette and looking out over the housetops. He watched her until she rose, looked about her with a disdainful, crafty smile, and turned out the light.

The next morning, when Miss Bower went out, Hedger followed her. Her white skirt gleamed ahead of him as she sauntered about the Square. She sat down behind the Garibaldi statue and opened a music book she carried. She turned the leaves carelessly, and several times glanced in his direction. He was on the point of going over to her, when she rose quickly and looked up at the sky. A flock of pigeons had risen from somewhere in the crowded Italian quarter to the south, and were wheeling rapidly up through the morning air, soaring and dropping, scattering and coming together, now grey, now white as silver, as they caught or intercepted the sunlight. She put up her hand to shade her eyes and followed them with a kind of defiant delight in her face.

Hedger came and stood beside her. "You've surely seen them before?"

"Oh, yes," she replied, still looking up. "I see them every day from my windows. They always come home about five o'clock. Where do they live?"

"I don't know. Probably some Italian raises them for the market. They were here long before I came, and I've been here four years."

"In that same gloomy room? Why didn't you take mine when it was vacant?"

"It isn't gloomy. That's the best light for painting."

"Oh, is it? I don't know anything about painting. I'd like to see your pictures sometime. You have such a lot in there. Don't they get dusty, piled up against the wall like that?"

"Not very. I'd be glad to show them to you. Is your name really Eden Bower? I've seen your letters on the table."

"Well, it's the name I'm going to sing under. My father's name is Bowers, but my friend Mr. Jones, a Chicago newspaper man who writes about music, told me to drop the 's.' He's crazy about my voice."

Miss Bower didn't usually tell the whole story,—about anything. Her first name, when she lived in Huntington, Illinois, was Edna, but Mr. Jones had persuaded her to change it to one which he felt would be worthy of her future. She was quick to take suggestions, though she told him she "didn't see what was the matter with 'Edna.' "

She explained to Hedger that she was going to Paris to study. She was waiting in New York for Chicago friends who were to take her over, but who had been detained. "Did you study in Paris?" she asked.

"No, I've never been in Paris. But I was in the south of France all last summer, studying with C——. He's the biggest man among the moderns,—at least I think so."

Miss Bower sat down and made room for him on the bench. "Do tell me about it. I expected to be there by this time, and I can't wait to find out what it's like."

Hedger began to relate how he had seen some of this Frenchman's work in an exhibition, and deciding at once that this was the man for him, he had taken a boat for Marseilles the next week, going over steerage. He proceeded at once to the little town on the coast where his painter lived, and presented himself. The man never took pupils, but because Hedger had come so far, he let him stay. Hedger lived at the master's house and every day they went out together to paint, sometimes on the blazing rocks down by the sea. They wrapped themselves in light woollen blankets and didn't feel the heat. Being there and working with C—— was being in Paradise, Hedger concluded; he learned more in three months than in all his life before.

Eden Bower laughed. "You're a funny fellow. Didn't you do anything but work? Are the women very beautiful? Did you have awfully good things to eat and drink?"

Hedger said some of the women were fine looking, especially one girl who went about selling fish and lobsters. About the food there was nothing remarkable,—except the ripe figs, he liked those. They drank sour wine, and used goat-butter, which was strong and full of hair, as it was churned in a goat skin.

"But don't they have parties or banquets? Aren't there any fine hotels down there?"

"Yes, but they are all closed in summer, and the country people are poor. It's a beautiful country, though."

"How, beautiful?" she persisted.

"If you want to go in, I'll show you some sketches, and you'll see."

Miss Bower rose. "All right. I won't go to my fencing lesson this morning. Do you fence? Here comes your dog. You can't move but he's after you. He always makes a face at me when I meet him in the hall, and shows his nasty little teeth as if he wanted to bite me."

In the studio Hedger got out his sketches, but to Miss Bower, whose favourite pictures were Christ Before Pilate and a redhaired Magdalen of Henner, these landscapes were not at all beautiful, and they gave her no idea of any country whatsoever. She was careful not to commit herself, however. Her vocal teacher had already convinced her that she had a great deal to learn about many things.

"Why don't we go out to lunch somewhere?" Hedger asked, and began to dust his fingers with a handkerchief—which he got out of sight as swiftly as possible.

"All right, the Brevoort," she said carelessly. "I think that's a good place, and they have good wine. I don't care for cocktails."

Hedger felt his chin uneasily. "I'm afraid I haven't shaved this morning. If you could wait for me in the Square? It won't take me ten minutes."

Left alone, he found a clean collar and handkerchief, brushed his coat and blacked his shoes, and last of all dug up ten dollars from the bottom of an old copper kettle he had brought from Spain. His winter hat was of such a complexion that the Brevoort hall boy winked at the porter as he took it and placed it on the rack in a row of fresh straw ones.

IV

That afternoon Eden Bower was lying on the couch in her music room, her face turned to the window, watching the pigeons. Reclining thus she could see none of the neighbouring roofs, only the sky itself and the birds that crossed and recrossed her field of vision, white as scraps of paper blowing in the wind. She was thinking that she was young and handsome and had had a good lunch, that a very easy-going, light-hearted city lay in the streets below her; and she was wondering why she found this queer painter chap, with his lean, bluish cheeks and heavy black eyebrows, more interesting than the smart young men she met at her teacher's studio.

Eden Bower was, at twenty, very much the same person that we all know her to be at forty, except that she knew a great deal less. But one thing she knew: that she was to be Eden Bower. She was like some one standing before a great show window full of beautiful and costly things, deciding which she will order. She understands that they will not all be delivered immediately, but one by one they will arrive at her door. She already knew some of the many things that were to happen to her; for instance, that the Chicago millionaire who was going to take her abroad with his sister as chaperone, would eventually press his claim in quite another manner. He was the most circumspect of bachelors, afraid of everything obvious, even of women who were too flagrantly handsome. He was a nervous collector of pictures and furniture, a nervous patron of music, and a nervous host; very cautious about his health, and about any course of conduct that might make him ridiculous. But she knew that he would at last throw all his precautions to the winds.

People like Eden Bower are inexplicable. Her father sold farming machinery in Huntington, Illinois, and she had grown up with no acquaintances or experiences outside of that prairie town. Yet from her earliest childhood she had not one conviction or opinion in common with the people about her,—the only people she knew. Before she was out of short dresses she had made up her mind that she was going to be an actress, that she would live far away in great cities, that she would be much admired by men and would have everything she wanted. When she was thirteen, and was already singing and reciting for church entertainments, she read in some illustrated magazine a long article about the late Czar of Russia, then just come to the throne or about to come to it. After that, lying in the hammock on the front porch on summer evenings, or sitting through a long sermon in the family pew, she amused herself by trying to make up her mind whether she would or would not be the Czar's mistress when she played in his Capital. Now Edna had met this fascinating word only in the novels of Ouida,—her hard-worked little mother kept a long row of them in the upstairs storeroom, behind the linen chest. In Huntington, women who bore that relation to men were called by a very different name, and their lot was not an enviable one; of all the shabby and poor, they were the shabbiest. But then, Edna had never lived in Huntington, not even before she began to find books like "Sapho" and "Mademoiselle de Maupin," secretly sold in paper covers throughout Illinois. It was as if she had come into Huntington, into the Bowers family, on one of the trains that puffed over the marshes behind their back fence all day long, and was waiting for another train to take her out.

As she grew older and handsomer, she had many beaux, but these small-town boys didn't interest her. If a lad kissed her when he brought her home from a dance, she was indulgent and she rather liked it. But if he pressed her further, she slipped away from him, laughing. After she began to sing in Chicago, she was consistently discreet. She stayed as a guest in rich people's houses, and she knew that she was being watched like a rabbit in a laboratory. Covered up in bed, with the lights out, she thought her own thoughts, and laughed.

This summer in New York was her first taste of freedom. The Chicago capitalist, after all his arrangements were made for sailing, had been compelled to go to Mexico to look after oil interests. His sister knew an excellent singing master in New York. Why should not a discreet, well-balanced girl like Miss Bower spend the summer there, studying quietly? The capitalist suggested that his sister might enjoy a summer on Long Island; he would rent the Griffith's place for her, with all the servants, and Eden could stay there. But his sister met this proposal with a cold stare. So it fell out, that between selfishness and greed, Eden got a summer all her own,—which really did a great deal toward making her an artist and whatever else she was afterward to become. She had time to look about, to watch without being watched; to select diamonds in one window and furs in another, to select shoulders and moustaches in the big hotels where she went to lunch. She had the easy freedom of obscurity and the consciousness of power. She enjoyed both. She was in no hurry.

While Eden Bower watched the pigeons, Don Hedger sat on the other side of the bolted doors, looking into a pool of dark turpentine, at his idle brushes, wondering why a woman could do this to him. He, too, was sure of his future and knew that he was a chosen man. He could not know, of course, that he was merely the first to fall under a fascination which was to be disastrous to a few men and pleasantly stimulating to many thousands. Each of these two young people sensed the future, but not completely. Don Hedger knew that nothing much would ever happen to him. Eden Bower understood that to her a great deal would happen. But she did not guess that her neighbour would have more tempestuous adventures sitting in his dark studio than she would find in all the capitals of Europe, or in all the latitude of conduct she was prepared to permit herself.

V

One Sunday morning Eden was crossing the Square with a spruce young man in a white flannel suit and a panama hat. They had been breakfasting at the Brevoort and he was coaxing her to let him come up to her rooms and sing for an hour.

"No, I've got to write letters. You must run along now. I see a friend of mine over there, and I want to ask him about something before I go up."

"That fellow with the dog? Where did you pick him up?" the young man glanced toward the seat under a sycamore where Hedger was reading the morning paper.

"Oh, he's an old friend from the West," said Eden easily. "I won't introduce you, because he doesn't like people. He's a recluse. Good-bye. I can't be sure about Tuesday. I'll go with you if I have time after my lesson." She nodded, left him, and went over to the seat littered with newspapers. The young man went up the Avenue without looking back.

"Well, what are you going to do today? Shampoo this animal all morning?" Eden enquired teasingly.

Hedger made room for her on the seat. "No, at twelve o'clock I'm going out to Coney Island. One of my models is going up in a balloon this afternoon. I've often promised to go and see her, and now I'm going."

Eden asked if models usually did such stunts. No, Hedger told her, but Molly Welch added to her earnings in that way. "I believe," he added, "she likes the excitement of it. She's got a good deal of spirit. That's why I like to paint her. So many models have flaccid bodies."

"And she hasn't, eh? Is she the one who comes to see you? I can't help hearing her, she talks so loud."

"Yes, she has a rough voice, but she's a fine girl. I don't suppose you'd be interested in going?"

"I don't know," Eden sat tracing patterns on the asphalt with the end of her parasol. "Is it any fun? I got up feeling I'd like to do something different today. It's the first Sunday I've not had to sing in church. I had that engagement for breakfast at the Brevoort, but it wasn't very exciting. That chap can't talk about anything but himself."

Hedger warmed a little. "If you've never been to Coney Island, you ought to go. It's nice to see all the people; tailors and bar-tenders and prize-fighters with their best girls, and all sorts of folks taking a holiday."

Eden looked sidewise at him. So one ought to be interested in people of that kind, ought one? He was certainly a funny fellow. Yet he was never, somehow, tiresome. She had seen a good deal of him lately, but she kept wanting to know him better, to find out what made him different from men like the one she had just left—whether he really was as different as he seemed. "I'll go with you," she said at last, "if you'll leave that at home." She pointed to Caesar's flickering ears with her sunshade.

"But he's half the fun. You'd like to hear him bark at the waves when they come in."

"No, I wouldn't. He's jealous and disagreeable if he sees you talking to any one else. Look at him now."

"Of course, if you make a face at him. He knows what that means, and he makes a worse face. He likes Molly Welch, and she'll be disappointed if I don't bring him."

Eden said decidedly that he couldn't take both of them. So at twelve o'clock when she and Hedger got on the boat at Desbrosses street, Caesar was lying on his pallet, with a bone.

Eden enjoyed the boat-ride. It was the first time she had been on the water, and she felt as if she were embarking for France. The light warm breeze and the plunge of the waves made her very wide awake, and she liked crowds of any kind. They went to the balcony of a big, noisy restaurant and had a shore dinner, with tall steins of beer. Hedger had got a big advance from his advertising firm since he first lunched with Miss Bower ten days ago, and he was ready for anything.

After dinner they went to the tent behind the bathing beach, where the tops of two balloons bulged out over the canvas. A red-faced man in a linen suit stood in front of the tent, shouting in a hoarse voice and telling the people that if the crowd was good for five dollars more, a beautiful young woman would risk her life for their entertainment. Four little boys in dirty red uniforms ran about taking contributions in their pillbox hats. One of the balloons was bobbing up and down in its tether and people were shoving forward to get nearer the tent.

"Is it dangerous, as he pretends?" Eden asked.

"Molly says it's simple enough if nothing goes wrong with the balloon. Then it would be all over, I suppose."

"Wouldn't you like to go up with her?"

"I? Of course not. I'm not fond of taking foolish risks."

Eden sniffed. "I shouldn't think sensible risks would be very much fun."

Hedger did not answer, for just then every one began to shove the other way and shout, "Look out. There she goes!" and a band of six pieces commenced playing furiously.

As the balloon rose from its tent enclosure, they saw a girl in green tights standing in the basket, holding carelessly to one of the ropes with one hand and with the other waving to the spectators. A long rope trailed behind to keep the balloon from blowing out to sea.

As it soared, the figure in green tights in the basket diminished to a mere spot, and the balloon itself, in the brilliant light, looked like a big silver-grey bat, with its wings folded. When it began to sink, the girl stepped through the hole in the basket to a trapeze that hung below, and gracefully descended through the air, holding to the rod with both hands, keeping her body taut and her feet close together. The crowd, which had grown very large by this time, cheered vociferously. The men took off their hats and waved, little boys shouted, and fat old women, shining with the heat and a beer lunch, murmured admiring comments upon the balloonist's figure. "Beautiful legs, she has!"

"That's so," Hedger whispered. "Not many girls would look well in that position." Then, for some reason, he blushed a slow, dark, painful crimson.

The balloon descended slowly, a little way from the tent, and the red-faced man in the linen suit caught Molly Welch before her feet touched the ground, and pulled her to one side. The band struck up "Blue Bell" by way of welcome, and one of the sweaty pages ran forward and presented the balloonist with a large bouquet of artificial flowers. She smiled and thanked him, and ran back across the sand to the tent.

"Can't we go inside and see her?" Eden asked. "You can explain to the door man. I want to meet her." Edging forward, she herself addressed the man in the linen suit and slipped something from her purse into his hand.

They found Molly seated before a trunk that had a mirror in the lid and a "make-up" outfit spread upon the tray. She was wiping the cold cream and powder from her neck with a discarded chemise.

"Hello, Don," she said cordially. "Brought a friend?"

Eden liked her. She had an easy, friendly manner, and there was something boyish and devil-may-care about her.

"Yes, it's fun. I'm mad about it," she said in reply to Eden's questions. "I always want to let go, when I come down on the bar. You don't feel your weight at all, as you would on a stationary trapeze."

The big drum boomed outside, and the publicity man began shouting to newly arrived boatloads. Miss Welch took a last pull at her cigarette. "Now you'll have to get out, Don. I change for the next act. This time I go up in a black evening dress, and lose the skirt in the basket before I start down."

"Yes, go along," said Eden. "Wait for me outside the door. I'll stay and help her dress."

Hedger waited and waited, while women of every build bumped into him and begged his pardon, and the red pages ran about holding out their caps for coins, and the people ate and perspired and shifted parasols against the sun. When the band began to play a two-step, all the bathers ran up out of the surf to watch the ascent. The second balloon bumped and rose, and the crowd began shouting to the girl in a black evening dress who stood leaning against the ropes and smiling. "It's a new girl," they called. "It ain't the Countess this time. You're a peach, girlie!"

The balloonist acknowledged these compliments, bowing and looking down over the sea of upturned faces,—but Hedger was determined she should not see him, and he darted behind the tent-fly. He was suddenly dripping with cold sweat, his mouth was full of the bitter taste of anger and his tongue felt stiff behind his teeth. Molly Welch, in a shirt-waist and a white tam-o'-shanter cap, slipped out from the tent under his arm and laughed up in his face. "She's a crazy one you brought along. She'll get what she wants!"

"Oh, I'll settle with you, all right!" Hedger brought out with difficulty.

"It's not my fault, Donnie. I couldn't do anything with her. She bought me off. What's the matter with you? Are you soft on her? She's safe enough. It's as easy as rolling off a log, if you keep cool." Molly Welch was rather excited herself, and she was chewing gum at a high speed as she stood beside him, looking up at the floating silver cone. "Now watch," she exclaimed suddenly. "She's coming down on the bar. I advised her to cut that out, but you see she does it first-rate. And she got rid of the skirt, too. Those black tights show off her legs very well. She keeps her feet together like I told her, and makes a good line along the back. See the light on those silver slippers,—that was a good idea I had. Come along to meet her. Don't be a grouch; she's done it fine!"

Molly tweaked his elbow, and then left him standing like a stump, while she ran down the beach with the crowd.

Though Hedger was sulking, his eye could not help seeing the low blue welter of the sea, the arrested bathers, standing in the surf, their arms and legs stained red by the dropping sun, all shading their eyes and gazing upward at the slowly falling silver star.

Molly Welch and the manager caught Eden under the arms and lifted her aside, a red page dashed up with a bouquet, and the band struck up "Blue Bell." Eden laughed and bowed, took Molly's arm, and ran up the sand in her black tights and silver slippers, dodging the friendly old women, and the gallant sports who wanted to offer their homage on the spot.

When she emerged from the tent, dressed in her own clothes, that part of the beach was almost deserted. She stepped to her companion's side and said carelessly: "Hadn't we better try to catch this boat? I hope you're not sore at me. Really, it was lots of fun."

Hedger looked at his watch. "Yes, we have fifteen minutes to get to the boat," he said politely.

As they walked toward the pier, one of the pages ran up panting. "Lady, you're carrying off the bouquet," he said, aggrievedly.

Eden stopped and looked at the bunch of spotty cotton roses in her hand. "Of course. I want them for a souvenir. You gave them to me yourself."

"I give 'em to you for looks, but you can't take 'em away. They belong to the show."

"Oh, you always use the same bunch?"

"Sure we do. There ain't too much money in this business."

She laughed and tossed them back to him. "Why are you angry?" she asked Hedger. "I wouldn't have done it if I'd been with some fellows, but I thought you were the sort who wouldn't mind. Molly didn't for a minute think you would."

"What possessed you to do such a fool thing?" he asked roughly.

"I don't know. When I saw her coming down, I wanted to try it. It looked exciting. Didn't I hold myself as well as she did?"

Hedger shrugged his shoulders, but in his heart he forgave her.

The return boat was not crowded, though the boats that passed them, going out, were packed to the rails. The sun was setting. Boys and girls sat on the long benches with their arms about each other, singing. Eden felt a strong wish to propitiate her companion, to be alone with him. She had been curiously wrought up by her balloon trip; it was a lark, but not very satisfying unless one came back to something after the flight. She wanted to be admired and adored. Though Eden said nothing, and sat with her arms limp on the rail in front of her, looking languidly at the rising silhouette of the city and the bright path of the sun, Hedger felt a strange drawing near to her. If he but brushed her white skirt with his knee, there was an instant communication between them, such as there had never been before. They did not talk at all, but when they went over the gang-plank she took his arm and kept her shoulder close to his. He felt as if they were enveloped in a highly charged atmosphere, an invisible network of subtle, almost painful sensibility. They had somehow taken hold of each other.

An hour later, they were dining in the back garden of a little French hotel on Ninth Street, long since passed away. It was cool and leafy there, and the mosquitoes were not very numerous. A party of South Americans at another table were drinking champagne, and Eden murmured that she thought she would like some, if it were not too expensive. "Perhaps it will make me think I am in the balloon again. That was a very nice feeling. You've forgiven me, haven't you?"

Hedger gave her a quick straight look from under his black eyebrows, and something went over her that was like a chill, except that it was warm and feathery. She drank most of the wine; her companion was indifferent to it. He was talking more to her tonight than he had ever done before. She asked him about a new picture she had seen in his room; a queer thing full of stiff, supplicating female figures. "It's Indian, isn't it?"

"Yes. I call it Rain Spirits, or maybe, Indian Rain. In the Southwest, where I've been a good deal, the Indian traditions make women have to do with the rain-fall. They were supposed to control it, somehow, and to be able to find springs, and make moisture come out of the earth. You see I'm trying to learn to paint what people think and feel; to get away from all that photographic stuff. When I look at you, I don't see what a camera would see, do I?"

"How can I tell?"

"Well, if I should paint you, I could make you understand what I see." For the second time that day Hedger crimsoned unexpectedly, and his eyes fell and steadily contemplated a dish of little radishes. "That particular picture I got from a story a Mexican priest told me; he said he found it in an old manuscript book in a monastery down there, written by some Spanish Missionary, who got his stories from the Aztecs. This one he called 'The Forty Lovers of the Queen,' and it was more or less about rain-making."

"Aren't you going to tell it to me?" Eden asked.

Hedger fumbled among the radishes. "I don't know if it's the proper kind of story to tell a girl."

She smiled; "Oh, forget about that! I've been balloon riding today. I like to hear you talk."

Her low voice was flattering. She had seemed like clay in his hands ever since they got on the boat to come home. He leaned back in his chair, forgot his food, and, looking at her intently, began to tell his story, the theme of which he somehow felt was dangerous tonight.

The tale began, he said, somewhere in Ancient Mexico, and concerned the daughter of a king. The birth of this Princess was preceded by unusual portents. Three times her mother dreamed that she was delivered of serpents, which betokened that the child she carried would have power with the rain gods. The serpent was the symbol of water. The Princess grew up dedicated to the gods, and wise men taught her the rain-making mysteries. She was with difficulty restrained from men and was guarded at all times, for it was the law of the Thunder that she be maiden until her marriage. In the years of her adolescence, rain was abundant with her people. The oldest man could not remember such fertility. When the Princess had counted eighteen summers, her father went to drive out a war party that harried his borders on the north and troubled his prosperity. The King destroyed the invaders and brought home many prisoners. Among the prisoners was a young chief, taller than any of his captors, of such strength and ferocity that the King's people came a day's journey to look at him. When the Princess beheld his great stature, and saw that his arms and breast were covered with the figures of wild animals, bitten into the skin and coloured, she begged his life from her father. She desired that he should practise his art upon her, and prick upon her skin the signs of Rain and Lightning and Thunder, and stain the wounds with herb-juices, as they were upon his own body. For many days, upon the roof of the King's house, the Princess submitted herself to the bone needle, and the women with her marvelled at her fortitude. But the Princess was without shame before the Captive, and it came about that he threw from him his needles and his stains, and fell upon the Princess to violate her honour; and her women ran down from the roof screaming, to call the guard which stood at the gateway of the King's house, and none stayed to protect their mistress. When the guard came, the Captive was thrown into bonds, and he was gelded, and his tongue was torn out, and he was given for a slave to the Rain Princess.

The country of the Aztecs to the east was tormented by thirst, and their king, hearing much of the rain-making arts of the Princess, sent an embassy to her father, with presents and an offer of marriage. So the Princess went from her father to be the Queen of the Aztecs, and she took with her the Captive, who served her in everything with entire fidelity and slept upon a mat before her door.

The King gave his bride a fortress on the outskirts of the city, whither she retired to entreat the rain gods. This fortress was called the Queen's House, and on the night of the new moon the Queen came to it from the palace. But when the moon waxed and grew toward the round, because the god of Thunder had had his will of her, then the Queen returned to the King. Drought abated in the country and rain fell abundantly by reason of the Queen's power with the stars.

When the Queen went to her own house she took with her no servant but the Captive, and he slept outside her door and brought her food after she had fasted. The Queen had a jewel of great value, a turquoise that had fallen from the sun, and had the image of the sun upon it. And when she desired a young man whom she had seen in the army or among the slaves, she sent the Captive to him with the jewel, for a sign that he should come to her secretly at the Queen's House upon business concerning the welfare of all. And some, after she had talked with them, she sent away with rewards; and some she took into her chamber and kept them by her for one night or two. Afterward she called the Captive and bade him conduct the youth by the secret way he had come, underneath the chambers of the fortress. But for the going away of the Queen's lovers the Captive took out the bar that was beneath a stone in the floor of the passage, and put in its stead a rush-reed, and the youth stepped upon it and fell through into a cavern that was the bed of an underground river, and whatever was thrown into it was not seen again. In this service nor in any other did the Captive fail the Queen.

But when the Queen sent for the Captain of the Archers, she detained him four days in her chamber, calling often for food and wine, and was greatly content with him. On the fourth day she went to the Captive outside her door and said: "Tomorrow take this man up by the sure way, by which the King comes, and let him live."

In the Queen's door were arrows, purple and white. When she desired the King to come to her publicly, with his guard, she sent him a white arrow; but when she sent the purple, he came secretly, and covered himself with his mantle to be hidden from the stone gods at the gate. On the fifth night that the Queen was with her lover, the Captive took a purple arrow to the King, and the King came secretly and found them together. He killed the Captain with his own hand, but the Queen he brought to public trial. The

Captive, when he was put to the question, told on his fingers forty men that he had let through the underground passage into the river. The Captive and the Queen were put to death by fire, both on the same day, and afterward there was scarcity of rain.

⋆ ⋆ ⋆

Eden Bower sat shivering a little as she listened. Hedger was not trying to please her, she thought, but to antagonize and frighten her by his brutal story. She had often told herself that his lean, big-boned lower jaw was like his bull-dog's, but tonight his face made Caesar's most savage and determined expression seem an affectation. Now she was looking at the man he really was. Nobody's eyes had ever defied her like this. They were searching her and seeing everything; all she had concealed from Livingston, and from the millionaire and his friends, and from the newspaper men. He was testing her, trying her out, and she was more ill at ease than she wished to show.

"That's quite a thrilling story," she said at last, rising and winding her scarf about her throat. "It must be getting late. Almost every one has gone."

They walked down the Avenue like people who have quarrelled, or who wish to get rid of each other. Hedger did not take her arm at the street crossings, and they did not linger in the Square. At her door he tried none of the old devices of the Livingston boys. He stood like a post, having forgotten to take off his hat, gave her a harsh, threatening glance, muttered "good-night," and shut his own door noisily.

There was no question of sleep for Eden Bower. Her brain was working like a machine that would never stop. After she undressed, she tried to calm her nerves by smoking a cigarette, lying on the divan by the open window. But she grew wider and wider awake, combating the challenge that had flamed all evening in Hedger's eyes. The balloon had been one kind of excitement, the wine another; but the thing that had roused her, as a blow rouses a proud man, was the doubt, the contempt, the sneering hostility with which the painter had looked at her when he told his savage story. Crowds and balloons were all very well, she reflected, but woman's chief adventure is man. With a mind over active and a sense of life over strong, she wanted to walk across the roofs in the starlight, to sail over the sea and face at once a world of which she had never been afraid.

Hedger must be asleep; his dog had stopped sniffing under the double doors. Eden put on her wrapper and slippers and stole softly down the hall over the old carpet; one loose board creaked just as she reached the ladder. The trap-door was open, as always on hot nights. When she stepped out on the roof she drew a long breath and walked across it, looking up at the sky. Her foot touched something soft; she heard a low growl, and on the instant Caesar's sharp little teeth caught her ankle and waited. His breath was like steam on her leg. Nobody had ever intruded upon his roof before, and he panted for the movement or the word that would let him spring his jaw. Instead, Hedger's hand seized his throat.

"Wait a minute. I'll settle with him," he said grimly. He dragged the dog toward the manhole and disappeared. When he came back, he found Eden standing over by the dark chimney, looking away in an offended attitude.

"I caned him unmercifully," he panted. "Of course you didn't hear anything; he never whines when I beat him. He didn't nip you, did he?"

"I don't know whether he broke the skin or not," she answered aggrievedly, still looking off into the west.

"If I were one of your friends in white pants, I'd strike a match to find whether you were hurt, though I know you are not, and then I'd see your ankle, wouldn't I?"

"I suppose so."

He shook his head and stood with his hands in the pockets of his old painting jacket. "I'm not up to such boy-tricks. If you want the place to yourself, I'll clear out. There are plenty of places where I can spend the night, what's left of it. But if you stay here and I stay here—" He shrugged his shoulders.

Eden did not stir, and she made no reply. Her head drooped slightly, as if she were considering. But the moment he put his arms about her they began to talk, both at once, as people do in an opera. The instant avowal brought out a flood of trivial admissions. Hedger confessed his crime, was reproached and forgiven, and now Eden knew what it was in his look that she had found so disturbing of late.

Standing against the black chimney, with the sky behind and blue shadows before, they looked like one of Hedger's own paintings of that period; two figures, one white and one dark, and nothing whatever distinguishable about them but that they were male and female. The faces were lost, the contours blurred in shadow, but the figures were a man and a woman, and that was their whole concern and their mysterious beauty,—it was the rhythm in which they moved, at last, along the roof and down into the dark hole; he first, drawing her gently after him. She came down very slowly. The excitement and bravado and uncertainty of that long day and night seemed all at once to tell upon her. When his feet were on the carpet and he reached up to lift her down, she twined her arms about his neck as after a long separation, and turned her face to him, and her lips, with their perfume of youth and passion.

⋆ ⋆ ⋆

One Saturday afternoon Hedger was sitting in the window of Eden's music room. They had been watching the pigeons come wheeling over the roofs from their unknown feeding grounds.

"Why," said Eden suddenly, "don't we fix those big doors into your studio so they will open? Then, if I want you, I won't have to go through the hall. That illustrator is loafing about a good deal of late."

"I'll open them, if you wish. The bolt is on your side."

"Isn't there one on yours, too?"

"No. I believe a man lived there for years before I came in, and the nurse used to have these rooms herself. Naturally, the lock was on the lady's side."

Eden laughed and began to examine the bolt. "It's all stuck up with paint." Looking about, her eye lighted upon a bronze Buddah which was one of the nurse's treasures. Taking him by his head, she struck the bolt a blow with his squatting posteriors. The two doors creaked, sagged, and swung weakly inward a little way, as if they were too old for such escapades. Eden tossed the heavy idol into a stuffed chair. "That's better," she exclaimed exultantly. "So the bolts are always on the lady's side? What a lot society takes for granted!"

Hedger laughed, sprang up and caught her arms roughly. "Whoever takes you for granted— Did anybody, ever?"

"Everybody does. That's why I'm here. You are the only one who knows anything about me. Now I'll have to dress if we're going out for dinner."

He lingered, keeping his hold on her. "But I won't always be the only one, Eden Bower. I won't be the last."

"No, I suppose not," she said carelessly. "But what does that matter? You are the first."

As a long, despairing whine broke in the warm stillness, they drew apart. Caesar, lying on his bed in the dark corner, had lifted his head at this invasion of sunlight, and realized that the side of his room was broken open, and his whole world shattered by change. There stood his master and this woman, laughing at him! The woman was pulling the long black hair of this mightiest of men, who bowed his head and permitted it.

VI

In time they quarrelled, of course, and about an abstraction,—as young people often do, as mature people almost never do. Eden came in late one afternoon. She had been with some of her musical friends to lunch at Burton Ives' studio, and she began telling Hedger about its splendours. He listened a moment and then threw down his brushes. "I know exactly what it's like," he said impatiently. "A very good department-store conception of a studio. It's one of the show places."

"Well, it's gorgeous, and he said I could bring you to see him. The boys tell me he's awfully kind about giving people a lift, and you might get something out of it."

Hedger started up and pushed his canvas out of the way. "What could I possibly get from Burton Ives? He's almost the worst painter in the world; the stupidest, I mean."

Eden was annoyed. Burton Ives had been very nice to her and had begged her to sit for him. "You must admit that he's a very successful one," she said coldly.

"Of course he is! Anybody can be successful who will do that sort of thing. I wouldn't paint his pictures for all the money in New York."

"Well, I saw a lot of them, and I think they are beautiful."

Hedger bowed stiffly.

"What's the use of being a great painter if nobody knows about you?" Eden went on persuasively. "Why don't you paint the kind of pictures people can understand, and then, after you're successful, do whatever you like?"

"As I look at it," said Hedger brusquely, "I am successful."

Eden glanced about. "Well, I don't see any evidences of it," she said, biting her lip. "He has a Japanese servant and a wine cellar, and keeps a riding horse."

Hedger melted a little. "My dear, I have the most expensive luxury in the world, and I am much more extravagant than Burton Ives, for I work to please nobody but myself."

"You mean you could make money and don't? That you don't try to get a public?"

"Exactly. A public only wants what has been done over and over. I'm painting for painters,—who haven't been born."

"What would you do if I brought Mr. Ives down here to see your things?"

"Well, for God's sake, don't! Before he left I'd probably tell him what I thought of him."

Eden rose. "I give you up. You know very well there's only one kind of success that's real."

"Yes, but it's not the kind you mean. So you've been thinking me a scrub painter, who needs a helping hand from some fashionable studio man? What the devil have you had anything to do with me for, then?"

"There's no use talking to you," said Eden walking slowly toward the door. "I've been trying to pull wires for you all afternoon, and this is what it comes to." She had expected that the tidings of a prospective call from the great man would be received very differently, and had been thinking as she came home in the stage how, as with a magic wand, she might gild Hedger's future, float him out of his dark hole on a tide of prosperity, see his name in the papers and his pictures in the windows on Fifth Avenue.

Hedger mechanically snapped the midsummer leash on Caesar's collar and they ran downstairs and hurried through Sullivan Street off toward the river. He wanted to be among rough, honest people, to get down where the big drays bumped over stone paving blocks and the men wore corduroy trowsers and kept their shirts open at the neck. He stopped for a drink in one of the sagging bar-rooms on the water front. He had never in his life been so deeply wounded; he did not know he could be so hurt. He had told this girl all his secrets. On the roof, in these warm, heavy summer nights, with her hands locked in his, he had been able to explain all his misty ideas about an unborn art the world was waiting for; had been able to explain them better than he had ever done to himself. And she had looked away to the chattels of this uptown studio and coveted them for him! To her he was only an unsuccessful Burton Ives.

Then why, as he had put it to her, did she take up with him? Young, beautiful, talented as she was, why had she wasted herself on a scrub? Pity? Hardly; she wasn't sentimental. There was no explaining her. But in this passion that had seemed so fearless and so fated to be, his own position now looked to him ridiculous; a poor dauber without money or fame,—it was her caprice to load him with favours. Hedger ground his teeth so loud that his dog, trotting beside him, heard him and looked up.

While they were having supper at the oysterman's, he planned his escape. Whenever he saw her again, everything he had told her, that he should never have told any one, would come back to him; ideas he had never whispered even to the painter whom he worshipped and had gone all the way to France to see. To her they must seem his apology for not having horses and a valet, or merely the puerile boastfulness of a weak man. Yet if she slipped the bolt tonight and came through the doors and said, "Oh, weak man, I belong to you!" what could he do? That was the danger. He would catch the train out to Long Beach tonight, and tomorrow he would go on to the north end of Long Island, where an old friend of his had a summer studio among the sand dunes. He would stay until things came right in his mind. And she could find a smart painter, or take her punishment.

When he went home, Eden's room was dark; she was dining out somewhere. He threw his things into a hold-all he had carried about the world with him, strapped up some colours and canvases, and ran downstairs.

VII

Five days later Hedger was a restless passenger on a dirty, crowded Sunday train, coming back to town. Of course he saw now how unreasonable he had been in expecting a Huntington girl to know anything about pictures; here was a whole continent full of people who knew nothing about pictures and he didn't hold it against them. What had such things to do with him and Eden Bower? When he lay out on the dunes, watching the moon come up out of the sea, it had seemed to him that there was no wonder in the world like the wonder of Eden Bower. He was going back to her because she was older than art, because she was the most overwhelming thing that had ever come into his life.

He had written her yesterday, begging her to be at home this evening, telling her that he was contrite, and wretched enough.

Now that he was on his way to her, his stronger feeling unaccountably changed to a mood that was playful and tender. He wanted to share everything with her, even the most trivial things. He wanted to tell her about the people on the train, coming back tired from their holiday with bunches of wilted flowers and dirty daisies; to tell her that the fish-man, to whom she had often sent him for lobsters, was among the passengers, disguised in a silk shirt and a spotted tie, and how his wife looked exactly like a fish, even to her eyes, on which cataracts were forming. He could tell her, too, that he hadn't as much as unstrapped his canvases,—that ought to convince her.

In those days passengers from Long Island came into New York by ferry. Hedger had to be quick about getting his dog out of the express car in order to catch the first boat. The East River, and the bridges, and the city to the west, were burning in the conflagration of the sunset; there was that great home-coming reach of evening in the air.

The car changes from Thirty-fourth Street were too many and too perplexing; for the first time in his life Hedger took a hansom cab for Washington Square. Caesar sat bolt upright on the worn leather cushion beside him, and they jogged off, looking down on the rest of the world.

It was twilight when they drove down lower Fifth Avenue into the Square, and through the Arch behind them were the two long rows of pale violet lights that used to bloom so beautifully against the grey stone and asphalt. Here and yonder about the Square hung globes that shed a radiance not unlike the blue mists of evening, emerging softly when daylight died, as the stars emerged in the thin blue sky. Under them the sharp shadows of the trees fell on the cracked pavement and the sleeping grass. The first stars and the first lights were growing silver against the gradual darkening, when Hedger paid his driver and went into the house,—which, thank God, was still there! On the hall table lay his letter of yesterday, unopened.

He went upstairs with every sort of fear and every sort of hope clutching at his heart; it was as if tigers were tearing him. Why was there no gas burning in the top hall? He found matches and the gas bracket. He knocked, but got no answer; nobody was there.

Before his own door were exactly five bottles of milk, standing in a row. The milk-boy had taken spiteful pleasure in thus reminding him that he forgot to stop his order.

Hedger went down to the basement; it, too, was dark. The janitress was taking her evening airing on the basement steps. She sat waving a palm-leaf fan majestically, her dirty calico dress open at the neck. She told him at once that there had been "changes." Miss Bower's room was to let again, and the piano would go tomorrow. Yes, she left yesterday, she sailed for Europe with friends from Chicago. They arrived on Friday, heralded by many telegrams. Very rich people they were said to be, though the man had refused to pay the nurse a month's rent in lieu of notice,—which would have been only right, as the young lady had agreed to take the rooms until October. Mrs. Foley had observed, too, that he didn't overpay her or Willy for their trouble, and a great deal of trouble they had been put to, certainly. Yes, the young lady was very pleasant, but the nurse said there were rings on the mahogany table where she had put tumblers and wine glasses. It was just as well she was gone. The Chicago man was uppish in his ways, but not much to look at. She supposed he had poor health, for there was nothing to him inside his clothes.

Hedger went slowly up the stairs—never had they seemed so long, or his legs so heavy. The upper floor was emptiness and silence. He unlocked his room, lit the gas, and opened the windows. When he went to put his coat in the closet, he found, hanging among his clothes, a pale, flesh-tinted dressing gown he had liked to see her wear, with a perfume—oh, a perfume that was still Eden Bower! He shut the door behind him and there, in the dark, for a moment he lost his manliness. It was when he held this garment to him that he found a letter in the pocket.

The note was written with a lead pencil, in haste: She was sorry that he was angry, but she still didn't know just what she had done. She had thought Mr. Ives would be useful to him; she guessed he was too proud. She wanted awfully to see him again, but Fate came knocking at her door after he had left her. She believed in Fate. She would never forget him, and she knew he would become the greatest painter in the world. Now she must pack. She hoped he wouldn't mind her leaving the dressing gown; somehow, she could never wear it again.

After Hedger read this, standing under the gas, he went back into the closet and knelt down before the wall; the knot hole had been plugged up with a ball of wet paper,—the same blue note-paper on which her letter was written.

He was hard hit. Tonight he had to bear the loneliness of a whole lifetime. Knowing himself so well, he could hardly believe that such a thing had ever happened to him, that such a woman had lain happy and contented in his arms. And now it was over. He turned out the light and sat down on his painter's stool before the big window. Caesar, on the floor beside him, rested his head on his master's knee. We must leave Hedger thus, sitting in his tank with his dog, looking up at the stars.

⋆ ⋆ ⋆

Coming, Aphrodite! This legend, in electric lights over the Lexington Opera House, had long announced the return of Eden Bower to New York after years of spectacular success in Paris. She came at last, under the management of an American Opera Company, but bringing her own *chef d'orchestre*.

One bright December afternoon Eden Bower was going down Fifth Avenue in her car, on the way to her broker, in Williams Street. Her thoughts were entirely upon stocks,—Cerro de Pasco, and how much she should buy of it,—when she suddenly looked up and realized that she was skirting Washington Square. She had not seen the place since she rolled out of it in an old-fashioned four-wheeler to seek her fortune, eighteen years ago.

"*Arrêtez, Alphonse. Attendez moi,*" she called, and opened the door before he could reach it. The children who were streaking over the asphalt on roller skates saw a lady in a long fur coat, and short, high-heeled shoes, alight from a French car and pace slowly about the Square, holding her muff to her chin. This spot, at least, had changed very little, she reflected; the same trees, the same fountain, the white arch, and over yonder, Garibaldi, drawing the sword for freedom. There, just opposite her, was the old red brick house.

"Yes, that is the place," she was thinking. "I can smell the carpets now, and the dog,—what was his name? That grubby bathroom at the end of the hall, and that dreadful Hedger—still, there was something about him, you know—" She glanced up and blinked against the sun. From somewhere in the crowded quarter south of the Square a flock of pigeons rose, wheeling quickly upward into the brilliant blue sky. She threw back her head, pressed her muff closer to her chin, and watched them with a smile of amazement and delight. So they still rose, out of all that dirt and noise and squalor, fleet and silvery, just as they used to rise that summer when she was twenty and went up in a balloon on Coney Island!

Alphonse opened the door and tucked her robes about her. All the way down town her mind wandered from Cerro de Pasco, and she kept smiling and looking up at the sky.

When she had finished her business with the broker, she asked him to look in the telephone book for the address of M. Gaston Jules, the picture dealer, and slipped the paper on which he wrote it into her glove. It was five o'clock when she reached the French Galleries, as they were called. On entering she gave the attendant her card, asking him to take it to M. Jules. The dealer appeared very promptly and begged her to come into his private office, where he pushed a great chair toward his desk for her and signalled his secretary to leave the room.

"How good your lighting is in here," she observed, glancing about. "I met you at Simon's studio, didn't I? Oh, no! I never forget anybody who interests me." She threw her muff on his writing table and sank into the deep chair. "I have come to you for some information that's not in my line. Do you know anything about an American painter named Hedger?"

He took the seat opposite her. "Don Hedger? But, certainly! There are some very interesting things of his in an exhibition at V——'s. If you would care to—"

She held up her hand. "No, no. I've no time to go to exhibitions. Is he a man of any importance?"

"Certainly. He is one of the first men among the moderns. That is to say, among the very moderns. He is always coming up with something different. He often exhibits in Paris, you must have seen—"

"No, I tell you I don't go to exhibitions. Has he had great success? That is what I want to know."

M. Jules pulled at his short grey moustache. "But, Madame, there are many kinds of success," he began cautiously.

Madame gave a dry laugh. "Yes, so he used to say. We once quarrelled on that issue. And how would you define his particular kind?"

M. Jules grew thoughtful. "He is a great name with all the young men, and he is decidedly an influence in art. But one can't definitely place a man who is original, erratic, and who is changing all the time."

She cut him short. "Is he much talked about at home? In Paris, I mean? Thanks. That's all I want to know." She rose and began buttoning her coat. "One doesn't like to have been an utter fool, even at twenty."

"*Mais, non!*" M. Jules handed her her muff with a quick, sympathetic glance. He followed her out through the carpeted showroom, now closed to the public and draped in cheesecloth, and put her into her car with words appreciative of the honour she had done him in calling.

Leaning back in the cushions, Eden Bower closed her eyes, and her face, as the street lamps flashed their ugly orange light upon it, became hard and settled, like a plaster cast; so a sail, that has been filled by a strong breeze, behaves when the wind suddenly dies. Tomorrow night the wind would blow again, and this mask would be the golden face of Aphrodite. But a "big" career takes its toll, even with the best of luck.

THE SHADOWY THIRD

by Ellen Glasgow

Ellen Anderson Gholson Glasgow's first novel, *The Descendant*, was published anonymously in 1897, when she was only 24. Her fiction dominated the bestseller lists in the United States during the first few decades of the twentieth century. Her novel *In This Our Life* won the Pulitzer Prize for Fiction in 1942. "The Shadowy Third" was first published in *Scribner's* in 1916.

When the call came I remember that I turned from the telephone in a romantic flutter. Though I had spoken only once to the great surgeon, Roland Maradick, I felt on that December afternoon that to speak to him only once—to watch him in the operating-room for a single hour—was an adventure which drained the colour and the excitement from the rest of life. After all these years of work on typhoid and pneumonia cases, I can still feel the delicious tremor of my young pulses; I can still see the winter sunshine slanting through the hospital windows over the white uniforms of the nurses.

"He didn't mention me by name. Can there be a mistake?" I stood, incredulous yet ecstatic, before the superintendent of the hospital.

"No, there isn't a mistake. I was talking to him before you came down." Miss Hemphill's strong face softened while she looked at me. She was a big, resolute woman, a distant Canadian relative of my mother's, and the kind of nurse I had discovered in the month since I had come up from Richmond, that Northern hospital boards, if not Northern patients, appear instinctively to select. From the first, in spite of her hardness, she had taken a liking—I hesitate to use the word "fancy" for a preference so impersonal—to her Virginia cousin. After all, it isn't every Southern nurse, just out of training, who can boast a kinswoman in the superintendent of a New York hospital.

"And he made you understand positively that he meant me?" The thing was so wonderful that I simply couldn't believe it.

"He asked particularly for the nurse who was with Miss Hudson last week when he operated. I think he didn't even remember that you had a name. When I asked if he meant Miss Randolph, he repeated that he wanted the nurse who had been with Miss Hudson. She was small, he said, and cheerful-looking. This, of course, might apply to one or two of the others, but none of these was with Miss Hudson."

"Then I suppose it is really true?" My pulses were tingling. "And I am to be there at six o'clock?"

"Not a minute later. The day nurse goes off duty at that hour, and Mrs. Maradick is never left by herself for an instant."

"It is her mind, isn't it? And that makes it all the stranger that he should select me, for I have had so few mental cases."

"So few cases of any kind," Miss Hemphill was smiling, and when she smiled I wondered if the other nurses would know her. "By the time you have gone through the treadmill in New York, Margaret, you will have lost a good many things besides your inexperience. I wonder how long you will keep your sympathy and your imagination? After all, wouldn't you have made a better novelist than a nurse?"

"I can't help putting myself into my cases. I suppose one ought not to?"

"It isn't a question of what one ought to do, but of what one must. When you are drained of every bit of sympathy and enthusiasm, and have got nothing in return for it, not even thanks, you will understand why I try to keep you from wasting yourself."

"But surely in a case like this—for Doctor Maradick?"

"Oh, well, of course—for Doctor Maradick." She must have seen that I implored her confidence, for, after a minute, she let fall carelessly a gleam of light on the situation: "It is a very sad case when you think what a charming man and a great surgeon Doctor Maradick is."

Above the starched collar of my uniform I felt the blood leap in bounds to my cheeks. "I have spoken to him only once," I murmured, "but he is charming, and so kind and handsome, isn't he?"

"His patients adore him."

"Oh, yes, I've seen that. Everyone hangs on his visits." Like the patients and the other nurses, I also had come by delightful, if imperceptible, degrees to hang on the daily visits of Doctor Maradick. He was, I suppose, born to be a hero to women. From my first day in his hospital, from the moment when I watched, through closed shutters, while he stepped out of his car, I have never doubted that he was assigned to the great part in the play. If I had been ignorant of his spell—of the charm he exercised over his hospital—I should have felt it in the waiting hush, like a drawn breath, which followed his ring at the door and preceded his imperious footstep on the stairs. My first impression of him, even after the terrible events of the next year, records a memory that is both careless and splendid. At that moment, when, gazing through the chinks in the shutters, I watched him, in his coat of dark fur, cross the pavement over the pale streaks of sunshine, I knew beyond any doubt—I knew with a sort of infallible prescience—that my fate was irretrievably bound up with his in the future. I knew this, I repeat, though Miss Hemphill would still insist that my foreknowledge was merely a sentimental gleaning from indiscriminate novels. But it wasn't only first love, impressionable as my kinswoman believed me to be. It wasn't only the way he looked. Even more than his appearance—more than the shining dark of his eyes, the silvery brown of his hair, the dusky glow in his face—even more than his charm and his magnificence, I think, the beauty and sympathy in his voice won my heart. It was a voice, I heard someone say afterwards, that ought always to speak poetry.

So you will see why—if you do not understand at the beginning, I can never hope to make you believe impossible things!—so you will see why I accepted the call when it came as an imperative summons. I couldn't have stayed away after he sent for me. However much I may have tried not to go, I know that in the end I must have gone. In those days, while I was still hoping to write novels, I used to talk a great deal about "destiny" (I have learned since then how silly all such talk is), and I suppose it was my "destiny" to be caught in the web of Roland Maradick's personality. But I am not the first nurse to grow love-sick about a doctor who never gave her a thought.

"I am glad you got the call, Margaret. It may mean a great deal to you. Only try not to be too emotional." I remember that Miss Hemphill was holding a bit of rose-geranium in her hand while she spoke—one of the patients had given it to her from a pot she kept in her room, and the scent of the flower is still in my nostrils—or my memory. Since then—oh, long since then—I have wondered if she also had been caught in the web.

"I wish I knew more about the case." I was pressing for light. "Have you ever seen Mrs. Maradick?"

"Oh, dear, yes. They have been married only a little over a year, and in the beginning she used to come sometimes to the hospital and wait outside while the doctor made his visits. She was a very sweet-looking woman then—not exactly pretty, but fair and slight, with the loveliest smile, I think, I have ever seen. In those first months she was so much in love that we used to laugh about it among ourselves. To see her face light up when the doctor came out of the hospital and crossed the pavement to his car, was as good as a play. We never tired of watching her—I wasn't superintendent then, so I had more time to look out of the window while I was on day duty. Once or twice she brought her little girl in to see one of the patients. The child was so much like her that you would have known them anywhere for mother and daughter."

I had heard that Mrs. Maradick was a widow, with one child, when she first met the doctor, and I asked now, still seeking an illumination I had not found, "There was a great deal of money, wasn't there?"

"A great fortune. If she hadn't been so attractive, people would have said, I suppose, that Doctor Maradick married her for her money. Only," she appeared to make an effort of memory, "I believe I've heard somehow that it was all left in trust away from Mrs. Maradick if she married again. I can't, to save my life, remember just how it was; but it was a queer will, I know, and Mrs. Maradick wasn't to come into the money unless the child didn't live to grow up. The pity of it——"

A young nurse came into the office to ask for something—the keys, I think, of the operating-room, and Miss Hemphill broke off inconclusively as she hurried out of the door. I was sorry that she left off just when she did. Poor Mrs. Maradick! Perhaps I was too emotional, but even before I saw her I had begun to feel her pathos and her strangeness.

My preparations took only a few minutes. In those days I always kept a suitcase packed and ready for sudden calls; and it was not yet six o'clock when I turned from Tenth Street into Fifth Avenue, and stopped for a minute, before ascending the steps, to look at the house in which Doctor Maradick lived. A fine rain was falling, and I remember thinking, as I turned the corner, how depressing the weather must be for Mrs. Maradick. It was an old house, with damp-looking walls (though that may have been because of the rain) and a spindle-shaped iron railing which ran up the stone steps to the black door, where I noticed a dim flicker through the old-fashioned fanlight. Afterwards I discovered that Mrs. Maradick had been born in the house—her maiden name was Calloran—and that she had never wanted to live anywhere else. She was a woman—this I found out when I knew her better—of strong attachments to both persons and places; and though Doctor Maradick had tried to persuade her to move uptown after her marriage, she had clung, against his wishes, to the old house in lower Fifth Avenue. I dare say she was obstinate about it in spite of her gentleness and her passion for the doctor. Those sweet, soft women, especially when they have always been rich, are sometimes amazingly obstinate. I have nursed so many of them since—women with strong affections and weak intellects—that I have come to recognize the type as soon as I set eyes upon it.

My ring at the bell was answered after a little delay, and when I entered the house I saw that the hall was quite dark except for the waning glow from an open fire which burned in the library. When I gave my name, and added that I was the night nurse, the servant appeared to think my humble presence unworthy of illumination. He was an old negro butler, inherited perhaps from Mrs. Maradick's mother, who, I learned afterwards, was from South Carolina; and while he passed me on his way up the staircase, I heard him vaguely muttering that he "wa'n't gwinter tu'n on dem lights twel de chile had done playin'."

To the right of the hall, the soft glow drew me into the library, and crossing the threshold timidly, I stooped to dry my wet coat by the fire. As I bent there, meaning to start up at the first sound of a footstep, I thought how cosy the room was after the damp walls outside to which some bared creepers were clinging; and I was watching the strange shapes and patterns the firelight made on the old Persian rug, when the lamps of a slowly turning motor flashed on me through the white shades at the window. Still dazzled by the glare, I looked round in the dimness and saw a child's ball of red and blue rubber roll towards me out of the gloom of the adjoining room. A moment later, while I made a vain attempt to capture the toy as it spun past me, a little girl darted airily, with peculiar lightness and grace, through the doorway, and stopped quickly, as if in surprise at the sight of a stranger. She was a small child—so small and slight that her footsteps made no sound on the polished floor of the threshold; and I remember thinking while I looked at her that she had the gravest and sweetest face I had ever seen. She couldn't—I decided this afterwards—have been more than six or seven years old, yet she stood there with a curious prim dignity, like the dignity of an elderly person, and gazed up at me with enigmatical eyes. She was dressed in Scotch plaid, with a bit of red ribbon in her hair, which was cut in a fringe over her forehead and hung very straight to her shoulders. Charming as she was, from her uncurled brown hair to the white socks and black slippers on her little feet, I recall most vividly the singular look in her eyes, which appeared in the shifting light to be of an indeterminate colour. For the odd thing about this look was that it was not the look of childhood at all. It was the look of profound experience, of bitter knowledge.

"Have you come for your ball?" I asked; but while the friendly question was still on my lips, I heard the servant returning. In my confusion I made a second ineffectual grasp at the play-thing, which had rolled away from me into the dusk of the drawing-room. Then, as I raised my head, I saw that the child also had slipped from the room; and without looking after her I followed the old negro into the pleasant study above, where the great surgeon awaited me.

Ten years ago, before hard nursing had taken so much out of me, I blushed very easily, and I was aware at the moment when I crossed Doctor Maradick's study that my cheeks were the colour of peonies. Of course, I was a fool—no one knows this better than I do—but I had never been alone, even for an instant, with him before, and the man was more than a hero to me, he was—there isn't any reason now why I should blush over the confession—almost a god. At that age I was mad about the wonders of surgery, and Roland Maradick in the operating-room was magician enough to have turned an older and more sensible head than mine. Added to his great reputation and his marvelous skill, he was, I am sure of this, the most splendid-looking man, even at forty-five, that one could imagine. Had he been ungracious—had he been positively rude to me, I should still have adored him; but when he held out his hand, and greeted me in the charming way he had with women, I felt that I would have died for him. It is no wonder that a saying went about the hospital that every woman he operated on fell in love with him. As for the nurses—well, there wasn't a single one of them who had escaped his spell—not even Miss Hemphill, who could have been scarcely a day under fifty.

"I am glad you could come, Miss Randolph. You were with Miss Hudson last week when I operated?"

I bowed. To save my life I couldn't have spoken without blushing the redder.

"I noticed your bright face at the time. Brightness, I think, is what Mrs. Maradick needs. She finds her day nurse depressing." His eyes rested so kindly upon me that I have suspected since that he was not entirely unaware of my worship. It was a small thing, heaven knows, to flatter his vanity—a nurse just out of a training-school—but to some men no tribute is too insignificant to give pleasure.

"You will do your best, I am sure." He hesitated an instant—just long enough for me to perceive the anxiety beneath the genial smile on his face—and then added gravely, "We wish to avoid, if possible, having to send her away."

I could only murmur in response, and after a few carefully chosen words about his wife's illness, he rang the bell and directed the maid to take me upstairs to my room. Not until I was ascending the stairs to the third storey did it occur to me that he had really told me nothing. I was as perplexed about the nature of Mrs. Maradick's malady as I had been when I entered the house.

I found my room pleasant enough. It had been arranged—at Doctor Maradick's request, I think—that I was to sleep in the house, and after my austere little bed at the hospital, I was agreeably surprised by the cheerful look of the apartment into which the maid led me. The walls were papered in roses, and there were curtains of flowered chintz at the window, which looked down on a small formal garden at the rear of the house. This the maid told me, for it was too dark for me to distinguish more than a marble fountain and a fir-tree, which looked old, though I afterwards learned that it was replanted almost every season.

In ten minutes I had slipped into my uniform and was ready to go to my patient; but for some reason—to this day I have never found out what it was that turned her against me at the start—Mrs. Maradick refused to receive me. While I stood outside her door I heard the day nurse trying to persuade her to let me come in. It wasn't any use, however, and in the end I was obliged to go back to my room and wait until the poor lady got over her whim and consented to see me. That was long after dinner—it must have been nearer eleven than ten o'clock—and Miss Peterson was quite worn out by the time she came for me.

"I'm afraid you'll have a bad night," she said as we went downstairs together. That was her way, I soon saw, to expect the worst of everything and everybody.

"Does she often keep you up like this?"

"Oh, no, she is usually very considerate. I never knew a sweeter character. But she still has this hallucination——"

Here again, as in the scene with Doctor Maradick, I felt that the explanation had only deepened the mystery. Mrs. Maradick's hallucination, whatever form it assumed, was evidently a subject for evasion and subterfuge in the household. It was on the tip of my tongue to ask, "What is her hallucination?"—but before I could get the words past my lips we had reached Mrs. Maradick's door, and Miss Peterson motioned me to be silent. As the door opened a little way to admit me, I saw that Mrs. Maradick was already in bed, and that the lights were out except for a night-lamp burning on a candle-stand beside a book and a carafe of water.

"I won't go in with you," said Miss Peterson in a whisper; and I was on the point of stepping over the threshold when I saw the little girl, in the dress of Scotch plaid, slip by me from the dusk of the room into the electric light of the hall. She held a doll in her arms, and as she went by she dropped a doll's work-basket in the doorway. Miss Peterson must have picked up the toy, for when I turned in a minute to look for it I found that it was gone. I remember thinking that it was late for a child to be up—she looked delicate, too—but, after all, it was no business of mine, and four years in a hospital had taught me never to meddle in things that do not concern me. There is nothing a nurse learns quicker than not to try to put the world to rights in a day.

When I crossed the floor to the chair by Mrs. Maradick's bed, she turned over on her side and looked at me with the sweetest and saddest smile.

"You are the night nurse," she said in a gentle voice; and from the moment she spoke I knew that there was nothing hysterical or violent about her mania—or hallucination, as they called it. "They told me your name, but I have forgotten it."

"Randolph—Margaret Randolph." I liked her from the start, and I think she must have seen it.

"You look very young, Miss Randolph."

"I am twenty-two, but I suppose I don't look quite my age. People usually think I am younger."

For a minute she was silent, and while I settled myself in the chair by the bed, I thought how strikingly she resembled the little girl I had seen first in the afternoon, and then leaving her room a few moments before. They had the same small, heart-shaped faces, coloured ever so faintly; the same straight, soft hair, between brown and flaxen; and the same large, grave eyes, set very far apart under arched eyebrows. What surprised me most, however, was that they both looked at me with that enigmatical and vaguely wondering expression—only in Mrs. Maradick's face the vagueness seemed to change now and then to a definite fear—a flash, I had almost said, of startled horror.

I sat quite still in my chair, and until the time came for Mrs. Maradick to take her medicine not a word passed between us. Then, when I bent over her with the glass in my hand, she raised her head from the pillow and said in a whisper of suppressed intensity:

"You look kind. I wonder if you could have seen my little girl?"

As I slipped my arm under the pillow I tried to smile cheerfully down on her. "Yes, I've seen her twice. I'd know her anywhere by her likeness to you."

A glow shone in her eyes, and I thought how pretty she must have been before illness took the life and animation out of her features. "Then I know you're good." Her voice was so strained and low that I could barely hear it. "If you weren't good you couldn't have seen her."

I thought this queer enough, but all I answered was, "She looked delicate to be sitting up so late."

A quiver passed over her thin features, and for a minute I thought she was going to burst into tears. As she had taken the medicine, I put the glass back on the candle-stand, and bending over the bed, smoothed the straight brown hair, which was as fine and soft as spun silk, back from her forehead. There was something about her—I don't know what it was—that made you love her as soon as she looked at you.

"She always had that light and airy way, though she was never sick a day in her life," she answered calmly after a pause. Then, groping for my hand, she whispered passionately, "You must not tell him—you must not tell any one that you have seen her!"

"I must not tell any one?" Again I had the impression that had come to me first in Doctor Maradick's study, and afterwards with Miss Peterson on the staircase, that I was seeking a gleam of light in the midst of obscurity.

"Are you sure there isn't any one listening—that there isn't any one at the door?" she asked, pushing aside my arm and raising herself on the pillows.

"Quite, quite sure. They have put out the lights in the hall."

"And you will not tell him? Promise me that you will not tell him." The startled horror flashed from the vague wonder of her expression. "He doesn't like her to come back, because he killed her."

"Because he killed her!" Then it was that light burst on me in a blaze. So this was Mrs. Maradick's hallucination! She believed that her child was dead— the little girl I had seen with my own eyes leaving her room; and she believed that her husband—the great surgeon we worshipped in the hospital—had murdered her. No wonder they veiled the dreadful obsession in mystery! No wonder that even Miss Peterson had not dared to drag the horrid thing out into the light! It was the kind of hallucination one simply couldn't stand having to face.

"There is no use telling people things that nobody believes," she resumed slowly, still holding my hand in a grasp that would have hurt me if her fingers had not been so fragile. "Nobody believes that he killed her. Nobody believes that she comes back every day to the house. Nobody believes—and yet you saw her——"

"Yes, I saw her—but why should your husband have killed her?" I spoke soothingly, as one would speak to a person who was quite mad. Yet she was not mad, I could have sworn this while I looked at her.

For a moment she moaned inarticulately, as if the horror of her thoughts were too great to pass into speech. Then she flung out her thin, bare arm with a wild gesture.

"Because he never loved me!" she said. "He never loved me!"

"But he married you," I urged gently while I stroked her hair. "If he hadn't loved you, why should he have married you?"

"He wanted the money—my little girl's money. It all goes to him when I die."

"But he is rich himself. He must make a fortune from his profession."

"It isn't enough. He wanted millions." She had grown stern and tragic. "No, he never loved me. He loved someone else from the beginning—before I knew him."

It was quite useless, I saw, to reason with her. If she wasn't mad, she was in a state of terror and despondency so black that it had almost crossed the border-line into madness. I thought once that I would go upstairs and bring the child down from her nursery; but, after a moment's hesitation, I realized that Miss Peterson and Doctor Maradick must have long ago tried all these measures. Clearly, there was nothing to do except soothe and quiet her as much as I could; and this I did until she dropped into a light sleep which lasted well into the morning.

By seven o'clock I was worn out—not from work but from the strain on my sympathy—and I was glad, indeed, when one of the maids came in to bring me an early cup of coffee. Mrs. Maradick was still sleeping—it was a mixture of bromide and chloral I had given her—and she did not wake until Miss Peterson came on duty an hour or two later. Then, when I went downstairs, I found the dining-room deserted except for the old housekeeper, who was looking over the silver. Doctor Maradick, she explained to me presently, had his breakfast served in the morning-room on the other side of the house.

"And the little girl? Does she take her meals in the nursery?"

She threw me a startled glance. Was it, I questioned afterwards, one of distrust or apprehension?

"There isn't any little girl. Haven't you heard?"

"Heard? No. Why, I saw her only yesterday."

The look she gave me—I was sure of it now—was full of alarm.

"The little girl—she was the sweetest child I ever saw—died just two months ago of pneumonia."

"But she couldn't have died." I was a fool to let this out, but the shock had completely unnerved me. "I tell you I saw her yesterday."

The alarm in her face deepened. "That is Mrs. Maradick's trouble. She believes that she still sees her."

"But don't you see her?" I drove the question home bluntly.

"No." She set her lips tightly. "I never see anything."

So I had been wrong, after all, and the explanation, when it came, only accentuated the terror. The child was dead—she had died of pneumonia two months ago—and yet I had seen her, with my own eyes, playing ball in the library; I had seen her slipping out of her mother's room, with her doll in her arms.

"Is there another child in the house? Could there be a child belonging to one of the servants?" A gleam had shot through the fog in which I was groping.

"No, there isn't any other. The doctors tried bringing one once, but it threw the poor lady into such a state she almost died of it. Besides, there wouldn't be any other child as quiet and sweet-looking as Dorothea. To see her skipping along in her dress of Scotch plaid used to make me think of a fairy, though they say that fairies wear nothing but white or green."

"Has any one else seen her—the child, I mean—any of the servants?"

"Only old Gabriel, the coloured butler, who came with Mrs. Maradick's mother from South Carolina. I've heard that negroes often have a kind of second sight—though I don't know that that is just what you would call it. But they seem to believe in the supernatural by instinct, and Gabriel is so old and doty—he does no work except answer the door-bell and clean the silver—that nobody pays much attention to anything that he sees——"

"Is the child's nursery kept as it used to be?"

"Oh, no. The doctor had all the toys sent to the children's hospital. That was a great grief to Mrs. Maradick; but Doctor Brandon thought, and all the nurses agreed with him, that it was best for her not to be allowed to keep the room as it was when Dorothea was living."

"Dorothea? Was that the child's name?"

"Yes, it means the gift of God, doesn't it? She was named after the mother of Mrs. Maradick's first husband, Mr. Ballard. He was the grave, quiet kind—not the least like the doctor."

I wondered if the other dreadful obsession of Mrs. Maradick's had drifted down through the nurses or the servants to the housekeeper; but she said nothing about it, and since she was, I suspected, a garrulous person, I thought it wiser to assume that the gossip had not reached her.

A little later, when breakfast was over and I had not yet gone upstairs to my room, I had my first interview with Doctor Brandon, the famous alienist who was in charge of the case. I had never seen him before, but from the first moment that I looked at him I took his measure almost by intuition. He was, I suppose, honest enough—I have always granted him that, bitterly as I have felt towards him. It wasn't his fault that he lacked red blood in his brain, or that he had formed the habit, from long association with abnormal phenomena, of regarding all life as a disease. He was the sort of physician—every nurse will understand what I mean—who deals instinctively with groups instead of with individuals. He was long and solemn and very round in the face; and I hadn't talked to him ten minutes before I knew he had been educated in Germany, and that he had learned over there to treat every emotion as a pathological manifestation. I used to wonder what he got out of life—what any one got out of life who had analyzed away everything except the bare structure.

When I reached my room at last, I was so tired that I could barely remember either the questions Doctor Brandon had asked or the directions he had given me. I fell asleep, I know, almost as soon as my head touched the pillow; and the maid who came to inquire if I wanted luncheon decided to let me finish my nap. In the afternoon, when she returned with a cup of tea, she found me still heavy and drowsy. Though I was used to night nursing, I felt as if I had danced from sunset to daybreak. It was fortunate, I reflected, while I drank my tea, that every case didn't wear on one's sympathies as acutely as Mrs. Maradick's hallucination had worn on mine.

Through the day I did not see Doctor Maradick; but at seven o'clock when I came up from my early dinner on my way to take the place of Miss Peterson, who had kept on duty an hour later than usual, he met me in the hall and asked me to come into his study. I thought him handsomer than ever in his evening clothes, with a white flower in his buttonhole. He was going to some public dinner, the housekeeper told me, but, then, he was always going somewhere. I believe he didn't dine at home a single evening that winter.

"Did Mrs. Maradick have a good night?" He had closed the door after us, and turning now with the question, he smiled kindly, as if he wished to put me at ease in the beginning.

"She slept very well after she took the medicine. I gave her that at eleven o'clock."

For a minute he regarded me silently, and I was aware that his personality—his charm—was focussed upon me. It was almost as if I stood in the centre of converging rays of light, so vivid was my impression of him.

"Did she allude in any way to her—to her hallucination?" he asked.

How the warning reached me—what invisible waves of sense perception transmitted the message—I have never known; but while I stood there, facing the splendour of the doctor's presence, every intuition cautioned me that the time had come when I must take sides in the household. While I stayed there I must stand either with Mrs. Maradick or against her.

"She talked quite rationally," I replied after a moment.

"What did she say?"

"She told me how she was feeling, that she missed her child, and that she walked a little every day about her room."

His face changed—how I could not at first determine.

"Have you seen Doctor Brandon?"

"He came this morning to give me his directions."

"He thought her less well to-day. He has advised me to send her to Rosedale."

I have never, even in secret, tried to account for Doctor Maradick. He may have been sincere. I tell only what I know—not what I believe or imagine—and the human is sometimes as inscrutable, as inexplicable, as the supernatural.

While he watched me I was conscious of an inner struggle, as if opposing angels warred somewhere in the depths of my being. When at last I made my decision, I was acting less from reason, I knew, than in obedience to the pressure of some secret current of thought. Heaven knows, even then, the man held me captive while I defied him.

"Doctor Maradick," I lifted my eyes for the first time frankly to his, "I believe that your wife is as sane as I am—or as you are."

He started. "Then she did not talk freely to you?"

"She may be mistaken, unstrung, piteously distressed in mind"—I brought this out with emphasis—"but she is not—I am willing to stake my future on it—a fit subject for an asylum. It would be foolish—it would be cruel to send her to Rosedale."

"Cruel, you say?" A troubled look crossed his face, and his voice grew very gentle. "You do not imagine that I could be cruel to her?"

"No, I do not think that." My voice also had softened.

"We will let things go on as they are. Perhaps Doctor Brandon may have some other suggestion to make." He drew out his watch and compared it with the clock—nervously, I observed, as if his action were a screen for his discomfiture or perplexity. "I must be going now. We will speak of this again in the morning."

But in the morning we did not speak of it, and during the month that I nursed Mrs. Maradick I was not called again into her husband's study. When I met him in the hall or on the staircase, which was seldom, he was as charming as ever; yet, in spite of his courtesy, I had a persistent feeling that he had taken my measure on that evening, and that he had no further use for me.

As the days went by Mrs. Maradick seemed to grow stronger. Never, after our first night together, had she mentioned the child to me; never had she alluded by so much as a word to her dreadful charge against her husband. She was like any woman recovering from a great sorrow, except that she was sweeter and gentler. It is no wonder that everyone who came near her loved her; for there was a mysterious loveliness about her like the mystery of light, not of darkness. She was, I have always thought, as much of an angel as it is possible for a woman to be on this earth. And yet, angelic as she was, there were times when it seemed to me that she both hated and feared her husband. Though he never entered her room while I was there, and I never heard his name on her lips until an hour before the end, still I could tell by the look of terror in her face whenever his step passed down the hall that her very soul shivered at his approach.

During the whole month I did not see the child again, though one night, when I came suddenly into Mrs. Maradick's room, I found a little garden, such as children make out of pebbles and bits of box, on the window-sill. I did not mention it to Mrs. Maradick, and a little later, as the maid lowered the shades, I noticed that the garden had vanished. Since then I have often wondered if the child were invisible only to the rest of us, and if her mother still saw her. But there was no way of finding out except by questioning, and Mrs. Maradick was so well and patient that I hadn't the heart to question. Things couldn't have been better with her than they were, and I was beginning to tell myself that she might soon go out for an airing, when the end came so suddenly.

It was a mild January day—the kind of day that brings the foretaste of spring in the middle of winter, and when I came downstairs in the afternoon, I stopped a minute by the window at the end of the hall to look down on the box maze in the garden. There was an old fountain, bearing two laughing boys in marble, in the centre of the gravelled walk, and the water, which had been turned on that morning for Mrs. Maradick's pleasure, sparkled now like silver as the sunlight splashed over it. I had never before felt the air quite so soft and springlike in January; and I thought, as I gazed down on the garden, that it would be a good idea for Mrs. Maradick to go out and bask for an hour or so in the sunshine. It seemed strange to me that she was never allowed to get any fresh air except the air that came through her windows.

When I went into her room, however, I found that she had no wish to go out. She was sitting, wrapped in shawls, by the open window, which looked down on the fountain; and as I entered she glanced up from a little book she was reading. A pot of daffodils stood on the window-sill—she was very fond of flowers and we tried always to keep some growing in her room.

"Do you know what I am reading, Miss Randolph?" she asked in her soft voice; and she read aloud a verse while I went over to the candle-stand to measure out a dose of medicine.

" 'If thou hast two loaves of bread, sell one and buy daffodils, for bread nourisheth the body, but daffodils delight the soul.' That is very beautiful, don't you think so?"

I said "Yes," that it was beautiful; and then I asked her if she wouldn't go downstairs and walk about in the garden.

"He wouldn't like it," she answered; and it was the first time she had mentioned her husband to me since the night I came to her. "He doesn't want me to go out."

I tried to laugh her out of the idea; but it was no use, and after a few minutes I gave up and began talking of other things. Even then it did not occur to me that her fear of Doctor Maradick was anything but a fancy. I could see, of course, that she wasn't out of her head; but sane persons, I knew, sometimes have unaccountable prejudices, and I accepted her dislike as a mere whim or aversion. I did not understand then and—I may as well confess this before the end comes—I do not understand any better to-day. I am writing down the things I actually saw, and I repeat that I have never had the slightest twist in the direction of the miraculous.

The afternoon slipped away while we talked—she talked brightly when any subject came up that interested her—and it was the last hour of day—that grave, still hour when the movement of life seems to droop and falter for a few precious minutes—that brought us the thing I had dreaded silently since my first night in the house. I remember that I had risen to close the window, and was leaning out for a breath of the mild air, when there was the sound of steps, consciously softened, in the hall outside, and

Doctor Brandon's usual knock fell on my ears. Then, before I could cross the room, the door opened, and the doctor entered with Miss Peterson. The day nurse, I knew, was a stupid woman; but she had never appeared to me so stupid, so armoured and encased in her professional manner, as she did at that moment.

"I am glad to see that you are taking the air." As Doctor Brandon came over to the window, I wondered maliciously what devil of contradictions had made him a distinguished specialist in nervous diseases.

"Who was the other doctor you brought this morning?" asked Mrs. Maradick gravely; and that was all I ever heard about the visit of the second alienist.

"Someone who is anxious to cure you." He dropped into a chair beside her and patted her hand with his long, pale fingers. "We are so anxious to cure you that we want to send you away to the country for a fortnight or so. Miss Peterson has come to help you to get ready, and I've kept my car waiting for you. There couldn't be a nicer day for a trip, could there?"

The moment had come at last. I knew at once what he meant, and so did Mrs. Maradick. A wave of colour flowed and ebbed in her thin cheeks, and I felt her body quiver when I moved from the window and put my arms on her shoulders. I was aware again, as I had been aware that evening in Doctor Maradick's study, of a current of thought that beat from the air around into my brain. Though it cost me my career as a nurse and my reputation for sanity, I knew that I must obey that invisible warning.

"You are going to take me to an asylum," said Mrs. Maradick.

He made some foolish denial or evasion; but before he had finished I turned from Mrs. Maradick and faced him impulsively. In a nurse this was flagrant rebellion, and I realized that the act wrecked my professional future. Yet I did not care—I did not hesitate. Something stronger than I was driving me on.

"Doctor Brandon," I said, "I beg you—I implore you to wait until to-morrow. There are things I must tell you."

A queer look came into his face, and I understood, even in my excitement, that he was mentally deciding in which group he should place me—to which class of morbid manifestations I must belong.

"Very well, very well, we will hear everything," he replied soothingly; but I saw him glance at Miss Peterson, and she went over to the wardrobe for Mrs. Maradick's fur coat and hat.

Suddenly, without warning, Mrs. Maradick threw the shawls away from her, and stood up. "If you send me away," she said, "I shall never come back. I shall never live to come back."

The grey of twilight was just beginning, and while she stood there, in the dusk of the room, her face shone out as pale and flower-like as the daffodils on the window-sill. "I cannot go away!" she cried in a sharper voice. "I cannot go away from my child!"

I saw her face clearly; I heard her voice; and then—the horror of the scene sweeps back over me!—I saw the door open slowly and the little girl run across the room to her mother. I saw the child lift her little arms, and I saw the mother stoop and gather her to her bosom. So closely locked were they in that passionate embrace that their forms seemed to mingle in the gloom that enveloped them.

"After this can you doubt?" I threw out the words almost savagely—and then, when I turned from the mother and child to Doctor Brandon and Miss Peterson, I knew breathlessly—oh, there was a shock in the discovery!—that they were blind to the child. Their blank faces revealed the consternation of ignorance, not of conviction. They had seen nothing except the vacant arms of the mother and the swift, erratic gesture with which she stooped to embrace some invisible presence. Only my vision—and I have asked myself since if the power of sympathy enabled me to penetrate the web of material fact and see the spiritual form of the child—only my vision was not blinded by the clay through which I looked.

"After this can you doubt?" Doctor Brandon had flung my words back to me. Was it his fault, poor man, if life had granted him only the eyes of flesh? Was it his fault if he could see only half of the thing there before him?

But they couldn't see, and since they couldn't see I realized that it was useless to tell them. Within an hour they took Mrs. Maradick to the asylum; and she went quietly, though when the time came for parting from me she showed some faint trace of feeling. I remember that at the last, while we stood on the pavement, she lifted her black veil, which she wore for the child, and said: "Stay with her, Miss Randolph, as long as you can. I shall never come back."

Then she got into the car and was driven off, while I stood looking after her with a sob in my throat. Dreadful as I felt it to be, I didn't, of course, realize the full horror of it, or I couldn't have stood there quietly on the pavement. I didn't realize it, indeed, until several months afterwards when word came that she had died in the asylum. I never knew what her illness was, though I vaguely recall that something was said about "heart failure"—a loose enough term. My own belief is that she died simply of the terror of life.

To my surprise Doctor Maradick asked me to stay on as his office nurse after his wife went to Rosedale; and when the news of her death came there was no suggestion of my leaving. I don't know to this day why he wanted me in the house. Perhaps he thought I should have less opportunity to gossip if I stayed under his roof; perhaps he still wished to test the power of his charm over me. His vanity was incredible in so great a man. I have seen him flush with pleasure when people turned to look at him in the street, and I know that he was not above playing on the sentimental weakness of his patients. But he was magnificent, heaven knows! Few men, I imagine, have been the objects of so many foolish infatuations.

The next summer Doctor Maradick went abroad for two months, and while he was away I took my vacation in Virginia. When we came back the work was heavier than ever—his reputation by this time was tremendous—and my days were so crowded with appointments, and hurried flittings to emergency cases, that I had scarcely a minute left in which to remember poor Mrs. Maradick. Since the afternoon when she went to the asylum the child had not been in the house; and at last I was beginning to persuade myself that the little figure had been an optical illusion—the effect of shifting lights in the gloom of the old rooms—not the apparition I had once believed it to be. It does not take long for a phantom to fade from the memory—especially when one leads the active and methodical life I was forced into that winter. Perhaps—who knows?—(I remember telling myself) the doctors may have been right, after all, and the poor lady may have actually been out of her mind. With this view of the past, my judgment of Doctor Maradick insensibly altered. It ended, I think, in my acquitting him altogether. And then, just as he stood clear and splendid in my verdict of him, the reversal came so precipitately that I grow breathless now whenever I try to live it over again. The violence of the next turn in affairs left me, I often fancy, with a perpetual dizziness of the imagination.

It was in May that we heard of Mrs. Maradick's death, and exactly a year later, on a mild and fragrant afternoon, when the daffodils were blooming in patches around the old fountain in the garden, the housekeeper came into the office, where I lingered over some accounts, to bring me news of the doctor's approaching marriage.

"It is no more than we might have expected," she concluded rationally. "The house must be lonely for him—he is such a sociable man. But I can't help feeling," she brought out slowly after a pause in which I felt a shiver pass over me, "I can't help feeling that it is hard for that other woman to have all the money poor Mrs. Maradick's first husband left her."

"There is a great deal of money, then?" I asked curiously.

"A great deal." She waved her hand, as if words were futile to express the sum. "Millions and millions!"

"They will give up this house, of course?"

"That's done already, my dear. There won't be a brick left of it by this time next year. It's to be pulled down and an apartment-house built on the ground."

Again the shiver passed over me. I couldn't bear to think of Mrs. Maradick's old home falling to pieces.

"You didn't tell me the name of the bride," I said. "Is she some-one he met while he was in Europe?"

"Dear me, no! She is the very lady he was engaged to before he married Mrs. Maradick, only she threw him over, so people said, because he wasn't rich enough. Then she married some lord or prince from over the water; but there was a divorce, and now she has turned again to her old lover. He is rich enough now, I guess, even for her!"

It was all perfectly true, I suppose; it sounded as plausible as a story out of a newspaper; and yet while she told me I felt, or dreamed that I felt, a sinister, an impalpable hush in the air. I was nervous, no doubt; I was shaken by the suddenness with which the housekeeper had sprung her news on me; but as I sat there I had quite vividly an impression that the old house was listening—that there was a real, if invisible, presence somewhere in the room or the garden. Yet, when an instant afterwards I glanced through the long window which opened down to the brick terrace, I saw only the faint sunshine over the deserted garden, with its maze of box, its marble fountain, and its patches of daffodils.

The housekeeper had gone—one of the servants, I think, came for her—and I was sitting at my desk when the words of Mrs. Maradick on that last evening floated into my mind. The daffodils brought her back to me; for I thought, as I watched them growing, so still and golden in the sunshine, how she would have enjoyed them. Almost unconsciously I repeated the verse she had read to me:

"If thou hast two loaves of bread, sell one and buy daffodils"—and it was at this very instant, while the words were still on my lips, that I turned my eyes to the box maze, and saw the child skipping rope along the gravelled path to the fountain. Quite distinctly, as clear as day, I saw her come, with what children call the dancing step, between the low box borders to the place where the daffodils bloomed by the fountain. From her straight brown hair to her frock of Scotch plaid and her little feet, which twinkled in white socks and black slippers over the turning rope, she was as real to me as the ground on which she trod or the laughing marble boys under the splashing water. Starting up from my chair, I made a single step to the terrace. If I could only reach her—only speak to her—I felt that I might at last solve the mystery. But with the first flutter of my dress on the terrace, the airy little form melted into the quiet dusk of the maze. Not a breath stirred the daffodils, not a shadow passed over the sparkling flow of the water; yet, weak and shaken in every nerve, I sat down on the brick step of the terrace and burst into tears. I must have known that something terrible would happen before they pulled down Mrs. Maradick's home.

The doctor dined out that night. He was with the lady he was going to marry, the housekeeper told me; and it must have been almost midnight when I heard him come in and go upstairs to his room. I was downstairs because I had been unable to sleep, and the book I wanted to finish I had left that afternoon in the office. The book—I can't remember what it was—had seemed to me very exciting when I began it in the morning; but after the visit of the child I found the romantic novel as dull as a treatise on nursing. It was impossible for me to follow the lines, and I was on the point of giving up and going to bed, when Doctor Maradick opened the front door with his latch-key and went up the staircase. "There can't be a bit of truth in it," I thought over and over again as I listened to his even step ascending the stairs. "There can't be a bit of truth in it." And yet, though I assured myself that "there couldn't be a bit of truth in it," I shrank, with a creepy sensation, from going through the house to my room in the third storey. I was tired out after a hard day, and my nerves must have reacted morbidly to the silence and the darkness. For the first time in my life I knew what it was to be afraid of the unknown, of the unseen; and while I bent over my book, in the glare of the electric light, I became conscious presently that I was straining my senses for some sound in the spacious emptiness of the rooms overhead. The noise of a passing motor-car in the street jerked me back from the intense hush of expectancy; and I can recall the wave of relief that swept over me as I turned to my book again and tried to fix my distracted mind on its pages.

I was still sitting there when the telephone on my desk rang, with what seemed to my overwrought nerves a startling abruptness, and the voice of the superintendent told me hurriedly that Doctor Maradick was needed at the hospital. I had become so accustomed to these emergency calls in the night that I felt reassured when I had rung up the doctor in his room and had heard the hearty sound of his response. He had not yet undressed, he said, and would come down immediately while I ordered back his car, which must just have reached the garage.

"I'll be with you in five minutes!" he called as cheerfully as if I had summoned him to his wedding.

I heard him cross the floor of his room; and before he could reach the head of the staircase, I opened the door and went out into the hall in order that I might turn on the light and have his hat and coat waiting. The electric button was at the end of the hall, and as I moved towards it, guided by the glimmer that fell from the landing above, I lifted my eyes to the staircase, which climbed dimly, with its slender mahogany balustrade, as far as the third storey. Then it was, at the very moment when the doctor, humming gaily, began his quick descent of the steps, that I distinctly saw—I will swear to this on my deathbed—a child's skipping-rope lying loosely coiled, as if it had dropped from a careless little hand, in the bend of the staircase. With a spring I had reached the electric button, flooding the hall with light; but as I did so, while my arm was still outstretched behind me, I heard the humming voice change to a cry of surprise or terror, and the figure on the staircase tripped heavily and stumbled with groping hands into emptiness. The scream of warning died in my throat while I watched him pitch forward down the long flight of stairs to the floor at my feet. Even before I bent over him, before I wiped the blood from his brow and felt for his silent heart, I knew that he was dead.

Something—it may have been, as the world believes, a misstep in the dimness, or it may have been, as I am ready to bear witness, an invisible judgment—something had killed him at the very moment when he most wanted to live.

GAL YOUNG UN

A Story in Two Parts

by Marjorie Kinnan Rawlings

After graduating from the University of Wisconsin in 1918, Marjorie Kinnan spent ten years trying to write fiction while supporting herself as a professional journalist. In 1928 she moved to backwoods Florida and devoted herself to creative writing. "Gal Young Un," her first successful story, was published in *Harper's* in 1932 and was awarded the O. Henry Memorial Prize the following year. In 1939 her novel *The Yearling* received the Pulitzer Prize for Fiction.

PART I

The house was invisible from the road which wound, almost untraveled, through the flat-woods. Once every five days a turpentine wagon creaked down the ruts, and negroes moved like shadows among the pines. A few hunters in season came upon them chipping boxes, scraping aromatic gum from red pots into encrusted buckets; inquired the way and whether quail or squirrel or turkey had been seen. Then hunters and turpentiners moved again along the road, stepping on violets and yellow pitcher-plants that rimmed the edges.

The negroes were aware of the house. It stood a few hundred yards away, hidden behind two live oaks, isolated and remote in a patch of hammock. It was a tall square two-stories. The woman who gave them water from her well when the nearby branch was dry looked to them like the house, tall and bare and lonely, weathered gray, like its unpainted cypress. She seemed forgotten.

The two white men, hunting lazily down the road, did not remember—if they had ever known—that a dwelling stood here. Flushing a covey of quail that flung themselves like feathered bronze discs at the cover of the hammock, their first shots flicked through the twin oaks. They followed their pointer dog on the trail of single birds and stopped short in amazement. Entering the north fringe of the hammock, they had come out on a sandy open yard. A woman was watching them from the back stoop of an old house.

"Shootin' mighty close, men," she called.

Her voice sounded unused, like a rusty iron hinge.

The older man whistled in the dog, ranging feverishly in the low palmettos. The younger swaggered to the porch. He pushed back the black slouch hat from his brazen eyes.

"Never knowed nobody lived in six miles o' here."

His tone was insolent. He drew a flattened package of cigarettes from his corduroy hunting jacket, lighted one, and waited for her to begin scolding. Women always quarreled with him. Middle-aged women, like this one, quarreled earnestly; young ones snapped at him playfully.

"It's a long ways from anybody, ain't it?" she agreed.

He stared at her between puffs.

"Jesus, yes."

"I don't keer about you shootin'," she said. "It's purely sociable, hearin' men-folks acrost the woods. A shot come thu a winder jest now, that's all the reason I spoke."

The intruders shifted their shotguns uneasily. The older man touched his finger to his cap.

"That's all right, ma'am."

His companion strolled to the stone curbing of an open well. He peered into its depths, shimmering where the sun of high noon struck vertically.

"Good water?"

"The finest ever. Leave me fetch you a clean cup."

She turned into the house for a white china coffee cup. The men wound up a bucket of water on creaking ropes. The older man drank politely from the proffered cup. The other guzzled directly from the bucket. He reared back his head like a satisfied hound, dripping a stream of crystal drops from his red mouth.

"Ain't your dog thirsty? Here—reckon my ol' cat won't fuss if he drinks outen his dish." The woman stroked the animal's flanks as he lapped. "Ain't he a fine feller."

The hunters began to edge away.

"Men, I jest got common rations, bacon an' biscuit an' coffee, but you're plumb welcome to set down with me."

"No, thank you, ma'am." They looked at the sun. "Got to be moseyin' home."

The younger man was already on his way, sucking a straw. The other fumbled in his game-pocket.

"Sorry we come so clost up on you, lady. How 'bout a bird fer your dinner?"

She reached out a large hand for the quail.

"I'd shore thank you fer it. I'm a good shot on squirrel, an' turkeys when I git 'em roosted. Birds is hard without no dog to point 'em. I gits hungry fer quail . . ."

Her voice trailed off as the hunters walked through the pines toward the road. She waved her hand in case they should turn around. They did not look back.

★ ★ ★

The man was hunting alone because he had been laughed at. His cronies in the Florida village, to which he had returned after a few years' wandering, knew that he detested solitude. It was alien to him, a silent void into which he sank as into quicksand. He had stopped at the general store to pick up a hunting partner. The men lounging there hours at a time were usually willing to go with him. This time none was ready.

"Come go with me, Willy," he insisted. "I cain't go by myself."

The storekeeper called over his shoulder, weighing out a quarter's worth of water-ground meal for a negro.

"You'll git ketched out alone in the woods sometime, Trax, an' nobody won't know who 'tis."

The men guffawed.

"Trax always got to git him a buddy."

His smoldering eyes flared at them. He spat furiously across the rough pine floor of the store.

"I ain't got to git me none o' these sorry catbirds."

He had clattered down the wooden steps, spitting angrily every few feet. They were jealous, he thought, because he had been over on the east coast. He had turned instinctively down the south road out of the village. Old man Blaine had brought him this way last week. He hunted carelessly for two or three hours, taking pot shots at several coveys that rose under his feet. His anger made him miss the birds widely. It was poor sport without a companion and a dog.

Now he realized that he was lost. As a boy he had hunted these woods, but always with other boys and men. He had gone through them unseeing, stretching his young muscles luxuriously, absorbing lazily the rich Florida sun, cooling his face at every running branch. His shooting had been careless, avid. He liked to see the brown birds tumble in midair. He liked to hunt with the pack, to gorge on the game dinners they cooked by lake shores under oak trees. When the group turned homeward, he followed, thinking of supper; of the 'shine his old man kept hidden in the smokehouse; of the girls he knew. Someone else knew north and south, and the cross patterns of the piney-woods roads. The lonely region was now as unfamiliar as though he had been a stranger.

It was an hour or two past noon. He leaned his 12-gauge shotgun against a pine and looked about him nervously. He knew by the sun that he had come continuously south. He had crossed and recrossed the road, and could not decide whether it now lay to the right or left. If he missed it to the right, he would come to cypress swamp. He licked his lips. If he picked the wrong road to the left, it would bring him out a couple of miles above the village. That would be better. He could always get a lift back. He picked up his gun and began to walk.

In a few minutes a flat gray surface flashed suddenly from a patch of hammock. He stopped short. Pleasure swept over him, cooling his hot irritation. He recognized the house where he and Blaine had drawn water. He had cursed Blaine for giving a quail to the woman. He wiped the sweat from his face. The woman would feed him and direct him out of the flat-woods. Instinctively he changed his gait from a shuffling drag to his customary swagger.

He rapped loudly on the smooth cypress front door. It had a halfmoon fanlight over it. The house was old but it was capacious and good. There was, for all its bareness, an air of prosperity. Clean white curtains hung at the windows. A striped cat startled him by rearing against his legs. He kicked it away. The woman must be gone. A twig cracked in the yard beyond the high piazza. He turned. The woman was stalking around the side of the house to see before she was seen. Her gray face lightened as she recognized him. She laughed.

"Mister, if you knowed how long it's been since I heerd a rap. Don't nobody knock on my front door. The turpentine niggers calls so's I won't shoot, and the hunters comes a-talkin' to the well."

She climbed the front steps with the awkwardness of middle age. She dried a hand on her flour-sacking apron and held it out to him. He took it limply, interrupting the talk that began to flow from her. He was ugly with hunger and fatigue and boredom.

"How 'bout a mess o' them rations you was offerin' me last week?"

His impatience was tempered with the tone of casual intimacy in which he spoke to all women. It bridged time and space. The woman flushed.

"I'd be mighty well pleased—"

She opened the front door. It stuck at the sill, and she threw a strong body against it. He did not offer to help. He strolled in ahead of her. As she apologized for the moments it would take to fry bacon and make coffee, he was already staring about him at the large room. When she came to him from the kitchen half an hour later, her face red with her hurry, the room had made an impress on his mind, as roads and forests could not do. The size of the room, of the clay fireplace, the adequacy of chairs and tables of a frontier period, the luxury of a Brussels carpet, although ancient, over wood, the plenitude of polished, unused kerosene lamps—the details lay snugly in his mind like hoarded money.

Hungry, with the smell of hot food filling his breath, he took time to smooth his sleek black hair at a walnut-framed mirror on the varnished matchboard wall. He made his toilet boldly in front of the woman. A close watching of his dark face, of the quickness of his hands moving over his affectation of clipped side-burns, could only show her that he was good to look at. He walked to the kitchen with a roll, sprawling his long legs under the table.

With the first few mouthfuls of food good humor returned to him. He indulged himself in graciousness. The woman served him lavishly with fried cornbread and syrup, coffee, white bacon in thick slices, and fruits and vegetables of her own canning. His gluttony delighted her. His mouth was full, bent low over his heaped plate.

"You live fine, ma'am, for anyone lives plumb alone."

She sat down opposite him, wiping back the wet gray hair from her forehead, and poured herself a convivial cup of coffee.

"Jim—that was my husband—an' Pa always did say if they was good rations in the house they'd orter be on the table. I ain't got over the habit."

"You been livin' alone quite some time?"

"Jim's fifteen year dead. Pa 'bout six."

"Don't you never go nowheres?"

"I got no way to go. I kep' up stock fer two-three year after Pa died, but 'twa'n't wuth the worry. They's a family lives two mile closer to town than me, has a horse an' wagon. I take 'em my list o' things 'bout oncet a month. Seems like . . ."

He scarcely listened.

A change of atmosphere in her narrative indicated suddenly to him that she was asking him about himself.

"You a stranger?"

She was eager, leaning on the table waiting for his answer.

He finished a saucer of preserved figs, scraping at the rich syrup with relish. He tilted back in his chair luxuriously and threw the match from his cigarette in the general direction of the wood stove. He was entirely at home. His belly well filled with good food, his spirit touched with the unfailing intoxication to him of a woman's interest, he teetered and smoked and talked of his life, of his deeds, his dangers.

"You ever heard the name o' Trax Colton?"

She shook her head. He tapped his chest significantly, nodding at her.

"That's me. You've heard tell, if you on'y remembered, o' me leavin' here a few years back on account of a little cuttin' fuss. I been on the east coast—Daytona, Melbourne, all them places. The fuss blowed over an' I come back. Fixin' to take up business here."

He frowned importantly. He tapped a fresh cigarette on the table, as he had learned to do from his companions of the past years. He thought with pleasure of all that he had learned, of the sophistication that lay over his Cracker speech and ways like a cheap bright coat.

"I'm an A-1 bootlegger, ma'am."

For the time being he was a big operator from the east coast. He told her of small sturdy boats from Cuba, of signal flares on the St. Augustine beach at midnight, of the stream of swift automobiles moving in and out just before high tide. Her eyes shone. She plucked at the throat of her brown-checked gingham dress, breathing quickly. It was fitting that this dark glamorous young man should belong to the rocket-lit world of danger. It was ecstasy painful in its sharpness, that he should be tilted back at her table, flicking his fragrant ashes on her clean, lonely floor.

He was entirely amiable as he left her. Pleased with himself, he was for a moment pleased with her. She was a good woman. He laid his hand patronizingly on her shoulder. He stroked the striped cat on his way down the steps. This time he turned to lift his hand to her. She waved heartily as long as his lithe body moved in sight among the pines.

An impulse took her to the mirror where he had smoothed his hair, as though it would bring him within her vision again. She saw herself completely for the first time in many years. Isolation had taken the meaning from age. She had forgotten until this moment that she was no longer young. She turned from the mirror and washed the dishes soberly. It occurred to her that the young man had not even asked her name.

The hammock that had been always a friendly curtain about the old house was suddenly a wall. The flat-woods that had been sunny and open, populous with birds and the voice of winds, grew dense and dark. She had been solitary. She had grieved for Jim and for the old man her father. But solitude had kept her company in a warm natural way, sitting cozily at her hearth, like the cat. Now loneliness washed intolerably over her, as though she were drowning in a cold black pond.

The young man's complacency lasted a mile or two. As his feet began to drag, fact intruded on the fiction with which he had enraptured the gray-haired woman. Memories seeped back into him like a poison: memories of the lean years as ignorant hanger-on of the prosperous bootleggers; of his peddling to small garages of lye-cut 'shine in ignominious pints. The world for which he considered himself fitted had evaded him. His condition was desperate. He thought of the woman who had fed him, whom he had entranced with his story. Distaste for her flooded him, as though it was her fault the story was a lie. He lifted his shotgun and blew the head from a redbird trilling in a wild plum tree.

* * *

The storekeeper in the village was the only person who recognized Mattie Syles. The store was packed with the Saturday-night buyers of rations. A layer of whites milled in front of the meat counter; a layer of blacks shifted behind them. At the far grocery counter along a side wall a wedge of negroes had worked in toward the meal and sugar barrels, where helpers weighed out the dimes' and quarters' worth with deliberately inaccurate haste. Two white women were buying percale of the storekeeper's wife at the dry-goods counter.

The woman came in defiantly, as though the store was a shameful place where she had no business. She looked searchingly from side to side. The storekeeper's wife called, "Evenin', ma'am," and the two white women wheeled to stare and whisper after her. She advanced toward the meat counter. The negroes parted to let her in. The storekeeper poised his knife over a pork backbone to look at her. He laid it down, wiped his hands with a flourish on his front, and shook hands across the counter.

"If this ain't a surprise! Must be four-five years since you been to town! Meat I been sendin' you by Lantrys been all right? What kin I do fer you? Butchered this mornin'—got fresh beef. How 'bout a nice thin steak?"

She made her purchases slowly and moved to the staples counter. She insisted on being left until the last.

"I ain't in no hurry."

The store was almost empty and ready to close when she gathered her sacks together and climbed into the Lantrys' wagon, waiting outside the door. As Lantry clicked to his horse and they moved off she did not notice that the man she had hoped desperately to see was just strolling into the store.

"Gimme a couple o' packs o' Camels to tide me over Sunday."

"Fifteen cents straight now, Trax."

"Jest one, then."

The storekeeper spoke across the vacant store to his wife, rolling up the bolts of cloth.

"Edna, you have better manners with the customers, or we'll be losing 'em. Why'n't you take up some time with Mis' Syles?"

"Who?"

"Mis' Syles—Jim Syles' widder—ol' man Terry's daughter—lives four-five mile south, out beyond Lantry's. You know her, Edna. Lantry's been buyin' fer her."

"I never knowed her. How'd I know her now? Why'n't you call her by name, so's I'd of knowed?"

"Well, you keep better track of her if she's goin' to take to comin' to town agin. She's rich."

Trax turned in the doorway.

"You talkin' about that gank-gutted woman left jest now?"

He had avoided going into the store until she left. He had not intended to bring her volubility upon him in public, have her refer to their meal together. He had half-guessed she had come looking for him. Women did.

"She live alone in a two-story house you cain't see from the road?"

"That's her," the storekeeper agreed. "That's Mis' Syles, a'right."

"She's rich?"

"I mean rich. Got her five dollars a week steady rent-money from turpentine, an' three thousand dollars insurance in the bank her daddy left her. An' then lives 'tother end o' nowhere. Won't leave the old house."

"'Bout time somebody was fixin' to marry all that, goin' to waste."

"She wouldn't suit you, Trax. You didn't git a good look at her. You been used to 'em younger an' purtier."

The man Colton was excited. He walked out of the store without the customary "Well, evenin'" of departure. He hurried to Blaine's, where he was boarding, but did not go in. It was necessary to sit alone on the bench outside and think. His luck had not deserted him. As he leaned his dark head back against the wall, the tropical stars glittering over him were the bright lights of city streets. Here and there a fat star flickered. These were the burnished kerosene lamps of the widow Syles. The big room—the fireplace that would heat it on the coolest nights—one by one he drew out the remembered details and tucked them into his plans.

The man courted the woman with the careless impatience of his quail hunting. He intended to be done with it as quickly as possible. There was, astonishingly, a certain pleasure in her infatuation. He responded to any woman's warmth as a hound does to a grate fire, stretching comfortably before it. The maternal lavishness of her emotion for him was satisfying. Younger women, pretty women, expected something of him, coaxed and coquetted.

On his several visits to the widow before he condescended to be married to her, he sprawled in the early spring nights before the big fireplace. He made it plain that he was not one to sit around the kitchen stove. His fastidiousness charmed her. She staggered into the room with her generous arms heaped with wood: live oak and hickory, and some cedar chips, because Trax liked the smell. From his chair he directed the placing of the heavy logs. A fire must crackle constantly to please him. She learned to roll cigarettes for him, bringing them to him to lick flickeringly, like a snake, with his quick tongue. The process stirred her. When she placed the finished cigarette between his lips and lighted it with a blazing lighter'd splinter; when he puffed languidly on it and half-closed his eyes, and laid his fingers perhaps on her large-boned hand, she shivered.

The courting was needlessly protracted because she could not believe that he would have her. It was miracle enough that he should be here at all in these remote flat-woods. It was unbelievable that he should be willing to prolong the favor, to stay with her in this place forever.

She said, "Cain't be you raly wants me."

Yet she drank in his casual insistence.

"Why not? Ain't a thing the matter with you."

She understood sometimes—when she wakened with a clear mind in the middle of the night—that something strange had happened to her. She was moving in a delirium, like the haze of malaria when the fever was on. She solaced herself by thinking that Trax too might be submerged in such a delicious fog.

When he left her one night in the Blaine Ford he had borrowed, the retreating explosions of the car left behind a silence that terrified her. She ran to the beginning of the pines to listen. There was no sound but the breath of the south wind in the needles. There was no light but the endless flickering of stars. She knew that if the man did not come back again she would have to follow him. Solitude she had endured. She could not endure desolation.

When he came the next day she was ready to go to the village with him to the preacher. He laughed easily at her hurry and climbed ahead of her into the borrowed car. He drove zestfully, with abandon, bouncing the woman's big frame over the ruts of the dirt road.

As they approached the village he said casually, "I keep my money in Clark City. We'd orter do our business together. Where's yours?"

"Mine's there too. Some's in the post office an' some in the bank."

"Supposin' we go git married there. An' reckon you kin lend me a hundred till I add up my account?"

She nodded an assent to both questions.

"Don't you go spendin' no money on me, Trax, if you ain't got it real free to spend." She was alarmed for his interests. "You leave me pay fer things a while."

He drew a deep breath of relief. He was tempted for a moment to get her cash and head for the east coast at once. But he had made his plans to stay. He needed the old house in the safe flatwoods to make his start. He could even use the woman.

When they came back through the village from the city she stopped at the store for supplies. The storekeeper leaned across the fresh sausage to whisper confidentially:

"Tain't my business, Mis' Syles, but folks is sayin' Trax Colton is sort o' courtin' you. You come of good stock, an' you'd orter step easy. Trax is purely trash, Mis' Syles."

She looked at him without comprehension.

She said, "Me and Trax is married."

* * *

The gray of the house was overlaid with the tenderness of the April sun. The walls were washed with its thin gold. The ferns and lichens of the shingled roof were shot through with light, and the wren's nest under the eaves was luminous. The striped cat sprawled flattened on the rear stoop, exposing his belly to the soft warmth. The woman moved quietly at her work, for fear of awakening the man. She was washing. When she drew a bucket of water from the well she steadied it with one hand as it swung to the coping, so that there should be no sound.

Near the well stood bamboo and oleander. She left her bucket to draw her fingers along the satin stoutness of the fresh green bamboo shoots, to press apart the new buds of the oleander in search of the pale pinkness of the first blossoms. The sun lay like a friendly arm across her square shoulders. It seemed to her that she had been chilled, year on year, and that now for the first time she was warmed through to her marrow. Spring after the snapping viciousness of February; Trax sleeping in the bed after her solitude. . . . When she finished her washing she slipped in to look at him. A boyish quiet wiped out the nervous shiftiness of his waking expression. She wanted to gather him up, sleeping, in her strong arms and hold him against her capacious breast.

When his breakfast was almost ready, she made a light clatter in the kitchen. It irritated him to be called. He liked to get up of his own accord and find breakfast smoking, waiting for him. He came out gaping, washed his face and hands in the granite basin on the water-shelf, combed his hair leisurely at the kitchen mirror, turning his face this way and that. Matt stood watching him, twisting her apron. When he was quite through, she came to him and laid her cheek against his.

"Mornin', Trax-honey."

Her voice was vibrant.

"Mornin'."

He yawned again as he dropped into his chair. He beat lightly on his down-turned plate with his knife and surveyed the table. He scowled.

"Where's the bacon?"

"Honey, I didn't think you'd want none with the squirrel an' eggs an' fish."

"My God, I cain't eat breakfast without bacon."

"I'm sorry, Trax. 'Twon't take me but a minute now."

She was miserable because she had not fried bacon and he wanted it.

He slid eggs and meat and biscuits to his plate, poured coffee with an angry jerk, so that it spilled on the table, shoveled the food in, chewing with his mouth open. When Matt put the crisp thick slices of white bacon before him, he did not touch them. He lighted a cigarette and strolled to the stoop, pushing off the cat so that he might sit down. He leaned back and absorbed the sun. This was fine.

He had deliberately allowed himself these few idle weeks. He had gone long without comfort. His body needed it. His swaggering spirit needed it. The woman's adoration fed him. He could have had no greater sense of well-being, of affluence if she had been a nigger servant. Now he was ready for business. His weasel mind was gnawing its hole into the world he longed for.

"Matt!"

She left her dishes and came to stand over him.

"Matt, you're goin' in business with me. I want you should git me three hundred dollars. I want to set up a eight-barrel still back o' the house, down by the branch."

Trax had crashed like a meteor into the flat-woods. It had not occurred to her that his world must follow him. That was detached from him, only a strange story that he had told. She had a sensation of dismay that any thing, any person, must intrude on her ecstasy.

She said anxiously, "I got enough to make out on, Trax. You don't need to go startin' up nothin' like that."

"All right—if you want I should put my outfit some'eres else—"

"No, no. Don't you do that. Don't you go 'way. I didn't know you was studyin' on nothin' like that—you jest go ahead an' put it clost as you like."

"Down by the branch, like I said."

He visioned the lay-out for her. She listened, distraught. The platform here, for the barrels of mash. There, the wood-pile for the slow fire. Here again, the copper still itself. The cover was dense, utterly concealing. The location was remote.

"The idee, Matt," he was hunched forward, glowing, "is to sell yer own stuff what they call retail, see? It costs you fifty, seventy-five cents a gallon to make. You sell by the five-gallon jug fer seven dollars, like they're doin' now, you don't make nothin'. That's nigger pay. But what do you git fer it by the drink? A quarter. A quarter a drink an' a dollar a pint. You let people know they kin git 'em a drink out here any time to Trax Colton's, you got 'em comin' in from twothree counties fer it. You git twenty gallons ahead an' color some up, cook it a whiles underground to darken it, an' you take it to places like Jacksonville an' Miami—you got you real money."

It was as though thunder and lightning threatened over the flatwoods. The darkness of impending violence filled them. She stared at him.

"'Course, if you don't want to invest in my business with me, I got to be gittin' back where I come from."

The smoke from his cigarette drifted across her.

"No, no! It's all right!"

His glamorousness enfolded her like the April sun.

"Honey, anything you want to do's all right."

* * *

Setting up the still was a week's work. Men began to come and go. Where there had been, once in five days, the silent turpentiners, once in a while the winter hunters, there were now negroes bringing in cut wood; a local mason putting together brick and mortar; a hack carpenter building a platform with a roof; men in trucks bringing in sacks of meal and sugar, glass demijohns and oak kegs.

The storekeeper brought five hundred pounds of sugar.

"Howdy, Mis' Colton. Reckon you never figgered you'd be 'shinin'."

"No."

"But you couldn't git you no better place fer it."

Her square face brightened.

"That's jest what Trax says."

That night she approached him.

"Trax, all these here men knowin' what you're doin'—reckon it's safe?"

"They got no reason to say nothin'. The only reason anybody'd turn anybody else up was if he'd done somethin' to him. Then they'd git at him that-a-way. Git his still, see? Git him tore up. That way they'd git him."

She made no further comment. Her silence made its way through the wall of his egotism.

"You don't talk as much as you did, Matt. Else I got used to it."

"I was alone so long, honey. Seemed like I had to git caught up."

But the spring warmth was no longer so loosening to the tongue. The alien life the man was bringing in chilled the exuberance that had made her voluble.

"I'm fixin' to learn you to make the whiskey, Matt."

She stared at him.

"Less help we have, knowin' how much I got an' where 'tis, better it suits me, see?"

She said finally, "I kin learn."

The work seemed strange, when all her folk had farmed and timbered. But her closest contact with Trax was over the sour, seething mash. When they walked together back of the house, down to the running branch, their bodies pushing side by side through the low palmettos, they were a unit. Except to curse her briefly when she was clumsy, he was good-natured at his work. Crouching by the fire burning under the copper drum, the slow dripping from the coils, of the distillate, the only sound except for small woods life, she felt themselves man and wife. At other times his lovely body and unlovely spirit both evaded her.

He was ready to sell his wares. He drove to the village and to neighboring towns and cities, inviting friends and acquaintances to have a drink from one of the gallon jugs under the rear seat of the borrowed car. They pronounced it good 'shine. To the favored few financially able to indulge themselves he gave a drink of the "aged" liquor. Accustomed to the water-clear, scalding rawness of fresh 'shine, they agreed gravely that no better whiskey ever came in from Cuba. He let it be known that both brands would be available at any time, day or night, at the old Terry house four miles south of the village. He made a profound impression. Most bootleggers sold stuff whose origin and maker were unknown. Most 'shiners had always made it, or drifted into it aimlessly. Trax brought a pomp and ceremony to the local business.

Men found their way out the deep-rutted road. They left their cars among the pines and stumbled through the hammock to the house. They gathered in the big room Trax had recognized as suitable for his purposes. The long trenchered table old man Terry had sliced from red bay, held the china pitcher of "corn" and the jelly glasses from which they drank. Their bird-dogs and hounds padded across the piazza and lay before the fire. Trax drank with them, keying their gatherings to hilarity. He was a convivial host. Sometimes Blaine brought along his guitar, and Trax clapped his hands and beat his feet on the floor as the old man picked the strings. But he was uneasy when a quarrel developed. Then he moved, white-faced among the men, urging someone else to stop it.

At first the woman tried to meet them hospitably. When, deep in the hammock at the still, she heard the vibration of a motor, she hurried up to the house to greet the guests. She smoothed back the gray hair from her worn face and presented her middle-aged bulk in a clean apron. If there was one man alone, Trax introduced her casually, insolently:

"This is my old woman."

When a group of men came together, he ignored her. She stood in the doorway, smiling vaguely. He continued his talk as though she were not there. Sometimes one of the group, embarrassed, acknowledged her presence.

"How do, ma'am."

For the most part they took their cue from Trax and did not see her. Once, on her withdrawal to the kitchen, a stranger had followed for a match.

"Don't you mind workin' way out here in the woods?"

But she decided that Trax was too delicate to want his wife mixing with men who came to drink. At night he sometimes invited her into the big room with conspicuous courtesy. That was when one or two women had come with the men. Her dignity established the place as one where they might safely come. She sat miserably in their midst while they made banal jokes and drank from the thick glasses. They were intruders. Their laughter was alien among the pine trees. She stayed at the still most of the time. The labor was heavy and exacting. The run must be made when the mash was ready, whether it was day or night. It was better for Trax to stay at the house to take care of the customers.

In the early fall he was ready to expand. Matt was alone, scrubbing the floors between runs of whiskey. She heard a powerful car throbbing down the dirt road. It blew a horn constantly in a minor key. Men usually came into this place silently. She went to the piazza, wet brush in hand. With the autumnal drying of foliage, the road was discernible. The scent of wild vanilla filled the flat-woods. She drew in the sweetness, craning her neck to see.

A large blue sedan of expensive make swerved and rounded into the tracks other cars had made to the house. Trax was driving. He swung past the twin live oaks and into the sandy yard. He slammed the door behind him as he stepped out. He had bought the car with the remainder of Matt's three thousand and most of the summer's profits. He was ready to flash across his old haunts, a big operator from the interior.

"I kin sell that hundred gallons of aged stuff now fer what it's worth."

He nodded wisely. He sauntered into the house, humming under his breath.

"Hi-diddy-um-tum—" He was vibrant with an expectancy in which she had no part.

She heard him curse because the floor was wet. The cat crossed his path. He lifted it by the tail and slid it along the slippery boards. The animal came to her on the piazza. She drew it into her lap and sat on her haunches a long time, stroking the smooth hard head.

Life was a bad dream. Trax was away a week at a time. He hired the two Lantry boys to take his place. Matt worked with them, for the boys unwatched would let the mash ferment too long. Trax returned to the flat-woods only for fresh supplies of liquor and of clean clothes. It pleased him to dress in blues that harmonized not too subtly with the blue sedan. He wore light-blue shirts and a red necktie that was a challenging fire under the dark insolent face. Matt spent hours each week washing and ironing the blue shirts. She protested his increasing absences.

"Trax, you jest ain't here at all. I hardly got the heart fer makin' the runs, an' you gone."

He smiled.

"Any time it don't suit you, I kin move my outfit to the east coast."

He laid the threat across her like a whip.

The young Lantrys too saw Trax glamorously. They talked of him to Matt as they mixed the mash, fired, and kept their vigils. This seemed all she had these days of the man: talk of him with the boys beside the still. She was frustrated, filled, not with resentment, but with despair. Yet she could not put her finger on the injustice. She flailed herself with his words, "Any time you don't like it, I kin move."

She waited on Trax' old customers as best she could, running up the slight incline from the still-site to the house when she heard a car. Her strong body was exhausted at the end of the week. Yet when she had finished her elaborate baking on Saturday night she built up a roaring fire in the front room, hung the hot water kettle close to it for his bath, and sat down to wait for him.

Sometimes she sat by the fire almost all night. Sometimes he did not come at all. Men learned they could get a drink at Colton's any hour of the night on Saturday. When the square dance at Trimtree's was done, they came out to the flat-woods at two or three o'clock in the morning. The woman was always awake. They stepped up on the piazza and saw her through the window. She sat brooding by the fire, the striped cat curled in her lap. Around her bony shoulders she hugged the corduroy hunting jacket Trax had worn when he came to her.

She existed for the Saturday nights when the throb of the blue sedan came close; the Sunday mornings when he slept late and arose, sulky, for a lavish breakfast and dinner. Then he was gone again, and she was waving after him down the road. She thought that her love and knowledge of him had been always nothing but this watching through the pine trees as he went away.

The village saw more of him. Occasionally he loitered there a day to show off before he headed for the coast. At times he returned in the middle of the week and picked up fifteen or twenty gallons cached at Blaine's and did not go out to the flat-woods at all. On these occasions he had invariably a girl or woman with him; cheap pretty things whose lightness brought them no more than their shoddy clothes. The storekeeper, delivering meal and sugar to Matt, lingered one day. The still needed her, but she could not with courtesy dismiss him. At last he drew courage.

"Mis' Matt, dogged if I don't hate to complain on Trax to you, but folks thinks you don't know how he's a-doin' you. You're workin' like a dog, an' he ain't never home."

"I know."

"You work at 'shinin', somethin' you nor your folks never done—not that it ain't all right— An' Trax off in that big fine car spendin' the money fast as he turns it over."

"I know."

"The Klan talks some o' givin' him down the country fer it."

" 'Tain't nobody's business but his an' mine."

"Mis' Matt"—he scuffled in the sand—"I promised I'd speak of it. D'you know Trax has got him women goin' round with him?"

"No. I didn't know that."

"Ev'ybody figgered you didn't know that." He mopped his forehead. "The day you an' Trax was married, I was fixin' to tell you 'twa'n't nothin' but your money an' place he wanted to git him set up."

"That's my business, too," she said stonily.

He dropped his eyes before the cold face and moved to his truck. She called after him defiantly:

"What else did I have he'd want anyway!"

She went into the house. She understood the quality of her betrayal. The injustice was clear. It was only this: Trax had taken what he had not wanted. If he had said, "Give me the money and for the time, the house," it would have been pleasant to give, solely because he wanted. This was the humiliation: that she had been thrown in on the deal, like an old mare traded in with a farm.

The Lantry boys called unanswered from the palmettos.

She had known. There was no need of pretense. There was no difference between to-day and yesterday. There was only the dissipation of a haze, as though a sheet had been lifted from a dead body, so that, instead of knowing, she saw.

* * *

The man came home late Saturday afternoon. Startled, Matt heard the purr of the motor and hurried to the house from the still. She thought the woman with him had come for liquor. She came to meet them, wiping her hands on her brown gingham apron. Trax walked ahead of his companion, carrying his own shiny patent leather bag and a smaller shabby one. As they came into the house, she saw that it was not a woman, but a girl.

The girl was close on his heels, like a dog. She was painted crudely, as with a haphazard conception of how it should be done. Stiff blond curls were bunched under a tilted hat. A flimsy silk dress hung loosely on an immature frame. Cheap silk stockings bagged on thin legs. She rocked, rather than walked, on incredibly spiked heels. Her shoes absorbed Matt's attention. They were pumps of blue kid, the precise blue of the sedan.

"I mean, things got hot fer me on the east coast." Trax was voluble. "Used that coastal highway oncet too often. First thing I knowed, down below New Smyrna, I seed a feller at a garage give the high sign, an' I'm lookin' into the end of a .45." He flushed. "I jest did git away. It'll pay me to work this territory a whiles, till they git where they don't pay me no mind over there agin."

The girl was watching Matt with solemn blue eyes. Beside the gray bulk of the older woman, she was like a small gaudy doll. Trax indicated her to Matt with his thumb.

"Elly here'll be stayin' at the house a while."

He picked up the shabby bag and started up the stairs.

"Long as you an' me is usin' the downstairs, Matt, she kin sleep upstairs in that back room got a bed in it."

She pushed past the girl and caught him by the sleeve.

"Trax! What's this gal?"

"Ain't no harm to her." He laughed comfortably. He tweaked a wisp of her gray hair.

"She's jest a little gal young un," he said blandly, " 's got no place to go." He drew the girl after him. The woman stared at the high-heeled blue slippers clicking on every step.

PART II

A warm winter rain thrummed on the roof. The light rush of water sank muffled into the moss that padded the shingles. The sharpest sound was a gurgling in the gutter over the rain-barrel. There had been no visible rising of the sun. Only the gray daylight had protracted itself, so that it was no longer dawn, but day. Matt sat close to the kitchen stove, her bulk shadowy in the dimness. Now and then she opened the door of the fire-box to push in a stick of pine, and the light of the flames flickered over her drawn face.

She could not tell how much of the night she had sat crouched by the range. She had lain long hours unsleeping, while Trax breathed regularly beside her. When the rain began, she left the bed and dressed by the fresh-kindled fire. The heat did not warm her. Her mouth was dry; yet every few minutes an uncontrollable chill shook her body. It would be easy to walk up the unused stairs, down the dusty hall to the back room with the rough pine bed in it, to open the door and look in, to see if anyone was there. Yet if she continued to sit by the fire, moving back the coffee pot when it boiled, surely Trax would come to the kitchen alone, and she would know that yesterday no woman had come home with him. Through the long days her distraught mind had been busy with imaginings. They might easily have materialized, for a moment, in a painted girl, small and very young, in blue kid slippers.

Trax was moving about. She put the frying pan on the stove, sliced bacon into it, stirred up cornmeal into a pone with soda and salt and water. Trax called someone. He came into the kitchen, warmed his hands at the stove. He poured water into the wash basin and soused his face in it. Matt set the coffee pot on the table. The girl pushed open the door a little way and came through. She came to the table uncertainly as though she expected to be ordered away. Matt did not speak.

Trax said, "How's my gal?"

The girl brought her wide eyes to him and took a few steps to his chair.

"Where your shoes, honey?"

She looked down at her stockinged feet.

"I gotta be keerful of 'em."

He laughed indulgently.

"You kin have more when them's gone. Matt, give the young un somethin' to eat."

The thought struck the woman like the warning whir of a rattler that if she looked at the girl in this moment she would be compelled to lift her in her hands and drop her like a scorpion on the hot stove. She thought, "I cain't do sich as that." She kept her back turned until the impulse passed and she could control her trembling. Her body was of metal and wood. It moved of itself, in jerks. A stiff wooden head creaked above a frame so heavy it seemed immovable. Her stomach weighed her down. Her ample breasts hurt her ribs, as though they were of lead. She thought, "I got to settle this now."

She said aloud slowly, "I'll not wait on her, nor no other woman."

The girl twisted one foot over the other.

She said, "I ain't hungry."

Trax stood up. His mouth was thin. He said to Matt, "You'll wait on her, old lady, or you'll git along without my comp'ny."

She thought, "I got to settle it. I got to say it."

But she could not speak.

The girl repeated eagerly, "I ain't a bit hungry."

Trax picked up a plate from the table. He held it out to his wife.

She thought, "Anyway, cornbread an' bacon's got nothin' to do with it."

She dished out meat and bread. Trax held out a cup. She filled it with coffee. The man sat down complacently. The girl sat beside him and pecked at the food. Her eyes were lowered. Between mouthfuls, she twisted her fingers in her lap or leaned over to inspect her unshod feet.

Matt thought, "Remindin' me."

The paint had been rubbed from the round face. The hair was yellow, like allamanda blooms. The artificial curls that had protruded from the pert hat had flattened out during the damp night, and hung in loose waves on the slim neck. She wore the blue silk dress in which she had arrived.

Trax said, "You eat up good, Elly. May be night 'fore we git back to eat agin." He turned to Matt. "Lantry boys been doin' all right?"

"They been doin' all right. Them's good boys. I heerd 'em come in a hour back. But they needs watchin' right on. They'll let the mash go too long, spite of everything, if I ain't right on top of 'em."

She hardened herself.

"You jest as good to stay home an' do the work yourself. I ain't goin' near the outfit."

"They kin make out by theirselves," he said easily.

He rose from the table, picking his teeth.

"Come on, Elly."

The girl turned her large eyes to the older woman, as though she were the logical recipient of her confession.

"I forgot to wash my hands an' face," she said.

Trax spoke curtly.

"Well, do it now, an' be quick."

He poured warm water in the basin for her and stood behind her, waiting. She washed slowly, with neat, small motions, like a cat. Trax handed her the clean end of the towel. They went upstairs together. Trax' voice was low and muffled. It dripped through the ceiling like thick syrup. Suddenly Matt heard the girl laugh.

She thought, "I figgered all thet owl-face didn't let on no more'n she meant it to."

In a few minutes they came down again. Trax called from the front room.

"Best to cook dinner to-night, Matt. We're like not to git back at noon."

They ran from the porch through the rain.

She walked after them. She was in time to see them step in the blue sedan. The high-heeled slippers flickered across the running-board. The car roared through the live oaks, down the tracks among the pines. Matt closed her eyes against the sight of it.

She thought, "Maybe she takened her satchel an' I jest didn't see it. Maybe she ain't comin' back."

She forced herself to go to the upstairs bedroom. The drumming on the roof sounded close and louder. The bed was awkwardly made. The shabby handbag stood open in a hickory rocker, exposing its sparse contents. A sound startled her. The cat had followed, and was sniffing the unfamiliar garments in the chair. The woman gathered the animal in her arms. They were alone together in the house, desolate and lonely in the rain-drenched flat-woods.

She thought of the Lantry boys under the palmettos. They were careless when they were cold and wet. They might not put the last five hundred pounds of sugar under cover. Shivering in the drizzle, they might use muddy water from the bank of the branch, instead of going a few yards upstream where it ran deep and clear. She threw Trax' corduroy jacket about her and went down the incline behind the house to oversee the work.

She had decided not to cook anything for the evening. But when the mist lifted in late afternoon, and the sun struck slantwise through the wet dark trees, she left the Lantry boys to finish and went to the house. She fried ham and baked soda biscuits and sweet potatoes. The meal was ready and waiting and she stirred up a quick ginger cake and put it in the oven.

She said aloud, desperately, "Might be he'll be back alone."

Yet when the dark gathered the bare house into its loneliness, as she had gathered the cat, and she lighted kerosene lamps in the long front room and a fire, the man and girl came together as she had known they would. Where she had felt only despair, suddenly she was able to hate. She picked up her anger like a stone and hurled it after the blue heels.

"Go eat your dinner."

She spoke to them as she would to negro field hands. Trax stared at her. He herded Elly nervously ahead of him, as though to protect her from an obscure violence. Matt watched them, standing solidly on big feet. She had not been whole. She had charred herself against the man's youth and beauty. Her hate was healthful. It waked her from a drugged sleep, and she stirred faculties hurt and long unused.

She sat by the clay fireplace in the front room while the pair ate. They spoke in whispers, shot through by the sudden laugh of the girl. It was a single high sound, like the one note of the thrush. Hearing it, Matt twisted her mouth. When the casual clatter of plates subsided, she went to the kitchen and began scraping the dishes to wash them. Trax sat warily in his place. The girl made an effort to hand Matt odds and ends from the table. The woman ignored her.

Trax said to Elly, "Le's go by the fire."

Matt cleaned up the kitchen and fed the cat. She stroked its arching back as it chewed sideways on scraps of meat and potato. She took off her apron, listened at the open door for sounds from the Lantrys, bolted the door, and walked to the front room to sit stiff and defiant by the blazing pine fire. The girl sat with thin legs tucked under her chair. She looked from the man to the woman and back again. Trax stretched and yawned.

He said, "Guess I'll go down back an' give the boys a hand. I ain't any too sure they run one batch soon enough. I got to keep up my stuff. I got high-class trade. Ain't I, Elly?" He touched her face with his finger as he passed her.

The woman and the girl sat silently after his going. The cat padded in and sat between them.

The girl called timidly. "Kitty!"

Matt turned savagely.

"Keep your hands off him."

The girl laced her fingers and studied the animal.

"Do he scratch?"

Matt did not answer. She loosened her gray hair and combed it by the fire with a side-comb, plaiting it into two thin braids over her shoulders. Inside the childish hairdressing her face was bony and haggard. She went into the adjoining bedroom, undressed and got into bed. She lay reared up on one elbow, straining for every sound. The fire popped and crackled. Once the juice oozed from a pine log faster than it could burn. It made a sizzling, like boiling fat. A chair scraped and Elly went up to the back bedroom. Her high heels clicked overhead. Matt thought with satisfaction that the girl had no light. She was floundering around in the dark in the unfamiliar house.

In a little while the front door opened and closed softly. Matt heard Trax creak cautiously up the stairs to the back room.

★ ★ ★

Trax was sleeping away the bright March morning. Matt made no effort to be silent about her washing. She dipped noisily into the rain barrel. When the soft water was gone she drew from the well, rattling galvanized buckets. Elly sat on the bottom step of the rear stoop, scuffling her bare toes in the sand. She wore the blue silk dress. Beside her was a handful of her own garments in need of washing, a pair of silk stockings and two or three pieces of underwear. Matt passed in front of her to go to the clothes line.

Elly said, "Trax give me this dress."

The woman did not seem to hear her.

Elly continued. "Reckon it'll wash? It's spotted."

Matt did not answer. She hung flour-sacking towels on the line. The girl picked up her small pile, looked uncertainly at the tub of soapsuds, laid down the clothes. She went to the tub and began rubbing on the first garment she drew from the suds. It was one of Matt's gingham aprons. She rubbed with energy, and Matt towered over her before she noticed that the woman had left the line.

"Take your dirty hands out o' my tub."

The girl drew back, dripping suds from her thin arms. She turned her hands back and forth.

"They ain't dirty," she protested.

Matt laughed shortly. "Mighty simple, ain't you?"

An obscure doubt brushed her, like a dove that wavers to a perch and is gone again without lighting.

"Who do you figger I am?"

The girl faced her across the wash-tub. She said gravely, "The lady lives in Trax' house."

"Trax' house? Well, he lives in mine. Never heerd tell o' no sich thing as his wife, eh?"

The girl hesitated. "Trax jest said the old woman."

Matt breathed heavily. The girl took her silence and her questions for a mark of interest.

"Trax said you'd romp on me," she offered confidentially, "but you ain't." She wrapped one bare leg around the other. "I been romped on," she went on brightly. "Pa romped on me reg'lar."

"You got you folks then!"

"Yessum, but I don't know where he is. He run a blacksmith shop an' garage offen the hard road, but he closed up an' goed to Georgia with a lady. Then I lived with another lady down the road a piece. Trax sold her liquor, that's how come him to know me. She moved off, an' he takened me with him from there. Now I'm gonna live with him," she finished, adding with studied tact "—and you."

Trax came yawning to the rear stoop in time to see Matt walk toward the girl. Elly stared uncomprehending. He jumped to the sand and caught the woman's muscular arms from behind.

"Don't you touch her." He cracked his familiar whip over her. "You hurt that gal young un an' you've seed the last o' me."

The woman shook free from him in the strength of her rage.

"You git out o' here before I hurts her an' you, too. You take yer gal young un an' git."

He adjusted his mind slowly. Inconceivably, he had gone too far. Bringing the girl to the flat-woods had been dangerously brazen. It was done now. He understood that his hold on this place had become suddenly precarious. He had the car and he could move the still. Yet the lay-out suited his needs too exactly to be relinquished. He could not give it up. If the gray-headed woman was done with her infatuation, he was in trouble.

He said boldly, "I got no idee o' goin'. Me an' Elly'll be here right on."

She said, "I kin break ary one o' you in two with my hands."

"Not me, you cain't. Leave me tell you, ol' woman, I'm too quick fer you. An' if you hurt Elly"—his dark face nodded at her—"if you crack down on her—with them big hands o' yourn—if you got any notion o' knifin' "—he paused for emphasis—"I'll git you sent to the chair, or up fer life—an' I'll be here in these flat-woods—in this house—right on."

He pushed the girl ahead of him and walked into the house, lighting a cigarette. He said over his shoulder, thickly between puffs, "An' that'd suit me jest fine."

She turned blindly to the wash-tub. She soaped the blue shirts without seeing them, rubbing them up and down automatically. Her life that had run like the flat-woods road, straight and untraveled, was now a maze, doubling back on itself darkly, twisted with confusion. The man stood with his neat trap at the end of every path; the girl with her yellow hair and big eyes, at the beginning.

She thought, "I got to settle it."

⋆ ⋆ ⋆

Trax and Elly came and went like a pair of bright birds. The blue kid slippers, scuffed by the sand, flashed in and out of the old house. Matt watched the comings and goings heavily, standing solidly on the hand-hewn pine-board floors.

She did not go near the still. Her absence did not make the difference she had imagined. The Lantrys had the work well in hand. Trax paid their wages, and their product was satisfactory. Often she did not hear them come to their work through the pines and past the hammock. A northwest wind sometimes brought the scent of the mash to her nose. The storekeeper brought in sugar and meal by a lower trail, and she seldom saw him. Trax was selling all his liquor at a high urban price, and local patronage dwindled away. The woods were quiet day and night.

Then Trax and Elly were back again, talking of hotels and highways, of new business, the talk pierced through now and again by the girl's single-noted laughter. She eyed Matt gravely, but the woman felt that the girl, oddly, had no fear. Trax was insolent, as always, his eyes narrow and his ways wary. Matt cut down on the table. She cooked scarcely enough for the three to eat. Elly ate with her catlike slowness, taking twice as long at her meager plate as the others. Matt took to rising and clearing the table as soon as she and Trax had finished. She picked up the plates casually, as though unaware that the third one still showed half its food uneaten. Trax did not seem to notice. The girl sometimes looked hungrily after the vanishing portion. She made no protest. Once Matt found her in the kitchen between meals, eating cold cornbread. Trax backed her up in her curt order to Elly to keep out.

It enraged Matt to see Elly feed the cat. Elly saved bits from her sparse helpings and held them under the table when she thought herself unobserved. Occasionally when the girl held the animal in her lap, and Matt ignored it, Trax stroked him too, because it was

Elly who held him. Matt knew they sometimes had food in Elly's room at night. She began to hear a soft padding up the stairs and on the bare floor overhead, and knew the cat went up to join them. In the morning he was smug, washing his whiskers enigmatically. His desertion was intolerable. She shut him out at night. He wailed for hours at the door, accustomed to sleeping snugly inside the house.

* * *

Suddenly Trax was not taking Elly with him any more. The village had become accustomed to the grave childish face beside him when it disappeared. Casually he left her behind with Matt in the flat-woods. He drove away one morning and did not come back that night or the next.

Matt took it for a taunt. It seemed to her that he was daring her to trap herself. Elly watched the road anxiously the first day. She accepted, hours before Matt, his solitary departure. At their first breakfast alone together, she said hesitantly:

"I had a idee Trax was fixin' to go off alone."

Matt thought, "The fool don't know enough to keep quiet about it."

After the second day, Elly devoted herself to exploring outside the house. Trax had kept her close to him, and the hammock had been only a cluster of shrubs and great trees through which they came and went. The Spanish moss was hazed with green by the early spring, and she discovered that the gray strands were alive with infinitesimal rosy blossoms. Matt saw her sitting at the far edge of the hammock, pulling the stuff apart.

The woman thought, "She better git herself out o' my sight."

Elly roamed through the pines as far as the road, staring up and down its silent winding, then scampered back toward the house like an alarmed squirrel. She walked stealthily to the palmettos where the Lantrys worked the still, and watched them for hours, unseen. Except when Matt stared directly at her, her round-eyed gravity lifted into a certain lightness, as though she felt newly free to move about in the sunlight. She seemed content.

On a rainy afternoon Matt, ironing in the kitchen, heard a steady snipping from the front room. She stole to the door and peered through a crack. Elly was cutting pictures from an old magazine and making an arrangement of rooms and figures of men and women and children. She was talking to herself and occasionally to them. The cat was curled in her lap, shifting lazily as she moved forward or back.

Their meals together were silent. Matt became aware at dinner one day that the pink oleanders in a jelly glass were not of her picking and placing. She had always a spray of flowers or greenery on the table. Because Elly had brought in the blooms, she snatched them from the water and stuffed them in the stove.

She allowed the girl a minimum of food. Once when she took away the plates before Elly had fairly begun, the girl reached after her desperately and said "Matt!" Again, when Matt moved from the table, leaving a plate of biscuits behind, Elly pounced on the largest and crammed it into her mouth. She began to laugh, poking in the crumbs.

She said, "You ain't romped on me yet."

Matt decided that Trax had put Elly up to goading her. She spoke for the first time in days.

"Don't you let Trax put no notions in yore head. I got no idee o' rompin' on you. That ain't what I'm fixin' to do."

For the most part, the girl was uncomplaining and strangely satisfied. The immature body, however, was becoming rapidly emaciated.

Trax was gone two weeks. He came in for an afternoon and loaded up with twenty gallon-jugs concealed under the large rear seat, and went hurriedly away. He called to the two women who stood watching on the piazza.

"Got a order."

Matt nodded grimly after him. She thought, "You got you one more chance, too, if you on'y knowed it." She turned to observe the girl beside her. There was apparent on the young face a faint wistfulness and no surprise. Matt thought, "She's got her orders jest to set tight."

Trax came home for the following week-end. He slept most of the time and was sulky. He paid no more attention to Elly than to the older woman. At no time in the two days or nights did he go to the upstairs room. When he was about, Elly followed him a few steps. Then, as he continued to ignore her, she dropped behind and took up her own simple affairs. Matt told herself that if he left this time without the girl, she was ready. On Monday morning, after loading, he went alone to the car.

She said carelessly, "I might take a notion to go some'eres or do somethin'. When you comin' back this time?"

He laughed insolently. "Steppin' out, Matt?" He was sure of himself. He was too quick for her. Whatever futilities she was planning, it would surprise her most to return on the day he named.

"Be back Sat'day."

He drove off smiling.

Matt was nervous all week. On Saturday morning she surprised the Lantry boys by appearing at the still. They had come and gone without contact with her for some weeks.

She said, "Boys, I jest got word the Pro-hi's is comin' lookin' fer Trax' outfit. Now I ain't quick as you-all, an' I want each one o' you should go down the road a good piece an' stay there all day, watchin', one to the north an' 'tother to the south. I'll tend the outfit, an' if I hears a whistle I'll know what it means an' it'll give me time to smash the jugs an' git to the house."

The boys were in instant alarm.

"Must be somebody's turned Trax up," they said.

Matt said, "Mighty likely. Somebody's likely got it in fer him. Trax hisself done tole me a long ways back, if anybody had it in fer a man, that was the way they'd git at him."

They nodded in agreement.

"That's about it, Mis' Matt. Git him tore up an' git at him that-a-way."

They hid several demijohns in near-by cover and hurried anxiously the two ways of the road. They reported later in the village that they heard no sound for an hour or so. Toward noon their straining ears caught the crash of an axe on metal. There was the high thin splintering of glass. The isolated crashes settled into a steady shattering of wood and iron and copper. A column of smoke began to rise from the vicinity of the still. The Lantry to the south skirted the road through the pines and joined his brother. They cut through the woods to the village and announced that the Pro-hi's had come in from the west and were tearing up Colton's outfit. The word went out to avoid the flat-woods road.

The Lantrys were waiting for Trax when he came through in late afternoon. They flagged him down. They drove with him as far as their own place, telling him what they knew.

"When we lit out we could hear 'em maulin' on the barrels an' purely see the smoke. Things is tore up an' burnt up all right."

They conjectured who, of his numerous enemies, might have betrayed him. He drove at a spring-breaking clip over the root-filled ruts of the sand road. His face was black and frightened. When he let the boys out of the car he had said nothing about the week's wages. They looked at each other.

One said, "How 'bout us gittin' ten dollars, anyway, Trax?"

"That's it. I ain't got it. I on'y got five myself. I was fixin' to turn over this lot quick."

"We hid out 'bout twenty gallons, if they ain't found it," they informed him eagerly. He listened tensely to a description of the location and was gone.

He drove into the yard and stopped the car in gear with a jerk. No one was in sight. He ran back of the house to the palmettos. A ring of fire had blackened palms and oaks and myrtle for a hundred feet around. A smoldering pile of bricks and barrel hoops and twisted metal in the center marked the site of the still. He began a frenzied search for the hidden jugs.

Matt peered from a window in the front room. She ordered Elly upstairs.

"You stay there till I tell you different."

The woman hurried into the yard with a jug of kerosene and a handful of papers. The sedan was twenty-five feet from the house, but the direction of the wind was safe. She soaked the hood and seats of the car with oil and piled papers on the floor. She tied a bundle of oil-soaked paper on the end of her longest clothes prop; touched a match to it. She lowered the pole to the machine. The oil caught fire. When the blaze reached the gas tank, the explosion disintegrated an already charring mass.

Trax heard the muffled roar up the incline behind him. The demijohns were where the Lantry boys had indicated. They were broken. He left the stench of over-turned mash and spilled alcohol and ran to the house. He could not for a moment comprehend that the twisting mass of metal and flame was the blue sedan.

Matt stood on the rear stoop. He looked at her in bewilderment. His stare dropped from her straggling gray hair down the length of her frame. Her apron was smudged and torn. Her hands were black and raw. He came back to her implacable cold eyes. He choked.

"You done it yourself!"

He burst into spasmodic curses, then broke off, overcome by their futility. The sweat ran into his eyes. He wiped it out and gaped about him in loose-mouthed confusion. He shuffled a few feet to the stoop and sank down on the bottom step. The woman looked down at him.

"Better git goin'."

He rose, swaying.

"You ol' . . ."

His obscenities fell away from her as rain washed from the weathered shingles of the old house. She towered over him. The tall house towered over him. He was as alien as on the bright day when he had first come hunting here.

He plunged up the steps toward her, his head low between his shoulders.

"Better git back."

His outstretched fists dropped at his sides. The fingers fell open. The woman lifted the shotgun.

"Better git—"

He shook his head, unbelieving. His eyes clung to the dark cavities of the pitted steel. He moved one foot slowly to the next step.

The woman aimed carefully at the shoe, as though it were some strange reptile creeping into the house. She fired a trifle to the left, so that the pattern of the double-ought buckshot shell sprayed in a close mass into the sand. One pellet clipped through the leather, and a drop of blood sank placidly into the pine step. The man stared fascinated. His hand jerked to his mouth, like a wooden toy moved by strings. He stifled a sound, or tried to make one. The woman could not tell. He lifted a face dry with fear and backed down the steps.

It was necessary to walk widely to the side to avoid the heat of the burned car. He threw out his hands hopelessly and hesitated. The sun slanted orange and gold through the hammock. Beyond, there were already shadows among the dark pines. It would be twilight before he could be out of the flat-woods. He found voice.

"Matt," he whined, "how'll I git to town?"

The woman wiped her streaked face with a corner of her apron.

"Reckon you'll have to git there on foot, Mister—the way you come in the first place."

She turned her back and went into the house. The girl had come down the stairs and was flattened against a wall. Her face was brushed with a desperate knowledge. Matt jerked her head at the open front door.

"All right. I'm thu. You kin go on with him now."

"Matt—"

"Go on. Git."

The girl did not move. Matt pushed her headlong to the door. Elly took hold of the big arm with both hands, drawing back, and Matt struck her away. She went confusedly down the steps. Trax was leaving the hammock. He struck wildly through the pines. The girl took a few steps after him, then turned toward the woman watching from the doorway. Matt called loudly:

"Go on. Git."

The man had reached the road and was plunging along it to the north. The girl ran three or four paces in his direction, then stopped again, like a stray dog or cat that would not be driven away. She hesitated at the edge of the hammock. The small uncertain figure was visible between the twin oaks beyond the high porch. Matt turned into the house and closed the door.

She was strong and whole. She was fixed, deep-rooted as the pine trees. They leaned a little, bent by an ancient storm. Nothing more could move them.

The car in the yard had settled into a smoking heap. The acrid smell of burned rubber and paint filled the house. Matt closed the north window to keep out the stench. The glass rattled in its frame. The air was gusty and the spring night would be cold. There were swift movements and rattlings among the oak boughs above the roof, as though small creatures were pattering across the floor of the wind.

Matt shivered and kindled a fire in the front room. She looked about for the cat. The noise and disorder of the day had driven him to distant hunting grounds and he had not yet ventured to return. She drew close to the fire in her rocker and held her smudged hands to the blaze.

She thought, "I've lit a bait o' fires to-day."

That was over and done with. There would be no more 'shining among the palmettos; no more coming and going of folk; no more Trax and his owl-faced girl. She was very tired. Her square frame relaxed in its exhaustion. She leaned back her head and drowsed deeply in her chair.

★ ★ ★

When she wakened, the fire had burned to ashes. The moon rode high over the flat-woods, with clouds scurrying underneath. The room was silver, then black, as the moonlight came and went. The chill wind sucked through the pines. There was another sound; the sobbing of a lighter breath. Suddenly Matt knew the girl was still there.

She rose in a plunge from the rocker. She wasn't done with them yet. . . . She opened the door a few inches and listened. The muffled sound was unmistakable. It was the choked gasping of a child that has cried itself breathless. It came from the edge of the hammock. Where the pines began she could distinguish a huddle on the ground that was neither stump nor bushes. She closed the door.

Trax was gone—and Elly was here.

He had flung away and left her behind. She was discarded, as Matt had been long discarded. He was through with Elly, too. For the first time the woman was able to conceive of them separately. And the one was gone, and the other was here. She groped her way stupefied to the kitchen, lighted a kerosene lamp, and made a fire in the range. She wanted a scalding pot of tea to stop her shivering. She split a cold biscuit and fried it and sat down with her plate and tea-cup. She breathed hard, and ate and drank mechanically.

"He was done with her a long ways back."

He had driven off alone in the blue sedan, not to infuriate, but because there was nothing else to do with the girl. Matt chewed her biscuit slowly. She laughed grimly.

"I give him too much credit fer smartness."

A flash of anger stirred her, like a spurt of flame from an old fire, that Elly should be now at the edge of the hammock.

"Trax wa'n't man enough to take off his mess with him."

She sipped her cooling tea.

She remembered grudgingly the girl's contentment. The shadow of the man, passing away, left clear the picture of a child, pulling moss apart and cutting paper dolls. Rage at Trax possessed her.

"I'd orter hided him fer takin' sech a young un along his low-down way."

In a burst of fury she conceded the girl's youth. Elly was too young . . .

"I'd orter been hided. Me an' Trax together."

Matt rose from the table and gathered up the few dishes. She stopped in the act. She looked at her hands as though their knotty strength were strange to her.

"Snatchin' off a young un's rations . . ."

She leaned heavily on the table, pondering. Emptiness filled the house—a living presence—appalling—still.

She strode abruptly out the door and through the hammock to the pines. The moon had swung toward its setting and the rays lay long under the trees. The girl lay crouched against a broad mottled trunk.

Matt said, "You kin come on back."

The emaciated figure wavered from the ground on spindling legs. It tried to crowd close to the warmth of the woman's body. As they moved toward the house, the girl stumbled in the run-over slippers.

Matt said, "Here. Gimme them crazy shoes."

Elly stooped and took them from her bare feet. The woman put them in her apron pockets. She went ahead of the girl into the front room and bent down to kindle a fire.

WHY I LIVE AT THE P.O.

by Eudora Welty

Eudora Welty was born, spent most of her life, and died in Jackson, Mississippi. Her first short story was published in 1936, when she was in her late twenties. "Why I Live at the P.O." was published in *The Atlantic Monthly* five years later; it's one of the seventeen stories in her collection entitled *A Curtain of Green and Other Stories* (1941), which also includes an introduction by Katherine Anne Porter.

I WAS GETTING along fine with Mama, Papa-Daddy and Uncle Rondo until my sister Stella-Rondo just separated from her husband and came back home again. Mr. Whitaker! Of course I went with Mr. Whitaker first, when he first appeared here in China Grove, taking "Pose Yourself" photos, and Stella-Rondo broke us up. Told him I was one-sided. Bigger on one side than the other, which is a deliberate, calculated falsehood: I'm the same. Stella-Rondo is exactly twelve months to the day younger than I am and for that reason she's spoiled.

She's always had anything in the world she wanted and then she'd throw it away. Papa-Daddy gave her this gorgeous Add-a-Pearl necklace when she was eight years old and she threw it away playing baseball when she was nine, with only two pearls.

So as soon as she got married and moved away from home the first thing she did was separate! From Mr. Whitaker! This photographer with the popeyes she said she trusted. Came home from one of those towns up in Illinois and to our complete surprise brought this child of two.

Mama said she like to made her drop dead for a second. "Here you had this marvelous blonde child and never so much as wrote your mother a word about it," says Mama. "I'm thoroughly ashamed of you." But of course she wasn't.

Stella-Rondo just calmly takes off this *hat*, I wish you could see it. She says, "Why, Mama, Shirley-T.'s adopted, I can prove it."

"How?" says Mama, but all I says was, "H'm!" There I was over the hot stove, trying to stretch two chickens over five people and a completely unexpected child into the bargain, without one moment's notice.

"What do you mean—'H'm!'?" says Stella-Rondo, and Mama says, "I heard that, Sister."

I said that oh, I didn't mean a thing, only that whoever Shirley-T. was, she was the spit-image of Papa-Daddy if he'd cut off his beard, which of course he'd never do in the world. Papa-Daddy's Mama's papa and sulks.

Stella-Rondo got furious! She said, "Sister, I don't need to tell you you got a lot of nerve and always did have and I'll thank you to make no future reference to my adopted child whatsoever."

"Very well," I said. "Very well, very well. Of course I noticed at once she looks like Mr. Whitaker's side too. That frown. She looks like a cross between Mr. Whitaker and Papa-Daddy."

"Well, all I can say is she isn't."

"She looks exactly like Shirley Temple to me," says Mama, but Shirley-T. just ran away from her.

So the first thing Stella-Rondo did at the table was turn Papa-Daddy against me.

"Papa-Daddy," she says. He was trying to cut up his meat. "Papa-Daddy!" I was taken completely by surprise. Papa-Daddy is about a million years old and's got this long-long beard. "Papa-Daddy, Sister says she fails to understand why you don't cut off your beard."

So Papa-Daddy l-a-y-s down his knife and fork! He's real rich. Mama says he is, he says he isn't. So he says, "Have I heard correctly? You don't understand why I don't cut off my beard?"

"Why," I says, "Papa-Daddy, of course I understand, I did not say any such of a thing, the idea!"

He says, "Hussy!"

I says, "Papa-Daddy, you know I wouldn't any more want you to cut off your beard than the man in the moon. It was the farthest thing from my mind! Stella-Rondo sat there and made that up while she was eating breast of chicken."

But he says, "So the postmistress fails to understand why I don't cut off my beard. Which job I got you through my influence with the government. 'Bird's nest'—is that what you call it?"

Not that it isn't the next to smallest P.O. in the entire state of Mississippi.

I says, "Oh, Papa-Daddy," I says, "I didn't say any such of a thing, I never dreamed it was a bird's nest, I have always been grateful though this is the next to smallest P.O. in the state of Mississippi, and I do not enjoy being referred to as a hussy by my own grandfather."

But Stella-Rondo says, "Yes, you did say it too. Anybody in the world could of heard you, that had ears."

"Stop right there," says Mama, looking at *me*.

So I pulled my napkin straight back through the napkin ring and left the table.

As soon as I was out of the room Mama says, "Call her back, or she'll starve to death," but Papa-Daddy says, "This is the beard I started growing on the Coast when I was fifteen years old." He would of gone on till nightfall if Shirley-T. hadn't lost the Milky Way she ate in Cairo.

So Papa-Daddy says, "I am going out and lie in the hammock, and you can all sit here and remember my words: I'll never cut off my beard as long as I live, even one inch, and I don't appreciate it in you at all." Passed right by me in the hall and went straight out and got in the hammock.

It would be a holiday. It wasn't five minutes before Uncle Rondo suddenly appeared in the hall in one of Stella-Rondo's flesh-colored kimonos, all cut on the bias, like something Mr. Whitaker probably thought was gorgeous.

"Uncle Rondo!" I says. "I didn't know who that was! Where are you going?"

"Sister," he says, "get out of my way, I'm poisoned."

"If you're poisoned stay away from Papa-Daddy," I says. "Keep out of the hammock. Papa-Daddy will certainly beat you on the head if you come within forty miles of him. He thinks I deliberately said he ought to cut off his beard after he got me the P.O., and I've told him and told him and told him, and he acts like he just don't hear me. Papa-Daddy must of gone stone deaf."

"He picked a fine day to do it then," says Uncle Rondo, and before you could say "Jack Robinson" flew out in the yard.

What he'd really done, he'd drunk another bottle of that prescription. He does it every single Fourth of July as sure as shooting, and it's horribly expensive. Then he falls over in the hammock and snores. So he insisted on zigzagging right on out to the hammock, looking like a half-wit.

Papa-Daddy woke up with this horrible yell and right there without moving an inch he tried to turn Uncle Rondo against me. I heard every word he said. Oh, he told Uncle Rondo I didn't learn to read till I was eight years old and he didn't see how in the world I ever got the mail put up at the P.O., much less read it all, and he said if Uncle Rondo could only fathom the lengths he had gone to to get me that job! And he said on the other hand he thought Stella-Rondo had a brilliant mind and deserved credit for getting out of town. All the time he was just lying there swinging as pretty as you please and looping out his beard, and poor Uncle Rondo was *pleading* with him to slow down the hammock, it was making him as dizzy as a witch to watch it. But that's what Papa-Daddy likes about a hammock. So Uncle Rondo was too dizzy to get turned against me for the time being. He's Mama's only brother and is a good case of a one-track mind. Ask anybody. A certified pharmacist.

Just then I heard Stella-Rondo raising the upstairs window. While she was married she got this peculiar idea that it's cooler with the windows shut and locked. So she has to raise the window before she can make a soul hear her outdoors.

So she raises the window and says, "*Oh!*" You would have thought she was mortally wounded.

Uncle Rondo and Papa-Daddy didn't even look up, but kept right on with what they were doing. I had to laugh.

I flew up the stairs and threw the door open! I says, "What in the wide world's the matter, Stella-Rondo? You mortally wounded?"

"No," she says, "I am not mortally wounded but I wish you would do me the favor of looking out that window there and telling me what you see."

So I shade my eyes and look out the window.

"I see the front yard," I says.

"Don't you see any human beings?" she says.

"I see Uncle Rondo trying to run Papa-Daddy out of the hammock," I says. "Nothing more. Naturally, it's so suffocating-hot in the house, with all the windows shut and locked, everybody who cares to stay in their right mind will have to go out and get in the hammock before the Fourth of July is over."

"Don't you notice anything different about Uncle Rondo?" asks Stella-Rondo.

"Why, no, except he's got on some terrible-looking flesh-colored contraption I wouldn't be found dead in, is all I can see," I says.

"Never mind, you won't be found dead in it, because it happens to be part of my trousseau, and Mr. Whitaker took several dozen photographs of me in it," says Stella-Rondo. "What on earth could Uncle Rondo *mean* by wearing part of my trousseau out in the broad open daylight without saying so much as 'Kiss my foot,' *knowing* I only got home this morning after my separation and hung my negligee up on the bathroom door, just as nervous as I could be?"

"I'm sure I don't know, and what do you expect me to do about it?" I says. "Jump out the window?"

"No, I expect nothing of the kind. I simply declare that Uncle Rondo looks like a fool in it, that's all," she says. "It makes me sick to my stomach."

"Well, he looks as good as he can," I says. "As good as anybody in reason could." I stood up for Uncle Rondo, please remember. And I said to Stella-Rondo, "I think I would do well not to criticize so freely if I were you and came home with a two-year-old child I had never said a word about, and no explanation whatever about my separation."

"I asked you the instant I entered this house not to refer one more time to my adopted child, and you gave me your word of honor you would not," was all Stella-Rondo would say, and started pulling out every one of her eyebrows with some cheap Kress tweezers.

So I merely slammed the door behind me and went down and made some green-tomato pickle. Somebody had to do it. Of course Mama had turned both the niggers loose; she always said no earthly power could hold one anyway on the Fourth of July, so she wouldn't even try. It turned out that Jaypan fell in the lake and came within a very narrow limit of drowning.

So Mama trots in. Lifts up the lid and says, "H'm! Not very good for your Uncle Rondo in his precarious condition, I must say. Or poor little adopted Shirley-T. Shame on you!"

That made me tired. I says, "Well, Stella-Rondo had better thank her lucky stars it was her instead of me came trotting in with that very peculiar-looking child. Now if it had been me that trotted in from Illinois and brought a peculiar-looking child of two, I shudder to think of the reception I'd of got, much less controlled the diet of an entire family."

"But you must remember, Sister, that you were never married to Mr. Whitaker in the first place and didn't go up to Illinois to live," says Mama, shaking a spoon in my face. "If you had I would of been just as overjoyed to see you and your little adopted girl as I was to see Stella-Rondo, when you wound up with your separation and came on back home."

"You would not," I says.

"Don't contradict me, I would," says Mama.

But I said she couldn't convince me though she talked till she was blue in the face. Then I said, "Besides, you know as well as I do that that child is not adopted."

"She most certainly is adopted," says Mama, stiff as a poker.

I says, "Why, Mama, Stella-Rondo had her just as sure as anything in this world, and just too stuck up to admit it."

"Why, Sister," said Mama. "Here I thought we were going to have a pleasant Fourth of July, and you start right out not believing a word your own baby sister tells you!"

"Just like Cousin Annie Flo. Went to her grave denying the facts of life," I remind Mama.

"I told you if you ever mentioned Annie Flo's name I'd slap your face," says Mama, and slaps my face.

"All right, you wait and see," I says.

"I," says Mama, "*I* prefer to take my children's word for anything when it's humanly possible." You ought to see Mama, she weighs two hundred pounds and has real tiny feet.

Just then something perfectly horrible occurred to me.

"Mama," I says, "can that child talk?" I simply had to whisper! "Mama, I wonder if that child can be—you know—in any way? Do you realize," I says, "that she hasn't spoken one single, solitary word to a human being up to this minute? This is the way she looks," I says, and I looked like this.

Well, Mama and I just stood there and stared at each other. It was horrible!

"I remember well that Joe Whitaker frequently drank like a fish," says Mama. "I believed to my soul he drank *chemicals*." And without another word she marches to the foot of the stairs and calls Stella-Rondo.

"Stella-Rondo? O-o-o-o-o! Stella-Rondo!"

"What?" says Stella-Rondo from upstairs. Not even the grace to get up off the bed.

"Can that child of yours talk?" asks Mama.

Stella-Rondo says, "Can she what?"

"Talk! Talk!" says Mama. "Burdyburdyburdyburdy!"

So Stella-Rondo yells back, "Who says she can't talk?"

"Sister says so," says Mama.

"You didn't have to tell me, I know whose word of honor don't mean a thing in this house," says Stella-Rondo.

And in a minute the loudest Yankee voice I ever heard in my life yells out, "OE'm Pop-OE the Sailor-r-r-r Ma-a-an!" and then somebody jumps up and down in the upstairs hall. In another second the house would of fallen down.

"Not only talks, she can tap-dance!" calls Stella-Rondo. "Which is more than some people I won't name can do."

"Why, the little precious darling thing!" Mama says, so surprised. "Just as smart as she can be!" Starts talking baby talk right there. Then she turns on me. "Sister, you ought to be thoroughly ashamed! Run upstairs this instant and apologize to Stella-Rondo and Shirley-T."

"Apologize for what?" I says. "I merely wondered if the child was normal, that's all. Now that she's proved she is, why, I have nothing further to say."

But Mama just turned on her heel and flew out, furious. She ran right upstairs and hugged the baby. She believed it was adopted. Stella-Rondo hadn't done a thing but turn her against me from upstairs while I stood there helpless over the hot stove. So that made Mama, Papa-Daddy and the baby all on Stella-Rondo's side.

Next, Uncle Rondo.

I must say that Uncle Rondo has been marvelous to me at various times in the past and I was completely unprepared to be made to jump out of my skin, the way it turned out. Once Stella-Rondo did something perfectly horrible to him—broke a chain letter from Flanders Field—and he took the radio back he had given her and gave it to me. Stella-Rondo was furious! For six months we all had to call her Stella instead of Stella-Rondo, or she wouldn't answer. I always thought Uncle Rondo had all the brains of the entire family. Another time he sent me to Mammoth Cave, with all expenses paid.

But this would be the day he was drinking that prescription, the Fourth of July.

So at supper Stella-Rondo speaks up and says she thinks Uncle Rondo ought to try to eat a little something. So finally Uncle Rondo said he would try a little cold biscuits and ketchup, but that was all. So *she* brought it to him.

"Do you think it wise to disport with ketchup in Stella-Rondo's flesh-colored kimono?" I says. Trying to be considerate! If Stella-Rondo couldn't watch out for her trousseau, somebody had to.

"Any objections?" asks Uncle Rondo, just about to pour out all the ketchup.

"Don't mind what she says, Uncle Rondo," says Stella-Rondo. "Sister has been devoting this solid afternoon to sneering out my bedroom window at the way you look."

"What's that?" says Uncle Rondo. Uncle Rondo has got the most terrible temper in the world. Anything is liable to make him tear the house down if it comes at the wrong time.

So Stella-Rondo says, "Sister says, 'Uncle Rondo certainly does look like a fool in that pink kimono!' "

Do you remember who it was really said that?

Uncle Rondo spills out all the ketchup and jumps out of his chair and tears off the kimono and throws it down on the dirty floor and puts his foot on it. It had to be sent all the way to Jackson to the cleaners and re-pleated.

"So that's your opinion of your Uncle Rondo, is it?" he says. "I look like a fool, do I? Well, that's the last straw. A whole day in this house with nothing to do, and then to hear you come out with a remark like that behind my back!"

"I didn't say any such of a thing, Uncle Rondo," I says, "and I'm not saying who did, either. Why, I think you look all right. Just try to take care of yourself and not talk and eat at the same time," I says. "I think you better go lie down."

"Lie down my foot," says Uncle Rondo. I ought to of known by that he was fixing to do something perfectly horrible.

So he didn't do anything that night in the precarious state he was in—just played Casino with Mama and Stella-Rondo and Shirley-T. and gave Shirley-T. a nickel with a head on both sides. It tickled her nearly to death, and she called him "Papa." But at 6:30 A.M. the next morning, he threw a whole five-cent package of some unsold one-inch firecrackers from the store as hard as he could into my bedroom and they every one went off. Not one bad one in the string. Anybody else, there'd be one that wouldn't go off.

Well, I'm just terribly susceptible to noise of any kind, the doctor has always told me I was the most sensitive person he had ever seen in his whole life, and I was simply prostrated. I couldn't eat! People tell me they heard it as far as the cemetery, and old Aunt Jep Patterson, that had been holding her own so good, thought it was Judgment Day and she was going to meet her whole family. It's usually so quiet here.

And I'll tell you it didn't take me any longer than a minute to make up my mind what to do. There I was with the whole entire house on Stella-Rondo's side and turned against me. If I have anything at all I have pride.

So I just decided I'd go straight down to the P.O. There's plenty of room there in the back, I says to myself.

Well! I made no bones about letting the family catch on to what I was up to. I didn't try to conceal it.

The first thing they knew, I marched in where they were all playing Old Maid and pulled the electric oscillating fan out by the plug, and everything got real hot. Next I snatched the pillow I'd done the needlepoint on right off the davenport from behind Papa-Daddy. He went "Ugh!" I beat Stella-Rondo up the stairs and finally found my charm bracelet in her bureau drawer under a picture of Nelson Eddy.

"So that's the way the land lies," says Uncle Rondo. There he was, piecing on the ham. "Well, Sister, I'll be glad to donate my army cot if you got any place to set it up, providing you'll leave right this minute and let me get some peace." Uncle Rondo was in France.

"Thank you kindly for the cot and 'peace' is hardly the word I would select if I had to resort to firecrackers at 6:30 A.M. in a young girl's bedroom," I says back to him. "And as to where I intend to go, you seem to forget my position as postmistress of China Grove, Mississippi," I says. "I've always got the P.O."

Well, that made them all sit up and take notice.

I went out front and started digging up some four-o'clocks to plant around the P.O.

"Ah-ah-ah!" says Mama, raising the window. "Those happen to be my four-o'clocks. Everything planted in that star is mine. I've never known you to make anything grow in your life."

"Very well," I says. "But I take the fern. Even you, Mama, can't stand there and deny that I'm the one watered that fern. And I happen to know where I can send in a box top and get a packet of one thousand mixed seeds, no two the same kind, free."

"Oh, where?" Mama wants to know.

But I says, "Too late. You 'tend to your house, and I'll 'tend to mine. You hear things like that all the time if you know how to listen to the radio. Perfectly marvelous offers. Get anything you want free."

So I hope to tell you I marched in and got that radio, and they could of all bit a nail in two, especially Stella-Rondo, that it used to belong to, and she well knew she couldn't get it back, I'd sue for it like a shot. And I very politely took the sewing-machine motor I helped pay the most on to give Mama for Christmas back in 1929, and a good big calendar, with the first-aid remedies on it. The thermometer and the Hawaiian ukulele certainly were rightfully mine, and I stood on the step-ladder and got all my watermelon-rind preserves and every fruit and vegetable I'd put up, every jar. Then I began to pull the tacks out of the bluebird wall vases on the archway to the dining room.

"Who told you you could have those, Miss Priss?" says Mama, fanning as hard as she could.

"I bought 'em and I'll keep track of 'em," I says. "I'll tack 'em up one on each side the post-office window, and you can see 'em when you come to ask me for your mail, if you're so dead to see 'em."

"Not I! I'll never darken the door to that post office again if I live to be a hundred," Mama says. "Ungrateful child! After all the money we spent on you at the Normal."

"Me either," says Stella-Rondo. "You can just let my mail lie there and *rot*, for all I care. I'll never come and relieve you of a single, solitary piece."

"I should worry," I says. "And who you think's going to sit down and write you all those big fat letters and postcards, by the way? Mr. Whitaker? Just because he was the only man ever dropped down in China Grove and you got him—unfairly—is he going to sit down and write you a lengthy correspondence after you come home giving no rhyme nor reason whatsoever for your separation and no explanation for the presence of that child? I may not have your brilliant mind, but I fail to see it."

So Mama says, "Sister, I've told you a thousand times that Stella-Rondo simply got homesick, and this child is far too big to be hers," and she says, "Now, why don't you just sit down and play Casino?"

Then Shirley-T. sticks out her tongue at me in this perfectly horrible way. She has no more manners than the man in the moon.

I told her she was going to cross her eyes like that some day and they'd stick.

"It's too late to stop me now," I says. "You should have tried that yesterday. I'm going to the P.O. and the only way you can possibly see me is to visit me there."

So Papa-Daddy says, "You'll never catch me setting foot in that post office, even if I should take a notion into my head to write a letter some place." He says, "I won't have you reachin' out of that little old window with a pair of shears and cuttin' off any beard of mine. I'm too smart for you!"

"We all are," says Stella-Rondo.

But I said, "If you're so smart, where's Mr. Whitaker?"

So then Uncle Rondo says, "I'll thank you from now on to stop reading all the orders I get on postcards and telling everybody in China Grove what you think is the matter with them," but I says, "I draw my own conclusions and will continue in the future to draw them." I says, "If people want to write their inmost secrets on penny postcards, there's nothing in the wide world you can do about it, Uncle Rondo."

"And if you think we'll ever *write* another postcard you're sadly mistaken," says Mama.

"Cutting off your nose to spite your face then," I says. "But if you're all determined to have no more to do with the U.S. mail, think of this: What will Stella-Rondo do now, if she wants to tell Mr. Whitaker to come after her?"

"Wah!" says Stella-Rondo. I knew she'd cry. She had a conniption fit right there in the kitchen.

"It will be interesting to see how long she holds out," I says. "And now—I am leaving."

"Good-bye," says Uncle Rondo.

"Oh, I declare," says Mama, "to think that a family of mine should quarrel on the Fourth of July, or the day after, over Stella-Rondo leaving old Mr. Whitaker and having the sweetest little adopted child! It looks like we'd all be glad!"

"Wah!" says Stella-Rondo, and has a fresh conniption fit.

"*He* left *her*—you mark my words," I says. "That's Mr. Whitaker. I know Mr. Whitaker. After all, I knew him first. I said from the beginning he'd up and leave her. I foretold every single thing that's happened."

"Where did he go?" asks Mama.

"Probably to the North Pole, if he knows what's good for him," I says.

But Stella-Rondo just bawled and wouldn't say another word. She flew to her room and slammed the door.

"Now look what you've gone and done, Sister," says Mama. "You go apologize."

"I haven't got time, I'm leaving," I says.

"Well, what are you waiting around for?" asks Uncle Rondo.

So I just picked up the kitchen clock and marched off, without saying "Kiss my foot" or anything, and never did tell Stella-Rondo good-by.

There was a nigger girl going along on a little wagon right in front.

"Nigger girl," I says, "come help me haul these things down the hill, I'm going to live in the post office."

Took her nine trips in her express wagon. Uncle Rondo came out on the porch and threw her a nickel.

⋆ ⋆ ⋆

And that's the last I've laid eyes on any of my family or my family laid eyes on me for five solid days and nights. Stella-Rondo may be telling the most horrible tales in the world about Mr. Whitaker, but I haven't heard them. As I tell everybody, I draw my own conclusions.

But oh, I like it here. It's ideal, as I've been saying. You see, I've got everything cater-cornered, the way I like it. Hear the radio? All the war news. Radio, sewing machine, book ends, ironing board and that great big piano lamp—peace, that's what I like. Butter-bean vines planted all along the front where the strings are.

Of course, there's not much mail. My family are naturally the main people in China Grove, and if they prefer to vanish from the face of the earth, for all the mail they get or the mail they write, why, I'm not going to open my mouth. Some of the folks here in town are taking up for me and some turned against me. I know which is which. There are always people who will quit buying stamps just to get on the right side of Papa-Daddy.

But here I am, and here I'll stay. I want the world to know I'm happy.

And if Stella-Rondo should come to me this minute, on bended knees, and *attempt* to explain the incidents of her life with Mr. Whitaker, I'd simply put my fingers in both my ears and refuse to listen.

THE LIFE YOU SAVE MAY BE YOUR OWN

by Flannery O'Connor

(Mary) Flannery O'Connor's first short stories were published in 1946, when she was 21 years old and living in Milledgeville, Georgia. By the time she died eighteen years later of complications from lupus, she had published a total of about thirty short stories (two of which were O. Henry Memorial Award winners) and two novels. "The Life You Save May Be Your Own," first published in the *Kenyon Review* in 1953, was included in *A Good Man Is Hard to Find and Other Stories*, published in 1955.

THE OLD WOMAN and her daughter were sitting on their porch when Mr. Shiftlet came up their road for the first time. The old woman slid to the edge of her chair and leaned forward, shading her eyes from the piercing sunset with her hand. The daughter could not see far in front of her and continued to play with her fingers. Although the old woman lived in this desolate spot with only her daughter and she had never seen Mr. Shiftlet before, she could tell, even from a distance, that he was a tramp and no one to be afraid of. His left coat sleeve was folded up to show there was only half an arm in it and his gaunt figure listed slightly to the side as if the breeze were pushing him. He had on a black town suit and a brown felt hat that was turned up in the front and down in the back and he carried a tin tool box by a handle. He came on, at an amble, up her road, his face turned toward the sun which appeared to be balancing itself on the peak of a small mountain.

The old woman didn't change her position until he was almost into her yard; then she rose with one hand fisted on her hip. The daughter, a large girl in a short blue organdy dress, saw him all at once and jumped up and began to stamp and point and make excited speechless sounds.

Mr. Shiftlet stopped just inside the yard and set his box on the ground and tipped his hat at her as if she were not in the least afflicted; then he turned toward the old woman and swung the hat all the way off. He had long black slick hair that hung flat from a part in the middle to beyond the tips of his ears on either side. His face descended in forehead for more than half its length and ended suddenly with his features just balanced over a jutting steel-trap jaw. He seemed to be a young man but he had a look of composed dissatisfaction as if he understood life thoroughly.

"Good evening," the old woman said. She was about the size of a cedar fence post and she had a man's gray hat pulled down low over her head.

The tramp stood looking at her and didn't answer. He turned his back and faced the sunset. He swung both his whole and his short arm up slowly so that they indicated an expanse of sky and his figure formed a crooked cross. The old woman watched him with her arms folded across her chest as if she were the owner of the sun, and the daughter watched, her head thrust forward and her fat helpless hands hanging at the wrists. She had long pink-gold hair and eyes as blue as a peacock's neck.

He held the pose for almost fifty seconds and then he picked up his box and came on to the porch and dropped down on the bottom step. "Lady," he said in a firm nasal voice, "I'd give a fortune to live where I could see me a sun do that every evening."

"Does it every evening," the old woman said and sat back down. The daughter sat down too and watched him with a cautious sly look as if he were a bird that had come up very close. He leaned to one side, rooting in his pants pocket, and in a second he brought out a package of chewing gum and offered her a piece. She took it and unpeeled it and began to chew without taking her eyes off him. He offered the old woman a piece but she only raised her upper lip to indicate she had no teeth.

Mr. Shiftlet's pale sharp glance had already passed over everything in the yard—the pump near the comer of the house and the big fig tree that three or four chickens were preparing to roost in—and had moved to a shed where he saw the square rusted back of an automobile. "You ladies drive?" he asked.

"That car ain't run in fifteen year," the old woman said. "The day my husband died, it quit running."

"Nothing is like it used to be, lady," he said. "The world is almost rotten."

"That's right," the old woman said. "You from around here?"

"Name Tom T. Shiftlet," he murmured, looking at the tires.

"I'm pleased to meet you," the old woman said. "Name Lucynell Crater and daughter Lucynell Crater. What you doing around here, Mr. Shiftlet?"

He judged the car to be about a 1928 or '29 Ford. " 'Lady," he said, and turned and gave her his full attention, "lemme tell you something. There's one of these doctors in Atlanta that's taken a knife and cut the human heart—the human heart," he repeated, leaning forward, "out of a man's chest and held it in his hand," and he held his hand out, palm up, as if it were slightly weighted with the human heart, "and studied it like it was a day-old chicken, and lady," he said, allowing a long significant pause in which his head slid forward and his clay-colored eyes brightened, "he don't know no more about it than you or me."

"That's right," the old woman said.

"Why, if he was to take that knife and cut into every corner of it, he still wouldn't know no more than you or me. What you want to bet?"

"Nothing," the old woman said wisely. "Where you come from, Mr. Shiftlet?"

He didn't answer. He reached into his pocket and brought out a sack of tobacco and a package of cigarette papers and rolled himself a cigarette, expertly with one hand, and attached it in a hanging position to his upper lip. Then he took a box of wooden matches from his pocket and struck one on his shoe. He held the burning match as if he were studying the mystery of flame while it traveled dangerously toward his skin. The daughter began to make loud noises and to point to his hand and shake her finger at him, but when the flame was just before touching him, he leaned down with his hand cupped over it as if he were going to set fire to his nose and lit the cigarette.

He flipped away the dead match and blew a stream of gray into the evening. A sly look came over his face. "Lady," he said, "nowadays, people'll do anything anyways. I can tell you my name is Tom T. Shiftlet and I come from Tarwater, Tennessee, but you never have seen me before: how you know I ain't lying? How you know my name ain't Aaron Sparks, lady, and I come from Singleberry, Georgia, or how you know it's not George Speeds and I come from Lucy, Alabama, or how you know I ain't Thompson Bright from Toolafalls, Mississippi?"

"I don't know nothing about you," the old woman muttered, irked.

"Lady," he said, "people don't care how they lie. Maybe the best I can tell you is, I'm a man; but listen lady," he said and paused and made his tone more ominous still, "what is a man?"

The old woman began to gum a seed. "What you carry in that tin box, Mr. Shiftlet?" she asked.

"Tools," he said, put back. "I'm a carpenter."

"Well, if you come out here to work, I'll be able to feed you and give you a place to sleep but I can't pay. I'll tell you that before you begin," she said.

There was no answer at once and no particular expression on his face. He leaned back against the two-by-four that helped support the porch roof. "Lady," he said slowly, "there's some men that some things mean more to them than money." The old woman rocked without comment and the daughter watched the trigger that moved up and down in his neck. He told the old woman then that all most people were interested in was money, but he asked what a man was made for. He asked her if a man was made for money, or what. He asked her what she thought she was made for but she didn't answer, she only sat rocking and wondered if a one-armed man could put a new roof on her garden house. He asked a lot of questions that she didn't answer. He told her that he was twenty-eight years old and had lived a varied life. He had been a gospel singer, a foreman on the railroad, an assistant in an undertaking parlor, and he come over the radio for three months with Uncle Roy and his Red Creek Wranglers. He said he had fought and bled in the Arm Service of his country and visited every foreign land and that everywhere he had seen people that didn't care if they did a thing one way or another. He said he hadn't been raised thataway.

A fat yellow moon appeared in the branches of the fig tree as if it were going to roost there with the chickens. He said that a man had to escape to the country to see the world whole and that he wished he lived in a desolate place like this where he could see the sun go down every evening like God made it to do.

"Are you married or are you single?" the old woman asked.

There was a long silence. "Lady," he asked finally, "where would you find you an innocent woman today? I wouldn't have any of this trash I could just pick up."

The daughter was leaning very far down, hanging her head almost between her knees, watching him through a triangular door she had made in her overturned hair; and she suddenly fell in a heap on the floor and began to whimper. Mr. Shiftlet straightened her out and helped her get back in the chair.

"Is she your baby girl?" he asked.

"My only," the old woman said, "and she's the sweetest girl in the world. I wouldn't give her up for nothing on earth. She's smart too. She can sweep the floor, cook, wash, feed the chickens, and hoe. I wouldn't give her up for a casket of jewels."

"No," he said kindly, "don't ever let any man take her away from you."

"Any man come after her," the old woman said, "I'll have to stay around the place."

Mr. Shiftlet's eye in the darkness was focused on a part of the automobile bumper that glittered in the distance. "Lady," he said, jerking his short arm up as if he could point with it to her house and yard and pump, "there ain't a broken thing on this plantation that I couldn't fix for you, one-arm jackleg or not. I'm a man," he said with a sullen dignity, "even if I ain't a whole one. I got," he said, tapping his knuckles on the floor to emphasize the immensity of what he was going to say, "a moral intelligence!" and his face pierced out of the darkness into a shaft of doorlight and he stared at her as if he were astonished himself at this impossible truth.

The old woman was not impressed with the phrase. "I told you you could hang around and work for food," she said, "if you don't mind sleeping in that car yonder."

"Why listen, lady," he said with a grin of delight, "the monks of old slept in their coffins!"

"They wasn't as advanced as we are," the old woman said.

★ ★ ★

The next morning he began on the roof of the garden house while Lucynell, the daughter, sat on a rock and watched him work. He had not been around a week before the change he had made in the place was apparent. He had patched the front and back steps, built a new hog pen, restored a fence, and taught Lucynell, who was completely deaf and had never said a word in her life, to say the word "bird." The big rosy-faced girl followed him everywhere, saying "Burrttddt ddbirrrttdt," and clapping her hands. The old woman watched from a distance, secretly pleased. She was ravenous for a son-in-law.

Mr. Shiftlet slept on the hard narrow back seat of the car with his feet out the side window. He had his razor and a can of water on a crate that served him as a bedside table and he put up a piece of mirror against the back glass and kept his coat neatly on a hanger that he hung over one of the windows.

In the evenings he sat on the steps and talked while the old woman and Lucynell rocked violently in their chairs on either side of him. The old woman's three mountains were black against the dark blue sky and were visited off and on by various planets and by the moon after it had left the chickens. Mr. Shiftlet pointed out that the reason he had improved this plantation was because he had taken a personal interest in it. He said he was even going to make the automobile run.

He had raised the hood and studied the mechanism and he said he could tell that the car had been built in the days when cars were really built. You take now, he said, one man puts in one bolt and another man puts in another bolt and another man puts in another bolt so that it's a man for a bolt. That's why you have to pay so much for a car: you're paying all those men. Now if you didn't have to pay but one man, you could get you a cheaper car and one that had had a personal interest taken in it, and it would be a better car. The old woman agreed with him that this was so.

Mr. Shiftlet said that the trouble with the world was that nobody cared, or stopped and took any trouble. He said he never would have been able to teach Lucynell to say a word if he hadn't cared and stopped long enough.

"Teach her to say something else," the old woman said.

"What you want her to say next?" Mr. Shiftlet asked.

The old woman's smile was broad and toothless and suggestive. "Teach her to say 'sugarpie,'" she said.

Mr. Shiftlet already knew what was on her mind.

The next day he began to tinker with the automobile and that evening he told her that if she would buy a fan belt, he would be able to make the car run.

The old woman said she would give him the money. "You see that girl yonder?" she asked, pointing to Lucynell who was sitting on the floor a foot away, watching him, her eyes blue even in the dark. "If it was ever a man wanted to take her away, I would say, 'No man on earth is going to take that sweet girl of mine away from me!' but if he was to say, 'Lady, I don't want to take her away, I want her right here,' I would say, 'Mister, I don't blame you none. I wouldn't pass up a chance to live in a permanent place and get the sweetest girl in the world myself. You ain't no fool,' I would say."

"How old is she?" Mr. Shiftlet asked casually.

"Fifteen, sixteen," the old woman said. The girl was nearly thirty but because of her innocence it was impossible to guess.

"It would be a good idea to paint it too," Mr. Shiftlet remarked. "You don't want it to rust out."

"We'll see about that later," the old woman said.

The next day he walked into town and returned with the parts he needed and a can of gasoline. Late in the afternoon, terrible noises issued from the shed and the old woman rushed out of the house, thinking Lucynell was somewhere having a fit. Lucynell was sitting on a chicken crate, stamping her feet and screaming, "Burrddttt! bddurrddtttt!" but her fuss was drowned out by the car. With a volley of blasts it emerged from the shed, moving in a fierce and stately way. Mr. Shiftlet was in the driver's seat, sitting very erect. He had an expression of serious modesty on his face as if he had just raised the dead.

That night, rocking on the porch, the old woman began her business at once. "You want you an innocent woman, don't you?" she asked sympathetically. "You don't want none of this trash."

"No'm, I don't," Mr. Shiftlet said.

"One that can't talk," she continued, "can't sass you back or use foul language. That's the kind for you to have. Right there," and she pointed to Lucynell sitting cross-legged in her chair, holding both feet in her hands.

"That's right," he admitted. "She wouldn't give me any trouble."

"Saturday," the old woman said, "you and her and me can drive into town and get married."

Mr. Shiftlet eased his position on the steps.

"I can't get married right now," he said. "Everything you want to do takes money and I ain't got any."

"What you need with money?" she asked.

"It takes money," he said. "Some people'll do anything anyhow these days, but the way I think, I wouldn't marry no woman that I couldn't take on a trip like she was somebody. I mean take her to a hotel and treat her. I wouldn't marry the Duchesser Windsor," he said firmly, "unless I could take her to a hotel and give her something good to eat.

"I was raised thataway and there ain't a thing I can do about it. My old mother taught me how to do."

"Lucynell don't even know what a hotel is," the old woman muttered. "Listen here, Mr. Shiftlet," she said, sliding forward in her chair, "you'd be getting a permanent house and a deep well and the most innocent girl in the world. You don't need no money. Lemme tell you something: there ain't any place in the world for a poor disabled friendless drifting man."

The ugly words settled in Mr. Shiftlet's head like a group of buzzards in the top of a tree. He didn't answer at once. He rolled himself a cigarette and lit it and then he said in an even voice, "Lady, a man is divided into two parts, body and spirit."

The old woman clamped her gums together.

"A body and a spirit," he repeated. "The body, lady, is like a house: it don't go anywhere; but the spirit, lady, is like a automobile: always on the move, always . . ."

"Listen, Mr. Shiftlet," she said, "my well never goes dry and my house is always warm in the winter and there's no mortgage on a thing about this place. You can go to the courthouse and see for yourself. And yonder under that shed is a fine automobile." She laid the bait carefully. "You can have it painted by Saturday. I'll pay for the paint."

In the darkness, Mr. Shiftlet's smile stretched like a weary snake waking up by a fire. After a second he recalled himself and said, "I'm only saying a man's spirit means more to him than anything else. I would have to take my wife off for the weekend without no regards at all for cost. I got to follow where my spirit says to go."

"I'll give you fifteen dollars for a weekend trip," the old woman said in a crabbed voice. "That's the best I can do."

"That wouldn't hardly pay for more than the gas and the hotel," he said. "It wouldn't feed her."

"Seventeen-fifty," the old woman said. "That's all I got so it isn't any use you trying to milk me. You can take a lunch."

Mr. Shiftlet was deeply hurt by the word "milk." He didn't doubt that she had more money sewed up in her mattress but he had already told her he was not interested in her money. "I'll make that do," he said and rose and walked off without treating with her further.

On Saturday the three of them drove into town in the car that the paint had barely dried on and Mr. Shiftlet and Lucynell were married in the Ordinary's office while the old woman witnessed. As they came out of the courthouse, Mr. Shiftlet began twisting his neck in his collar. He looked morose and bitter as if he had been insulted while someone held him. "That didn't satisfy me none," he said. "That was just something a woman in an office did, nothing but paper work and blood tests. What do they know about my blood? If they was to take my heart and cut it out," he said, "they wouldn't know a thing about me. It didn't satisfy me at all."

"It satisfied the law," the old woman said sharply.

"The law," Mr. Shiftlet said and spit. "It's the law that don't satisfy me."

He had painted the car dark green with a yellow band around it just under the windows. The three of them climbed in the front seat and the old woman said, "Don't Lucynell look pretty? Looks like a baby doll." Lucynell was dressed up in a white dress that her mother had uprooted from a trunk and there was a Panama hat on her head with a bunch of red wooden cherries on the brim. Every now and then her placid expression was changed by a sly isolated little thought like a shoot of green in the desert. "You got a prize!" the old woman said.

Mr. Shiftlet didn't even look at her.

They drove back to the house to let the old woman off and pick up the lunch. When they were ready to leave, she stood staring in the window of the car, with her fingers clenched around the glass. Tears began to seep sideways out of her eyes and run along the dirty creases in her face. "I ain't ever been parted with her for two days before," she said.

Mr. Shiftlet started the motor.

"And I wouldn't let no man have her but you because I seen you would do right. Good-by, Sugarbaby," she said, clutching at the sleeve of the white dress. Lucynell looked straight at her and didn't seem to see her there at all. Mr. Shiftlet eased the car forward so that she had to move her hands.

The early afternoon was clear and open and surrounded by pale blue sky. Although the car would go only thirty miles an hour, Mr. Shiftlet imagined a terrific climb and dip and swerve that went entirely to his head so that he forgot his morning bitterness. He had always wanted an automobile but he had never been able to afford one before. He drove very fast because he wanted to make Mobile by nightfall.

Occasionally he stopped his thoughts long enough to look at Lucynell in the seat beside him. She had eaten the lunch as soon as they were out of the yard and now she was pulling the cherries off the hat one by one and throwing them out the window. He became depressed in spite of the car. He had driven about a hundred miles when he decided that she must be hungry again and at the next small town they came to, he stopped in front of an aluminum-painted eating place called The Hot Spot and took her in and ordered her a plate of ham and grits. The ride had made her sleepy and as soon as she got up on the stool, she rested her head on the counter and shut her eyes. There was no one in The Hot Spot but Mr. Shiftlet and the boy behind the counter, a pale youth with a greasy rag hung over his shoulder. Before he could dish up the food, she was snoring gently.

"Give it to her when she wakes up," Mr. Shiftlet said. "I'll pay for it now."

The boy bent over her and stared at the long pink-gold hair and the half-shut sleeping eyes. Then he looked up and stared at Mr. Shiftlet. "She looks like an angel of Gawd," he murmured.

"Hitchhiker," Mr. Shiftlet explained. "I can't wait. I got to make Tuscaloosa."

The boy bent over again and very carefully touched his finger to a strand of the golden hair and Mr. Shiftlet left.

He was more depressed than ever as he drove on by himself. The late afternoon had grown hot and sultry and the country had flattened out. Deep in the sky a storm was preparing very slowly and without thunder as if it meant to drain every drop of air from the earth before it broke. There were times when Mr. Shiftlet preferred not to be alone. He felt too that a man with a car had a responsibility to others and he kept his eye out for a hitchhiker. Occasionally he saw a sign that warned: "Drive carefully. The life you save may be your own."

The narrow road dropped off on either side into dry fields and here and there a shack or a filling station stood in a clearing. The sun began to set directly in front of the automobile. It was a reddening ball that through his windshield was slightly flat on the bottom and top. He saw a boy in overalls and a gray hat standing on the edge of the road and he slowed the car down and stopped in front of him. The boy didn't have his hand raised to thumb the ride, he was only standing there, but he had a small cardboard suitcase and his hat was set on his head in a way to indicate that he had left somewhere for good. "Son," Mr. Shiftlet said, "I see you want a ride."

The boy didn't say he did or he didn't but he opened the door of the car and got in, and Mr. Shiftlet started driving again. The child held the suitcase on his lap and folded his arms on top of it. He turned his head and looked out the window away from Mr. Shiftlet. Mr. Shiftlet felt oppressed. "Son," he said after a minute, "I got the best old mother in the world so I reckon you only got the second best."

The boy gave him a quick dark glance and then turned his face back out the window.

"It's nothing so sweet," Mr. Shiftlet continued, "as a boy's mother. She taught him his first prayers at her knee, she give him love when no other would, she told him what was right and what wasn't, and she seen that he done the right thing. Son," he said, "I never rued a day in my life like the one I rued when I left that old mother of mine."

The boy shifted in his seat but he didn't look at Mr. Shiftlet. He unfolded his arms and put one hand on the door handle.

"My mother was a angel of Gawd," Mr. Shiftlet said in a very strained voice. "He took her from heaven and giver to me and I left her." His eyes were instantly clouded over with a mist of tears. The car was barely moving.

The boy turned angrily in the seat. "You go to the devil!" he cried. "My old woman is a flea bag and yours is a stinking pole cat!" and with that he flung the door open and jumped out with his suitcase into the ditch.

Mr. Shiftlet was so shocked that for about a hundred feet he drove along slowly with the door still open. A cloud, the exact color of the boy's hat and shaped like a turnip, had descended over the sun, and another, worse looking, crouched behind the car. Mr. Shiftlet felt that the rottenness of the world was about to engulf him. He raised his arm and let it fall again to his breast. "Oh Lord!" he prayed. "Break forth and wash the slime from this earth!"

The turnip continued slowly to descend. After a few minutes there was a guffawing peal of thunder from behind and fantastic raindrops, like tin-can tops, crashed over the rear of Mr. Shiftlet's car. Very quickly he stepped on the gas and with his stump sticking out the window he raced the galloping shower into Mobile.

EVERYDAY USE

for your grandmama

by Alice Walker

"Everyday Use" is one of the thirteen short stories included in Alice Walker's first collection, *In Love and Trouble*, published in 1973, when she was almost 30 years old and living in Jackson, Mississippi (where Eudora Welty also lived). Ten years later, her masterpiece *The Color Purple* won both the Pulitzer Prize and the National Book Award.

I WILL WAIT for her in the yard that Maggie and I made so clean and wavy yesterday afternoon. A yard like this is more comfortable than most people know. It is not just a yard. It is like an extended living room. When the hard clay is swept clean as a floor and the fine sand around the edges lined with tiny, irregular grooves, anyone can come and sit and look up into the elm tree and wait for the breezes that never come inside the house.

Maggie will be nervous until after her sister goes: she will stand hopelessly in corners, homely and ashamed of the burn scars down her arms and legs, eying her sister with a mixture of envy and awe. She thinks her sister has held life always in the palm of one hand, that "no" is a word the world never learned to say to her.

* * *

You've no doubt seen those TV shows where the child who has "made it" is confronted, as a surprise, by her own mother and father, tottering in weakly from backstage. (A pleasant surprise, of course: What would they do if parent and child came on the show only to curse out and insult each other?) On TV mother and child embrace and smile into each other's faces. Sometimes the mother and father weep, the child wraps them in her arms and leans across the table to tell how she would not have made it without their help. I have seen these programs.

Sometimes I dream a dream in which Dee and I are suddenly brought together on a TV program of this sort. Out of a dark and soft-seated limousine I am ushered into a bright room filled with many people. There I meet a smiling, gray, sporty man like Johnny Carson who shakes my hand and tells me what a fine girl I have. Then we are on the stage and Dee is embracing me with tears in her eyes. She pins on my dress a large orchid, even though she has told me once that she thinks orchids are tacky flowers.

In real life I am a large, big-boned woman with rough, man-working hands. In the winter I wear flannel nightgowns to bed and overalls during the day. I can kill and clean a hog as mercilessly as a man. My fat keeps me hot in zero weather. I can work outside all day, breaking ice to get water for washing; I can eat pork liver cooked over the open fire minutes after it comes steaming from the hog. One winter I knocked a bull calf straight in the brain between the eyes with a sledge hammer and had the meat hung up to chill before nightfall. But of course all this does not show on television. I am the way my daughter would want me to be: a hundred pounds lighter, my skin like an uncooked barley pancake. My hair glistens in the hot bright lights. Johnny Carson has much to do to keep up with my quick and witty tongue.

But that is a mistake. I know even before I wake up. Who ever knew a Johnson with a quick tongue? Who can even imagine me looking a strange white man in the eye? It seems to me I have talked to them always with one foot raised in flight, with my head turned in whichever way is farthest from them. Dee, though. She would always look anyone in the eye. Hesitation was no part of her nature.

* * *

"How do I look, Mama?" Maggie says, showing just enough of her thin body enveloped in pink skirt and red blouse for me to know she's there, almost hidden by the door.

"Come out into the yard," I say.

Have you ever seen a lame animal, perhaps a dog run over by some careless person rich enough to own a car, sidle up to someone who is ignorant enough to be kind to him? That is the way my Maggie walks. She has been like this, chin on chest, eyes on ground, feet in shuffle, ever since the fire that burned the other house to the ground.

Dee is lighter than Maggie, with nicer hair and a fuller figure. She's a woman now, though sometimes I forget. How long ago was it that the other house burned? Ten, twelve years? Sometimes I can still hear the flames and feel Maggie's arms sticking to me, her hair smoking and her dress falling off her in little black papery flakes. Her eyes seemed stretched open, blazed open by the flames reflected in them. And Dee. I see her standing off under the sweet gum tree she used to dig gum out of; a look of concentration on her face as she watched the last dingy gray board of the house fall in toward the red-hot brick chimney. Why don't you do a dance around the ashes? I'd wanted to ask her. She had hated the house that much.

I used to think she hated Maggie, too. But that was before we raised money, the church and me, to send her to Augusta to school. She used to read to us without pity; forcing words, lies, other folks' habits, whole lives upon us two, sitting trapped and ignorant underneath her voice. She washed us in a river of make-believe, burned us with a lot of knowledge we didn't necessarily need to know. Pressed us to her with the serious way she read, to shove us away at just the moment, like dimwits, we seemed about to understand.

Dee wanted nice things. A yellow organdy dress to wear to her graduation from high school; black pumps to match a green suit she'd made from an old suit somebody gave me. She was determined to stare down any disaster in her efforts. Her eyelids would not flicker for minutes at a time. Often I fought off the temptation to shake her. At sixteen she had a style of her own: and knew what style was.

* * *

I never had an education myself. After second grade the school was closed down. Don't ask me why: in 1927 colored asked fewer questions than they do now. Sometimes Maggie reads to me. She stumbles along good-naturedly but can't see well. She knows she is not bright. Like good looks and money, quickness passes her by. She will marry John Thomas (who has mossy teeth in an earnest face) and then I'll be free to sit here and I guess just sing church songs to myself. Although I never was a good singer. Never could carry a tune. I was always better at a man's job. I used to love to milk till I was hooked in the side in '49. Cows are soothing and slow and don't bother you, unless you try to milk them the wrong way.

I have deliberately turned my back on the house. It is three rooms, just like the one that burned, except the roof is tin; they don't make shingle roofs any more. There are no real windows, just some holes cut in the sides, like the portholes in a ship, but not round and not square, with rawhide holding the shutters up on the outside. This house is in a pasture, too, like the other one. No doubt when Dee sees it she will want to tear it down. She wrote me once that no matter where we "choose" to live, she will manage to come see us. But she will never bring her friends. Maggie and I thought about this and Maggie asked me, "Mama, when did Dee ever *have* any friends?"

She had a few. Furtive boys in pink shirts hanging about on washday after school. Nervous girls who never laughed. Impressed with her they worshiped the well-turned phrase, the cute shape, the scalding humor that erupted like bubbles in lye. She read to them.

When she was courting Jimmy T she didn't have much time to pay to us, but turned all her faultfinding power on him. He *flew* to marry a cheap city girl from a family of ignorant flashy people. She hardly had time to recompose herself.

⋆ ⋆ ⋆

When she comes I will meet—but there they are!

Maggie attempts to make a dash for the house, in her shuffling way, but I stay her with my hand. "Come back here," I say. And she stops and tries to dig a well in the sand with her toe.

It is hard to see them clearly through the strong sun. But even the first glimpse of leg out of the car tells me it is Dee. Her feet were always neat-looking, as if God himself had shaped them with a certain style. From the other side of the car comes a short, stocky man. Hair is all over his head a foot long and hanging from his chin like a kinky mule tail. I hear Maggie suck in her breath. "Uhnnnh," is what it sounds like. Like when you see the wriggling end of a snake just in front of your foot on the road. "Uhnnnh."

Dee next. A dress down to the ground, in this hot weather. A dress so loud it hurts my eyes. There are yellows and oranges enough to throw back the light of the sun. I feel my whole face warming from the heat waves it throws out. Earrings gold, too, and hanging down to her shoulders. Bracelets dangling and making noises when she moves her arm up to shake the folds of the dress out of her armpits. The dress is loose and flows, and as she walks closer, I like it. I hear Maggie go "Uhnnnh" again. It is her sister's hair. It stands straight up like the wool on a sheep. It is black as night and around the edges are two long pigtails that rope about like small lizards disappearing behind her ears.

"Wa-su-zo-Tean-o!" she says, coming on in that gliding way the dress makes her move. The short stocky fellow with the hair to his navel is all grinning and he follows up with "Asalamalakim, my mother and sister!" He moves to hug Maggie but she falls back, right up against the back of my chair. I feel her trembling there and when I look up I see the perspiration falling off her chin.

"Don't get up," says Dee. Since I am stout it takes something of a push. You can see me trying to move a second or two before I make it. She turns, showing white heels through her sandals, and goes back to the car. Out she peeks next with a Polaroid. She stoops down quickly and lines up picture after picture of me sitting there in front of the house with Maggie cowering behind me. She never takes a shot without making sure the house is included. When a cow comes nibbling around the edge of the yard she snaps it and me and Maggie and the house. Then she puts the Polaroid in the back seat of the car, and comes up and kisses me on the forehead.

Meanwhile Asalamalakim is going through motions with Maggie's hand. Maggie's hand is as limp as a fish, and probably as cold, despite the sweat, and she keeps trying to pull it back. It looks like Asalamalakim wants to shake hands but wants to do it fancy. Or maybe he don't know how people shake hands. Anyhow, he soon gives up on Maggie.

"Well," I say. "Dee."

"No, Mama," she says. "Not 'Dee,' Wangero Leewanika Kemanjo!"

"What happened to 'Dee'?" I wanted to know.

"She's dead," Wangero said. "I couldn't bear it any longer, being named after the people who oppress me."

"You know as well as me you was named after your aunt Dicie," I said. Dicie is my sister. She named Dee. We called her "Big Dee" after Dee was born.

"But who was *she* named after?" asked Wangero.

"I guess after Grandma Dee," I said.

"And who was she named after?" asked Wangero.

"Her mother," I said, and saw Wangero was getting tired. "That's about as far back as I can trace it," I said. Though, in fact, I probably could have carried it back beyond the Civil War through the branches.

"Well," said Asalamalakim, "there you are."

"Uhnnnh," I heard Maggie say.

"There I was not," I said, "before 'Dicie' cropped up in our family, so why should I try to trace it that far back?"

He just stood there grinning, looking down on me like somebody inspecting a Model A car. Every once in a while he and Wangero sent eye signals over my head.

"How do you pronounce this name?" I asked.

"You don't have to call me by it if you don't want to," said Wangero.

"Why shouldn't I?" I asked. "If that's what you want us to call you, we'll call you."

"I know it might sound awkward at first," said Wangero.

"I'll get used to it," I said. "Ream it out again."

Well, soon we got the name out of the way. Asalamalakim had a name twice as long and three times as hard. After I tripped over it two or three times he told me to just call him Hakim-a-barber. I wanted to ask him was he a barber, but I didn't really think he was, so I didn't ask.

"You must belong to those beef-cattle peoples down the road," I said. They said "Asalamalakim" when they met you, too, but they didn't shake hands. Always too busy: feeding the cattle, fixing the fences, putting up salt-lick shelters, throwing down hay. When the white folks poisoned some of the herd the men stayed up all night with rifles in their hands. I walked a mile and a half just to see the sight.

Hakim-a-barber said, "I accept some of their doctrines, but farming and raising cattle is not my style." (They didn't tell me, and I didn't ask, whether Wangero (Dee) had really gone and married him.)

We sat down to eat and right away he said he didn't eat collards and pork was unclean. Wangero, though, went on through the chitlins and corn bread, the greens and everything else. She talked a blue streak over the sweet potatoes. Everything delighted her. Even the fact that we still used the benches her daddy made for the table when we couldn't afford to buy chairs.

"Oh, Mama!" she cried. Then turned to Hakim-a-barber. "I never knew how lovely these benches are. You can feel the rump prints," she said, running her hands underneath her and along the bench. Then she gave a sigh and her hand closed over Grandma Dee's butter dish. "That's it!" she said. "I knew there was something I wanted to ask you if I could have." She jumped up from the table and went over in the corner where the churn stood, the milk in it clabber by now. She looked at the churn and looked at it.

"This churn top is what I need," she said. "Didn't Uncle Buddy whittle it out of a tree you all used to have?"

"Yes," I said.

"Uh huh," she said happily. "And I want the dasher, too."

"Uncle Buddy whittle that, too?" asked the barber.

Dee (Wangero) looked up at me.

"Aunt Dee's first husband whittled the dash," said Maggie so low you almost couldn't hear her. "His name was Henry, but they called him Stash."

"Maggie's brain is like an elephant's," Wangero said, laughing. "I can use the churn top as a centerpiece for the alcove table," she said, sliding a plate over the churn, "and I'll think of something artistic to do with the dasher."

When she finished wrapping the dasher the handle stuck out. I took it for a moment in my hands. You didn't even have to look close to see where hands pushing the dasher up and down to make butter had left a kind of sink in the wood. In fact, there were a lot of small sinks; you could see where thumbs and fingers had sunk into the wood. It was beautiful light yellow wood, from a tree that grew in the yard where Big Dee and Stash had lived.

After dinner Dee (Wangero) went to the trunk at the foot of my bed and started rifling through it. Maggie hung back in the kitchen over the dishpan. Out came Wangero with two quilts. They had been pieced by Grandma Dee and then Big Dee and me had hung them on the quilt frames on the front porch and quilted them. One was in the Lone Star pattern. The other was Walk Around the Mountain. In both of them were scraps of dresses Grandma Dee had worn fifty and more years ago. Bits and pieces of Grandpa

Jarrell's Paisley shirts. And one teeny faded blue piece, about the size of a penny matchbox, that was from Great Grandpa Ezra's uniform that he wore in the Civil War.

"Mama," Wangero said sweet as a bird. "Can I have these old quilts?"

I heard something fall in the kitchen, and a minute later the kitchen door slammed.

"Why don't you take one or two of the others?" I asked. "These old things was just done by me and Big Dee from some tops your grandma pieced before she died."

"No," said Wangero. "I don't want those. They are stitched around the borders by machine."

"That'll make them last better," I said.

"That's not the point," said Wangero. "These are all pieces of dresses Grandma used to wear. She did all this stitching by hand. Imagine!" She held the quilts securely in her arms, stroking them.

"Some of the pieces, like those lavender ones, come from old clothes her mother handed down to her," I said, moving up to touch the quilts. Dee (Wangero) moved back just enough so that I couldn't reach the quilts. They already belonged to her.

"Imagine!" she breathed again, clutching them closely to her bosom.

"The truth is," I said, "I promised to give them quilts to Maggie, for when she marries John Thomas."

She gasped like a bee had stung her.

"Maggie can't appreciate these quilts!" she said. "She'd probably be backward enough to put them to everyday use."

"I reckon she would," I said. "God knows I been saving 'em for long enough with nobody using 'em. I hope she will!" I didn't want to bring up how I had offered Dee (Wangero) a quilt when she went away to college. Then she had told me they were old-fashioned, out of style.

"But they're *priceless!*" she was saying now, furiously; for she has a temper. "Maggie would put them on the bed and in five years they'd be in rags. Less than that!"

"She can always make some more," I said. "Maggie knows how to quilt."

Dee (Wangero) looked at me with hatred. "You just will not understand. The point is these quilts, *these* quilts!"

"Well," I said, stumped. "What would *you* do with them?"

"Hang them," she said. As if that was the only thing you *could* do with quilts.

Maggie by now was standing in the door. I could almost hear the sound her feet made as they scraped over each other.

"She can have them, Mama," she said, like somebody used to never winning anything, or having anything reserved for her. "I can 'member Grandma Dee without the quilts."

I looked at her hard. She had filled her bottom lip with checkerberry snuff and it gave her face a kind of dopey, hangdog look. It was Grandma Dee and Big Dee who taught her how to quilt herself. She stood there with her scarred hands hidden in the folds of her skirt. She looked at her sister with something like fear but she wasn't mad at her. This was Maggie's portion. This was the way she knew God to work.

When I looked at her like that something hit me in the top of my head and ran down to the soles of my feet. Just like when I'm in church and the spirit of God touches me and I get happy and shout. I did something I never done before: hugged Maggie to me, then dragged her on into the room, snatched the quilts out of Miss Wangero's hands and dumped them into Maggie's lap. Maggie just sat there on my bed with her mouth open.

"Take one or two of the others," I said to Dee.

But she turned without a word and went out to Hakim-a-barber.

"You just don't understand," she said, as Maggie and I came out to the car.

"What don't I understand?" I wanted to know.

"Your heritage," she said. And then she turned to Maggie, kissed her, and said, "You ought to try to make something of yourself, too, Maggie. It's really a new day for us. But from the way you and Mama still live you'd never know it."

She put on some sunglasses that hid everything above the tip of her nose and chin.

Maggie smiled; maybe at the sunglasses. But a real smile, not scared. After we watched the car dust settle I asked Maggie to bring me a dip of snuff. And then the two of us sat there just enjoying, until it was time to go in the house and go to bed.

HEAT

by Joyce Carol Oates

Joyce Carol Oates published her first book in 1963, when she was 25 years old; since then she has published over forty widely acclaimed novels and many volumes of short stories. Her novel *them* won the National Book Award in 1970. Two of her short stories have been O. Henry first-prize winners (1967 and 1973). "Heat" was first published in *The Paris Review* in 1989.

It was midsummer, the heat rippling above the macadam roads, cicadas screaming out of the trees, and the sky like pewter, glaring.

The days were the same day, like the shallow mud-brown river moving always in the same direction but so low you couldn't see it. Except for Sunday: church in the morning, then the fat Sunday newspaper, the color comics, and newsprint on your fingers.

Rhea and Rhoda Kunkel went flying on their rusted old bicycles, down the long hill toward the railroad yard, Whipple's Ice, the scrubby pastureland where dairy cows grazed. They'd stolen six dollars from their own grandmother who loved them. They were eleven years old; they were identical twins; they basked in their power.

Rhea and Rhoda Kunkel: it was always Rhea-and-Rhoda, never Rhoda-and-Rhea, I couldn't say why. You just wouldn't say the names that way. Not even the teachers at school would say them that way.

We went to see them in the funeral parlor where they were waked; we were made to. The twins in twin caskets, white, smooth, gleaming, perfect as plastic, with white satin lining puckered like the inside of a fancy candy box. And the waxy white lilies, and the smell of talcum powder and perfume. The room was crowded; there was only one way in and out.

Rhea and Rhoda were the same girl; they'd wanted it that way. Only looking from one to the other could you see they were two.

The heat was gauzy; you had to push your way through like swimming. On their bicycles Rhea and Rhoda flew through it hardly noticing, from their grandmother's place on Main Street to the end of South Main where the paved road turned to gravel leaving town. That was the summer before seventh grade, when they died. Death was coming for them, but they didn't know.

They thought the same thoughts sometimes at the same moment, had the same dream and went all day trying to remember it, bringing it back like something you'd be hauling out of the water on a tangled line. We watched them; we were jealous. None of us had a twin. Sometimes they were serious and sometimes, remembering, they shrieked and laughed like they were being killed. They stole things out of desks and lockers but if you caught them they'd hand them right back; it was like a game.

There were three floor fans in the funeral parlor that I could see, tall whirring fans with propeller blades turning fast to keep the warm air moving. Strange little gusts came from all directions, making your eyes water. By this time Roger Whipple was arrested, taken into police custody. No one had hurt him. He would never stand trial; he was ruled mentally unfit and would never be released from confinement.

He died there, in the state psychiatric hospital, years later, and was brought back home to be buried—the body of him, I mean. His earthly remains.

Rhea and Rhoda Kunkel were buried in the same cemetery, the First Methodist. The cemetery is just a field behind the church.

In the caskets the dead girls did not look like anyone we knew, really. They were placed on their backs with their eyes closed, and their mouths, the way you don't always look in life when you're sleeping. Their faces were too small. Every eyelash showed, too perfect. Like angels, everyone was saying, and it was strange it was *so*. I stared and stared.

What had been done to them, the lower parts of them, didn't show in the caskets.

Roger Whipple worked for his father at Whipple's Ice. In the newspaper it stated he was nineteen. He'd gone to DeWitt Clinton until he was sixteen; my mother's friend Sadie taught there and remembered him from the special education class. A big slow sweet-faced boy with these big hands and feet, thighs like hams. A shy gentle boy with good manners and a hushed voice.

He wasn't simpleminded exactly, like the others in that class. He was watchful, he held back.

Roger Whipple in overalls squatting in the rear of his father's truck, one of his older brothers driving. There would come the sound of the truck in the driveway, the heavy block of ice smelling of cold, ice tongs over his shoulder. He was strong, round-shouldered like an older man. Never staggered or grunted. Never dropped anything. Pale washed-looking eyes lifting out of a big face, a soft mouth wanting to smile. We giggled and looked away. They said he'd never been the kind to hurt even an animal; all the Whipples swore.

Sucking ice, the cold goes straight into your jaws and deep into the bone.

People spoke of them as the Kunkel twins. Mostly nobody tried to tell them apart: homely corkscrew-twisty girls you wouldn't know would turn up so quiet and solemn and almost beautiful, perfect little dolls' faces with the freckles powdered over, touches of rouge on the cheeks and mouths. I was tempted to whisper to them, kneeling by the coffins, *Hey, Rhea! Hey, Rhoda! Wake up!*

They had loud slip-sliding voices that were the same voice. They weren't shy. They were always first in line. One behind you and one in front of you and you'd better be wary of some trick. Flamey-orange hair and the bleached-out skin that goes with it, freckles like dirty raindrops splashed on their faces. Sharp green eyes they'd bug out until you begged them to stop.

Places meant to be serious, Rhea and Rhoda had a hard time sitting still. In church, in school, a sideways glance between them could do it. Jamming their knuckles into their mouths, choking back giggles. Sometimes laughter escaped through their fingers like steam hissing. Sometimes it came out like snorting and then none of us could hold back. The worst time was in assembly, the principal up there telling us that Miss Flagler had died, we would all miss her. Tears shining in the woman's eyes behind her goggle glasses and one of the twins gave a breathless little snort; you could feel it like flames running down the whole row of girls, none of us could hold back.

Sometimes the word "tickle" was enough to get us going, just that word.

I never dreamt about Rhea and Rhoda so strange in their caskets sleeping out in the middle of a room where people could stare at them, shed tears and pray over them. I never dream about actual things, only things I don't know. Places I've never been, people I've never seen. Sometimes the person I am in the dream isn't me. Who it is, I don't know.

Rhea and Rhoda bounced up the drive on their bicycles behind Whipple's Ice. They were laughing like crazy and didn't mind the potholes jarring their teeth or the clouds of dust. If they'd had the same dream the night before, the hot sunlight erased it entirely.

When death comes for you, you sometimes know and sometimes don't.

Roger Whipple was by himself in the barn, working. Kids went down there to beg him for ice to suck or throw around or they'd tease him, not out of meanness but for something to do. It was slow, the days not changing in the summer, heat sometimes all night long. He was happy with children that age, he was that age himself in his head—sixth-grade learning abilities, as the newspaper stated, though he could add and subtract quickly. Other kinds of arithmetic gave him trouble.

People were saying afterward he'd always been strange. Watchful like he was, those thick soft lips. The Whipples did wrong to let him run loose.

They said he'd always been a good gentle boy, went to Sunday school and sat still there and never gave anybody any trouble. He collected Bible cards; he hid them away under his mattress for safekeeping. Mr. Whipple started in early disciplining him the way you might discipline a big dog or a horse. Not letting the creature know he has any power to be himself exactly. Not giving him the opportunity to test his will.

Neighbors said the Whipples worked him like a horse, in fact. The older brothers were the most merciless. And why they all wore coveralls, heavy denim and long legs on days so hot, nobody knew. The thermometer above the First Midland Bank read 98 degrees F. on noon of that day, my mother said.

Nights afterward my mother would hug me before I went to bed. Pressing my face hard against her breasts and whispering things I didn't hear, like praying to Jesus to love and protect her little girl and keep her from harm, but I didn't hear; I shut my eyes tight and endured it. Sometimes we prayed together, all of us or just my mother and me kneeling by my bed. Even then I knew she was a good mother, there was this girl she loved as her daughter that was me and loved more than that girl deserved. There was nothing I could do about it.

Mrs. Kunkel would laugh and roll her eyes over the twins. In that house they were "double trouble"—you'd hear it all the time like a joke on the radio that keeps coming back. I wonder did she pray with them too. I wonder would they let her.

In the long night you forget about the day; it's like the other side of the world. Then the sun is there, and the heat. You forget.

We were running through the field behind school, a place where people dumped things sometimes, and there was a dead dog there, a collie with beautiful fur, but his eyes were gone from the sockets and the maggots had got him where somebody tried to lift him with her foot, and when Rhea and Rhoda saw they screamed a single scream and hid their eyes.

They did nice things—gave their friends candy bars, nail polish, some novelty key chains they'd taken from somewhere, movie stars' pictures framed in plastic. In the movies they'd share a box of popcorn, not noticing where one or the other of them left off and a girl who wasn't any sister of theirs sat.

Once they made me strip off my clothes where we'd crawled under the Kunkels' veranda. This was a large hollowed-out space where the earth dropped away at one end and you could sit without bumping your head; it was cool and smelled of dirt and stone. Rhea said all of a sudden, *Strip!* and Rhoda said at once, *Strip! Come on!* So it happened. They wouldn't let me out unless I took off my clothes, my shirt and shorts, yes, and my panties too. *Come on,* they said, whispering and giggling; they were blocking the way out so I had no choice. I was scared but I was laughing too. This is to show our power over you, they said. But they stripped too just like me.

You have power over others you don't realize until you test it.

Under the Kunkels' veranda we stared at each other but we didn't touch each other. My teeth chattered, because what if somebody saw us, some boy, or Mrs. Kunkel herself? I was scared but I was happy too. Except for our faces, their face and mine, we could all be the same girl.

The Kunkel family lived in one side of a big old clapboard house by the river; you could hear the trucks rattling on the bridge, shifting their noisy gears on the hill. Mrs. Kunkel had eight children. Rhea and Rhoda were the youngest. Our mothers wondered why Mrs. Kunkel had let herself go: she had a moon-shaped pretty face but her hair was frizzed ratty; she must have weighed two hundred pounds, sweated and breathed so hard in the warm weather. They'd known her in school. Mr. Kunkel worked construction for the county. Summer evenings after work he'd be sitting on the veranda drinking beer, flicking cigarette butts out into the yard; you'd be fooled, almost thinking they were fireflies. He went bare-chested in the heat, his upper body dark like stained wood. Flat little purplish nipples inside his chest hair the girls giggled to see. Mr. Kunkel teased us all; he'd mix Rhea and Rhoda up the way he'd mix the rest of us up, like it was too much trouble to keep names straight.

Mr. Kunkel was in police custody; he didn't even come to the wake. Mrs. Kunkel was there in rolls of chin fat that glistened with sweat and tears, the makeup on her face so caked and discolored you were embarrassed to look. It scared me, the way she grabbed me as soon as my parents and I came in, hugging me against her big balloon breasts, sobbing. All the strength went out of me; I couldn't push away.

The police had Mr. Kunkel for his own good, they said. He'd gone to the Whipples, though the murderer had been taken away, saying he would kill anybody he could get his hands on: the old man, the brothers. They were all responsible, he said; his little girls were dead. Tear them apart with his bare hands, he said, but he had a tire iron.

Did it mean anything special, or was it just an accident Rhea and Rhoda had taken six dollars from their grandmother an hour before? Because death was coming for them; it had to happen one way or another.

If you believe in God you believe that. And if you don't believe in God it's obvious.

Their grandmother lived upstairs over a shoe store downtown, an apartment looking out on Main Street. They'd bicycle down there for something to do and she'd give them grape juice or lemonade and try to keep them awhile, a lonely old lady but she was nice, she was always nice to me; it was kind of nasty of Rhea and Rhoda to steal from her but they were like that. One was in the kitchen talking with her and without any plan or anything the other went to use the bathroom, then slipped into her bedroom, got the money out of her purse like it was something she did every day of the week, that easy. On the stairs going down to the street Rhoda whispered to Rhea, What did you *do*? knowing Rhea had done something she hadn't ought to have done but not knowing what it was or anyway how much money it was. They started in poking each other, trying to hold the giggles until they were safe away.

On their bicycles they stood high on the pedals, coasting, going down the hill but not using their brakes. *What did you do! Oh, what did you do!*

Rhea and Rhoda always said they could never be apart. If one didn't know exactly where the other was that one could die. Or the other could die. Or both.

Once they'd gotten some money from somewhere, they wouldn't say where, and paid for us all to go to the movies. And ice cream afterward too.

You could read the newspaper articles twice through and still not know what he did. Adults talked about it for a long time but not so we could hear. I thought probably he'd used an ice pick. Or maybe I heard somebody guess who didn't know any more than me.

We liked it that Rhea and Rhoda had been killed, and all the stuff in the paper, and everybody talking about it, but we didn't like it that they were dead; we missed them.

Later, in tenth grade, the Kaufmann twins moved into our school district: Doris and Diane. But it wasn't the same thing.

Roger Whipple said he didn't remember any of it. Whatever he did, he didn't remember. At first everybody thought he was lying; then they had to accept it as true, or true in some way: doctors from the state hospital examined him. He said over and over he hadn't done anything and he didn't remember the twins there that afternoon, but he couldn't explain why their bicycles were at the foot of his stairway and he couldn't explain why he'd taken a bath in the middle of the day. The Whipples admitted that wasn't a practice of Roger's or of any of them, ever, a bath in the middle of the day.

Roger Whipple was a clean boy, though. His hands always scrubbed so you actually noticed, swinging the block of ice off the truck and, inside the kitchen, helping to set it in the icebox. They said he'd got crazy if he got bits of straw under his nails from the icehouse or inside his clothes. He'd been taught to shave and he shaved every morning without fail; they said the sight of the beard growing in, the scratchy feel of it, seemed to scare him.

A few years later his sister Linda told us how Roger was built like a horse. She was our age, a lot younger than him; she made a gesture toward her crotch so we'd know what she meant. She'd happened to see him a few times, she said, by accident.

There he was squatting in the dust laughing, his head lowered, watching Rhea and Rhoda circle him on their bicycles. It was a rough game where the twins saw how close they could come to hitting him, brushing him with their bike fenders, and he'd lunge out, not seeming to notice if his fingers hit the spokes; it was all happening so fast you maybe wouldn't feel pain. Out back of the icehouse, the yard blended in with the yard of the old railroad depot next door that wasn't used any more. It was burning hot in the sun; dust rose in clouds behind the girls. Pretty soon they got bored with the game, though Roger Whipple even in his heavy overalls wanted to keep going. He was red-faced with all the excitement; he was a boy who loved to laugh and didn't have much chance. Rhea said she was thirsty, she wanted some ice, so Roger Whipple scrambled right up and went to get a big bag of ice cubes! He hadn't any more sense than that.

They sucked on the ice cubes and fooled around with them. He was panting and lolling his tongue pretending to be a dog, and Rhea and Rhoda cried, Here, doggie! Here, doggie-doggie! tossing the ice cubes at Roger Whipple he tried to catch in his mouth. That went on for a while. In the end the twins just dumped the rest of the ice onto the dirt, then Roger Whipple was saying he had some secret things that belonged to his brother Eamon he could show them, hidden under his bed mattress; would they like to see what the things were?

He wasn't one who could tell Rhea from Rhoda or Rhoda from Rhea. There was a way some of us knew: the freckles on Rhea's face were a little darker than Rhoda's, and Rhea's eyes were just a little darker than Rhoda's. But you'd have to see the two side by side with no clowning around to know.

Rhea said OK, she'd like to see the secret things. She let her bike fall where she was straddling it.

Roger Whipple said he could only take one of them upstairs to his room at a time, he didn't say why.

OK, said Rhea. Of the Kunkel twins, Rhea always had to be first.

She'd been born first, she said. Weighed a pound or two more.

Roger Whipple's room was in a strange place: on the second floor of the Whipple house above an unheated storage space that had been added after the main part of the house was built. There was a way of getting to the room from the outside, up a flight of rickety wooden stairs. That way Roger could get in and out of his room without going through the rest of the house. People said the Whipples had him live there like some animal, they didn't want him tramping through the house, but they denied it. The room had an inside door too.

Roger Whipple weighed about one hundred ninety pounds that day. In the hospital he swelled up like a balloon, people said, bloated from the drugs; his skin was soft and white as bread dough and his hair fell out. He was an old man when he died aged thirty-one.

Exactly why he died, the Whipples never knew. The hospital just told them his heart had stopped in his sleep.

Rhoda shaded her eyes, watching her sister running up the stairs with Roger Whipple behind her, and felt the first pinch of fear, that something was wrong or was going to be wrong. She called after them in a whining voice that she wanted to come along too, she didn't want to wait down there all alone, but Rhea just called back to her to be quiet and wait her turn, so Rhoda waited, kicking at the ice cubes melting in the dirt, and after a while she got restless and shouted up to them—the door was shut, the shade on the window was drawn—saying she was going home, damn them, she was sick of waiting, she said, and she was going home. But nobody came to the door or looked out of the window; it was like the place was empty. Wasps had built one of those nests that look like mud in layers under the eaves, and the only sound was wasps.

Rhoda bicycled toward the road so anybody who was watching would think she was going home; she was thinking she hated Rhea! hated her damn twin sister! wished she was dead and gone, God damn her! She was going home, and the first thing she'd tell their mother was that Rhea had stolen six dollars from Grandma: she had it in her pocket right that moment.

The Whipple house was an old farmhouse they'd tried to modernize by putting on red asphalt siding meant to look like brick. Downstairs the rooms were big and drafty; upstairs they were small, some of them unfinished and with bare floorboards, like Roger Whipple's room, which people would afterward say based on what the police said was like an animal's pen, nothing in it but a bed shoved into a corner and some furniture and boxes and things Mrs. Whipple stored there.

Of the Whipples—there were seven in the family still living at home—only Mrs. Whipple and her daughter Iris were home that afternoon. They said they hadn't heard a sound except for kids playing in the back; they swore it.

Rhoda was bent on going home and leaving Rhea behind, but at the end of the driveway something made her turn her bicycle wheel back . . . so if you were watching you'd think she was just cruising around for something to do, a red-haired girl with whitish skin and freckles, skinny little body, pedaling fast, then slow, then coasting, then fast again, turning and dipping and crisscrossing her path, talking to herself as if she was angry. She hated Rhea! She was furious at Rhea! But feeling sort of scared too and sickish in the pit of her belly, knowing that she and Rhea shouldn't be in two places; something might happen to one of them or to both. Some things you know.

So she pedaled back to the house. Laid her bike down in the dirt next to Rhea's. The bikes were old hand-me-downs, the kick-stands were broken. But their daddy had put on new Goodyear tires for them at the start of the summer, and he'd oiled them too.

You never would see just one of the twins' bicycles anywhere, you always saw both of them laid down on the ground and facing in the same direction with the pedals in about the same position.

Rhoda peered up at the second floor of the house, the shade drawn over the window, the door still closed. She called out, Rhea? Hey, Rhea? starting up the stairs, making a lot of noise so they'd hear her, pulling on the railing as if to break it the way a boy would. Still she was scared. But making noise like that and feeling so disgusted and mad helped her get stronger, and there was Roger Whipple with the door open staring down at her flush-faced and sweaty as if he was scared too. He seemed to have forgotten her. He was wiping his hands on his overalls. He just stared, a lemony light coming up in his eyes.

Afterward he would say he didn't remember anything. Just didn't remember anything. The size of a grown man but round-shouldered so it was hard to judge how tall he was, or how old. His straw-colored hair falling in his eyes and his fingers twined together as if he was praying or trying with all the strength in him to keep his hands still. He didn't remember the twins in his room and couldn't explain the blood but he cried a lot, acted scared and guilty and sorry like a dog that's done bad, so they decided he shouldn't be made to stand trial; there was no point to it.

Afterward Mrs. Whipple kept to the house, never went out, not even to church or grocery shopping. She died of cancer just a few months before Roger died; she'd loved her boy, she always said; she said none of it was his fault in his heart, he wasn't the kind of boy to injure an animal; he loved kittens especially and was a good sweet obedient boy and religious too and Jesus was looking after him and whatever happened it must have been those girls teasing him; everybody knew what the Kunkel twins were like. Roger had had a lifetime of being teased and taunted by children, his heart broken by all the abuse, and something must have snapped that day, that was all.

The Whipples were the ones, though, who called the police. Mr. Whipple found the girls' bodies back in the icehouse hidden under some straw and canvas. Those two look-alike girls, side by side.

He found them around 9 P.M. that night. He knew, he said. Oh, he knew.

The way Roger was acting, and the fact that the Kunkel girls were missing: word had gotten around town. Roger taking a bath like that in the middle of the day and washing his hair too and not answering when anyone said his name, just sitting there staring at the floor. So they went up to his room and saw the blood. So they knew.

The hardest minute of his life, Mr. Whipple said, was in the icehouse lifting that canvas to see what was under it.

He took it hard too; he never recovered. He hadn't any choice but to think what a lot of people thought—it had been his fault. He was an old-time Methodist, he took all that seriously, but none of it helped him. Believed Jesus Christ was his personal savior and He never stopped loving Roger or turned His face from him, and if Roger did truly repent in his heart he would be saved and they would be reunited in Heaven, all the Whipples reunited. He believed, but none of it helped in his life.

The icehouse is still there but boarded up and derelict, the Whipples' ice business ended long ago. Strangers live in the house, and the yard is littered with rusting hulks of cars and pickup trucks. Some Whipples live scattered around the county but none in town. The old train depot is still there too.

After I'd been married some years I got involved with this man, I won't say his name, his name is not a name I say, but we would meet back there sometimes, back in that old lot that's all weeds and scrub trees. Wild as kids and on the edge of being drunk. I was crazy for this guy, I mean crazy like I could hardly think of anybody but him or anything but the two of us making love the way we did; with him deep inside me I wanted it never to stop. Just fuck and fuck and fuck, I'd whisper to him, and this went on for a long time, two or three years, then ended the way these things do and looking back on it I'm not able to recognize that woman, as if she was someone not even not-me but a crazy woman I would despise, making so much of such a thing, risking her marriage and her kids finding out and her life being ruined for such a thing, my God. The things people do.

It's like living out a story that has to go its own way.

Behind the icehouse in his car I'd think of Rhea and Rhoda and what happened that day upstairs in Roger Whipple's room. And the funeral parlor with the twins like dolls laid out and their eyes like dolls' eyes too that shut when you tilt them back. One night when I wasn't asleep but wasn't awake either I saw my parents standing in the doorway of my bedroom watching me and I knew their thoughts, how they were thinking of Rhea and Rhoda and of me their daughter wondering how they could keep me from harm, and there was no clear answer.

In his car in his arms I'd feel my mind drift, after we'd made love or at least after the first time. And I saw Rhoda Kunkel hesitating on the stairs a few steps down from Roger Whipple. I saw her white-faced and scared but deciding to keep going anyway, pushing by Roger Whipple to get inside the room, to find Rhea; she had to brush against him where he was standing as if he meant to block her but not having the nerve exactly to block her and he was smelling of his body and breathing hard but not in imitation of any dog now, not with his tongue flopping and lolling to make them laugh. Rhoda was asking where was Rhea? She couldn't see well at first in the dark little cubbyhole of a room because the sunshine had been so bright outside.

Roger Whipple said Rhea had gone home. His voice sounded scratchy as if it hadn't been used in some time. She'd gone home, he said, and Rhoda said right away that Rhea wouldn't go home without her and Roger Whipple came toward her saying, Yes she did, yes she *did,* as if he was getting angry she wouldn't believe him. Rhoda was calling, *Rhea, where are you?* Stumbling against something on the floor tangled with the bedclothes.

Behind her was this big boy saying again and again, Yes she did, yes she *did,* his voice rising, but it would never get loud enough so that anyone would hear and come save her.

I wasn't there, but some things you know.

THE SHAWL

by Louise Erdrich

In 1984 Louise Erdrich won the National Book Critics Circle Award for her first novel, *Love Medicine*; in 2012 she received the National Book Award for Fiction for *The Round House*. "The Shawl" was first published in *The New Yorker* in 2001; it is included in *The Red Convertible*, an anthology of her work published in 2009.

AMONG THE ANISHINAABEG on the road where I live, it is told how a woman loved a man other than her husband and went off into the bush and bore his child. Her name was Aanakwad, which means cloud, and like a cloud she was changeable. She was moody and sullen one moment, her lower lip jutting and her eyes flashing, filled with storms. The next, she would shake her hair over her face and blow it straight out in front of her to make her children scream with laughter. For she also had two children by her husband, one a yearning boy of five years and the other a capable daughter of nine.

When Aanakwad brought the new baby out of the trees that autumn, the older girl was like a second mother, even waking in the night to clean the baby and nudge it to her mother's breast. Aanakwad slept through its cries, hardly woke. It wasn't that she didn't love her baby; no, it was the opposite—she loved it too much, the way she loved its father, and not her husband. This passion ate away at her, and her feelings were unbearable. If she could have thrown off that wronghearted love, she would have, but the thought of the other man, who lived across the lake, was with her always. She became a gray sky, stared monotonously at the walls, sometimes wept into her hands for hours at a time.

Soon, she couldn't rise to cook or keep the cabin neat, and it was too much for the girl, who curled up each night exhausted in her red-and-brown plaid shawl, and slept and slept, until the husband had to wake her to awaken her mother, for he was afraid of his wife's bad temper, and it was he who roused Aanakwad into anger by the sheer fact that he was himself and not the other.

At last, even though he loved Aanakwad, the husband had to admit that their life together was no good anymore. And it was he who sent for the other man's uncle. In those days, our people lived widely scattered, along the shores and in the islands, even out on the plains. There were no roads then, just trails, though we had horses and wagons and, for the winter, sleds. When the uncle came around to fetch Aanakwad, in his wagon fitted out with sled runners, it was very hard, for she and her husband had argued right up to the last about the children, argued fiercely until the husband had finally given in. He turned his face to the wall, and did not move to see the daughter, whom he treasured, sit down beside her mother, wrapped in her plaid robe in the wagon bed. They left right away, with their bundles and sacks, not bothering to heat up the stones to warm their feet. The father had stopped his ears, so he did not hear his son cry out when he suddenly understood that he would be left behind.

As the uncle slapped the reins and the horse lurched forward, the boy tried to jump into the wagon, but his mother pried his hands off the boards, crying *Gego, gego,* and he fell down hard. But there was something in him that would not let her leave. He jumped up and, although he was wearing only light clothing, he ran behind the wagon over the packed drifts. The horses picked up speed. His chest was scorched with pain, and yet he pushed himself on. He'd never run so fast, so hard and furiously, but he was determined, and he refused to believe that the increasing distance between him and the wagon was real. He kept going until his throat closed, he saw red, and in the ice of the air his lungs shut. Then, as he fell onto the board-hard snow, he raised his head. He watched the back of the wagon and the tiny figures of his mother and sister disappear, and something failed in him. Something broke. At that moment he truly did not care if he was alive or dead. So when he saw the gray shapes, the shadows, bounding lightly from the trees to either side of the trail, far ahead, he was not afraid.

* * *

The next the boy knew, his father had him wrapped in a blanket and was carrying him home. His father's chest was broad and, although he already spat the tubercular blood that would write the end of his story, he was still a strong man. It would take him many years to die. In those years, the father would tell the boy, who had forgotten this part entirely, that at first when he talked about the shadows the father thought he'd been visited by manidoog. But then, as the boy described the shapes, his father had understood that they were not spirits. Uneasy, he had decided to take his gun back along the trail. He had built up the fire in the cabin, and settled his boy near it, and went back out into the snow. Perhaps the story spread through our settlements because the father had to tell what he saw, again and again, in order to get rid of it. Perhaps as with all frightful dreams, amaaniso, he had to talk about it to destroy its power—though in this case nothing could stop the dream from being real.

The shadows' tracks were the tracks of wolves, and in those days, when our guns had taken all their food for furs and hides to sell, the wolves were bold and had abandoned the old agreement between them and the first humans. For a time, until we understood and let the game increase, the wolves hunted us. The father bounded forward when he saw the tracks. He could see where the pack, desperate, had tried to slash the tendons of the horses' legs. Next, where they'd leaped for the back of the wagon. He hurried on to where the trail gave out at the broad empty ice of the lake. There, he saw what he saw, scattered, and the ravens, attending to the bitter small leavings of the wolves.

For a time, the boy had no understanding of what had happened. His father kept what he knew to himself, at least that first year, and when his son asked about his sister's torn plaid shawl, and why it was kept in the house, his father said nothing. But he wept when the boy asked if his sister was cold. It was only after his father had been weakened by the disease that he began to tell the story, far too often and always the same way: he told how when the wolves closed in, Aanakwad had thrown her daughter to them.

When his father said those words, the boy went still. What had his sister felt? What had thrust through her heart? Had something broken inside her, too, as it had in him? Even then, he knew that this broken place inside him would not be mended, except by